NIGHT & DAY

THE CHARLIE PARKER STORIES

Every Dead Thing
Dark Hollow
The Killing Kind
The White Road
The Reflecting Eye
(Novella in the Nocturnes Collection)
The Black Angel
The Unquiet
The Reapers
The Lovers
The Gates
The Whisperers
The Burning Soul
The Wrath of Angels
The Wolf in Winter
A Song of Shadows
A Time of Torment
A Game of Ghosts
The Woman in the Woods
A Book of Bones
The Dirty South
The Nameless Ones
The Furies
The Instruments of Darkness

OTHER WORKS

Bad Men
Nocturnes
Night Music
The Book of Lost Things
The Land of Lost Things
he: A Novel

THE SAMUEL JOHNSON STORIES
(FOR YOUNG ADULTS)

The Gates
The Infernals
The Creeps

THE CHRONICLES OF THE INVADERS
(WITH JENNIFER RIDYARD)

Conquest
Empire
Dominion

NONFICTION

Books to Die For: The World's Greatest Mystery Writers on the World's Greatest Mystery Novels (edited by John Connolly and Declan Burke)
Parker: A Miscellany
Midnight Movie Monographs: Horror Express
Shadow Voices: 300 Years of Irish Genre Fiction, A History in Stories

NIGHT & DAY

JOHN CONNOLLY

EMILY BESTLER BOOKS
ATRIA
NEW YORK LONDON TORONTO SYDNEY NEW DELHI

EMILY BESTLER BOOKS

ATRIA

An Imprint of Simon & Schuster, LLC
1230 Avenue of the Americas
New York, NY 10020

Lines from *Northern Elegies*, "Third," from *The Complete Poems of Anna Akhmatova* (2000), edited by Roberta Reeder, reproduced by kind permission of Canongate.

First Emily Bestler Books/Atria Paperback edition October 2024

"The Bear" first published in The Little Island anthology, *Once Upon a Place*, edited by Eoin Colfer, published by Children's Books Ireland, 2015.
"The Evenings with Evans" first published in *Trouble Is Our Business*, edited by Declan Burke, published by New Island Books, Ireland, 2016.
Horror Express first published by Electric Dreamhouse, an imprint of PS Publishing Ltd, Great Britain, 2018.
"Unquiet Slumbers: A Tale of the Caxton Private Lending Library & Book Depository" first published in *Goldsboro Books First Edition 21*, published by The Dome Press, Great Britain, 2020.
Illustrations in *The Bear* by P. J. Lynch, first published in The Little Island anthology, *Once Upon a Place*, edited by Eoin Colfer, published by Children's Books Ireland, 2015.

EMILY BESTLER BOOKS / ATRIA PAPERBACK and colophon are trademarks of Simon & Schuster, LLC

Simon & Schuster: Celebrating 100 Years of Publishing in 2024

For information about special discounts for bulk purchases, please contact Simon & Schuster Special Sales at 1-866-506-1949 or business@simonandschuster.com.

The Simon & Schuster Speakers Bureau can bring authors to your live event. For more information or to book an event, contact the Simon & Schuster Speakers Bureau at 1-866-248-3049 or visit our website at www.simonspeakers.com.

Interior design by Erika R. Genova

Manufactured in the United States of America

1 3 5 7 9 10 8 6 4 2

Library of Congress Control Number: 2024944070

ISBN 978-1-6680-8167-9
ISBN 978-1-6680-8168-6 (ebook)

For Desmond Thomas Connolly (1929–91)

CONTENTS

The Pilgrims' Progress: A Tale of the Caxton Private Lending Library & Book Depository *1*

And All the Graves of All the Ghosts *33*

The Evenings with Evans *43*

Abelman's Line *59*

The Mire at Fox Tor *107*

The Bear *117*

The Flaw *127*

Unquiet Slumbers: A Tale of the Caxton Private Lending Library & Book Depository *151*

Our Friend Carlton *163*

Horror Express: Extended Edition *181*

Bibliography *347*

Afterword and Acknowledgments *349*

NIGHT
&
DAY

THE PILGRIMS' PROGRESS:
A TALE OF THE CAXTON
PRIVATE LENDING LIBRARY
& BOOK DEPOSITORY

THE LIBRARY

Fifth Series, Vol. XII, No. 3, September 1957

William Caxton's Houses at Westminster

By LAWRENCE E. TANNER, C.V.O.
Keeper of the Muniments, Westminster Abbey

(*Read before the Bibliographical Society on 21 February 1956*)

It is now just over sixty years ago that my predecessor at Westminster, the late Dr. Edward J. L. Scott, sometime Keeper of the Manuscripts and Egerton Librarian at the British Museum, first made known the existence of new material concerning William Caxton among the Muniments at Westminster Abbey. This material consisted of nearly 350 documents[1] relating to the Causton or Caxton family and their lands at Edmonton, Enfield, and Tottenham in the fourteenth century, together with a series of entries in the account rolls of the Prior, Sacrist, and Almoner of Westminster Abbey recording the payment of rent by William Caxton himself, and his assistant and successor Wynkyn de Worde, for the successive houses which they occupied within the precincts of the Monastery between the years 1477 and 1499.

The Causton documents remain something of a puzzle. The properties to which they refer were never owned by the Abbot and Convent of Westminster, and there appears to be no reason why they should be among the Abbey Muniments.

Miss Haining, the latest custodian of the Caxton Private Lending Library & Book Depository, had resigned herself to never understanding entirely the institution's intricacies. It was some consolation to her that she was, in this matter, as in many others, following in a proud tradition of Caxton librarianship. At some critical juncture in their involvement with the Caxton, each of her predecessors had thrown up their hands in defeat when it came to comprehending its workings, dating back to William Caxton himself, the library's somewhat unwilling founder, and therefore the first in a long line of baffled conservators.

On a basic level, the operation of the Caxton was easily explained. When a novel achieved a singular status with the reading public (generally after the death of its author), a first edition of the book in question, wrapped in brown paper and tied with string, would appear on the Caxton's doorstep, soon to be followed by the fictional character or characters responsible for its popularity. Now and again, due to some fault in the system, a character might arrive before the book, causing confusion or even mild shock for the librarian. Whatever the order of delivery, the physical environs of the Caxton—which, like a novel, were capable of containing multitudes—would already have conjured living quarters to accommodate them, always with a window through which could be glimpsed the world of their respective book, just in case a character should feel the urge to wander among the familiar. Funding for the library, involving the rounding up or down of fractions of pennies, was so ingrained in the systems of publishing that even the most scrupulous of accountants often failed to notice it. If they did, they never succeeded in establishing the cause, or the ultimate destination of the nubbins, and subsequently gave up—or, on occasion, went mad, and then gave up.

How Caxton came to establish the library that bore his name was one of the first stories passed down to their successors by departing librarians. Mr. Berger had shared it with Miss Haining over tea and scones, just as Mr. Gedeon had shared it with Mr. Berger some two decades earlier. It was a valuable introduction to what was to follow, since it was so improbable that everything else seemed marginally more acceptable by comparison.

As Miss Haining approached retirement, it had fallen to her to pass on the founding narrative of the Caxton to one Marjorie Dobbs, who had found her way to the library after having her purse pinched by the Artful Dodger. (The library had a way of choosing—or luring—replacement librarians. Some of Marjorie's predecessors had variously arrived there on the trail of Anna Karenina, Robinson Crusoe, Hamlet, and on one particularly memorable and confusing occasion, an enormous white rabbit cursing a pocket watch.)

Here, then, as told by Miss Haining to Miss Dobbs, is the origin story of the Caxton Private Lending Library & Book Depository.

• • • • • • •

Following the success of his first printing of *The Canterbury Tales*, William Caxton—writer, merchant, and, most importantly, printer of books—woke one morning in 1477 to find five individuals dressed as characters from that same work arguing among themselves in his yard in London's Almonry, by Westminster, seemingly with no idea as to how they'd come to be there, or so they claimed. They were respectively dressed as the Knight, the Miller, the Wife of Bath, the Summoner, and the Nun's Priest.

The popularity of his edition of Chaucer had taken William by surprise, albeit pleasantly. Discovering five ne'er-do-wells—or worse, four players and their bawd—loitering on his premises, apparently with some fixation on the text, was less welcome.

"Look," said William, "is this some kind of joke?"

"I shouldn't have thought so," said the Knight. "And if it was, what kind of joke would it be?"

He looked genuinely perturbed, like one who laughed little and didn't quite understand the concept of japery.

"We're meant to be here," said the Nun's Priest. "We may not know the 'how' of it but the 'why' is clear enough."

"Not to me it isn't," said William.

"The book," explained the Summoner. "You offered life to the book, and so offered life to us."

So sincerely did he speak that he gave William pause.

"You're not telling me—"

"We are," confirmed the Summoner.

"No, it can't—"

"It can," said the Wife of Bath.

"And it is," concluded the Miller. "Now," he added, to a murmur of agreement from the rest, "how about some breakfast?"

William gaped. He was an imaginative man—he could not have loved stories and been otherwise—but he was not a gullible one, or else he would have long since become a failure in business. He had a nose for dishonesty, and it wasn't twitching. If the five people before him weren't telling the truth, it wasn't because they didn't believe themselves to be. Furthermore, it was obvious from their stance that they weren't going anywhere for the time being, or not before being fed.

William sent for a kitchen boy.

"Inform the kitchen that we will have guests for breakfast," he told the boy. "And be so good as to wake Master Wynkyn from his rest."

After the food had been served, followed by extensive questioning by William and his assistant, Wynkyn de Worde, it began to creep up on the printer that if these were not lunatics, there was a possibility, however unlikely, that they might actually be who they professed to be—five of Chaucer's pilgrims. William didn't want to accept it, for reason alone dictated that it couldn't be so, but he felt a creeping sense of unease. He was a writer and printer. He gave physical form to stories. If a tale could assume length, breadth, and weight in the world, why not also the characters it contained?

William hurriedly ushered the pilgrims into an empty storage shed before anyone could begin asking awkward questions, not that he was short of further awkward questions of his own. Once the five were settled, with a trusted retainer watching the door, William and Wynkyn sat down over cheese and small beer to decide what was to be done with a group of fictional personages who had, it seemed, stepped off the page and into the real world. Wynkyn, like William, understood the power of books and had required surprisingly little convincing to fall into step with his master. For Wynkyn, there had always been a magic to the Caxton press—it gave material form to ideas and made tangible the intangible—and this latest development merely confirmed it.

The five pilgrims couldn't be permitted to wander the streets of London, that much was clear, not least because they included the Knight, in full regalia; the Miller, complete with bagpipes; and the Wife of Bath, who had already felt up a stable boy before marking the cook as a candidate for husband number six. Given free rein in the city, they'd end up attracting the attention of a justice of the peace. From there, it would be a short hop to the Marshalsea or Bedlam, with a strong chance of William and Wynkyn joining them in one or the other.

"Then there's the question of what happens should the rest of them arrive," said Wynkyn.

"The rest?" William barely avoided choking on a piece of hard cheese. He hadn't even considered that more of them might show up. "What are we supposed to do with thirty-one pilgrims?"

"I suppose we could direct them to the Archbishop of Canterbury," offered Wynkyn. "I mean, Canterbury was always their destination."

"Old Bourchier will have us arrested," said William, glumly. "Or worse, burned at the stake for sorcery."

Wynkyn paled and touched a hand to his neck. He hadn't considered that. When it came to the pyre, the lucky ones were strangled to death before the fires got started, but the words "lucky" and "strangled" did not properly belong together in his mind.

"It's hardly our fault they're here," said Wynkyn. "It's not as if we deliberately conjured them up."

"No, but we set them down on paper."

"Geoffrey Chaucer did that. By rights, the blame should be laid at his grave."

"Perhaps you could go about presenting that argument to the late poet, and thus add 'consorting with spirits' to our list of offenses," said William. "God's bones, I wonder how slowly the executioners can let a man burn."

Still, he thought that Wynkyn had a point about Chaucer's culpability, though it wasn't one he fancied making while someone measured them up for the stake. Chaucer might have written *The Canterbury Tales*, but he hadn't disseminated it. Initially, that had been the responsibility of the scribes who painstakingly copied it for distribution, but they hadn't been able to reproduce it at the pace of the Caxton press. Nobody in England, and few elsewhere, had been capable of such replication until now. Why, William's compositors and pressmen had already managed the previously unthinkable feat of printing hundreds of nearly identical copies of *The Canterbury Tales* in a fraction of the time it would have taken a scribe to create only part of a single copy, and at a similar fraction of the cost.

Now William understood. He might not have created the pilgrims, but he had popularized them, making them accessible beyond oral storytelling in a way that would have seemed fantastical to Chaucer less than a century earlier. And this was only the beginning: with more workers, and faster presses, a printer might be able to offer books not in the hundreds but the thousands. Johann Veldener, the creator of William's typeface, had suggested as much to him the night before William left Flanders for England, and William had laughed in his face.

"But who will read all these books, Johann?" William asked. "There are only so many lettered men."

Johann placed his hands on William's, gripping them tightly.

"Soon, William, there will be more. Books will make men lettered."

But even Johann had not anticipated what might happen as books became more accessible, and the characters became as real to readers as their own family and neighbors—and sometimes more beloved, too.

No, Johann, books will not alone make men lettered. They will give life to their characters.

"Bring me my coat," William told Wynkyn. "We must talk with Richard."

Richard Caxton was one of the Benedictine monks of Westminster Abbey, where he held the position of sacrist. He was a relative of William's through complex layers of marriage that even the most committed of later Caxton librarians had never been able to trace with certainty. He had also admired William's printing shop from its inception, unlike a vocal minority of his fellow clerics who believed that books should be for the elite, regarding the Caxton press as a threat to their position and, indeed, their scriptorium. Richard, by contrast, associated learning with civilization: the more learned the populace, the more civilized they might become, and the highest civilizing influence of all was the word of God. Richard still did not say it aloud, for fear of mockery or worse, but he envisaged a day when every household—or every household with a grasp of Latin—might have its own affordable copy of the Bible, and only presses like William's could make that possible. Following a period of discord, Richard's contingent at Westminster had prevailed, aided by the fact that the abbot, John Esteney, was one of William's patrons and had facilitated the establishment of his press in the abbey's precincts. The monks were now among William's customers for liturgical works and letters of indulgence, which provided the shop with a welcome source of guaranteed income.

William and Wynkyn walked with Richard by Long Ditch and tried to explain, as best they could, how they came to be harboring five fictional characters in a shed, with the expectation of more to follow. Richard, naturally, proved skeptical at first, and was hardly less so when introduced to the pilgrims, believing himself to be the victim of an elaborate practical joke concocted either by the five themselves or by William, with or without the connivance of Wynkyn. Yet gradually, over two days of interrogation and exposure to their company, Richard, despite himself, began to come around to the same opinion as William. What swayed him was the five's understanding that they *were* fictional characters, and therefore as bewildered as anyone else to discover themselves outside the book that had birthed them.

Any final doubts that Richard might have entertained were dispelled when, as he departed the shed on the second afternoon with William and Wynkyn, the Reeve materialized in the yard in front of them. One moment, the closed space was empty, the next, it was occupied by a thin, confused old man with closely cropped hair and a pinched, argumentative face. He was armed with a sword composed more of rust than clean metal.

"I warned you," said Wynkyn to William.

"You wouldn't be named Oswald, would you?" William asked the stranger.

"I am," came the reply. "How did you know that?"

"Because I know your story," William replied. "Now, I believe there are some people here with whom you might wish to renew acquaintance."

Wynkyn, Richard, and William sat at William's dining table. Small beer had been set aside in favor of red wine, more potent stuff being required to tackle the problem at hand.

"No one can find out the truth," said Richard. "If they do, they'll burn your shop to ash, and you and Wynkyn with it. As for the six—"

"Six and counting," Wynkyn interrupted.

"Yes, thank you—six and counting—I can see no good end for them unless a place of sanctuary can be found."

"Something strange has happened," said William.

"We're very aware of that," said Richard. "We'd hardly be here otherwise."

"No, something else strange. Yesterday, a copy of *The Canterbury Tales*, wrapped in brown paper and string, was left on the doorstep of the shop."

"By whom?"

"Nobody knows. It was just lying there, addressed to me."

"A dissatisfied customer, perhaps?" suggested Richard.

William bridled. While proud of his edition of Chaucer, he had been made aware of defects in the text on which he had based his version and had since come into possession of a superior manuscript. The errors—including a wrongly positioned Merchant's tale, a missing exchange between the Franklin and the Squire, and most embarrassingly, the omission or transposition of lines throughout the Knight's tale, distorting it horribly—galled William. Already, he was contemplating a second edition, illustrated throughout with woodcuts, once a thorough comparison of the two texts could be completed. The buyers of the first edition had, by and large, been understanding.

"We have no dissatisfied customers." William shifted in his chair, physically modifying his position before doing so metaphorically. "Or when we do, we try to rectify any error that might have been made, for we have a reputation to uphold. But I can see no flaw in the volume. It's perfect: even the naturally occurring irregularities in the binding are no longer detectable, and the pages are without blemish. I could tell from the first that it came from this shop, but it's as though it has been elevated by hands more skilled than any I have known."

"Why would someone return an improved copy of one of your publications to you?" asked Richard. "Other than as an object lesson, of course."

That tug on the line again, but William did not rise to the bait.

"I cannot say," he replied.

"What will you do with it?"

"Keep it, I suppose, in case whoever left it decides to seek its return."

Wynkyn coughed.

"I have some questions," he said.

"Out with them," said Richard, with more bite than he'd intended. He liked the Alsatian, who had arrived in England some years earlier as William's apprentice. Wynkyn shared Richard's vision of cheaper editions that might help spread God's word and was trying to persuade William to source his paper at home instead of from the Low Countries, which would cut costs. William, an artist, preferred the continental paper, but Richard thought that given time, Wynkyn might prove to be the better businessman.

Wynkyn was trying to choose his words carefully.

"I'm wary of appearing, um, blasphemous," he said.

William and Richard exchanged a look.

"It would be best avoided," said Richard, "but the door is closed, and what is said will stay between God and us."

"Well," continued Wynkyn, "my master has suggested that the appearance of the six pilgrims may have been caused by our making their parent volume more easily available. In working on the imagination of readers, we have, in turn, given physical life to those who previously existed only in manuscript reproductions. I have heard estimates of how many of those manuscripts there might be, and none has ever exceeded a hundred."

"Go on."

"*The Canterbury Tales* will hardly be the only such volume we print, so first of all, I'm wondering what further publications, if any, might precipitate a similar influx of characters? After all, the *Recuyell of the Historyes of Troye*, which my master printed in Bruges, did not result in Hector or Priam turning up at the door."

"Thank the Lord," said William. A bad situation might always be made worse. "Could it be that the heroes of the Trojan War were real, or likely so, while the pilgrims are not? Or they weren't until they showed up here."

"That would be my hope," said Wynkyn.

"Your 'hope'?" William didn't like the sound of that. "Then why do I detect such a note of doubt?"

"This is where things become delicate." Wynkyn looked like a man nominated to deliver bad news to a ruler not famed for his tolerance. "My master has spoken in the past of his intention to publish *The Golden Legend*, being, as we know, a collection of saints' lives. Should we discover that only fictional characters may be lent flesh and blood by the public passions, that's one thing. But were we to find that real figures, through the printed account of them, should similarly be given form—"

Richard grew noticeably worried, while William buried his face in his hands. The latter did not want to be responsible for an influx of holy men and women, many of whom had passed away under challenging circumstances and might diversely manifest as beheaded, dismembered, or pierced by a multiplicity of sharp objects.

"And," Wynkyn went on, "we have also considered the profitability of certain books of hours, containing short extracts from the Bible, both the Old and New Testaments." He paused meaningfully. "In English, rather than the less accessible Latin."

William let out a low moan. Whatever the drawbacks of saints materializing in his place of business, he most certainly did not want to precipitate the Second Coming.

"What am I supposed to do?" he asked. "If I refuse to print religious works, I'll go out of business, or be accused of apostasy."

"Thus," said Wynkyn, "my tentative use of the word 'hope.'"

"Look," said Richard, "if the credence of the populace was alone sufficient to cause the Son of God to reappear, it would have happened already."

"But we've never had printed books until now," said Wynkyn, "or not in such numbers. And this is only the beginning. The world is going to change. It's already changing. The arrival of the pilgrims is proof of that."

"Nevertheless, the idea that a book produced by men might compel God's son to manifest is—"

"Blasphemous?" William offered.

"I did warn you," said Wynkyn. "Someone had to say it."

Wynkyn had more to share but decided it might be politic to keep it to himself for fear of testing Richard's patience. Wynkyn was a man of letters. He spent his days surrounded by blocks, each bearing a symbol, and from those symbols, an infinitude of ideas was capable of being expressed. The more lettered a man, the more complex those ideas became, and with complexity came doubt. Wynkyn believed in God, but prized faith over evidence. The former possessed a higher quality, a grace, because it required a capacity to imagine and accept something beyond the ordinary; it was, according to Hebrews, the substance of things hoped for, the evidence of things not seen.

But when it came to forming and exploring ideas, doubt was always a fellow traveler. In fact, faith could not exist without it, because to reach that state of conviction required the overcoming of doubt. For a wise man, who reflected before acting, doubt was a necessary step on the path to conviction. Yet faith was not fixed. It wavered in times of trial or adversity, as when a loved one was taken before their time, in the face of war, plague, and famine, or when the innocent suffered. Wynkyn was familiar with the doctrine of original sin, but it didn't mean he was prepared to accept it without question. Man, not God, was responsible for the formation of doctrine, and men were, in all things, fallible. God might try to guide them, but in Wynkyn's experience, men sometimes misheard Him, or chose not to listen. To be informed, as the more uncompromising of clerics argued, that an infant had died of ague, or at the point of a spear, because they carried with them the taint of Adam's act of disobedience, was difficult for Wynkyn to countenance. Likewise, to hear that such torment was God's will, which was beyond human understanding, was less an answer than avoidance of the question, leaving unexamined the issue of the kind of God that would will misery on His creation.

But Wynkyn wasn't about to question church doctrine openly. The punishments for heresy were more severe than those for blasphemy. One might blaspheme out of drunkenness or anger, but heresy required the exercise of reason. It was a willed offense. On the other hand, Wynkyn was in no hurry to engage in outright blasphemy either, being quite content to avoid branding, flogging, or the piercing of his tongue. Yet an alternative answer to the question of God's nature could only be blasphemous: grave misfortune befell the deserving and undeserving alike because there was no God.

So Wynkyn had gone through periods of equivocation in his faith. Now, at his master's table, he was experiencing another such crisis, one that, if disclosed aloud, even only in present company, might cause him to lose his position, which he loved, and, should Richard's patience snap, his liberty, even his life. If God was not real, and Caxton's shop commenced publishing multiple copies of the Bible, was there yet not a chance that, on some morning in the future, the printers might awake to discover in the yard a figure bearing a startling resemblance to the risen Christ? If God did not make man, man must have made God. But then, by bringing God into being, whether in the form of the Father, Son, or Holy Spirit, would the Caxton press not simply have confirmed what everyone believed anyway? In that case, no harm would have been done—or not beyond changing the world, potentially for the better, although the First Coming hadn't ended so well. Who was to say that a man preaching kindness and tolerance would be better received in present-day England than he had been in the Holy Land almost fifteen hundred years earlier? If he didn't end up beaten to death in the street, he'd find a home in Bedlam with the six pilgrims.

If we become responsible for the Second Coming, Wynkyn decided, *it had better be a spectacle to remember.*

"Wynkyn, are you still with us?" asked Richard.

"Yes, sorry," Wynkyn replied. *Unfortunately.*

"I was saying that I'd prefer to use the word 'unlikely' to describe the invocation of the Savior," said Richard. "But let us assume for now that you, Wynkyn, are right about the impact of the printed word, and correct in imputing its powers of conjuration solely to those who might not otherwise have enjoyed a corporeal existence, aided by an unusual degree of renown caused by the proliferation of specific texts. We currently have only six pilgrims with whom to contend, not the full complement. Those under discussion are, I would hazard, among the more crowd-pleasing of Chaucer's characters, by virtue of their personalities or the quality of the stories they told.

"In the sciences," Richard went on, "what has occurred with *The Canterbury Tales* might be referred to as an unplanned experiment. I propose, therefore, that we undertake a planned one. We produce two pamphlets to be circulated as widely as possible within one mile of Westminster. The first pamphlet will concern a person known to be real, the other a person fanciful but with the potential to capture the imagination. We'll then wait to see what happens. If both appear, we have a grave difficulty, but if only the unreal one is made manifest, we'll better understand what's happening."

"What if neither of them appears?" asked Wynkyn.

Richard tugged at an earlobe.

"Then the pilgrims may be considered an anomaly—which would be a relief."

From his tone, Wynkyn suspected Richard might be growing more conflicted about the affair than he was willing to concede. If handled properly, the ability to summon saints on demand would be good for the Church, and the Benedictines of Westminster in particular. They were comparatively few in number, and the abbey, though an enduring tribute to the glory of God, was not a site of pilgrimage. The monks currently didn't even have enough funds to complete the construction of the West Towers, but if it became known that saints were popping up in the abbey's precincts, the Benedictines could raise towers to their hearts' content. Obviously, there was still the matter of avoiding the Second Coming, but should a middle ground be found—

"I have another question," said Wynkyn.

"Wynkyn," said Richard, summoning all his forbearance, "I begin to fear that Thomas Aquinas might have struggled to formulate so many questions as you."

Wynkyn, though, was not intimidated. In his view, foolish questions did not exist; even if they did, it was better to pose them than remain silent and later reap regrets.

"Isn't inventing a person potentially a breach of the Ninth Commandment?" asked Wynkyn. It was the politest way he could find of suggesting that Richard was intent upon deceiving a section of the populace. "After all, did not Aquinas himself state that it is unlawful to lie to deliver another from any danger whatsoever?"

Richard stared hard at Wynkyn.

"God preserve us," he said, "from educated men."

"Our press would be worthless were we otherwise," replied Wynkyn.

"If easier to control. But that, Wynkyn, is a headache for another day. In answer to your question, Aquinas affirms that to lie is to speak deliberately against one's own mind. I am in accordance with myself in the matter of the invented candidate, and so my conscience is at peace."

Wynkyn thought that Richard might be wasted at Westminster, since such sophistry more appropriately belonged in Rome. Were

Wynkyn a cardinal, he might already have advocated that Richard be measured for the relevant papal attire just to save time later.

For his part, Richard understood that what was real and what was true might not be one and the same, as the Church's scholars had long speculated on the differences between the literal and the figurative. For example, Richard was not convinced that Saint Denis, founder of the See of Paris, following his execution by decapitation, had walked the seven miles from Montmartre to the Roman settlement of Catulliacus with his severed head in his hands, the head continuing to preach for the duration. Neither did he believe Saint George had slain an actual dragon. Yet both stories, while not in accordance with reality, contained truths: the former regarding the impossibility of silencing the word of God, and the latter—as Richard had preached on the saint's most recent feast day—about standing up to evil, whether represented by Roman emperors or Satan himself. On a more practical level, Richard was one of those who knew that the charter of King Offa, dating from AD 785, which referred to "that terrible place which is known as Westminster"—terrible, that is, in the sense of inspiring holy awe—was a forgery authorized by Osbert of Clare, abbot of Westminster in the twelfth century, its purpose being to emphasize the abbey's historical importance and thus secure its position, ensuring it became that which the charter had foretold. As far as Richard was concerned, absolute truth was for God alone. Man, by contrast, was obliged to mold truth to fit a fallen world.

"Producing so many pamphlets will be an expensive undertaking," said William, returning the conversation to the pragmatic.

"Funds are scarce at present," said Richard, "but I'll speak with the abbot. He is fascinated by the potential of saints as exemplars, and retains a devotion, fittingly enough, to Saint Thomas of Canterbury."

William looked uneasy. The current king, Edward IV, came from the Plantagenet House of York. Henry II, a Plantagenet, had precipitated Becket's murder in 1170, and William wondered if it would be wise to remind Edward of his ancestor's failings. As a monarch, Edward left much to be desired. His morals were poor, and he had a short temper. Most recently, he had ordered his brother George, Duke of Clarence, to be executed on charges of treason, so it could at least be said that he was keeping up a family custom—indeed, a royal one—of sporadic yet pragmatic homicide. Nevertheless, Edward's wife, Elizabeth, enjoyed good relations with Abbot Esteney, who had consoled her on the death of her nine-month-old daughter, Margaret. Elizabeth might be prevailed upon to intercede if difficulties arose over a Becket pamphlet.

"There remains," said Wynkyn, "the question of what to do with the pilgrims."

"The abbey has more property within its precincts than it knows what to do with," said Richard. "If my cousin William is willing, we could arrange for a dwelling to be rented at a favorable rate, where the pilgrims can be housed while we await the outcome of our experiment."

William didn't particularly want to add to his outgoings by renting another property, but it was better than keeping the pilgrims where they were. They were quite garrulous, and some of his employees were growing too curious about the visitors.

"Won't they attract attention?" asked Wynkyn. "My master and I were concerned about being accused of sorcery were their true nature to be revealed."

"Not if the building in question is distant from the abbey," said Richard, "and they don't go making a spectacle of themselves."

"The Miller owns a set of bagpipes," said William. "It's hard not to make a spectacle of yourself with bagpipes."

"Well, take them away from him. The others will certainly thank you for it. And accusations of sorcery, should they arise, can easily be dealt with by declaring the pilgrims gently, harmlessly mad, and requiring only Christian care. Just because we believe something doesn't mean everyone else has to believe it too."

William refilled their cups, and the three men raised them to the success of their venture. The following evening, the pilgrims were relocated to a house by Thieving Lane, the Miller protesting the temporary seizure of his bagpipes, and the Wife of Bath enquiring of Richard whether he had any single male relatives and how committed to celibacy the novices might be. Once the pilgrims were safely in place, Richard returned to his quarters, put on his night coat, and set to work on the first of the pamphlets.

John Esteney, the abbot of Westminster, was a scholarly man. If he had a weakness, it took the form of a vanity customary to his tribe: he was reluctant to admit his ignorance, particularly of areas where he was regarded as possessing specialist knowledge.

Thus, when Richard Caxton approached him with the idea of publishing two pamphlets on saints—to be shared among clerics and read aloud from the abbey's pulpit—Esteney was most eager to write the Becket broadside. While the content of his sermons, in common with those of many learned preachers of his time, were often circulated among the faithful, this dissemination was primarily oral and prey to the vagaries of memory, bias, and even the listener's position in the congregation. Caxton's press assured Esteney of something approaching consistency of expression and communication regarding his ideas. He did, however, confess to being perturbed at Richard's selection of the Venerable Cominatus of Skopelos as a suitable subject for the second pamphlet.

"Isn't he a little, you know—"

"Obscure?" offered Richard.

"Indeed."

"Of course, but that's just the point."

"Is it?" Esteney appeared confused. "Why?"

"It is said that, in Rome, he is being posited as a potential patron saint of obscurity."

"Is he? I mean, the name is somewhat familiar," said Esteney, backtracking, "but the nature of his possible heavenly advocacy must have slipped my mind."

"It's hardly surprising, Father Abbot, since Cominatus did almost nothing of note. He helped secure the remains of Bishop Riginos following his martyrdom by Julian the Apostate in 362, then vanished from the record for centuries. But by his intercession, several minor liturgical volumes, long believed lost, were discovered on the nearby islands of Skiathos and Alonissos in 765. Even if their contents were so abstruse as to be of virtually no interest, it was very nice to have them back. Prayers to him also revealed the location of two overgrown roads leading to a pair of unmarked tombs that may or may not have contained the bones of martyrs. At the same time, he is credited with aiding the recovery of the key to a vault believed to have contained important documents or artifacts. It didn't, unfortunately, but it saved everyone from worrying about what might be inside. Cominatus is additionally set to become the patron saint of unsuccessful poets, which is most of them; composers of songs that are never sung; and playwrights who manage to write just a single play that is quickly forgotten. Even should he not achieve sainthood or the condition of the blessed, he would remain a useful addition to the Church's spiritual reserves."

The abbot raised an index finger.

"Which rather begs the question," he said, "of why, venerable though his name may be, Cominatus merits a pamphlet."

"Because," said Richard, "most people are destined to live in obscurity. They may work hard and raise families, but these are noble achievements, not necessarily noteworthy ones. In all likelihood, history will fail to recall such men and women, and in a few generations even their descendants will have forgotten them. In that sense, Cominatus could become one of the most useful of saints, for it is with him that the masses will have most in common. He would be *their* saint."

The abbot worried at his bottom lip.

"Look," he said, "it's not going to be a very long pamphlet, is it?"

"I should think that improbable," said Richard. "Your meditations on Becket ought to be substantial, but my reflections on Cominatus can be slight. Still, together they but offer a lesson greater than the sum of their individual parts: that all, whether major or minor, have their place at the Lord's table, and all will be remembered on the Last Day."

"All right," said the abbot, "but indicate to your cousin William that the Church would appreciate a favorable price."

When he was not at the press, Wynkyn ensured that the pilgrims remained safe and well. He found them quickly becoming listless, even after only a few days in the new lodgings, and so offered to accompany them on a series of walks around the city once less cumbersome clothing had been arranged for the Knight. Regrettably, the first of these expeditions also proved to be the last. The pilgrims were not so much overwhelmed by London as disengaged from it, as though they had been invited to walk through a simulacrum of a world instead of the world itself, and all were relieved to return to the calm of Westminster.

Later, over a meal of bread and mortrews, Wynkyn discussed the day's events with William.

"I thought they'd be happy to be out and about," Wynkyn concluded. "Instead, they couldn't wait to get back indoors."

William removed a sprig of something unidentifiable from between his teeth and set it aside.

"Because it's not their realm," he said. "You might have taken them to Canterbury itself and they wouldn't have been content. It's not even that our London is too real for them. It may be that it's not real enough."

"So what is to be done?"

"We'll just have to wait and see," said William.

The abbot, mindful of economies, was restricting his ruminations on Becket to twelve pages. Richard, as instructed, was doing his best to fit his contemplation of Cominatus into two, with most of the text devoted to what the saint represented more than what he might actually have done, given that the latter, even in fictional form, was negligible.

But as he wrote, Richard grew increasingly engaged with the idea of Cominatus. His presentation to the abbot was not intended as entirely facetious. Why should there not be a patron of the insignificant and anonymous? It was all very well to hold up Saint Elmo as a model of Christian fortitude: tortured in prison, sealed in a spiked barrel and rolled down a hill, set on fire, imprisoned and tortured again, over and over, until eventually his intestines were removed and tied around a pole, putting an end to him; or Symeon the Stylite, who decided to spend his life on top of a series of increasingly tall pillars. But what did such examples offer the ordinary man? True, Saint Elmo was a reminder that, unless one was especially unfortunate, there was always someone worse off than oneself, but one only had to walk the streets of London to see that. As for Symeon the Stylite, Richard privately suspected that Symeon just didn't like people very much and God provided a convenient excuse for getting away from them.

Cominatus, on the contrary, presented an instance of the everyday. He didn't do much, and most of what he did wasn't of any use, but he muddled along as best he could until he departed the world. His lifespan was unclear. His burial place remained unknown. Someone had probably mourned his passing, but he might also have been watched over only by a priest and a grave digger as he was consigned to the dirt. In fact, the more unremarkable the details, the more worthy of note Cominatus became, and Richard's days were consumed by thoughts of him. He began to devise a picture of Cominatus in his mind: average height and average build; hair and beard untrimmed, but not to the point of neglect; eyes blue, complexion olive; features resigned but not hopeless.

When Richard was happy with his work, he shared it with the abbot. The abbot smiled.

"Now I understand," he said, "and so will others."

William and Wynkyn supervised the printing of the pamphlets once Richard and the abbot declared themselves content with the arrangement and lettering, which used a black-letter typeface with handwritten paragraph marks inserted in red ink. For the experiment to have purpose, the pamphlets needed a wide circulation, so Richard prevailed upon the abbot to loosen his purse strings. This required him to play upon Esteney's ego, which itself might have been regarded as sinful manipulation of a good man, though Richard preferred to regard the fault more as the abbot's than his own. It was also decided that each pamphlet should continue to be read at services throughout the following month, so that none of the unlettered might be deprived of these insights into two distinct ways of serving God by two very different men.

As the days and weeks passed, William's sleep became increasingly disturbed. He came to fear the dawn, worried at what the morning might reveal. He had returned to the eyewitness account of Becket's murder by Edward Grim, which recalled how a blow from one of the killers had caused the top of Becket's skull to be "separated from his head, so that the blood turned white from the brain yet no less did the brain turn red from the blood." Worse followed when a traitorous monk "scattered the brains with the blood across the floor." This, William feared, was the image of Becket that lingered in the public imagination. If the saint did return, it was possible he might not do so in the fullest bloom of health. As for Cominatus, the picture painted of him by Richard was of a man so innocuous that even if he did materialize, there was a good chance no one would notice.

Meanwhile, so absorbed was Wynkyn with the press, and so tired was he at the conclusion of his labors, that four days passed without his finding time to visit the pilgrims. When he did, it was on Sunday after Mass, when he'd had to listen—again—to the stories of Becket and Cominatus. Interestingly, he'd begun to notice woodcuts of the latter being offered for sale, as well as trinkets featuring the saint's image, even locks of the saint's hair, cuttings from his finger- and toenails, and flakes of his skin "all the way from the Aegean." Richard was advocating that Westminster should intervene to prevent the more extreme manifestations of profiteering and protect the Venerable Cominatus's reputation, even if Wynkyn thought that both Richard and the abbot saw an opportunity to bolster the monastery's coffers and didn't want others drinking from the same trough, or not without paying a percentage for the privilege. The abbot had sent an emissary to the sacrist at Glastonbury Abbey to establish if, among its many relics—which included the complete skeletons of numerous holy men and women—there might be something relating to Cominatus with which the abbey was willing to part. The whole business, Wynkyn fretted, was getting out of hand.

He took a moment at the south transept to pause by the plain slab marking the grave of Geoffrey Chaucer. The poet had spent his final months at the abbey, living in a tenement in the garden of the Lady Chapel. The lease was granted to him for fifty-three years, but he died before the first year was out. Now, six figures who had sprung from his imagination were inhabiting a house not far from his resting place. So it was that Wynkyn and his master had unwittingly conspired with a dead man to usurp natural law. Once again, Wynkyn felt the first of the flames licking at the bare soles of his feet.

Such were his reflections as he left the abbey to walk to the pilgrims' house. Only four people had keys: Wynkyn, William, Richard, and the Knight, regarded as the most trustworthy of the six. But when Wynkyn entered, only the Wife of Bath was present. She was seated by a window at the back of the house, absorbed in a piece of embroidery that, to Wynkyn, initially appeared to show a naked man pushing a wheelbarrow, until he realized the wheelbarrow was actually a woman and—

Oh dear.

"Where is everyone?" Wynkyn asked.

The Wife of Bath drew the needle through an area of particular intimacy and contemplated Wynkyn, as though trying to decide what she should or should not share with him.

"Gone," she said at last.

"Gone where?"

The Wife of Bath indicated the door behind her, which led into a small yard that usually smelled strongly of the privy.

"Gone out."

"But there's nothing out there," said Wynkyn.

"There is now."

Wynkyn went to the door. His hand was on the latch when the Wife of Bath said, "I'd be careful if I were you."

"Why?"

She returned to her embroidery by the pale light filtering through the panes of flattened cow horn.

"You'll see," she said.

Wynkyn opened the door.

And he saw.

What was already being spoken of as the "Cult of Cominatus" was gathering adherents beyond Westminster. Richard Caxton had heard mention of him across the river in Southwark and as far east as Cornhill and Aldgate. It wouldn't be long before his name was carried beyond the walls, over St. Giles, Clerkenwell, Mile End, and The Moor. While the abbot awaited word from Glastonbury about the availability of relics, he had commissioned, to frustrate the profiteers, the striking of medals of both Saint Thomas and the Venerable Cominatus. The fact that Cominatus outsold Becket by three-to-one troubled Esteney only mildly, especially as Richard had advised his fellow monks to compliment the abbot on his Becket pamphlet at every opportunity and had arranged, at his own expense, for William to bind a presentation copy in stamped leather over wooden boards.

Yet, for all the talk of him, Cominatus had not materialized. While Richard appreciated that this might be for the best, he could not help but feel slightly disappointed. Perhaps, he concluded, he simply wasn't a good enough writer. Not everyone could be a Chaucer.

The Wife of Bath had produced a bottle of sack, from which she poured Wynkyn a generous cup before replenishing her own. Wynkyn preferred French wine, but since the loss some two decades earlier of Gascony, the last of England's wine-producing French provinces, Spanish wine was more common, not to mention cheaper. Then again, after what he'd just glimpsed, Wynkyn would have settled for the residue at the bottom of the lowliest tavern barrel as long as it contained alcohol.

Upon opening the door, Wynkyn had been greeted not by the sight of the yard and not by the odors of the street or the dung heap but by a vista of fields, with cattle grazing on the common ground and smoke rising from a pair of cottages. In the distance, surrounded by buildings, were the famed twin towers of Canterbury Cathedral, familiar to Wynkyn from engravings. He heard the calming buzz of bees and the yipping of an unseen dog. He thought he had never beheld a landscape so beautiful, so easeful. Even as he struggled to comprehend how he could be viewing it from the back of a house in

Westminster, his left foot was already leaving the step. He wanted to walk on the grass. He wanted to find the dog and pat it. He wanted to enter the cathedral and pray at Becket's shrine. But the Wife of Bath gripped his arm before he could do any of those things.

"Like I told you," she said, "I wouldn't. Well, *I* would, but you shouldn't."

"How can this be?" asked Wynkyn.

"Sit down and try, against your male instincts, to listen."

Which was how Wynkyn came to be holding a cup of sack in a hand that, he was relieved to note, didn't tremble, or not much.

The Wife of Bath pointed at the door through which Wynkyn had entered the house.

"Out there," she said, "is your world." She pointed to the back door. "But out there is our world, the world of the book, or that's as best as I can figure it. We've been watching it take form since the day we arrived but didn't want to say anything, not until we had some idea of what was happening."

"You mean Chaucer's book is changing the world?"

"The Bible changed the world," said the Wife of Bath. "The Quran, too, whether you're a Saracen or not."

Wynkyn's frame contorted in frustration.

"It's not the same thing," he said.

"Maybe not, but it's a version of it. Surely, once a book is out in the world, and being read, the world is altered, for better or worse."

Wynkyn took a deep draft of wine.

"We're in so much trouble," he said.

"Only if someone finds out."

"How are they *not* going to find out? Kent is currently outside our back door, where it's very much not supposed to be. There should be a yard, a wall, and a privy. Instead, we have fields, cottages, and Canterbury Cathedral."

The Wife of Bath patted Wynkyn's hand.

"But," she said, "not everyone can see it."

"What?"

"One of Richard's trusted monks brought us fresh rushes and a bag of whelks the day before yesterday. The back door was open because the Reeve had gone to find honey. I saw what you saw, but the monk saw nothing at all, or not beyond the yard. He even asked me to close the door on account of how the privy stank. I'm sure if your master William came here, he'd see the fields and the cathedral, and it might be that Brother Richard would too though I wouldn't bet on it. It was you and your master who printed *The Canterbury Tales*, not Richard. That's why we found ourselves here, next to the printing press, and not somewhere down by Canterbury itself."

Wynkyn looked to the closed door, which now marked a boundary between domains.

"Will the others come back?" he asked.

"They'll return soon enough. It's more restful here. It's exhausting being part of that world all the time. You feel this urge to revert, to become what the book wants you to be. But in this house, we're more at peace. The author's hand doesn't rest so heavily on us."

Wynkyn finished his wine.

"I'll have to inform William," he said, "though it might be easier just to show him."

The Wife of Bath returned to her embroidery.

"I'm not going anywhere," she said. "I have a pin to prick."

That evening, Wynkyn returned to the pilgrims' house with William. By then, the wandering pilgrims had reappeared and the sun was setting, casting a golden glow over the cottages, the fields, and the distant cathedral spires.

"We're in so much trouble," said William, unconsciously echoing Wynkyn's words as he stood on the doorstep and took in the vista.

"It may be," said Wynkyn, "that not everyone can see what we see."

"Can we—? I mean, would we be able to—?"

"Go outside?" interrupted the Wife of Bath. "No, as I explained to Master Wynkyn, you don't want to go getting lost in a book."

While the Knight might have been the most senior and distinguished of the pilgrims, Wynkyn noted that, in day-to-day matters, all five deferred to the Wife of Bath. They probably didn't have a lot of choice. Now William turned to face her.

"This is never going to end, is it?" he said.

So desolate did he look that the Wife of Bath was overcome by pity. She hugged William to her bosom, so that for a moment he resembled a man being smothered by pillows. When she consented to release him—which took longer than Wynkyn considered strictly necessary and seemed first to involve drawing William deeper into her folds—she had a tear in her eye, while William had to take a moment to recover his breath.

"Not unless you intend to uninvent the printing press," said the Wife of Bath, "and that's not going to happen. It may be that there won't be many books like ours, but there'll be a good deal of them, enough that you'll need to plan for what's to come. In the meantime, you don't have to worry about us. What we need, we'll find out there, and we'll live between two worlds."

Three months went by. Saint Thomas of Canterbury did not reveal himself, and neither did the Venerable Cominatus, despite depictions of him appearing regularly in places frequented by the commonest of the common folk.

Finally, William, Wynkyn, and Richard gathered again at William's table, a flask of good French wine before them, thanks to Richard's access to the abbey's cellars.

"So what did we learn?" asked William.

"That one can invent a person," replied Richard, "and even make others believe in the idea of him, to a degree. But to enchant a reader, to cause the line between what is actual and imagined to blur so that a character becomes almost as real to them as their own selves, a part of their lives—well, I don't think that can be forced. It's a combination of skill, luck—and magic, for want of a better word."

"We can't stop the act of printing," said Wynkyn. "It's in the world."

"Or the worlds," said Richard. He, too, had seen what lay beyond the back door of the pilgrims' house. He had glimpsed it more faintly than William and Wynkyn, like an image painted on muslin and overlaid, but glimpsed it nonetheless.

"I've started work on a translation of *The Golden Legend*," said William. "I'm going to include some Old Testament stories and begin, like de Voragine, with tales from the life of Christ, but I—like you, Richard—am no great storyteller, no Chaucer."

"And that's for the best," said Richard. "Planning for the future, I've identified more properties that might be suited to our purposes, since they're not technically owned by the abbey."

"Then who does own them?" asked William.

"Curiously, you and I may. The deeds were deposited with the abbey's muniments for safekeeping in the last century by one William de Causton, a mercer—a distant relative of ours, or so it seems. The deeds became confused, deliberately or otherwise, with the abbey's holdings, and are now so enmeshed that disentangling them might require all parties to resort to law. It is the abbot's proposal, then, that in return for the abbey informally accepting the likelihood of our ownership, we might accede to paying a nominal rent for the properties for so long as they are in use. That way, we can enjoy the protection of Westminster while avoiding any difficult questions. Should the properties be sold at a future date, a donation from the proceeds would be sufficient to satisfy the abbot."

William looked to Wynkyn. "What do you think?"

"It'll do," said Wynkyn. "For now."

And so the Caxton Private Lending Library & Book Depository came into being, though a century would pass before that name was formally appended to it. The agreement with Westminster Abbey stood from 1477 until 1499, when construction in its precincts, and the advent of the laborers required to complete it, necessitated the library's relocation. By then, William Caxton had been dead for eight years, and responsibility for both the care of the pilgrims and the running of the press—the latter soon to be moved to Fleet Street, birthing an entire industry—lay with Wynkyn de Worde.

The characters' numbers were first swelled by the arrival of Robin Hood, following the publication early in the sixteenth century of Wynkyn's *A Lytell Geste of Robyn Hode*, and then by Sir Tryamour, after popular rival editions of the eponymous old Middle English romance were issued by Wynkyn and his main competitor, Richard Pynson. What the Wife of Bath foresaw had come to pass, and the influx of characters had begun in earnest.

Aided by Richard Caxton, Wynkyn secured new premises near the old Caxton family lands at Enfield. A guardian was appointed in the form of one of Wynkyn's more bookish single male relatives, and thus Henry de Worde is regarded as the Caxton's first official librarian.

Richard Caxton died in 1504, still the sacrist at Westminster Abbey, and loyal to the characters to his very end. One of his most beloved possessions was a fine altar cloth of white damask, decorated with gold flowers and the arms of St. Edward the Confessor, which had been gifted to him by the Wife of Bath. Upon his death, it was bequeathed to the monastery.

One odd postscript remains to the tale of the founding of the Caxton Public Lending Library & Book Depository, discovered among

Richard's papers after his death. In April 1479, while walking along the banks of Clowson Stream, Richard heard a voice calling. He turned to see a man seated by the water, diverted by ducks and the possibilities of pigeons. He was of average height and build, with hair and beard untrimmed, though not to the point of neglect. His eyes were blue, his complexion olive, and his features were resigned but not hopeless. He was dressed in what looked like an old sack, tied with rope at the waist.

"I think you dropped something," he said.

Richard saw a square of plain cloth caught on a bush.

"It's not mine," he replied.

Richard was irritated by the distraction, having taken time alone to consider how best to adjudicate an unfortunate falling-out between two of his assistants—the *matricularius*, the monastery's timekeeper, and the *revestiarius*, who looked after the vestments—over a dozen misplaced cinctures.

"Never mind," said the man. "Probably not very important anyway."

"No, probably not."

"Still, you never know, do you? Little things matter. Sometimes, they're all we have."

He stood, wiped some stray blades of grass from his robe, and wished Richard a good day.

Richard walked on for a time. The *matricularius* was the problem, he thought. He was too quick to point the finger of—

Richard looked back, but the stranger had vanished, contentedly lost to the ordinary.

AND ALL THE GRAVES OF ALL THE GHOSTS

Now that you're there, where everything is known—tell me:
What else lived in that house besides us?

Anna Akhmatova, *Northern Elegies*, #3

It was almost funny at the start. Well, I say funny, when what I mean is odd, but there was an amusing aspect to it nonetheless. Not anymore—we're long past that—but for a while, when the children were still young and living in the house. It's only me now; me, and the Presence in the room upstairs. It has a name, or I think it does, even if it's one I'm reluctant to use. I suppose you might call it a ghost, although it's not dead, not yet.

But I'm getting ahead of myself. That's what happens when one has lived alone, or nearly alone, for too long: one falls out of the habit of explaining. It's rendered more difficult in this case by the fact that I don't have an explanation. It has yet to be revealed, but it will, in time. I'll form part of it, I think. It's this aspect of the situation that frightens me. It frightens me very much.

We bought the house from the Millards, but they certainly didn't advise us of any strangeness, some eccentricities of plumbing aside, and those were factored into the asking price. Of course, if one is trying to sell a property, the last thing one ought to do is suggest to potential purchasers that it might be haunted. I suppose it could be an attraction for a certain type of buyer, but it's certainly a niche interest, and most sensible folk would consider it a disincentive to proceeding.

So I don't think the Millards were trying to hide anything from us. They were simply a perfectly ordinary couple seeking to downsize. Neither was the house priced to sell, far from it. We had to bargain them down, and even then we ended up paying more than we'd intended, but they did leave the mirrors and chandeliers, which was nice of them. I've heard of sellers who've stripped houses to the boards, leaving the new occupants to eat under a bare bulb hanging from a length of exposed wire. The Millards weren't like that, and expressed concern upon hearing of our problem with the dining room. Perhaps they were just being polite. My wife suspected they thought us mad, as they changed their telephone number shortly after and went ex-directory. I can't blame them, really. Under the circumstances, I might have adopted a similar precaution.

We had been in the house for a couple of months when Lawrence, our younger child, complained of a draft in the dining room. He'd set up his toy fort there because the room was primarily for entertaining, and we weren't going to be doing much of that until the house was given a fresh coat of paint, the Millards not having put much money into the decor recently. Lawrence was permitted to occupy the expanse from the dining room fireplace to the Persian rug, just as long as he put everything away in time for the cleaning lady to dust and mop every Wednesday. Of course, he never did manage to get things cleared up in time, but that's boys for you. At least we weren't tripping over armies elsewhere or impaling our stockinged feet on lead bayonets.

It was a Saturday morning when Lawrence mentioned the draft (or so we thought it at first): a wind coming up through the floorboards, or down the chimney, except there was no wind, none at all. Rather, it was like one of those damp chills that settle in the late January air, burrowing into the bone. We tried to trace the source, with no luck. Eventually, we called the builder who had repaired some of the damaged plaster in that room, but he declared he couldn't feel any breeze; and it wasn't as though our breath was visibly pluming to give him the lie because, as I've said, the nip wasn't of that type. One might even have said that we were somehow carrying it inside us, like an infection transmitted solely within our little family group. We were the locus, but also the only carriers.

After that, Lawrence relocated the fort to his bedroom, but I noticed he didn't play with it as much anymore, and ultimately it was disassembled and consigned to the attic. When I asked him about it, he declared that the soldiers felt uncomfortably cold to the touch. More probably, it was the associations for which he didn't care, because by then our condition had changed. Worsened, you might say.

The first I learned of it was one Sunday evening, while I was sitting in the basement kitchen listening to Alan Keith on the Light Programme. If I remember correctly, he was playing the "Sanctus" from Gounod's *St. Cecilia Mass*. Actually, I don't know why I say that. Of course I remember correctly: I haven't been able to listen to Gounod since, probably for the same reason Lawrence dispensed with his fort and soldiers. It's just one of those phrases one uses when telling a story. As I've said, I'm unused to sharing in this way, and little fragments of the ordinary keep trying to intrude into what is, by any standard, an extraordinary narrative. Regardless, there I was, a glass of sherry in one hand, the other conducting Gounod, when I heard my wife cry out. It was an expression more of surprise than terror—a startled yelp, one might have said—but it was enough to draw me upstairs.

Susanna was standing in the doorway of the dining room, looking in the direction of what we had come to refer to as the Odd Corner. At first I thought someone might have lit a fire in the grate, because a pale smoke or mist, about five feet in height, hung in the air. But the fireplace was empty and the substance did not diffuse, instead remaining fixed, like a blurred image on a photographic plate. As we watched, it moved ever so slightly, and a column extruded horizontally before being subsumed once again into the whole. After a few seconds, the pattern was repeated, and this continued for a good five minutes. By then the children had joined us, but they seemed more fascinated than frightened until, at last, it dispersed.

Once it was gone, I approached the Odd Corner, my wife exhorting me to take care. I passed my hand through the place where the episode had occurred and noticed that the air was even colder than usual. I didn't know what to make of it, so I ordered the children to stay out of the room before locking the door behind us and placing the key in my jacket pocket. But that night, as I followed my wife to bed, the door was open again. The children, who were still awake, denied all knowledge, as did Susanna, and the key had remained in my pocket the entire evening. I had not slept or dozed, so no one could have taken it from me without my noticing. Puzzled, I secured the dining room once more.

But when we rose the next morning, the door was ajar. Short of nailing it closed, there appeared to be nothing for it but to leave it unlocked thereafter, which we did.

There were no further disturbances that week, and the coldness in the Odd Corner was less pronounced. But the following Sunday, the mist was back and the pattern was repeated: an extrusion, an absorption, the sequence repeated for five minutes. This time, though, I was prepared. I had our Brownie box camera to hand and shot an entire roll from various angles while the form was visible. But when the pictures were developed and returned, they showed only an empty space. It was most peculiar and frustrating.

So it continued, week in, week out, every Sunday—not always at the same time, but usually about a half hour either side of 6 p.m. We had Susanna's father and mother over for drinks one Sunday and tried to explain to them what had been happening, but they probably thought it was some form of unfunny joke on my part, as my in-laws and I had never really enjoyed a happy relationship. We invited them to view the phenomenon for themselves, yet they saw nothing, and their attendance only added to the general chill in the room. The anomaly was for us to witness, and us alone.

Then, some weeks after, we invited our local vicar to dine at our house while his junior curate was taking evensong. He was High Anglican, which we rather liked, but quite modern in his thinking, to the extent that some of the congregation regarded him as dangerously liberal. He listened sympathetically as we sat at the dining table, waiting for the cloud to appear. We informed him when it did, and he made a circuit of the spot, testing it with an index finger. He didn't see anything either, but admitted that the air seemed frosty. Then again, he didn't have much meat on him, and confessed that a great many places gave him the shivers, so he was always suffering or recovering from a cold.

We spoke with him about the possibility of an exorcism, but he told us that the Anglican Church didn't really go in for that business, even at the High end. That would change a decade or so later, but by then I had decided against any attempt at banishment, even had the relevant authorities permitted it. You see, nothing like this had ever happened to me before. I led what many might have considered a dull, middle-class existence, first as the assistant manager, and later the manager, of a high street bank. I was perfectly content, but little of note distinguished my days, or nothing upon which anyone might have felt obliged to comment after my death. My eulogy was not, I thought, destined to shock the congregation.

Truth be told, the Presence made me feel special.

It's strange what one can get used to: illness, pain, loss, grief. We're resilient creatures, we humans, and can grow habituated to almost anything. The Odd Corner became another idiosyncrasy in an already quirky old house, like the gurgling of the pipes or the slight incline to the floor of the main bedroom. The children told their friends about it, daring them to run through the spot, which some did until we discouraged the practice. It struck me as rude. I didn't want to go about offending or provoking whatever was there. It wasn't as though it was bothering us. No crockery was being thrown around, and neither were we being disturbed by unearthly wailing in the dead of night. It was just an area of coldness, and a mist, or something like one. We even began using the dining room more frequently, but never on Sundays. Occasionally, I'd trot along to take in the show with my pipe and a glass of sherry, but it didn't change much during the early years and the novelty quickly wore off. The children became bored with it sooner than I, and stopped referring to it, but Susanna remained bothered. She took to suggesting that we sell up, until the market took a dip and forced us to make do with what we had.

We rarely referred to the Presence in the Odd Corner—and it was an entity, of that we had no doubt—as a ghost, nor did we like to describe our experience as a haunting or an infestation. The algor apart, it didn't correspond to any descriptions of ghosts in fiction, or the supposedly true experiences recounted in the more sensationalist periodicals. I can't say it was harmless, exactly, because we were always aware of it, subconsciously or otherwise, and the tension between Susanna and me would ratchet up as the weekend approached, causing us to bicker over the most inconsequential of issues. For Susanna, the Presence was emotionally and psychologically disruptive; for me, it was a problem to be analyzed. What was it that we were seeing? What was the extrusion? And why did the event occur only on Sunday evenings? I investigated the history of the house, which had been built early in the nineteenth century, and of the land on which it sat, but found no record of a murdered servant girl or an ancient cemetery to suggest a cause for the phenomenon.

But perhaps it was because I spent more time considering the puzzle and found myself seated more regularly in the dining room come Sunday evening, waiting for the Presence to manifest, that I noticed the refinement before anyone else. Slowly, over the space of a decade, the Presence began to assume a more pronounced form: a woman. I could make out the shape of her hips, and her shoulder-length hair. She wore trousers, not a skirt, which struck me as important somehow. Had she been a revenant from some previous century, would a dress or skirt not have been the more likely mode of attire? The movement in the mist, it became clear, was the raising of her right arm to point a finger at something, followed by the lifting of both hands to her face in startlement, though whether delighted or appalled, I could not say. For some reason that was more to do with feeling than observation, I surmised it was the latter, especially when a dark hole started appearing where her mouth ought to be, gaping in what I identified as horror.

I mentioned these developments to Susanna, though only very reluctantly did she consent to observe them. Before turning away, she did concede that, yes, we were now looking at a woman, probably young, and wearing what looked like a sweater and trousers, even if no colors showed themselves beyond the yellowish tinge to the mist itself, the woman consistent in her insubstantiality.

She stares at something in the center of the room.

She points, before putting her hands to her face.

Silently, she screams.

Two years later, I succumbed to appendicitis. After the operation, I caught an infection that kept me hospitalized for two weeks and left me virtually incapacitated for a further fortnight upon my return home. I was unable to tackle the stairs without help, so my recuperation was conducted largely in the bedroom I shared with Susanna. There I took my meals; there I read; there I listened to the wireless; and there I slept. The Odd Corner barely crossed my mind, so absorbed was I by my own discomfort, so intent on my recovery.

Finally, when I could trust myself on the stairs, and the pain and exhaustion had become occasional and irritating rather than persistent and debilitating, I reimmersed myself in the tidal flow of family life. More than a month had passed since I last set foot in the dining room. Lawrence told me that he had poked his head in once or twice and could confirm that the Presence was still with us. He shared this information in the manner of a man explaining the mowing habits of a neighbor, or some mundane occurrence equally unworthy of note.

By contrast, my daughter Juliet, in common with Susanna, had now conceived a profound aversion to the room and refused to set foot there. I put this down to her age—she was seventeen—and the influence of her mother. My wife and I had been drifting apart for some years, and my recent illness had done nothing to bring us closer. She and Juliet had always been confidantes, so I was not surprised to discover the daughter taking the mother's side. I did not resent either of them for it, or so I told myself, even as the shadow of divorce loomed larger.

By then, Juliet had been accepted at Oxford, where she would read Classics, and so was not likely to be with us in the house for much longer. Lawrence, one year younger than his sister, and not as academic, was making noises about a career in the army, the prospect of military service appealing to the child in him. Our finances had improved dramatically, thanks to some astute early investments coming to fruition, leaving us in a comfortable position even as Susanna and I consulted our respective solicitors. There was no bitterness between us, only the sadness of two people who retained a fondness for each other but acknowledged that this was not the same as love: recalling the latter, Susanna was unwilling to settle for only the former. We agreed on wording acceptable to the lawyers—there is a boilerplate to it, so I asked only that I not be depicted as a cheat, bigamist, or wife-beater—and thus the matter was settled.

I could have sold the house. Susanna encouraged it, but I resisted. This decision caused the sole raising of voices between us during proceedings. She couldn't understand my attachment to the property and made it obvious that she ascribed some of the blame for the collapse of our marriage to the Presence in the Odd Corner. She termed it an obsession on my part, but I begged to differ. Now I realize that she and Juliet—yes, particularly Juliet—had recognized an aspect to it that took me longer to discern. That was why they had to leave: because the Presence continued to change, growing more defined, enabling them—us—to see it for who it was, or who it would become.

I am alone in the house now, except for the Presence. Susanna has remarried and lives with her new husband in Scotland. We are more than civil to each other, but the subject of the Presence never arises when we meet, nor is it discussed with Juliet and Lawrence. It haunts us all, though. This has, at last, become a haunting.

I spend most of my time in the dining room, waiting. Each Sunday the Presence appears. It is a woman, perhaps in her early twenties. She points in horror at something on the floor. She raises her hands to her face. She screams. She resembles Juliet.

What is a ghost? I have pondered this question. Indeed, of late I have been thinking of little else. I have concluded that it may be an echo—or a premonition—given rudimentary form, unbound by time, but tied to place. I believe the Presence has always occupied this space and will always occupy it. When we entered the house, we roused it and made it visible, but only to ourselves. It is a part of us. It is past, present, and future, all at once. It is a Juliet that was, is, and has yet to be.

I admit that I am afraid. I have come to understand what it is that lies unseen on the floor. Sometimes I can even glimpse it. I see no point in trying to leave, even should I wish to, since I would only be drawn back. It has to be this way, because otherwise there would be no Presence. I am part of it, for I, too, have always been here and will always be. I fear that great pain lies ahead for me, even violence. I see it reflected in the face of the Presence. This will not be a good death, and it is close. The room is always cold now.

The Presence appears. Juliet is here again.

Together, we stare.

THE EVENINGS WITH EVANS

What is grief? Grief is the suit that fitted once, but no longer. It is the jacket billowing, the waistband gaping. Grief is the house that went from too big to just right, then became too big again. Grief is the thing that feeds upon itself. Grief is the fire and the fuel.

Grief is a fox.

They died on December 23, although not all at the same time. His wife died first—instantly—when the car left the road. His daughter was still alive when a passerby staggered down the steep bank to offer help, and held her hand as the life left her. For that much, he was grateful. His son passed away later that evening in the hospital, with his father seated beside him. He lived long enough to tell the story of what happened: a fox on the road, an instinctive twist of the wheel to avoid it, and then—

Nothing, or next to nothing. Just a house with too many rooms and a man lost at the heart of it, like a rat in a maze, as grief reduced him to a repository of memories.

He did not have the energy to sell up—and anyway, where would he have gone? Wherever he went, he would bring his grief with him. At least here he found a kind of comfort, thin gruel declared sustenance. The house still bore traces of his wife and children, but there was more of his daughter than his son because Simon had been living in Berlin for the final two years of his life, helping to clean up after the Nazis. That Christmas was also likely to have been Caroline's last in permanent residence. She planned to study medicine in Edinburgh—to her mother's combined pride and dismay, as that city seemed so far away.

Gone. All gone.

Each day he would walk his estate, always with a shotgun hanging broken over one arm. He was searching for the fox. His son had described it before he died. The animal bore a distinctive white mark on its right side, Simon had whispered, perhaps caused by barbed wire.

So he became determined to find the fox and kill it, because had it not existed, his family would still be with him. But the fox refused to present itself and accept its fate. He spotted others, but not the one he sought. Nevertheless, each day he filled a pocket of his jacket with shells and stalked the woods and fields with the gun over his right arm.

It was the closest thing to hope he had left.

Mrs. Hoggart, who had been engaged as a housekeeper by his wife, continued to come by every day except Sunday. He tried to convince himself that she needed the work more than he needed her, but in reality, he knew better. She represented his only regular point of contact with the world beyond his estate. If she were to vanish, he would likely lapse into almost total silence. Mrs. Hoggart also advised him on the steps necessary to maintain the property, and took care of the payments to the craftsmen and temporary workers required to prevent it from lapsing further into decay. The Manse was not vast, or not by the standards of some of the great houses, but it was still sufficiently old and grand to swallow as much money as might be poured into it. And money he had: the City had been good to him, his investments had flourished, and they would continue to do so now that the war was over. Keeping an eye on his wealth was what passed for work these days.

On the first anniversary of their deaths, something came apart inside him. He could not have said why, or pointed to what might have changed. He simply felt the fracture in his being widen, and grief, as though envious of the few powers of speech he retained, seized his tongue and sought to still it.

And each day he roamed his lands, seeking the fox, while each night thereafter, he wept.

The Manse boasted a very distinctive wine cellar, one of the reasons he and his wife had bought the property. Parts of the cellar dated back to Norman times, with carvings on the walls and pillars suggesting that it might, at one point, have functioned as a place of worship or contemplation. Many of the bottles had been acquired by the Manse's previous owner and were included in the sale, while others were purchased in the years before the death of his family. Since then, he had neither added to nor depleted its stock. He did not entertain, and now rarely imbibed alcohol beyond an occasional restorative whisky or brandy to keep out the cold. He was afraid that if he began drinking seriously, he would never stop. For the most part, the door to the wine cellar remained closed, and even Mrs. Hoggart rarely ventured down there for long, content to make only occasional forays to keep the worst of the cobwebs at bay.

So it was that one evening after Mrs. Hoggart had departed, a pie left in the oven for him to consume when he saw fit, he was surprised to see the cellar door standing open and what appeared to be candlelight flickering in its depths. The cellar was wired for electricity, so no cause existed for anyone to be lighting candles. It could only have been the work of Mrs. Hoggart, even if he could not imagine why she might have chosen to set a flame. He tried the switch but the cellar remained dark: a blown bulb, perhaps, which would explain the use of the candle. Odd, though, that Mrs. Hoggart had not mentioned it to him or replaced the bulb instead of leaving a candle burning. Perhaps she had forgotten, even if this would have been so out of character as to suggest some form of otherworldly possession.

He took the winding stone staircase down. There, in the center of the floor, facing the lines of shelves that blended gently into the shadows, a table had been placed, and beside it, a chair. Both were familiar, as they formed part of the furnishings that had come with the house. They were constructed from oak so dark as to be almost black, the legs of the table decorated with carved curls of ivy, the chair with arms worn smooth by centuries of use, and an impressive curved back that enveloped the occupant in a way both comfortable and comforting. When last he had paid any attention to the table and chair, they had been heaped with old boxes, but both were now unburdened. On the table stood a bottle of red wine, a glass, a decanter, a corkscrew, and a single candle in a pewter candlestick.

He picked up the bottle: a 1929 Château Beychevelle, a fine Bordeaux. The dust had been blown from it, not wiped, and visible was the mark of the hand that had plucked it from the rack. He looked closely at the fingerprints, the grip wide, the fingers large. Mrs. Hoggart had hands like a bird's talons: strong, but small and thin. It struck him, somewhat uneasily, that it might not have been she who removed the bottle and set it on the table. But if not Mrs. Hoggart, then who?

Suddenly, the cellar seemed threatening to him.

He listened but could hear no sound beyond his own breathing and the sputtering of the candle. He lifted the candlestick from the table and held the light before him. He walked forward—one step, then two, slowly forcing back the shadows—and yet with each step he took he created darkness behind him, and the light was not quite strong enough to reach as far as the walls to either side of him, so he felt himself suspended in a fragile cocoon of illumination, one that would not save him in the event of an attack.

Slowly, and not before unsettling himself profoundly, he confirmed that he was the only occupant of the cellar, and finally found himself back at the table, staring at the wine bottle, the decanter, the corkscrew, and the clean glass. He discovered the niche from which the bottle had been removed and returned it to its place. Taking the candle with him, he climbed the stairs back to the landing and closed the door behind him. Only then did he extinguish the flame.

The following morning he questioned Mrs. Hoggart about the bottle and the candle. She professed ignorance and informed him that it had been at least a week since her last visit to the cellar. He thought that she gave him a peculiar look when she finished speaking. She had little idea of what he got up to when she left, and might well have suspected him of indulging in the odd tipple of an evening—not that she would have blamed him, not in the slightest. Her concerns about him might have been confirmed by the fact that the lights in the cellar now appeared to be working perfectly, even though he had not managed to get around to replacing the bulb, and had not asked Mrs. Hoggart to do so either.

So there they left the affair, each puzzled by the other. But that evening, when Mrs. Hoggart, as usual, departed for home, he checked the cellar. The table stood bare and the wine bottles remained undisturbed. He ate his meal—a stuffed capon with potatoes—and put a record on the gramophone while he read in the library, but had difficulty concentrating on the words before him. At last, he set the book aside and walked to the hall.

The cellar door was open, and he caught the flickering of a candle from below.

He kept his shotgun in a locked cabinet by the boot room. He retrieved it now, loaded the chambers, then waited until he was at the top of the stairs before locking the weapon, the click of it echoing against the stone walls.

"You hear that?" he called out. "That's the sound of a London Best, and you'd damn well better believe I'll use it if you don't show yourself!"

But no reply came from the cellar.

His mouth was dry. The shotgun wavered in his hands. He was dreadfully afraid. Still, he set the stock against his shoulder and took the stairs carefully until he reached the cellar. There, as before, stood a bottle of wine—a different selection, a 1920 Château Cheval Blanc—along with a decanter, a glass, a corkscrew, and a candle in a different candleholder, one that was unfamiliar to him but clearly old. A final additional detail had changed: the wine bottle was empty, but the decanter was full, the cork lying beside it.

"I'm warning you," he said, scanning the cellar, his eyes following the twin barrels of the gun. "Come out, or you'll be sorry."

But nobody appeared, and the depths of the cellar remained dark. He could hold either the candle or the shotgun, but not both, so a second search of the cellar was beyond him. He stepped to the very edge of the candle's reach, squinting into the murk, half expecting a pale hand to reach out and grab the weapon.

"Who are you?" he asked. He did not like the tone of his voice. It betrayed his fear, although he could not have said which he dreaded more—a continuing silence, or a possible reply to his question. In the end, he was left with the former.

A secret passage, he thought: somewhere in the cellar had to be a false wall, unsuspected and undiscovered, and an unknown person was using it to play a nasty game. Come morning, he would call Crichton & Sons, the local builders, and have them conduct a thorough test of the cellar floor and walls. In the meantime, he would keep the door locked, so that no intruder could penetrate farther.

He retreated toward the stairs. He glanced at the table in passing and froze. The wineglass had been empty when he first came down. He was certain that was the case. But it was half-full now.

He stared around him. No one could have managed to get behind him while he had the cellar under his gun, and he would have heard any footsteps on the stone floor, yet the wineglass had somehow been filled while his back was turned.

"No," he said. It was a denial of it all: the intruder, the glass filling, and the invitation to drink—for clearly an invitation it was. He would not accept it, and neither would he linger. He left the candle burning and kept his back to the wall as he made his way up the stairs, his finger against the trigger, the pressure heavy enough to fire a shot instantly if he detected even the hint of attack. When he reached the hall, he slammed the door behind him. The key hung from a hook on the wall: a big iron thing, more ornamental than anything else, but now pressed into service again. It stuck in the lock and seemed reluctant to turn. He shuddered, expecting at any moment to see the handle forced down from the other side. Then, mercifully, the key rotated and the door locked. He stepped back, taking up the shotgun once again. He waited, but all was quiet.

That night, he made up a bed for himself in the library. He kept the shotgun beside him and the key beneath the cushion on which his head rested. He did not sleep, only dozed a little, but each time his eyes closed, it seemed to him that he jerked awake immediately, his ears alert for the sound of some unseen entity testing the cellar door. Only when dawn came did he finally rest, to be woken some hours later by the arrival of Mrs. Hoggart. If she was surprised to find him sleeping on the couch, she chose not to comment, and he was grateful he had been given enough time to hide the shotgun from her sight. She prepared breakfast while he performed his ablutions, but before he ate, he called Crichton & Sons, and old

Albert Crichton, the paterfamilias, agreed to come round sometime after 1 p.m. to take a look at the cellar, drawn on the pretext that a rat might have found a means of ingress. The Crichton family had worked on the Manse for generations, and Albert had helped his father with remedial work on the cellar decades earlier.

When, at last, Albert and his son did arrive, he unlocked the cellar door and led the way down the stairs. The table was empty. The candle and candlestick were gone. The decanter—one of three—was back in the sideboard, with no sign that it had ever been moved. All the glasses were present and correct. As for the bottle, the untasted wine had been poured back inside, its cork restored, and it now stood on the sideboard. This detail was perhaps the most surprising of all. His nocturnal visitor appeared reluctant to waste a fine bottle of wine. The temperature in the cellar would keep it cool, and so it would be drinkable for a while longer.

The Crichtons could find no hole or other flaw in the cellar floor or walls and were perturbed when he asked them to check for some concealed door, as though wondering how a rat might use one, even if it existed. Albert believed that the cellar's walls and floor were sound, and any kind of priest hole or passage would have been discovered long ago. Nevertheless, the current owner's money was good, and work was work, so he offered to return the next day with two men and begin a thorough examination of the cellar, stone by stone.

When Crichton and his son left, Mrs. Hoggart departed with them, accepting a lift, and he could only imagine the conversation they would be having as they returned to the village. He had half a mind to stay at the village inn for the night, but that would hardly stem the gossip that would surely flow from whatever tales the Crichtons would tell, Mrs. Hoggart being—he hoped—more discreet.

Just as he was about to eat his evening meal—shin of beef—he checked the cellar door to ensure it remained locked. The key was in his jacket pocket, the weight of it threatening to tear the lining, but he did not want to leave it anywhere he could not see or feel it.

He had just stepped into the dining room, plate in hand, when he heard the sound of the cellar door opening. He put the plate on the table, picked up the shotgun, and went to the hall. As before, he could see the stairs winding down and the distant candlelight. Now, though, a kind of rage infected his fear. He was tiring of the game.

"Damn you," he said, and he repeated the words over and over as he stamped down the stairs. "Damn you, damn you, damn you . . ."

The same bottle of Château Cheval stood opened and decanted on the table, the same candle had been set in the candleholder, and the same darkness occupied the depths of the cellar, but the atmosphere had changed. He could not have said why, but he was acutely aware of no longer being alone, and felt that, whatever the company, it was watching him closely and curiously. Strangest of all—and for the first time since this peculiar ritual had begun—he noticed his fear ebbing, and his anger fading with it. Whatever was regarding him wished him no harm, but neither did it want to be seen, or not clearly. He thought he caught the slightest blur of movement just beyond the circumference of the candlelight, a hint of gray and white against black, but when he moved closer it receded.

"Who are you?" he asked.

The interloper did not answer.

"What do you want?"

Yet that, at least, was obvious: it wanted him to drink.

Almost resignedly, he lowered the shotgun.

"Fine, then," he said, "if I must."

He placed the weapon against the wall, and a thought struck him. He didn't want to consume the wine without food, so he returned to the dining room, retrieved his dinner, and, after only a moment's hesitation, descended again. He took the seat that had been prepared for him and picked up the decanter. His hand was heavy, and he filled the glass slightly higher than was advisable. From the darkness came an audible intake of breath, followed by a sniff of mild disapproval.

"Sorry," he said, and wondered to whom—or what—he was apologizing. He sniffed the wine and took a sip, swilling it in his mouth to release the flavors. It was wonderful. He had forgotten how good a glass of wine could taste.

He ate and drank slowly, now and again staring awkwardly into the dark, and the presence stared back at him. Oddly, it assumed more definition if he did not look directly at it. If he tried to pick it out of the murk, it might have been mistaken for a trick of the light caused by the movement of the candle's flame. But if he glanced aside, in the direction of the racks or the cellar walls, it had a degree of clarity. A man, quite tall, dressed in the manner of a butler or valet: a black suit, a white shirt with a Windsor collar, and a black tie in a classic simple knot.

The glass was empty. He refilled it. A peace settled over him. He should get a dog, he decided. He and his wife hadn't wanted another after the last one died. It was just too hard to say farewell to them, and with Simon gone and Caroline about to leave, there didn't seem to be much point. They had talked about traveling more once the children were settled, and—

He realized, quite gradually, that he was speaking aloud.

He stopped talking and put the glass down. Emotions constrained for too long suddenly threatened to overwhelm him.

"Enough," he said.

He stood, abandoning the shotgun, and went up the stairs, not caring that he had turned his back on whatever had taken up occupancy in the cellar. He just wanted to be gone from there. As he closed the door behind him, the candle was put out. He might once have attributed it to his own actions, or the draft from the door, except he knew better. The entity preferred the dark.

The next day, he retrieved the shotgun and tramped his fields and forests with a new urgency. More than ever, he wanted that fox. He was certain it was not dead. Had it been removed from the world, he would have sensed its absence. But the fox, as always, eluded him. Crichton and his men arrived to commence a *tap-tap* examination of the walls and floor, but again found nothing untoward beyond the odd hole that they filled in to discourage rodents.

That night, the cellar door stood open, even though he had the only key in his pocket, having used it to lock up after Crichton left. A candle burned, but he did not go down, and in time the light was blown out. The second night, the same.

On the third, he relented.

The bottle—a Saint Préfert from Châteauneuf-du-Pape, one of the first such wines bottled in the previous decade—stood unopened but the glass, the decanter, and the candle were all in place. He experienced a moment of disappointment at the sight of the corked bottle until he recovered himself and saw reflected in its intact nature the decision of someone who cared for wine and, after two nights without the appearance of the awaited guest, did not wish to waste a good bottle by decanting it only to watch it go undrunk. He turned his head, taking in the racks, before allowing his gaze to shift to the right, where the figure of a man shimmered. He could just make out his face, and the gray hair above it.

He opened the bottle, checked the cork, and decanted the wine. He waited a while before carefully filling the glass to the correct level. He sniffed, tasted, and—satisfied—took his seat.

"It's very good," he said.

If this was madness, it was a fine one.

He thought that the figure shifted slightly, its head inclining in acknowledgment.

He leaned forward in his chair, cupping the glass in his hands, warming it. He spoke.

"The first time I saw her," he said, "she was wearing a blue dress . . ."

Later, he could barely remember stumbling up the stairs. The house was in darkness, but he was not frightened. He renounced the couch, spurned the shotgun, and took to his bed. His throat hurt, and he knew he had been crying. He slept, and when he woke, his sorrow had eased.

And so it went, evening after evening: a bottle waiting for him, a glass, a candle, movement somewhere in the cellar, and a man listening.

"Simon was always a quiet child . . ."

"I thought Caroline might have become a surgeon . . ."

"My wife once had a new variety of rose named after me as a birthday gift . . ."

He even established a possible identity for his confessor, buried deep in the records of the Manse and those who had served in it over the years. No first name, no clue as to his origins, just a surname: Evans, who had supervised the transformation of the cellar into a suitable repository for wine and assembled the original collection in the early part of the nineteenth century. When he asked Mrs. Hoggart about him, she claimed to know nothing. She made inquiries in the village, but no one could recall an Evans.

"Not from around here, whoever he was," Mrs. Hoggart told him. "Someone would have tales to tell of him otherwise."

It took him three days to speak the name aloud in the cellar, and when he did so, he detected a change, a kind of closing of the distance between himself and the other, and he thought that he could somehow see the man more markedly, but still only if he did not gaze directly at him.

Two weeks after he had begun speaking to Evans, he was walking in the woods, the shotgun over his arm, when he came across the fox. He knew it from the marking on its side. A female: he could see its teats. It was standing in the path before him, perhaps a dozen feet away at most. The shotgun was loaded. He brought the barrels up and closed the break.

The click was loud, and the animal's ears twitched in response, but it did not run. Instead, it remained where it was, as though to say *Here I am. You have sought me for so long, and I am tired of hiding. Do what you will. Do what you must.*

He leveled the gun at the fox and put his finger on the trigger. He felt it give beneath the weight. Slowly, slowly . . .

He closed his eyes, willing himself to relax. When he opened them again, the fox had altered position. It was now sitting on its haunches, regarding him closely. They remained like that, man and beast, until the former lowered the shotgun, opened the break, and let the shells fall to the palm of his hand. Perhaps he had always known it would end this way. If he were to kill the animal, what would he have left?

The fox rose and trotted away. He watched it vanish into the undergrowth, and then it was lost to him.

He never saw the creature again.

The days went by. Each evening, he descended to the cellar, but often he did not drink, and sometimes did not even speak. But always, Evans was waiting, and if he wished to talk, Evans would listen.

The pains began to intensify a month after he saw the fox. He had been enduring them for a year but chose to ignore them until they started to come between him and his sleep. The doctors spoke of tumors that had spread through his system and admitted that surgery would be of little benefit at this late stage. He would be helped with his suffering; they would do their best to make the end as comfortable as possible. But death is rarely accommodating, and so he suffered.

A team of nurses cared for him in his final weeks, and during that time he managed a final visit to the cellar, on Christmas Eve. A nurse helped him down the stairs before leaving him alone, as requested. A bottle stood on the table, and a glass, but the candle had not been lit.

Evans, being careful.

He lit the candle himself with a match. The shadows retreated. At the very periphery of the illumination, he picked out the toes of a pair of polished shoes, a servant's livery, and a face hovering above it like a waning moon.

He poured himself a glass of wine. It was a 1928 Château Mouton Rothschild, a jewel of the cellar, but he could only manage a few mouthfuls. It seemed a shame to waste it, so he replaced the cork and determined to give it to the nurse to take home when she left the next morning. He wiped his mouth with a handkerchief and saw bright blood beside the deeper crimson of the wine.

"I came to say thank you, Evans," he said, "and goodbye. These evenings with you have meant a great deal to me. They have helped in ways I cannot even begin to explain. I shall miss our times together."

He felt a strange sense of disappointment that, even now, when they were about to be parted, Evans would not permit himself to be seen. The feeling passed. He had no right to be disappointed with Evans, no right at all.

He stood. He called for the nurse and heard her footsteps on the stairs. He wondered if she had been listening. No matter.

"Farewell, Evans," he said.

He blew out the candle, and Evans was gone.

Shortly before midnight, he lay on his deathbed and dreamed. He was on the forest path and saw the fox. When the animal trotted into the woods, he followed it.

He slept, and he died.

Darkness visible through a gap in the curtains. Starlight and moonlight. Sounds, voices. His robe hanging from a hook on the door.

He rose from his bed and put on the robe. The room smelled of fresh pine and woodsmoke. He opened the door and walked to the landing. The stairs stretched down to the hall, where a woman was adjusting the position of a Christmas ribbon around a mirror.

She looked up.

"You're awake."

"Yes."

"We've been waiting for you, the children and I."

He started to cry. He could not stop himself.

"Oh," she said. "Oh, oh."

She went to him and held him until he was ready to speak again.

"Where are they?" he asked.

"Walking in the woods, but they won't be long. Breakfast will be served soon, so you'll have to hurry up and get dressed. Why don't you choose a bottle of champagne and set it to chill? After all, it is Christmas. And," she added, "I think there is someone you might like to greet."

The cellar door stood open. A candle flickered. He descended.

A bottle stood on the table: Krug, 1928, one of the greatest vintages. Beside it was a tray with four champagne flutes. A man emerged from the shadows, both strange and familiar.

"Hello, Evans."

"Hello, sir. I took the liberty of selecting a bottle."

"I see that. An excellent choice."

"And I've set aside a claret to go with the goose later."

"I expect it will be very well received."

He looked at the Krug. "Why don't you open that now, so we might share a glass?"

"Most kind, sir."

He watched as Evans uncorked the champagne, the candlelight illuminating the spectral cloud of the vapor. Evans poured, they toasted, and they drank.

"All is well," he said.

"Yes, sir. All is well."

And the evenings with Evans stretch on forever.

ABELMAN'S LINE

Having dined alone, the man who goes by the name of Helmut Gregor finishes his coffee at the ABC Restaurant on Calle Lavalle in Buenos Aires. Uli Rudel should have been with him, but Rudel's bad leg, or what's left of it, has been acting up. Gregor might have stayed in his lodgings or visited his favorite brothel, but he chooses instead to go to the ABC, where he can listen to German being spoken and pretend he is not so far from home.

Gregor thanks the waiter in halting, heavily accented Spanish, and picks a stray piece of food from the distinctive gap between his front teeth before heading into the night. He pauses at the door to adjust his coat and examine the evening sky for the possibility of rain, which also allows him to check the street for anything out of the ordinary: a van parked too long, its driver unmoving; a man and woman kissing in a doorway that only the most desperate of lovers would deem acceptable; a car with its hood raised, a motorist peering into its workings.

Gregor sometimes worries that he is becoming a creature of routine, which would make him more vulnerable, but all men, as they grow older, take comfort from repetition. Novelty is for the young, but it is also the case that a man with routines of his own gains knowledge of the routines of others. Gregor already knows every crack in the pavement of this area of the city, the eccentricities of every streetlight, the names of residents, shopkeepers, road sweepers, and policemen, and any alteration to its customs will therefore be immediately apparent. In this way, he has survived, remaining concealed from his enemies while hiding in plain sight, for some here are aware that Helmut Gregor is an invention, a fiction. In private, they may even utter his true name aloud, although only among intimates and not often.

Gregor starts to walk, with only the song of the night birds to disturb his thoughts.

"We're holding," says Lavron.

"Confirm," says Falk.

Lavron runs the images from the Eye again. By now he's lost count of the number of times he's been through them, but as with Helmut Gregor and his environment, repetition and an immersion in the familiar make the uncommon stand out.

Before Lavron, a hologram of the timeline appears. With its nexus of branches, it resembles the crown of a tree, a similarity heightened by the decision to limit the line to a two-minute window, significantly below maximum capacity, so that the hologram assumes the shape of a sphere, as though a woodcutter gifted with divine precision has pruned branches into a perfect circle.

"Give me the overlay," says Falk.

Lavron superimposes a second hologram over the first, this one mapping the line on a subatomic level. The match appears perfect to the naked eye, but more is required for the go-ahead. Under the sphere, a horizontal feed slowly runs the numbers. The two-dozen people in the room monitor its progress, unspeaking. Only when the feed turns entirely green is there a collective release of breath.

"It's stable," says Lavron. "No deviation."

He turns to Falk.

"We have him."

Let's rewind—which, as you'll learn, is appropriate under the circumstances. First of all, the Eye. That's how everyone refers to it, though it's actually a subatomic mapper, so "the SAM" might be more correct, except nobody has ever called it that, not even those responsible for its invention. Right from the start, it was "the Eye." If you believed in God, you might have described it as miraculous. I'm not sure I believe in God, so I'm disinclined to use the word, but I still think it's as close to miraculous as anything man-made has ever come, even more than the Splitter, and the Splitter is pretty fucking amazing in itself.

I never tire of looking at those spheres because of what they represent: the sheer complexity of one tiny section of the universe, captured in a snapshot. Occasionally, I imagine what would happen if the system could be adapted to show us not just a fragment of a single timeline, but all of them: an infinite forest of infinite trees, infinitely growing. But that's not likely to happen anytime soon because four minutes is the current limit of the system. There's a reason why we've never gone to four, though, and only once increased to three. And what's the reason?

Money.

Okay, science lesson. I'll do my best to keep it painless, mainly because I admit I don't understand it all, even if that's nothing to be ashamed of. As far as I can tell, maybe a dozen people claim to comprehend fully the mechanics of what we do, and half of them are lying. As for the rest, you can ask them to explain the science, but you'll regret it. Either you'll walk away after thirty seconds or die of boredom. I mean, the whole business is beyond fascinating, but only on the macro level. Once you get down to the math, it's as dull to the layman as it is unintelligible. Basically, what we're dealing with here is block universe theory: every possible timeline happening simultaneously, everywhere. No past, present, or future—well, there is, or rather, there are, but the distinctions cease to have meaning. If it makes it simpler, think of past, present, and future as being overlaid, like the compressed layers of a sandwich, but all occupying the same space. Yet that's just one timeline, because here's where it gets really interesting, not to mention complicated.

So, you woke this morning—at 5:45, early riser that you are. You like to have a little time to yourself before the kids get up, or emails start cluttering your inbox. You climbed out of bed—except perhaps you didn't. It could be that you stayed where you were for a few minutes longer, waiting for the clock to hit 5:50, because nobody gets out of bed at 5:47 or 5:48, unless they're crazy, just as we like to make sure our total for a tank of gas ends in a zero.

Now we have two timelines: one in which you got up at 5:45 a.m., and another in which you rose to face the day at 5:50. But even within that five-minute gap, an abundance of further timelines exists: the one where you closed your eyes for a second or two, and the one where you didn't; the one where you turned over on your left side, and the one where you remained as you were; the one where your wife snored beside you, causing you to glance at her in annoyance; and the one where you didn't bother to look, since you've been married for twenty years and those little snores are part of the deal.

Meanwhile, those are just *your* timelines, because we haven't even begun to factor in your wife's timeline, or the timelines of the fly currently buzzing by the window and the spider curled in a corner hoping that same fly ends up in its web. We haven't considered the timelines of your kids, your neighbors, the birds on the branches of the oak in your yard, or the leaves on that same tree, some of which are poised to fall. And don't even get me started on the atomic level—or, God forbid, the subatomic level, because that's the point where the intricacy of the universe threatens to drive a person insane. We flourish as a series of potentialities that are also actualities, because for everything that happens, something doesn't happen—

except the thing that doesn't happen also happens, but on a separate timeline.

Which is where the Eye comes in.

Back in the control center, Lavron is looking at Meyer, and Meyer is looking at me, while I'm looking at Uri Hoch. (And, yes, on another timeline none of us is looking at anyone, or some of us are while others aren't. See, now you're getting the hang of it.) Hoch is currently in touch with Leela Tamor, but only unofficially, although I can listen in because all three of us have to sign off on what's about to occur. (Or not occur. I'll stop now.) Tamor keeps her distance from what we do, which gives her deniability. She's convinced that sometime in the future, distant or otherwise, the truth of what we've been engaged in will emerge, and there'll be investigations and interrogations, with jail sentences to follow. But Tamor is sixty-four and in poor health. I've tried to convince her that by the time they get around to asking her anything, she'll probably be dead, to which her response is that being dead hasn't saved any of the targets. This is a fair point, but whatever Tamor might or might not know, it wouldn't be worth putting an Eye on her to find out. There are better ways to spend the money, and more worthy dead people on whom to spend it.

"*Geldscheißerin*, what's your view?"

Tamor often refers to me as the banker, or occasionally—like now—as the gold shitter. I'm the finance person, the moneywoman, hence *Geldscheißerin*—though technically, I'm the one who squeezes the wealthy and collects the result. Whatever the truth may be, I can tell that Hoch wishes Tamor weren't talking to me at all, but that battle was fought and lost years ago.

"I want to run the Tree one more time," I tell her.

Hoch's expression suggests someone has just fed him a piece of bad fish.

"We've run it five times already," he says. "We're so far within the margin of error, we can't see the edges."

"But what's a sixth between friends?" I reply.

"We're not friends," says Hoch.

Which is true. But then, nobody in this room likes me. I'm the nonscientist, and scientists hate it when nonscientists can stop them from having fun. On the other hand, they wouldn't be here if it wasn't for what I do. I persuade rich people to hand over vast amounts of cash without asking too many questions or demanding to witness the results. I'm good at it, too—so fuck you, scientists.

"If Ari wants to run it once more, then we let it run," says Tamor.

"It'll cost us time," says Hoch. "And money."

"Time we have," I said. "The target isn't going anywhere. We know where to find him. After all, he's been dead for a century."

"What about money?"

"If you're wrong about the margin of error, it'll cost us a whole lot more."

"We're not wrong."

"Yeah," I say, "I've heard that before."

I know that Hoch would like to punch my lights out, woman or not. He's told me often enough how much pleasure it would give him, and it's true that I enjoy goading him. Tamor has taken me to task about it, but a girl shouldn't be denied her small pleasures. More to the point, you don't want to be the chump who has to tell someone who coughed up an eight-figure donation that they might as well have set their money on fire and laughed while it burned. I know, because I was that chump, and it was fucking Hoch's fault—well, not his alone, because Tamor concluded that it was a systemic failure, and a whole new series of checks and balances were required to ensure it didn't happen again. Nevertheless, the buck should have stopped with Hoch as senior operator—that's my view, if a minority one—and in any normal operation he'd have been out on his ass.

Unfortunately, Hoch is one of the handful of people I mentioned earlier who actually understand what we do, so it's not like we can fire him and then pull someone from the line at the employment office to fill the position. We're stuck with Hoch.

But I do appreciate his unhappiness. As far as Hoch and his people are concerned, I'm a bean counter, an obstacle to scientific, even moral, progress, although the ethics of what we do are gray at best, and I wouldn't like to be called upon to justify them in a court of law. With luck, as I told Tamor, that won't happen, and we'll all be yellowing bone before anyone begins unpicking our history.

But if our luck doesn't hold, I'm going to lawyer up or head for the hills, most likely the latter. I have three passports, only one of them in my own name, and enough cash squirreled away to keep me in comfort, if not luxury, for a decade or more. After that, I'll see what happens. I might kill myself, because once the truth has been revealed, the technology will be acquired by others and exploited in ways that Abelman would never have condoned. Then I suspect the world will probably come to an end, because I guarantee that the first rule to be broken will be the only one that matters: Maintain Temporal Integrity.

Or, to put it more prosaically: Don't Fuck with the Line.

The father of our work is Isaac Abelman, an Ashkenazi Jew. Abelman is a patronymic of Abel, meaning "vanity," and if, or when, everything heads south, you can bet the media will leap on that one. Abelman was a theoretical physicist, attached to CERN in Geneva, and was present on the day the first artificial black hole was created. That was Abelman's second-to-last day at the office, not that anyone was going to get all weepy at his absence. Abelman was said to have alienated more coworkers than there were actual operatives at CERN, which takes some doing. He was brilliant, of course, a genius's genius, but not what you'd call a people person, even by the low standards of the scientific community. He was also running his own personal research project on the side, siphoning money from the tank. That's the difficulty with a project run by more than twenty different member states, entailing an annual budget of billions of euros: there's a lot of scope for cash to slip between the floorboards. But the precise nature of Abelman's pet enterprise was destined to remain hidden from his employers, because as soon as they tried to access his records, his drives went into meltdown.

By then, of course, Abelman had left the building, never to be seen again in Europe or North America—or pretty much anywhere else, in fact. We knew where he was, though. We'd been in contact with him for years, and we gave him shelter when the time came, as well as laboratories, funding, and personnel. The ground had been prepared long before, and the switch, when it happened, went smoothly.

There were rumors, of course. There are always rumors. As long as they stay that way, everything is fine. Abelman wasn't big on Michelin-starred restaurants, five-star hotels, and diving weekends at the Red Sea. He didn't even like sunlight, so the only time I ever saw him outdoors was at night. "Nosferabel," that's what some of the technicians called him, though not to his face. Abelman wasn't your stereotypical scientist. He stood six four in his stocking feet, could bench two-fifty, even in his early sixties, and took out his frustrations on a punching bag every morning. Abelman could seriously fuck a person up.

But he didn't hate everyone, just nearly everyone. He tolerated about five people, and actively liked two. Strange to relate, I was one of them, because I never questioned what he did, only ensured that the checks cleared. Neither did I speak to him about his work, and in the evenings and on weekends I was happy to watch football matches with him—soccer, for you Americans out there, not that stop-start local shit you've misnamed. Abelman didn't have any particular team loyalty. He followed lots of sports, but football more than most; and he also enjoyed gambling, but we'll come back to that.

The other person Abelman liked was Bina Hannen, who was a decade younger than him and almost as smart, but with a better developed set of social skills. Bina claimed there was never anything sexual between her and Abelman, no matter what some might have whispered. Personally, my feeling is that there was, but they very sensibly tried to keep it quiet. The only reason I suspect they did get it together is that some mornings Abelman had a weird, satisfied smile on his face, and not even Hoch screwing up a whole series of calculations could wipe it off. Bina once told me that she had never met a man who got her the way Abelman did. It was, she said, as though he could see into her mind.

Abelman was never the same after Bina died. When her cancer was first diagnosed, he struggled to maintain focus. We had to stop him reaching out to doctors and researchers, like he could somehow whip them into doing something for her. We made sure she had the best treatment and kept her free from pain until close to the end. But if Abelman could have saved her, he would have, whatever the cost to himself. When she died, we monitored his research activities more closely than before, out of concern that he might try something foolish, but generally, he came across as no more than disengaged.

I spoke to him about it. Someone had to. He must have known he was being watched, though it was only polite to be open about it. He told me we didn't have to worry, and I believed him, but he added that it was only because the science wasn't yet precise enough. That was the word he used: precise. I don't think he was lying to me, either, but if he could hide his research from CERN, he could hide God knows what from us too, no matter how closely we kept tabs on him. I think that's what happened. Abelman kept something back. The precision wasn't there yet, but that didn't mean it couldn't be. If anyone was capable of advancing the science, it was Abelman.

I miss him. I miss him every day.

In the lab we've recalibrated, and Helmut Gregor is once again inside the restaurant. In a few minutes, he'll pay his bill, his coat will be brought, and he'll step out into the evening. He'll take a little time to adjust his collar and fasten his coat before deciding it's too warm for a buttoned-up coat, and he has to go to the trouble of unbuttoning it all over again. But it's a pantomime, a distraction. I don't know how many times I've watched Gregor perform the same exercise, even before this week, but it's a lot, and in an ideal world I wouldn't be watching it again. Nevertheless, I made the call, backed by Tamor, and so it's incumbent on me to pretend to be engaged, if only at the start. The run-through will take a couple of hours, and at some point, I'll slip away for a cup of coffee. Tamor will probably call me to talk about nothing, because that's what she does when we're about to stage an intervention.

That's how we refer to it, by the way: staging an intervention. It started as a joke at Lavron's expense, after he confessed to us that his wife and kids had trapped him in the living room to complain about the amount of time and money he was spending on his toy soldier collection and the space his battlefields were taking up in the basement. It keeps him calm, he says, and we should be thankful for small mercies, because even a calm Barak Lavron is a disquieting figure to behold.

But he'd also been acquiring antique pieces at auction, which he kept on a shelf in his den. He figured his wife wouldn't notice. Lavron has never really understood women—not that he's had much opportunity, since his wife is the only woman he's ever slept with, but that's no excuse. If you only have one problem to solve, the least you can do is come up with something approaching the right answer.

Lavron has been married to Sophia for nearly twenty years, and she remains barely less of an enigma to him now than she was when they first met. Sophia isn't even a particularly enigmatic woman. Like all women, and fewer men, she undoubtedly has hidden depths, but my guess is that, in her case, there aren't many, and someone would first have to paddle in a lot of shallows to find them. But I also have three failed marriages behind me, so it may be that I'm not one to preach, even if what led to my matrimonial collapses wasn't a failure of comprehension but an absence of faithfulness. I was a lousy spouse, but I remain on good terms with two of my ex-wives, and my children continue to be fond of me. Some people just don't belong married. It's not good for anyone involved.

But to return to Barak Lavron and his toy soldiers—sorry, "military miniatures," because if there's one thing guaranteed to incite Lavron to barely suppressed rage, it's referring to his treasures as "toys." So: his wife spots a red box on his shelf, and thinks, huh, that looks pretty. But she doesn't have her glasses with her—the woman wears spectacles with lenses like the base of a whisky tumbler—and can't read the writing on the front, which is too ornate for her to figure out unaided. She takes down the box, inside of which are twelve painted men on horseback, in mint condition, and an alarm bell goes off in her brain. She picks up one of her husband's magnifying glasses, which he uses for close-up painting work, and examines the label, revealing the contents to be Life Guards, created by the Britains company to mark the Diamond Jubilee of Queen Victoria in 1897. In other words, these are old soldiers—veterans, if you will.

A quick online search produces results from an auction in Toronto a month earlier, in which a record was set for a mint box of miniatures remarkably like the one on the desk before her, described in the catalogue as "Britains Set No. 72, Life Guards Past and Present, 1st version." The sale price was the equivalent of a year of mortgage payments for the Lavron household, and then some, this at a time when Barak Lavron had been complaining about the hole that two sets of college tuition were making in their savings, and how everyone needed to be more careful with their spending because Papa Lavron wasn't made of fucking money.

The immediate consequence was that Lavron was forced to sleep in one of the on-site cubicles for four days, and when he was finally permitted to return home, Sophia and the kids were waiting to pounce. Lavron is now on an allowance, which enables him to keep body and soul together while leaving him with enough to buy a few beers at the end of the week, if he's been frugal. He was free to keep the Life Guards set, though, which was some consolation. The downside is that he won't receive any more birthday presents before he dies, but I don't think he minds so much. Lavron loves that little red box of mounted soldiers. If he had to choose between saving it or his children in the event of a fire, he'd opt for the kids, but only after a potentially fatal hesitation.

Lavron's hobby/obsession might seem like an irrelevant digression in this narrative, even if—and forgive me for going back on my word, but I can't pass up these opportunities—the scientists on the team would argue that there's no such thing as an irrelevant digression, only a variation, and everything has relevance, especially if you follow the Line. Whether Archimedes takes a bath doesn't appear to be very interesting on a base level, unless you happen to be living with him and are wondering how to break it to him that, you know, a wash and brush up might be on the cards. Similarly, Isaac Newton's decision to kill an hour in the shade of a tree wouldn't have been worth alerting the newspapers about at the time, but you only have to spend a few minutes in our staff restaurant before you'll hear one of the team discussing the relativistic theory of gravitation, along with Minkowski space, Riemannian space, and a whole slate of further arcana that will, if you have any concern for the preservation of your good humor, lead you to find a quieter table elsewhere.

What I'm trying to say is that Lavron's argument with his wife over the painted soldiers, and his brief enforced separation from his family, caused him to be edgier than usual on the day the green light was given for the first intervention—our intervention, that is, not the one involving the soldiers. You know, I'll just capitalize "Intervention," to distinguish one from another. I should have done that earlier, but we don't capitalize it in reports, although I've always contended that we should. After all, it's the most important aspect of what we do. The scientists, and Hoch in particular, differ, arguing that the process is what's most interesting, and the Interventions—fuck you, Hoch—are just the end product, a demonstration of the technology's current capabilities at this early stage. For them, celebrating a successful Intervention is like cheering the second Ford Model T to roll off the line when you've already begun making sketches for a rocket to the stars. That's the problem with scientists, or one of the problems, because it's not like we're going to run out of questionable aspects to their disposition anytime soon: they're always in a hurry to get to the next stage without taking time to a) enjoy what's already happened and b) consider whether it is, in fact, a good idea to move to that next stage.

This is another reason I wish Abelman were still here. He took a different view, which is why he installed the safeguards. In a bunker somewhere, a specialist group of which perhaps even Tamor remains unaware, or about which she doesn't want to know, is working on a means of identifying Abelman's trip wires and disarming them. It'll take them years, even decades, because Abelman was smarter than all of them put together, Bina Hannen excepted, and Bina is dead. If the group screws up, causing the system to crash—or worse, self-erase—they'll struggle to get work teaching math to kindergarten kids, assuming they don't end up in a cell.

Or killed, because that's a possibility, too. Nobody talks about Krakauer. The official version is that he's in a secret prison following a star chamber trial for treason. But while there are undoubtedly secret prisons, there was no trial, not for Krakauer. He was questioned by experts and gave up everything he knew, including the names of his contacts. Krakauer wasn't good with pain, or certainly not the level of it to which he was subjected. When they were done with him, he was led to a tiled room with a sloped floor, which made it easier to clean, and shot in the back of the head. Within a week, seven foreign operatives either disappeared or were assassinated, even though Krakauer hadn't told them much. He was still at the stage of baiting the hook when he was escorted from his quarters at 4 AM. We'd been monitoring him, of course. We monitor everyone. Somewhere, someone is monitoring me, and someone is monitoring them, and all those people need to be paid. Since I'm responsible for securing funding, I'm effectively paying for my own surveillance. If that isn't the definition of a team player, I don't know what is.

But to return to Lavron: on that day, the day of the first Intervention, he panicked. Nobody blames him for it—as I said before, I blame Hoch—because whatever else Lavron might have done, he didn't freeze, and as any good soldier will tell you, the worst thing you can do in a crisis is nothing. Lavron made a decision and followed through on it. The result was a mess, physical as well as logistical, but we learned from it, which is why we're now running the Tree for a sixth time, over Hoch's objections, and we'll run it a seventh and an eighth if I'm not happy. Tamor will go along with it. We don't have an infinite supply of money, and I still have scabs on my knees from the amount of begging I had to do after the first fuckup, but that's the primary lesson we took from the disaster: check the Tree, then check it again, and again. The secondary lesson was this: always have a mop and bucket to hand, and a big bottle of bleach, because blood and bone are a bitch to clean up.

I keep circling what we do, and how we do it, but no explanation really conveys how extraordinary the technology is, and as I've already admitted, I lack the scientific or mathematical language required. But let's grasp the nettle, shall we? This is the process. We find a satisfactory timeline and, using the Abelman-Hannen Bridge, insert the Eye, a device that maps the locale and covers the variables so there are no surprises. We replay the footage from the Eye over and over, analyzing the data until we become exhaustingly acquainted with the movements of the target, the insects in the air, the leaves on the trees, the drifting of clouds, the actions of every particle down to neutrino level, which is serious number-crunching, a neutrino having almost no mass—an electron has near-zero mass, but still weighs five hundred thousand times more than a neutrino—and being capable of moving at close to the speed of light. Finally, a moment of Intervention is designated, and with the agreement of the three principals, the Splitter is activated. This creates an artificial timeline, a temporal dead end. The target is then trapped, and we have seventeen minutes and twenty-two seconds to move them along, before—

But I'm leaping ahead. I'll get to Walter Rauff and what happened to him, I promise, but I'll have to talk about Gerhard Bohne first, and Helmut Gregor is also obviously on my mind. There's a lot to keep track of, and not all of it good.

Anyway, that's what we do. How we do it is by creating miniature black holes, which is both more and less impressive than it sounds. More because, well, it's a black hole, which shouldn't be underestimated. Less because a) it's sealed deep in a bunker a mile belowground and b) it is, as the product description suggests, black, trapping all light, so that what we are privy to is an unsatisfactory visual representation on a series of screens, based on mathematical models of the black hole's effect on the light emitted by matter. Basically, it's a show for the rubes, no matter what Hoch may claim to the contrary. Don't get me wrong, it's a very good show, but it comes with a certain sense of anticlimax. Then again, if I was actually down in the bunker when the black hole opened, I'd be torn apart before being crushed to a point of infinite density, so I'll settle for a representation that comes without the promise of a rapid if original death. The black hole is created using exotic matter—in our case, negative mass particles—and involves a risk profile so great that no one ever speaks of it, and therefore it doesn't exist.

So far, we've only staged Interventions in the past, although, again, Abelman's beloved block universe theory proposes that past, present, and future all exist somewhere in that universe, and what we think of as "now" is an arbitrary judgment based on perception. We should, conjecturally, be able to insert an Eye into the future of a timeline as well as the past, but we can't, or not yet. The difficulty is the number of variables. Because it's the future, we can't map it accurately, not from our position on the timeline—obviously, there are no records—so we're reduced to speculation or educated guesses. Given the massive processing power and consequent costs involved in accessing a point on a timeline about which we do, in fact, know more than nothing at all, the future remains out of bounds—so far. Those shadowy figures I mentioned earlier, the ones working on dismantling Abelman's security, are doubtless hoping to pave the way for insertions into the future, in the future, but my suspicion is that Abelman had some ideas about that as well. He's stymied them at every turn, and I hear the whispers of frustration at how he seems to have anticipated each move they might make. It's as though he didn't just guess what they'd try—he knew.

I have my thoughts about that as well. Unless the shadow research group consists entirely of idiots, which it does not, then some of them are entertaining similar thoughts, centering on Abelman's love of gambling.

You'll have to forgive the fragmented nature of this account. It's not as linear as some might wish, but that serves as an analogy for time itself. A linear account would be a misrepresentation of the temporal reality, with its multiplicity of possibilities, its fathomless branches. While it may appear that I'm jumping around, there's a logic to it, or that's the defense I'll use. I'm not a storyteller, just as I'm not a scientist. But I'm also not sure what happened, so I'm still piecing it all together. I have clues, but no solution. Abelman's gambling is one of those clues.

The gambling was undoubtedly a vice, but one we were prepared to indulge. It seemed to be Abelman's only one, and the amounts involved were not so large as to set off alarm bells. I should know, because my father was a gambler. He worked as a taxi driver, and his tips were used to fund his jones, so he was that rare bird: the responsible gambler. For my father, the pleasure lay not in winning or losing, but in the moment before the final card was turned or the roulette ball came to rest in the slot. He thrived on the uncertainty, the anticipation. (Schrödinger would have applauded.) Patterns applied, but only to a point, because chance played a more significant part, and provided the excitement. That's why casinos are always looking for patterns in wins, because they're usually a sign that someone is cheating.

Abelman liked betting only on sporting events: horse races, football games, basketball, tennis, even golf. He was promiscuous in his fascinations, to that extent. Since he couldn't leave the compound, he gambled online, spreading his bets over a range of sites and providers, and we had access to his activities. After a while, Tamor and the others stopped keeping an eye on him. As long as the sums were modest, they didn't care, because any losses wouldn't leave Abelman exposed.

But I continued to be curious, because Abelman didn't react to his triumphs and reverses like any gambler I'd ever met, and I couldn't detect a logic to his wagers. Overall, he won considerably more than he lost, but there were occasions when I felt he might have made poor bets deliberately to disrupt a sequence of wins, and others when the opposite occurred, and a bet that made no sense produced a significant return. Frequently, Abelman was happiest when he lost, or when a seemingly sure thing went against the odds.

I realized that he liked unanticipated outcomes. Rather than being disturbed by the anomaly, he was amused.

Lavron and Hoch are huddled with a pair of technicians, whispering among themselves, which is always a concern. If it's worth saying, it should be shared with the whole group, but I don't worry about these confabs as much as I used to, because for all his bitching, Hoch is nearly as anxious to avoid screwups as I am. He knows that his reputation and his job depend on successful Interventions. On the screens, a pixelated version of Helmut Gregor stands frozen while another continues along the street, which means that the Eye has identified an anomoly that may have been missed during the previous passes. If that's the case, I'll stand vindicated, even if I doubt Hoch will acknowledge it.

I look again at Gregor, who has been dead since 1979. He drowned following a stroke while swimming in Bertioga, in the state of Sáo Paulo, Brazil. By then he was living under his final alias of Wolfgang Gerhard, which he'd inherited following the actual Gerhard's return to Germany in 1971. Gerhard, or Gerhard Mark II, was in poor health when he drowned, but the man on the screen is reasonably fit and healthy. As Gregor, he's been performing illegal abortions, which he may regard as a step up from his day-to-day duties running a carpentry and furniture firm, and acting as the South American agent for his family's farm equipment company.

Amid all this, Uli Rudel is a welcome distraction for Gregor. There is much to admire about Rudel: his war record as a fighter ace; his Knight's Cross, awarded to him personally by the Führer; and his unwavering commitment to the Nazi cause. But Rudel is also one of the few men in Buenos Aires whom Gregor considers a friend. They are bound by misfortune—displacement and unfaithful wives—and console each other at the ABC Restaurant. But not tonight. On this night, Gregor has eaten alone.

So many names, so many identities: Helmut Gregor, Fritz Ullman, Fritz Hollman, Peter Hochbichler, Josi Aspiazu, Dr. Fausto Rindón, each adopted and discarded as circumstances required. Life became harder for him after Eichmann was captured. Eichmann tried to sell Gregor out—no honor among thieves and murderers—even if the address Eichmann gave under interrogation was a disused mail drop. Our understanding is that Gregor followed Eichmann's trial with interest, though the two men were never close, even during their common exile. Eichmann was careless, boastful, too quick to share his past. Gregor avoided his company out of self-preservation as much as personal hostility. When Eichmann was hanged, Gregor must have experienced a tightening around his own neck, and I doubt he wore ties for a while. After all, a reward had been offered for his capture—and by the Germans, no less, who had also issued an arrest warrant. It was one thing to be hunted by Jews, but to be betrayed by his own people must have caused him serious distress, as well as no small inconvenience. He had to abandon Argentina for Paraguay, and then Paraguay for Brazil, each location less comfortable and more dangerous than the last. No wonder his health began to suffer. But for that first decade or so after the war ended, Gregor lived relatively openly and occasionally consented to share with the faithful his real name: Josef Mengele.

It was Abelman who theorized that it might be possible to bridge two timelines. The important word here is "theorized," because much of the practical work was credited to Bina Hannen, and so the link is known as an Abelman-Hannen Bridge. But shortly before her death, Bina admitted to Tamor and me that Abelman had been responsible for ninety percent of the practical side as well, and she had always felt guilty about taking more credit than she believed was her due. But Abelman insisted, and she had gone along with it. When confronted, Abelman denied this was the case and suggested that

Bina's pain medication might be affecting her memory and judgment. Bina subsequently recanted, arguing that she had been confused. Abelman got to her, I have no doubt about it. Right from the start, he was trying to hide how much he knew. He was the cleverest of clever men, one who didn't want anyone to know just how clever he really was. But let's leave the question of who did what aside. It doesn't matter, except insofar as it may have relevance to Abelman's subsequent disappearance.

The official chronicle, the one to which Tamor and her superiors adhere, is that while at CERN, Abelman, whose field of research was S-matrix theory, came up with the mathematical proof for the Bridge, elements of which were then forwarded to us. We arranged to meet Abelman in Paris, where he produced further details of the proof, enough to convince us not only that he wasn't a fraud but also that the Bridge might be more than a theoretical possibility. When we asked Abelman why he had approached us instead of the Americans, we were informed of the conditions that would be attached to the creation of the Bridge, and one in particular. Some might have called it revenge. We, like Abelman, preferred to think of it as delayed justice.

It took us a year to establish the facility and recruit the team, which was remarkably fast under the circumstances. We were helped by the fact that Abelman had supplied us with a list of his requirements and the names of prospective scientists and technicians. Hoch was low down on that list, although, in his defense, it was a short set of names. Bina Hannen, incidentally, was right at the top, although she didn't have much of a reputation, gifted though she was. Someone should have looked more closely at Bina's inclusion, even if it was better for Abelman that they didn't.

Abelman, as he had requested, was given a week's notice when we were ready to move. On the day he left CERN, he put on his coat and hat, told his colleagues he would see them in the morning, took the number 18 tram to Gare Cornavin, and promptly vanished. By midnight, he was in Tel Aviv, and by the following Monday he had commenced work on the first Bridge. Our estimate was that it could take decades to construct. In fact, it took just five years, but consumed money like a fire in a bank vault. But I had faith. I trusted Abelman. I know that may sound odd, given the views I've already expressed about scientists, but Abelman was exceptional. There was a serenity to him, and a conviction that never leaned into delusion. Without him, the project would not have existed. He was its creator, its instigator, but also its visionary, and its moral voice.

Many of the initial discussions about the project focused on morality, which may sound curious for a venture that some might brand as profoundly immoral. Occasionally, even I have doubts—if this is justice, has it not assumed a wild form?—though I keep them to myself. To express doubt, or show signs of distress, is to invite an intervention by our resident psychologist, a woman whose tediousness is matched only by her doggedness. It's better to suffer in silence.

Abelman repeatedly invoked morals during the selection of targets for Intervention, and in response to any questions about what limits might, or should, be placed on the uses of the technology. We resembled children to whom Abelman, in loco parentis, was trying to explain the realities of life, while we endeavored to chip away at his authority. Ultimately, it was a futile effort, because we would always be obliged to follow Abelman's lead. He was the head scientist and had constructed his conceptual edifices carefully, just as he would the physical infrastructure, but with an awareness of potential abuses. Because of this, his dominion was both scientific and ethical, and we deferred to it, some more willingly than others.

That latter cohort is now trying to pick their way through Abelman's traps and barriers in an attempt to wrest control of the technology from his invisible grasp, but I suppose they had always anticipated it would come to this. They went along with Abelman because it suited them—they got to see the system in action, and knew it worked—but hoped either to wear him down as time went on, or have his knowledge bequeathed to them upon his death. Should neither come to pass, they had assembled the shadow group, which worked to mirror the processes of Abelman and his people. Abelman was aware of that, too, of course. He was no innocent, yet he didn't even attempt to hide information from them, no matter how crucial. The members of the shadow group must have been rubbing their hands with glee while wondering how Abelman could be so naive, so remiss. In reality, he only ever let them see what he wanted them to see, and as they watched him, so also did he watch them. Mirrors reflecting mirrors reflecting—what?

Abelman's will, that's what.

So Abelman discovered that it was theoretically, then actually, possible to create a link between two timelines. In forming the link between Line 1 and Line 2, a reaction occurred in the second timeline. Abelman described it as a temporal flare, an unexpected variation on Newton's third law of motion: to every action, there is an equal and opposite reaction. Because I'm an idiot and would have to explain it to other idiots to induce them to hand over money, I was presented with the analogy of a sealed bladder of water. Poke it with a finger, and some of the liquid gets displaced, causing the bladder to bulge. This was, in effect, what was happening on the second timeline, except with a caveat. A temporal disparity occurred, an abnormality, and even Abelman struggled to understand why. It lasted only seventeen minutes and twenty-two seconds, and no amount of mathematical tinkering could establish a cause.

I came up with one but was afraid to raise it during those exploratory sessions, because I didn't care to be labeled dumber than I was already assumed to be by taking an analogy literally. What, I wondered, if there was a hole in the bladder, right at the bulge? I very nearly asked the question aloud, before biting my tongue. Looking back, I don't know that it would have made a great deal of difference if I had spoken. Walter Rauff would still have died—again. He'd just have died again differently.

Abelman was fascinated by the temporal flare. Even then, I'm convinced he was considering the possibilities it offered, although to everyone else it was just a dead end, like someone constructing a one-inch cul-de-sac on a transnational highway. But it was the dead-end nature of the flare, or what seemed like a dead end, that caught Abelman's fancy. That was why he was a genius, and the rest of us are not geniuses. Because that dead end would become the nucleus of the project: the black hole.

"We're talking about time travel, right?" someone asked—it might have been Hoch.

I can still remember the look on Abelman's face, the way he raised his eyes to heaven as though to ask, *God, am I forever to be surrounded by small minds? Does no one listen to a word I say?*

"No, not time travel," Abelman replied patiently, or patiently for him, once he'd mastered his emotions. "Temporal manipulation."

Abelman could call it what he wanted, but it was time travel, of a sort. Admittedly, the people moving unexpectedly through time weren't going willingly, and it didn't end well for them, but I always viewed them as time travelers. Toward the end, Abelman grudgingly admitted that it might be the case. What irritated him was the way that the non-eggheads talked about shifting the targets forward in time, which he regarded as entirely inaccurate, and would inevitably lead him to lecture some unfortunate on the nature of the block universe.

"You know why I like you?" he once asked me, during halftime in a football match of no consequence.

"Because I always pay for the beer? Because I'm a lesbian, and therefore of no sexual interest to you beyond prurience, if even that?"

"Those things, too. Principally, I like you because you don't say stupid shit. You may think stupid shit, but you don't say it, and *that* is smart."

Which was what passed for a compliment in Abelman's world and might help explain why he was not universally adored.

We selected Gerhard Bohne as the first target because the logistics were simple. Bohne was the head of the Third Reich's Work Group of Sanatoriums and Nursing Homes, responsible for the systematic extermination of the physically and mentally disabled: the substandard Aryans, by the Reich's reckoning. Bohne's program, Aktion T4, murdered about two hundred thousand Germans by gassing followed by cremation, and provided a blueprint for the mass slaughter that followed in the concentration camps. After the war, Bohne made his way to Argentina, protected by the dictator Juan Perón, but returned to Germany when a coup ousted his benefactor, where he was indicted in Frankfurt in 1963. Upon his release on bail, Bohne immediately headed back to Argentina, where he thought he might yet be safe, or safer than at home. But he was extradited to Germany in 1966, only to be declared unfit to stand trial, thus permitting him to live at liberty for another fifteen years.

To be honest, we regarded Bohne as small fry, and some of us openly expressed the view that since he had killed mostly Germans, he was their problem, not ours. They'd had their chance to deal with him and botched it. Let them build their own underground laboratories and create their own artificial black holes. But our first major billionaire donor had lost relatives to Aktion T4, and promised to support our project unto death and beyond if Bohne got what should have been coming to him back in the 1960s.

We also had to take into account the fact that we had a great deal of information on Bohne's movements, including, crucially, film of his extradition from Argentina in 1966. (We could also pin him down to various spots before the war, but at that stage he had yet to commit his crimes. The program forbids Intervention before commission. We can't punish a man for something he hasn't done, or not without abdicating moral authority.) The footage from 1966 is just one minute and ten seconds long, but at forty-one seconds Bohne emerges from a police car at the airport, a coat draped over his arms to hide the handcuffs. He is then led to the steps of the plane, and escorted into the cabin, before we catch a final glimpse of him at one of the windows. The film meant we would not be working blind from the off. We could place Bohne in a definite location, and at a specific moment in time, which made it easier to decide on the positioning of the Eye. We also had pictures of him disembarking under escort at Frankfurt Airport on November 14, and assembled further footage of his movements before the decision was made not to try him. The quandary, as Abelman noted, was that Bohne was never alone. He was always surrounded by people, or under the observation of a camera.

"So?" someone asked. If I remember correctly, it was Mizrahi, Tamor's deputy, who fathomed even less about the project than I did but was too arrogant to hide it. "You've assured us that the Intervention will be instantaneous."

"I never used that word," Abelman replied.

"Close enough."

"This is science. Close enough doesn't suffice."

Words that would come back to haunt us—and Bohne, too, though not for very long.

"Oh, for God's sake," resumed Mizrahi.

Tamor tutted. She was an observant Jew and did not believe in unnecessary invocations of the Divine. On the other hand, my sexuality did not trouble her—either because the Torah limited its abhorrence of same-sex activity to males and Tamor was too busy to consult later rabbinical commentaries, or I was so good at procuring money that any perceived failings were rendered immaterial. I leave it to you to decide on the correct answer. (Hint: it's the second.)

"My apologies," said Mizrahi, with some vague gesture of repentance toward the ceiling, which probably wouldn't have satisfied the requirements of the Torah, but never mind. "I still don't understand why the presence of people around Bohne is such a problem."

"What if something goes wrong?" asked Abelman. "Then we will have witnesses. Given the presence of cameras, we might even have a record of it on any number of new timelines."

Witnesses would be bad. Even Mizrahi could grasp that much.

"What do you suggest?" Tamor asked Abelman.

"We keep gathering information on Bohne's routines after his release, until we're satisfied that we have him alone at a fixed point."

"Which could take weeks, or months," said Mizrahi. "Every delay costs money."

"If we blow our first shot badly enough," I pointed out, "it might cost us more than money. Remember: Maintain Temporal Integrity."

I was always careful to use that terminology around Tamor. When I'd expressed it in our more prosaic terms at a previous meeting, Tamor had lectured me afterward about my language.

"Get him alone," said Tamor.

Tamor's word was law, so we spent another eight weeks on surveillance and mapping before finally deciding on the optimal position for the Eye.

And still we fucked up.

Right. I've given you the dummy's version of the process, and we've talked about the integrity of the Line(s), which means I can't really prevaricate any longer about what happened to Bohne and Rauff: two different outcomes, each unpleasant in its own way. Let's take them in order of appearance, which means Bohne comes first.

First off, Lavron panicked, and I maintain it was the fault of

Hoch, Dr. Fucking Nearly Right, although Abelman could be said to bear some responsibility as well. However, I'm reluctant to blame Abelman because he was still distraught over Bina Hannen, and had trusted Hoch and the rest to dot every final *i* and cross every last *t*. They didn't, but then they were also under pressure from Tamor to demonstrate that the process worked, and Tamor, in turn, had people breathing down her neck. I accept, too, that there were unknown unknowns, including a tiny fault in the calibration of the Tree that led to an error in the final mapping. The technical term is "clusterfuck," which meant that collective responsibility kicked in, and Hoch kept his job. Even Lavron was forgiven for hitting the button a second time, since the system, which instantly recalibrated once the error was recognized, indicated it was safe. Had he taken a moment, Lavron might have questioned whether the error had been corrected or compounded by the recalibration and wouldn't have attempted a second Intervention until he was satisfied with the answer. A whole lot of people in that room later had to put up their hands and admit that, yes, they could have done better, none of which would have been a source of much consolation to Gerhard Bohne, though it really couldn't have happened to a nicer man.

Abelman looked drawn, but he wasn't so distracted that he would have failed to spot a divergence had the math not been off to begin with. There were nerves, but no more than might have been anticipated when a black hole was about to be created a mile below everyone's feet. I'm being a bit overdramatic here, perhaps, since we'd already created one black hole to permit the insertion of the Eye, but that was a much smaller black hole—though still capable of destroying all life on Earth had someone messed up the math on that as well—while the second would have to be considerably larger to power the Splitter and permit the Intervention.

I was the only one advocating for another run-through—do you see a pattern?—because I knew that Abelman wasn't functioning at the top of his game; that Hoch and his team were both overworked and excessively eager finally to run the process all the way through; and that Tamor faced the possibility of being shut down if she didn't begin producing something better than speculative models of successful outcomes. Under such pressures, the potential for mistakes or poor decisions increases. Unfortunately, the momentum was against me and in favor of continuing, so continue we did.

I don't want to make this sound as though I was smart and everybody else was in error. It's not like that at all. I'm just naturally prudent, like any good accountant. It's in my nature. I know that three broken marriages might appear to contradict this, but I prefer to take the view that they support it: I'm good at setting emotion to one side. You want a garden party? Great, let's have one, but we ought to wait until tomorrow when the weather's going to be better. I don't care that it's your birthday today and the guests are already primed to attend. Tell them to stay home, and they can come out when the sun is shining—or, alternatively, when the first Intervention in a multibillion-dollar temporal manipulation project doesn't feel as though it may be about to end in disaster.

But we had Bohne isolated on a stretch of the River Main in Sachsenhausen, and all the indicators checked out. Tamor was on a secure line, and when she gave the order to proceed, Abelman didn't demur. He did pause momentarily to glance at Hoch, who nodded like one of those toy dogs kept by morons in the rear windows of their cars, but that was as far as any expression of doubt went.

"We have assent," said Abelman. "Lock on the target."

"Target locked," said Lavron.

"On my mark: Three. Two. One. Take him."

Which was when Lavron hit the button.

And nothing happened.

Okay, that's not completely true. The Eye operated as it should have, but instead of creating an artificial timeline to isolate a new iteration of Gerhard Bohne while the original went about his affairs, it sent us a cloud of pollen and a few flies. Worse, a facet of the action of the Eye drew Bohne's attention. It might have been a flash, or just something subliminal, but he knew it was there, whatever "it" might be: a wrongness, for want of a better word. Later, we'd observe the original iteration of targets similarly pause at the instant of activation and look slightly confused after the creation of the new timeline. Abelman theorized that they might be experiencing a form of déjà vu. Once more, I wonder how much he really knew.

Anyway, we now had an ex-Nazi peering into the undergrowth, where, in a thicket of rhododendrons, lay a piece of tech that should not have existed for another century.

"What just happened?" asked Abelman. Tamor's voice was so loud in his ear that even I could hear it, and I was five desks away.

"The calibration was off," said Lavron.

"Then recalibrate!" urged Hoch, while all around him great minds tried to find the error they'd missed the first time around. On the main screen, the Tree displayed a shadow, as though an unseen sun were shining on it from the east. Suddenly, the shadow vanished.

"I have it," said Lavron. "We're locked."

"Then take him," ordered Hoch, before Abelman could object. It should have been for Abelman to decide, but Hoch had been unnerved, and now all he could see was Bohne's face looming over the rhododendrons, and his own career ending in ruin.

Without waiting for the go-ahead from Abelman, Lavron hit the button again as, belowground, the black hole was pressed into service for the second time in a matter of minutes without first ensuring it was stable. Never mind beta testing, this hadn't even been alpha-tested. I can recall closing my eyes. I prayed that the end, if it came, would be quick. I opened them again when Lavron uttered a hushed, horrified "Fuuuuuccccck." A few of the people in the room were staring at the containment chamber. The rest were looking at the screen. Neither scene could have been described as pretty.

The containment chamber, or Cage, was designed to hold the

target: sterile environment, reinforced plexiglass, and absolutely no admittance while in use. Any contact with the target was to be conducted by electronic means only, from outside the chamber. Right now, in addition to the earlier pollen and some dying flies, the Cage contained half of Gerhard Bohne—the bottom half, if it matters, Bohne having been neatly bisected. Unfortunately, the action of the Eye hadn't cauterized the wound, so he was making a mess. On the screen, meanwhile, the top half of Gerhard Bohne was making a similar mess in a patch of Frankfurt grass. Incredibly, he was still alive. He was unlikely to remain that way for long, but he seemed to be working up whatever reserves of strength remained to indulge himself in a final scream.

Lavron recalibrated again and hit the button a third time. He didn't wait to be told. If the world came to an end because of what he was doing, there'd be no one left to blame him; and if it didn't, he'd be able to claim that he had prevented a disaster from becoming a calamity, or some variation on the same. By his action, Lavron managed to extract Bohne's top half, in addition to all traces of his DNA, leaving only the original Bohne, tottering on his heels in his own timeline, wondering what had just happened. Which was the last we saw of that version of Bohne, because the Eye collapsed as intended, its remnants joining the two halves of the Bohne variant in the containment chamber.

That Bohne, our Bohne, then exploded.

If you've never seen a man explode, you should consider yourself lucky. It's not a memory to be shared with the grandchildren. The reason for the explosion of Gerhard Bohne had to do with the air pressure in the chamber, which was designed to cope with the results of a single Intervention, not three Interventions in rapid succession. Frankly, we were lucky we hadn't cut corners on containment, or else we might have all been picking pieces of old Nazi out of our hair.

There was complete silence for a while. Inside the Cage, the walls ran striking shades of red, interspersed with shards of pinkish-white matter. Lavron was puking in a paper-only recycling container. He had only himself to blame.

"Shut it down," said Abelman, finally. He sounded tired rather than angry, a disappointed teacher let down by his pupils.

"At least we know it works," I said. "Kind of."

From the beginning, Abelman emphasized the importance of recognizing what could, or should, be changed and what should remain unaltered. Tamor was present for only some of those discussions because she had a low boredom threshold. I think it also frustrated her that Abelman held all the cards. He dictated the pace of our progress, even as the floor and walls vibrated during the initial years of construction belowground.

According to Abelman, our future couldn't be altered, because somewhere in the block universe it was already written. But that was just *a* future, one of many. Take the famous grandfather paradox, so beloved of murderous grandchildren everywhere. A person travels back in time and kills their grandfather before he can sire offspring. Logically, that person would cease to exist as a consequence of their actions, since their birth would now never happen. But they do exist, because they were able to travel back in time in the first place. This is known as a consistency paradox.

Abelman argued that should a homicidal grandchild travel back in time and kill their grandfather, a new timeline would be created, in which one of the near-infinite variations of the grandchild would not be born. On their own timeline, though, they would continue to exist, because they occupied a line in which they had been born, even if it was hard to see how they could ever look a grandparent in the eye again.

Similarly, one might go back to December 12, 1980, to buy

$10,000 worth of Apple shares, in the expectation of returning to one's own time to find oneself a millionaire—assuming, of course, that the difficulties of zipping backward and forward in time had been addressed to everyone's satisfaction. According to Abelman, our intrepid investor wouldn't be a millionaire upon their return because they hadn't been a millionaire when they left, or if they were, it wasn't because they dropped $10,000 on Apple shares on the day of the company's IPO. Instead, that purchase would have created a new timeline in which a different version of themselves was an Apple millionaire—or maybe not, because the timeline created by the investment would not necessarily conclude with the desired outcome. There was no way of anticipating the direction of the new timeline, or how the addition of the investor might affect the company's development.

This brought us to Adolf Hitler. It was inevitable that it would, in a quantum version of Godwin's law. In fact, he came up on the first day, thanks to Abelman, who just wanted to get him out of the way. I doubt there was one person in that room, Abelman excepted, who hadn't considered the possibility of using the technology to kill Hitler in the hope of, if not avoiding the Second World War, then preventing the Holocaust; that, or finding a way to target him before he swallowed a cyanide pill and shot himself in the head, thereby gaining some measure of retribution. Given our rule about not punishing someone for crimes not yet committed, the second option was deemed more just, if not more acceptable.

"Indeed," said Abelman, with a certain obvious effort at retaining his patience, "preventing the Holocaust might be one of the results of killing Hitler. So, too, might be the removal of the Second World War from that timeline. But suppose the Soviet Union, undamaged by conflict, then becomes ever more powerful, accelerating a confrontation with the West. We don't have a conventional war from 1939 to 1945, but we do have a nuclear war in, to pick a year, 1951, in the course of which large swaths of the planet are scoured to ash, and tens of millions of people die. And these aren't theoretical people, but real human beings, just existing on a different timeline from us. Do you really want those lives on your conscience? No, you do not. Therefore, we have a moral obligation not to interfere with the timelines. Do you understand? Because if you don't, you have no business being in this room."

The debate continued for a time, but in the end, most of us got the message: Don't Fuck with the Line. The ones who didn't get the message, the ones in the shadows—well, we shall see, won't we? Now you know why that little temporal cul-de-sac is so important. It's the least intrusive means of achieving our ends. We can't change what's occurred, or have decided not to try, but we can punish those responsible, or a variant of them.

Oh, and we still haven't targeted Hitler. Some of the groundwork has been done, but no further headway has been made. It may be a case of saving the best—or worst—for last. Some of us might prefer to leave him untouched. We've spoken of it among ourselves and share a similar take. We don't want to spend all that time and money to confront a possibly syphilitic fantasist, forcing us to accept that this wreck of a man might bear ultimate responsibility for destroying us in our millions. Let him remain a monster of myth. Better to tackle those who were involved in mass murder and torture on a practical level. Hence Mengele, Rauff, and their ilk: monstrous, but not monsters.

And Bohne, of course, but you now know how that played out.

The meeting following the Bohne Intervention was a fractious one, involving a lot of finger-pointing, shouting, and varying degrees of refusal or acceptance of blame. Hoch and his confederates were in a particularly foul mood, since they'd had to mop up the Cage. The core team, the one that identifies and researches the targets and performs the Interventions, is small, and doesn't discuss its work beyond the walls of what we call (outside of Tamor's hearing) the Holy of Holies. We prepare our own food, make our own beds, and scrub our own bathrooms. If you spill a pot of coffee, you get rid of the mess, because there's no janitor. We maintain a roster, and everyone, no matter how senior, sticks to it. If you're busy, you find someone who'll agree to swap places with you. But nobody had anticipated the necessity of including a duty labeled CLEAN DEAD NAZI FROM CAGE, and there was an understandable degree of reluctance to get suited and booted before grabbing a mop, a bucket, a hose, and two gallons of bleach. I made it clear that I hadn't been in favor of proceeding with the Intervention in the first place, so I was off the hook. Ultimately, sanitizing the Cage fell to Lavron and six others, all selected by Hoch, who—to his credit—became the eighth man on the cleanup crew. It took hours to get the Cage ready for sterilization, in part because no one had seen fit to have a drain installed at the design stage.

My only involvement was to request a tissue sample for my own use. The principal investor in the Bohne Intervention didn't know anything about the particulars of what we were doing and didn't ask. Her grandfather had lost a sister and brother to him, and she had a Down syndrome child of her own. She also served as a riposte to those among us who viewed Bohne as a strictly Aryan problem, since her great-grandfather was Jewish. I had promised only that I would provide her with physical evidence that Bohne had been located and punished, and thanks to some faulty calibration, I had no shortage of material.

I can recall visiting her after a very private and discreet laboratory had analyzed the sample and confirmed that it matched a specimen previously forwarded to them by our investor: a couple of Bohne's hair follicles—though how she had obtained them, I couldn't say. If the lab was curious as to why the age-associated DNA methylation markers indicated that the fresh sample came from a subject who now appeared to be younger than he was when the original material was obtained, they knew better than to inquire further. They were also paid enough not to ask why the older specimen had come from a dead person—based on the mRNA in the cells—and the more recent one from the same individual when he was alive. Money can buy silence, and a lot of money buys a lot of silence.

The investor, when I arrived, was sitting in a chair by her window. By then, she was a very old woman, and would live only for another two years. In her right hand she held a glass vial containing what was, I assumed, some of Gerhard Bohne.

"I have one question," she said.

"Ask it," I said, "although I can't promise an answer."

"Did he suffer?"

I thought of Bohne's bisected corpse, and how, during the postmortem analysis of what went wrong, we had replayed the footage from the Cage. In the seconds before he exploded, Gerhard Bohne had definitely blinked.

"I think," I said, "that it's safe to say he did."

We didn't try again until eleven months after Bohne's death. Tamor ordered a full post-incident review, which took five months, with a further three required to address deficiencies exposed by data capture and analytics, followed by a series of dry runs. The delay worked in our favor, because it allowed me time to build up a war chest. The first investor, Bohne's nemesis, was generous with her introductions—and discreet, too. A great deal of money began to flow into my hands, and while Abelman's people did their best to spend it as quickly as it was sourced, they were defeated in the end, and we accumulated a useful surplus.

Abelman's interest in the endeavor was flagging, though. He was absorbed in what was described as "next-stage development," but since he was secretive by nature, and using ever more advanced homomorphic encryption to protect his research, what precisely that next stage might entail was known only to himself. Tamor, in an unguarded moment, confirmed to me that it was time travel, but I could have told her that, whatever Abelman's persnicketiness about definitions.

By that stage, Abelman and I weren't spending so much downtime together. We'd still watch the occasional game, but I would be more engaged in the action. As I said, Bina's death had fundamentally altered him, but I wouldn't have called him depressed any longer. Yes, there was residual grief, but also a renewed focus. Abelman had moved on. His mind was working on fresh marvels, though he remained interested enough in the old ones to take his seat in the control room for the Rauff Intervention, and admitted later that he was glad he did, because watching it on a screen wouldn't have been the same. Thankfully, the outcome was less messy than the Bohne Intervention, although that wouldn't have been difficult. We also learned more from it, including that I might be smarter than I'd been given credit for.

Let me say from the start that Walter Rauff was a source of some embarrassment to us. He had been one of Reinhard Heydrich's aides, first in the SD, or Security Service, and subsequently in the Reich Security Main Office. He and Heydrich had both joined the Kriegsmarine as young men, and Rauff had served in Spain and South America, which proved useful when he later went on the run. His principal contribution to the Nazi war effort, and the reason he was on our list, was his instrumental role in the development of mobile gas chambers through his work with the Criminal Technical Institute of the Main Office.

Rauff's efforts had a humanitarian aspect, if you were a Nazi. He observed that the act of shooting thousands of unarmed civilians was having a detrimental effect on the emotional and psychological well-being of the German military, and the use of gas vans would exact a lesser toll on those soldiers involved in the operation. Rauff was not merely a theoretician, but also a hands-on manager, leading mobile killing squads in North Africa and Italy. Along the way, he accrued a tidy nest egg from gold and jewelry stolen from dead Jews, because Rauff was an inveterate thief. There was a rodent-like aspect to him in appearance and disposition. He wasn't the most intelligent of men, but he was sly and slippery. That he escaped justice, and thrived after the war, should not have come as a surprise to anyone. What was a surprise—and our source of shame—was that we helped him do it. This killer of Jews, directly responsible for the murders of a hundred thousand or more of us, and indirectly responsible for the deaths of many times that number, worked for us after the war. This was how low we had sunk.

I say "we," but our service had not been constituted when Rauff was recruited at the end of the 1940s. At that time it was still the Shai, short for Sherut Yediot, the Information Service of the Haganah, the armed wing of the Jewish Agency in Palestine, and was not in the best condition. The British had raided Jewish Agency headquarters in Jerusalem on June 29, 1946—known as Black Sabbath—resulting in the arrest of a number of its leaders, along with some 2,700 operatives. Following partition in 1948, the Shai was cut off from its Arab contacts, or those still willing to work with it. Desperate times called for desperate measures—and unsavory bedfellows.

After the war, Rauff had assisted and advised Syrian president Husni al-Za'im during fighting against the fledgling state of Israel, but Rauff was always vulnerable because nobody trusted him. When Za'im was toppled in 1949, Rauff needed help, which we provided in return for whatever intelligence he could offer about his soon-to-be former employers. I've heard it said that we facilitated his Ecuadorean transit visa, though I've never been able to find proof in writing. I can confirm that we didn't try to prevent Rauff from leaving for South America, and he and his family eventually settled in Chile, where he spied for a time for the Bundesnachrichtendienst, the West German intelligence service, before they too cut him loose, finally recognizing him for the liar and fraud that he was.

Whatever friends Rauff still possessed in German intelligence circles advised him to curtail a trip to the homeland in 1960, where plans were already afoot to have him arrested. Once he was safely huddled in Chile, he proved impossible to extradite, with both Allende and, later, Pinochet resisting requests to ship him back to Germany for trial. Eventually, Mossad grew so frustrated that they considered killing him, but that plan, too, came to nothing, and Rauff died of a heart attack in 1984. During his lifetime, our every effort to punish him was overshadowed by the awareness that we had, briefly, worked with our people's executioner. Now, thanks to Abelman, we had a chance to make up for the failings of a previous generation.

Because of the various attempts to bring him to justice, conventional or otherwise, and the fact that he lived quite openly in Chile, not even bothering to change his name, we had assembled a detailed file on Rauff's movements. We settled on an Intervention in Punta Arenas, where Rauff operated a king crab cannery. The Intervention went like a dream. The Eye located Rauff on an empty stretch of street near the Austral brewery, with a thirty-second window of opportunity when he would be alone. On the day of the Intervention, the Eye flashed, the Splitter activated, the Bridge opened, and moments later a confused Walter Rauff, aged fifty-four, was in the Cage. He had not been bisected, and showed no signs of exploding—at least, not literally.

Once he'd recovered his composure, Rauff began testing the plexiglass, and asking what was happening and where he was, which were perfectly reasonable questions. We could see him, but he could not see us. We did need him to hear us, though. We let Hoch do the talking. Abelman was content to watch and Tamor, as usual, was elsewhere. But most of us were also tongue-tied. Rauff was the first of the old breed we had encountered in person, even if we felt we knew him, so long had we been watching and researching him. We probably knew more about Rauff than he did about himself.

"You're in a facility north of Tel Aviv," Hoch told him.

"That's a lie," said Rauff.

"What do you remember last?"

"I'm not answering your questions until you stop lying."

Hoch killed the mike. "Restrict his air," he ordered.

The Cage's design permitted the air supply to be cut off, reduced, or rapidly expelled in the event of contamination. Within a minute, Rauff was slumped against the glass, gasping.

"We'll restore your oxygen supply," Hoch informed him, "if you agree to answer our questions. Do you so agree?"

Rauff waved his left hand, which we took for assent, and the oxygen restriction was lifted.

"So," repeated Hoch, "what do you remember last?"

"A flash," said Rauff, still struggling for breath. "A red flash."

"And then?"

"I was watching myself walk away."

"Nothing else?"

"Blackness. Dizziness. Then I was here, wherever here is."

"We told you. You're north of Tel Aviv."

"How can that be possible?"

"Because it's the middle of the twenty-first century," said Hoch, "and a great many things are possible that once were not."

"No, that's not true," said Rauff, but he sounded unsure.

"Let him look," said Hoch.

Inside the containment chamber, the screen was activated. Rauff could now see us: two dozen faces, all hostile, regarding him from behind a series of virtual displays.

"It's a trick," said Rauff.

"No, it's science," said Hoch.

A drone camera circled Rauff, running a secondary medical scan. The Cage itself could do most of the work, but the camera was useful for close-ups. It also served as a piece of theater. This was technology unknown to Rauff and might help bring the "It's True/Isn't True" exchanges to a rapid conclusion. First of all, they served no purpose, and second, there was the matter of the seventeen minutes and twenty-two seconds to be considered, because that was where we entered the unknown.

As far as Hoch was concerned, Rauff was no longer in the temporal dead end, because he was now part of our timeline. The dead end existed only to allow us to extract Rauff without interfering with his own timeline in Punta Arenas, 1960. But Abelman wasn't as convinced as Hoch about the dead end. The seventeen minutes and twenty-two seconds troubled him, since he could find nothing in his models to account for the disparity. This was why, unseen by Rauff but obvious to us, a clock was counting down from 17:22. We were now at 9:05. What happened when it reached zero was of interest to all concerned.

"Why have you brought me here?" asked Rauff.

That was another very good question. One of the first issues to be addressed when the program was in its planning stages was what to do with the targets once they'd successfully been extracted. An ordinary trial was out of the question, and Abelman was against involving the military, with which Tamor concurred. Nobody on the team wanted to be responsible for executing the targets, even though the Cage would have done the job cleanly through suffocation. Neither did we want to have to remove the bodies afterward, as that smacked too much of the crimes these men had committed against us in the first place. As usual, it was Abelman who came up with a solution—although that wasn't the word we used, for obvious reasons.

Abelman proposed a second Bridge.

The clock was now at eight minutes, fifty-five seconds. The second Bridge wouldn't activate until the count reached zero. Until then, Rauff would remain where he was.

It was Abelman who answered Rauff's question.

"You've been brought here to answer for your crimes."

"Crimes?" said Rauff. "What crimes? I was an administrator. I moved papers on a desk."

"You were integral to the development of mobile gas chambers."

Rauff shrugged. "Does the rat blame the man who helps build the trap?"

"These rats do."

"I was ordered to work on the mobile units: by Nebe, by Heydrich, by Himmler."

"You could have refused."

"I would have been shot."

"That's untrue, a lie unworthy even of you."

"No proof was ever offered that my design was put into practice. Not one single S-wagen was produced to support the allegations."

"Because they were all destroyed to hide the evidence."

"If that's the case, I knew nothing about it."

"Do you deny that they were built?"

"If my testimony is to be used in a court of law, I am entitled to legal representation."

"There will be no court of law."

"Summary justice?" Rauff laughed. "That's no justice at all."

"You'd know. Returning to the S-wagen, you supervised the modifications personally. Not only that, you watched as the victims were herded inside, and waited while they died, which took ten minutes, sometimes longer. The drivers had to plug their ears against the screams. You did not. You were untroubled."

"More fabrications, concocted by men trying to save themselves from the noose."

"Display the document," said Abelman.

A magnified image appeared in the air before Rauff: a letter to SS-Obersturmbannführer Walter Rauff, dated June 5, 1942, informing him of modifications proposed for ten Saurer vehicles, to be delivered to the Chelmno extermination camp in Poland. The letter confirmed that ninety-seven thousand had already been processed—*verarbeit*—in the camp's three existing vans since the previous December, although at no time were the words "persons," "people," or "human beings" employed. Instead, the letter referred only to "pieces," "merchandise," and "load." Rauff picked up on this instantly.

"This refers only to the difficulty of transporting supplies safely," he said. "All damage to goods and matériel had to be accounted for."

"Show him the 'damage,' " said Abelman.

Initially, I had been against the use of the Eye for this purpose. I saw no reason to disperse funds in a manner that would not benefit us, but Abelman felt it was important, and he persuaded the others. As with most things, he ended up persuading me as well. The Eye got what we wanted on the second attempt. God, said Tamor, must have been smiling on our efforts. Where God was when the Jews and gypsies from the Łódź ghetto were being systematically gassed by Rauff and his men—well, that was another matter.

The Eye had not been able to record the entry of the victims, because they were made to undress inside the main building before being directed to its cellar, from which a ramp led directly to the van. Once the load space was full, the doors were closed and the engine started. The Eye had registered what happened when that engine was subsequently turned off. The vehicle was ordered to pull away for Rauff's benefit, as otherwise he'd have been forced to check the results from inside the cellar, which wouldn't have been pleasant. His face was clearly visible to the right of the screen for five seconds before he put a white handkerchief to his nose and mouth, waved a hand, and the doors were opened. Once the exhaust fumes had started pumping into the van, the victims naturally moved toward the rear to escape them. Now the corpses tumbled out like cordwood, all under Rauff's watchful eye.

The countdown read one minute exactly. Abelman checked with

the team. He no longer had any interest in what Rauff might say. Hoch took up the baton.

"That's you," said Hoch.

"A later insertion," said Rauff. "A crude attempt to implicate me. I demand to speak to a lawyer. Do you hear me?" His voice grew louder. "I want a lawyer!"

Abelman killed the speaker. He was trying to concentrate on whatever Tamor was communicating through his earpiece.

"The Bridge is ready," he told her.

I let out a deep breath. Two Bridges: I'd be making a lot of phone calls, and twisting a great many arms, to fill the hole this would leave in our funds.

We watched the clock tick toward zero. In the Cage, Rauff continued to rage soundlessly. I heard someone counting down the final seconds and realized it was me.

"—two, one."

And Walter Rauff crumbled to dust.

Abelman had his own designation for it, "temporal infiltration," but it came down to what I intimated earlier when referencing the bladder analogy: a seepage of time, as though a tiny fissure in the structure of the Cage had permitted seconds to leak out. To our list of lessons learned, we could now add that we would only have the pleasure of our targets' company for, at most, seventeen minutes, twenty-one seconds before we had to send them on their way, or else resign ourselves to sweeping out the Cage. 17:22 was, we accepted, cutting it too fine. Thankfully, DNA from the detritus of Walter Rauff was sufficient to provide proof of extraction, so the three donors who had jointly funded the Intervention could be satisfied that their money was well spent. The downside was that Abelman had not been allowed to activate the second Bridge. That would come with the next target: Otto Rasch.

If Walter Rauff was more cunning than intelligent, Otto Rasch was proof that sometimes the most cultivated and learned of men can be capable of the worst barbarism. Rasch, who held doctorates in political economy and law, was the commander of Einsatzgruppe C, one of the most notorious of the SS death squads, and had helped supervise the murder of over thirty-three thousand Jews at Babi Yar, in what is now modern Ukraine. The Jews were told they were to be resettled, but instead were ordered to undress before being led naked into a ravine, in batches of ten, and machine-gunned to death. Once a layer of bodies accumulated, the next group of victims was ordered to lie on the remains of the first to utilize the forty-nine-feet deep ravine to its maximum capacity. The executioners had to walk across a carpet of corpses to do their work. After two days of killing, from September 29 to 30, 1941, the ravine was collapsed by the Germans, burying the executed as well as the wounded, who suffocated to death.

So successful was the Babi Yar experiment that the Nazis reverted to the ravine repeatedly during the occupation, eventually leaving more than a hundred thousand bodies buried. Unfortunately for the perpetrators, Operation Barbarossa was destined to end in failure, and Babi Yar constituted evidence of war crimes that could end badly for those responsible. The decision was made in the summer of 1943 to disinter the bodies, using Russian slave labor, and burn them on pyres, but the effort didn't prevent the ringleaders of the massacre from being called to account after the war. Friedrich Jeckeln and Paul Blobel were hanged, and Kurt Eberhard committed suicide while in custody. Only Rasch, the most ruthless of them all, escaped justice. His trial was discontinued due to ill health, and he died of Parkinson's disease in 1948.

We located a photograph of Rasch in his office at the Reich-controlled Continental Oil Company, or "Konti," in Berlin, where he worked as a director following his discharge from the SS at the end of 1941. We then sourced a blueprint of the building and a record of meetings attended by Rasch during that year. The Eye was inserted into Rasch's office twenty minutes before he was due to leave for a consultation with Ernst Rudolf Fischer and Alfred Bentz, the principal movers behind the establishment of Konti. We extracted him from his otherwise empty office as he walked from his desk to the door. Once we had him safely in the Cage, he was ordered to undress. When he refused, we cut off his air until he complied. That was the only conversation we had with him. After that, we turned off the speaker. Rasch had nothing to say worth hearing.

As soon as he was naked, the second Bridge was activated. The placement of the Eye for Rasch's redirection was always going to be a difficult, traumatic affair. Abelman had accepted the duty. I stayed with him, even though he assured me that it wasn't necessary. It didn't take us long, but still, I didn't sleep that night, or the next, and subsisted on coffee and dry bread for three days after. Sometimes I don't think I'll ever recover from those thirty-six hours spent with Abelman.

The Cage had harvested DNA from Rasch—skin cells and a pinprick blood sample taken remotely from the sole of his foot before he left—enabling us to provide that all-important proof of extraction. It still amazes me how little the donors wanted to know about the specifics. It was enough that they had achieved *naqam naqamath*: not vengeance alone, which would have involved meeting evil with evil, but a vengeance of vindication.

"Send him on his way," said Abelman.

The second Bridge was activated. One moment Rasch was in the Cage, and the next he was buried under a pile of corpses at Babi Yar.

Now we are back where we began, with Helmut Gregor, or the elusive Mengele. He will be our fourth Intervention, and thanks to Abelman, we have a special *naqam naqamath* for him. I suspect its aptness means that we will use it again in the future. My only regret is that Abelman is no longer here to bear witness.

Abelman vanished last month, during the standard testing of the black hole. Tamor and the shadow team are still trying to establish precisely what happened, but I doubt they ever will. Once again, Abelman was too many steps ahead of us. There was more than one Cage, just as there were always multiple Bridges, and not every dead end was as dead as it appeared to be. As for the seventeen minutes and twenty-two seconds, Abelman found a way to use those, too, even if we haven't, so far. He discovered something about them, something we failed to notice; that, or he knew it already, like the outcome of certain horse races and football games.

This is what I suspect, as does Tamor: Abelman, or this Abelman, was not from our timeline. He was moving between lines, trying to find the perfect one. Let us call it Abelman's Line, but also Bina Hannen's. He was searching for a line in which she did not have cancer, or a point on that line where his involvement might make a difference to her fate. Each time he failed, he made subtle modifications and adjusted minor variables, all contributing to the discovery or creation of a line where he and Bina could be together. How long he had been trying, I could not say. He was aging, obviously, so each Intervention came at a later stage. Ultimately, he would die, but before he did, he wanted to find a line where Bina survived.

I may be wrong, of course, but by the nature of the block universe, I may also be right. And yes, some might detect an element of hypocrisy in what Abelman was doing, because he was definitely Fucking with the Line. But as Samuel Johnson observed, no man is a hypocrite in his pleasures, and anyway, Abelman had invented the technology. It was his Line.

Abelman's Line.

I am waiting. Lavron is waiting. Hoch is waiting. Finally, Tamor gives her assent.

"Take him," she says, and hangs up.

On a street in Buenos Aires, Mengele is briefly permitted to watch a version of himself continuing home before he—this version, our version—is transported to the Cage. There was some dialogue about whether we might wish to interrogate him, if only briefly, but all indications are that he was an unrepentant Nazi to the end, so we are unlikely to learn anything of note.

Like Rasch, Mengele is instructed to undress, and like Rasch, he is initially reluctant to oblige. Lavron is already sucking the air from the Cage before Mengele has finished refusing. Mengele is then mildly sedated while a drone shaves what's left of his hair and stores it for proof of extraction. At the same time, a needle inserts Abelman's final gift to us into the ball of Mengele's foot: a temporal repeater. Danny Haddad, one of our theoretical physicists, had agreed to be the guinea pig, and later informed us that it had enabled him to experience the same orgasm with his girlfriend five times in a row before he started to get bored, and not a little tender. The repeater has a limited time span—just two minutes—but that's sufficient for our present purpose and can be set to replicate the phase as often as desired. We have no idea how long the power supply lasts. That's for the next stage of testing. Abelman left three repeaters, along with instructions for their use. We'll employ one today and try to figure out how the technology works from the remaining two. Meanwhile, Mengele is in the Cage, looking gray.

"Send him on his way," Hoch says, consciously echoing Abelman's words.

We will continue Abelman's work. We will make him proud. We will undermine the shadow operatives, thanks to a stick drive left to me by Abelman. The drive is a primitive piece of tech, but then I'm not very bright, as Abelman never ceased to inform me, so he deemed it best to give me something I could easily use to frustrate their efforts.

Lavron and I took responsibility for the installation of the second Eye, assisted by a stripped-down team. It was more horrific even than Babi Yar, because all those we saw were still alive. But in addition to being a *naqam naqamath*, it was a *chesed shel emet*, the truest act of kindness, one for the dead. I think you can guess the number at which the repeater was set. I doubt it will last that long, but it will last long enough.

Mengele vanishes from the Cage, and an instant later is engulfed by a press of two thousand naked bodies in the underground gas chamber by Crematorium III at Birkenau. It takes two minutes for the average human being to die from inhalation of Zyklon B. Mengele will endure it many times over until the repeater fails.

The Eye ceases to function as the Bridge closes. We move on. The list is long, as long as time.

THE MIRE AT FOX TOR

I had this from Tenley, which is important to note from the beginning because Tenley had no interest in tall tales, being almost entirely lacking in imagination. He never read a book unless it contained numbers or tables and always began *The Times* at the financial pages. He wasn't a dull man, exactly, but he was a passionless one, and a little of his company went a long way. Tenley was, though, an enthusiastic if solitary hiker, and each autumn would take a week's holiday to go traipsing through some desolate part of the British landscape with a pack on his back and a walking staff in his right hand. He had a special fondness for moors—Marsden, Bodmin, Kinder, Denbigh—and stayed at the remotest inns he could find in their vicinity, where he dined alone and spoke to no one, unless it was to order a drink or ask for the salt. I suspect he was never more contented than during those excursions.

It was with some surprise, therefore, that I encountered Tenley one evening at the Bodega Wine House, or the Marble Halls as it was more colloquially known, which had a reputation for conviviality. I was keeping an eye on Ewer in those days. Ewer was fond of the Halls, and I had made a point of becoming a regular there, whether he was present or not. By then, we were convinced that Ewer, as well as writing for the *Daily Herald*, was passing information to the Soviets, even if it would be another six months before we caught him in the act.

On this particular evening Ewer was nowhere to be seen, but Tenley was occupying a corner table. The Bodega was very quiet, but Tenley had still contrived to find himself a spot as far removed as possible from the rest of the clientele. I nodded to him, he nodded back, and—mirabile dictu—indicated that I should join him if I wished. With alternatives for company, I might have declined, but I didn't want to appear rude. Also, it would strengthen my claim as a habitué, thus aiding me in the Ewer business. So I made a point of informing the barman that I would sit with a friend, and ordered a refill for Tenley and a glass of the same for myself.

Tenley and I were at school together, and his mother and mine were distant cousins. He knew that I was something or other in military intelligence, but no more than that, and had never pressed me on the matter, as much out of a general lack of curiosity as any innate discretion. It had been about six months since last we'd met, and it struck me that he'd put on some weight—not a great deal, but enough to suggest that perhaps he was not hiking as much as he once did. I saw, too, that a cane with a heavy brass head stood in the corner beside our table. Tenley caught me looking at it.

"I've been carrying an injury," he said. "It's made walking difficult."

I told him I was sorry to hear it and hoped it was only a temporary setback. "After all," I added, "you must miss your moors."

"Not as much as you might think," and I could have sworn that he shuddered as he spoke. "I'm less sure of the world now."

It was an odd statement, and I said so.

"Are you minded to listen to a story?" he asked.

These were words I never expected to hear from Tenley's lips, but what's seldom is wonderful, or so we hope.

"Of course," I replied.

Here, then, is the tale Tenley told me.

• • • • • • •

Tenley had decided that his annual hike should take in some of Fox Tor, hundreds of acres of bogland on Dartmoor in Devon, said to have inspired Grimpen Mire in Conan Doyle's *The Hound of the Baskervilles*. Not that Tenley had ever read the book; what attracted him to Fox Tor was its wildness and the difficulty of negotiating a safe path through it. Fox Tor had claimed several lives, and not all who went missing were found. It offered a challenge, and one unlikely to be shared with many others, Fox Tor discouraging all but the most determined of hikers. What marker posts there were would sometimes be hidden by rising waters or lost altogether to the mud, and it was best to cross it only after extended periods of dry weather.

The preceding summer had been somewhat mixed, but after some consultation with locals by letter, Tenley felt confident that his experience would see him through. He had planned a route that would take him to Fox Tor itself before continuing to Childe's Tomb at the southeast extreme, after which he would proceed to his lodgings for the night. The tomb was said to mark the spot where a wealthy hunter perished during a blizzard in the eleventh century, his body subsequently being retrieved and buried by the monks of Tavistock Abbey. It was, apparently, not much to see—a reconstruction of the original, according to Tenley, which had been plundered to build a house—but if one were walking the moor, visiting the tomb was one of the things one did. I suppose it broke up the monotony.

While he was an experienced hiker, Tenley had underestimated the rigors of Fox Tor. The going was hard, the mud sucking so insistently at his boots that, after only a few hours, his thighs ached, and he grew short of breath. Visibility was poor, not that there was much to see, not even Childe's Tomb; despite all his preparations and the use of a compass, Tenley had somehow missed the landmark entirely. Having stopped to assess his situation, he concluded that the tomb must be within a mile of his present position, but whether north or south of it, he could not be sure, for he had strayed badly from the path. He began to wonder if there might not be a taint to the air of the mire that had caused him to become disoriented, because his sense of direction was usually as unfailing as his compass needle. Something certainly smelled unpleasant, and not in a vegetal way. Tenley guessed that a sheep or goat had become trapped in the mud and died there, its slow decay contaminating the environment.

It was then that Tenley heard a voice calling out from nearby. It sounded like a child in distress, an impression confirmed when, moments later, Tenley saw a muddied boy stagger from the mire onto firmer ground. The boy was perhaps five or six, and wore shorts and a tattered sweater over an open-collared shirt. He had a sock only on his left foot, the other being bare, though it took Tenley a little while to realize this, so begrimed were the new arrival's legs from the knees down. He had clearly been crying, the tears cutting channels through the dirt on his face.

"Help us," he said. "Please."

"Us?"

Tenley squatted before the boy and gripped him by the shoulders. The sweater was damp, indicating the boy had been out there for some time, long enough for the mist to have penetrated his clothing. If he didn't get warm soon, he'd catch his death.

"We were walking across the mire when Mummy fell in the water," said the boy. "Now she can't get out."

"Where?" asked Tenley. "Show me, quickly."

The boy took Tenley's hand, and it was all the man could do not to yank it back instinctively. Tenley did not relish intimate contact with strangers, and could not recall the last time a child's hand had touched his own; probably not since his school days, he decided. Still, he let the boy's cold fingers clasp his own and walked with him farther into the mire. The boy, anxious for his mother, tried to hurry Tenley along, hauling so hard that he traveled with his body at an angle to the ground, his shoeless feet vanishing up to the ankles in the mud, to be released only reluctantly. But Tenley, unwilling to end up in the same situation as the boy's mother, kept them to a slower pace, testing the way as he went.

"How much longer?" he asked the boy, but received no answer. It struck Tenley that, were the boy as disoriented as he himself had been, they might have no luck finding his mother. She could already be dead; while the boy's cries had carried clearly enough, Tenley had heard nothing that sounded like a woman. Of course, she was possibly so weak that it was all she could do to keep herself from sinking. Tenley hoped this was the case. He did not know whether he was capable of consoling a distraught child who had just lost his mother.

Also, the day was waning, and soon the dark would come. Tenley had sufficient food and water in his pack for two days, even three at a push, and matches to light a fire, but nevertheless, he did not fancy spending a night on Fox Tor. Doring, a colleague and fellow hiker, had broken his ankle on the North York Moors late one February afternoon and was forced to shelter as best he could until a farmer came by early the following morning. The cold had got into Doring's bones and he had never been the same after.

"I said," Tenley repeated, "how much farther?"

The boy stopped walking, and his hand slipped free from Tenley's.

"We're here," said the boy. "This is where she fell in."

Tenley saw that they were standing between two small pools of dark, peaty water, separated by a narrow ridge upon which Tenley was now standing. He might almost have missed the pools had the boy not alerted him, so thick was the moss and greenery around them and so poor the fading light. There was no sign of a woman clinging to the bank of either, and Tenley felt any optimism die.

"Which one was it?" he asked, and the boy pointed to the pool on the right. Tenley knelt to peer into the water, but could see nothing. He had no idea how deep it might be and no intention of wading in to find out. He looked around for a long branch; the woman, if she was down there, might somehow, with the final flickers of consciousness, be capable of grabbing hold of it. At worst, if the branch hit something fleshy, Tenley would at least know where she was.

"Find a stick," he told the boy. "We need to—"

But the boy had retreated and was now watching Tenley from a distance, his hands in his pockets—and he was humming, as though what was unfolding was of no more than passing interest. It might have been a trick of the light, but to Tenley, he seemed paler than before, and older too: his hair thinner, his skin wrinkled, his eyes more knowing.

"What's wrong with you?" Tenley asked. "Your mother is somewhere down there."

"Actually, she's not," said the boy. "She's behind you."

Which was when a hand emerged from the second pool and gripped Tenley's right ankle. Tenley cried out in pain as much as shock, for the nails on the hand were very long and dug deep into his flesh. A second hand appeared, clawing at his left boot. Tenley felt a strong tug, and suddenly, he was lying flat on his belly. He tried to gain a handhold, but the grass came away in his fingers as he was dragged toward the pool. He managed to roll onto his back, dig in his elbows, and lean back, but while this slowed his progress, it failed to arrest it. By now, his calves were hanging over the edge of the ridge, and the heels of his boots were touching water. One female hand was entangled in the laces of his left boot, and the other was gouging at his right calf, having torn through the sock and the wool trousers tucked inside.

Tenley could now see into the pool itself and thought he could make out the lineaments of a woman's face in the murk, her hair undulating, garlanded with weeds. Tenley believed the boy's mother to be panicking in her efforts to save herself from drowning, and if he could just find his grip, he could yet rescue her. But if he ended up in that pool with her, she might well do for them both.

Then Tenley's laces broke, freeing his left leg. At the same moment, his right hand, which had been scrabbling at the mud, discovered the roots of a bush. He held on tight and hauled hard with his right foot, hoping to drag the woman from the pool and have done with her, because the pain in his calf was becoming unbearable.

The woman came up all right, her entire upper body emerging from the pool—which was when Tenley realized his mistake. He couldn't have said how long she'd been down there, but it wasn't a matter of minutes, or even hours. Her eye sockets were empty, and her skin was gray-green. Holes had been nibbled in her face and chest, and in places the flesh was worn away to the bone. As Tenley stared, her mouth opened wide, and a black eel wriggled from the maw only to fall into the water and swim off.

Tenley drew back his left leg and sent the full force of his boot into her face. He thought he felt her nose break, though she made no sound. He struck again. This time, the impact was enough to cause her to let go of him. She dropped below the water as Tenley clambered onto the ridge and remained there on all fours, his body trembling. He could still see the woman, though. She was staring up at him from just below the surface, if an eyeless entity could be said to stare. Blind or not, she knew where he was, and he thought she might be readying herself for another attempt at him.

A small bare, rotting foot entered his field of vision. Tenley looked up to find the boy glaring at him, now barely less ruined than his mother, but unlike her, still capable of speech.

"That was my mummy," he said.

Tenley rose as quickly as his injured leg would allow. He'd had enough. He was cold and wet, his calf was lacerated, and he'd ruined a perfectly good pair of wool trousers. Strangely, he was angrier with the boy than with the woman. Without him, she would have been forced to hunt for herself or, more probably, go without, which Tenley concluded might be best for all concerned. The boy was her facilitator, confirming Tenley's long-held suspicion that, while you knew where you stood with adults, you really couldn't trust a child.

Tenley grabbed the boy by the scruff of the neck.

"Then join her, damn you."

With considerable venom, Tenley swept the boy into the pool, and the two, mother and son, sank together until they became twin glimmers in the gloom, and then were lost to sight. Tenley remained by the bank until he was certain that they weren't about to surface again soon, before picking up his pack and slowly, painfully, making his way from Fox Tor.

In the Marble Halls, Tenley finished his glass of wine.

"I can see you don't believe me," he said.

"Not a word of it," I replied, "though I admit it's quite the tale. To be honest, I didn't know you had such a story in you. Were you to write it down, Smith might consider it for the *Strand*."

Tenley didn't take offense, only stood, located his cane, and prepared to leave. He took his wallet from his pocket, but I told him I was happy to pay. The story had helped pass some of what might otherwise have been an entirely dull evening. Tenley nodded his thanks.

"What if I showed you the marks left by the woman's nails?" he asked.

"That wouldn't help. They might have been caused by something else: a misstep through rotten wood, for example, or a broken bottle discarded on the moor."

"I suppose you're right," said Tenley. "You always were of a skeptical bent."

"Have you shared this story with anyone else?" I asked. "I should be careful about claiming it was true, you know. You'll get yourself a reputation."

"I informed the landlord of the Forest Inn at Hexworthy, since it was he who had to summon a doctor to treat my wounds. They were deep, you see, and already showed signs of infection. I told the doctor, too."

"And how did they take it?"

Tenley put on his hat. "They were incredulous—at first."

"At first? What caused them to reconsider?"

From his wallet, Tenley produced a single long, greenish fingernail, which he laid on the table. I didn't touch it. I didn't care to. It looked old and lethal, more like the talon of some extinct predatory bird that anything human, yet human it was; I knew enough of anatomy to make that judgment. I couldn't imagine how a man like Tenley could have come by it, unless what he'd related contained some measure of truth.

Tenley picked up the fingernail and restored it to his wallet, while I took a strengthening mouthful of wine. There was something about that fingernail: the color, the jaggedness, even the smell—because it did smell, of stagnancy and decay, so much so that I immediately spat my wine back in the glass. It now tasted foul, though it had been fine before. I wanted Tenley to be gone, and his blasted fingernail with him.

"I suppose," I said, as a prelude to farewell, "that the whole experience has rather put you off hiking."

Tenley buttoned his coat and tapped his cane to his hat in salute. "Not at all," he said, "but it's put me off children for life."

THE BEAR

The bear appeared shortly after they arrived at the cottage in North Kerry. Steven was surprised to see the bear, mainly because there weren't supposed to be any bears in Kerry, or not that he knew of. Of course, it was possible that the bear was the last of its kind and had been keeping a low profile for fear of being sent to a zoo—or worse, shot. If so, it must have been a remarkable bear, because it wasn't as if there were many places for a bear to hide in the townland of Ballyline. As far as Steven could tell, the whole area was short on caves and woods, which was where he understood many bears liked to live.

Steven hadn't been anticipating the arrival of a bear at their new home. In fact, he hadn't been anticipating very much at all. His newly reduced family—his mum, his brother, and him—had come down to Kerry to stay for a while in their grandmother's old house after their dad left. It was the start of the summer holiday, so school wasn't a problem. His mum said she just wanted a little time to think. Steven thought that she missed his dad. He didn't know why his dad had gone away. He felt that his dad didn't want to leave, and his mum didn't really want him to go either, but everything between his parents had grown angry and confused, and now the household was condensed to three.

Their grandmother had been dead for a couple of years. Steven couldn't remember much about her because he was only little when she died. The house had mostly been standing empty ever since, except when his mum or one of her sisters decided to use it for a holiday. It was dusty, and smelled of old clothes, but the fields behind it stretched for miles and the sun shone more brightly than it did in the city.

The house also had shelves and shelves of books. A few days before the bear came, Steven found a volume titled *500 Fascinating Facts About Kerry!* It was written by someone named A. Mohan. The book was very odd. To begin with, A. Mohan seemed to struggle to find five hundred fascinating facts about Kerry, and so had settled for 499. A. Mohan also had a strange idea of what a fact might be.

Fascinating Fact No. 17: Kerry is the only county in Ireland to contain the same letter occurring twice in succession.

Hang on, thought Steven, that's not right. What about Roscommon, and Offaly? What about Derry, and Kilkenny?

Fascinating Fact No. 97: Kerry is Cork spelled backward.

Seriously?

Fascinating Fact No. 123: Kerry was once part of Gibraltar.

Now, wait a minute . . .

Fascinating Fact No. 156: Kerry once boasted the highest mountain in Ireland, Carrauntoohil, until the discovery of Mount Tully in County Kildare.

Steven knew for certain that Kildare was the flattest county in Ireland. If a man stood on a chair in Kildare, you'd be able to see him on the horizon, never mind unexpected mountains suddenly popping up there. Steven had begun to view *500 Fascinating Facts About Kerry!* with a degree of caution, even mild concern. He suspected that A. Mohan might be mad. He was just about to compose a letter to the publishers, advising them to be more careful in their choice of authors, when his brother returned home, closely followed by the bear.

David, Steven's brother, was the older by three years. Ever since they'd arrived in Ballyline, David had started bringing various creatures into the house: earwigs that he kept in a glass case in his bedroom, and to which he gave the names of Roman emperors;

a three-legged mouse that quickly vanished through a hole in the floorboards and could still be heard running about behind the bookshelves; and a plump pigeon that David claimed was unable to fly, but which turned out simply to be lazy. After a short nap and a peck at some breadcrumbs, the pigeon realized that, wherever it was, it wasn't where it was supposed to be and flew headfirst into a window, temporarily stunning itself. Ever since, it had remained in its box, emerging only for short walks around the bedroom, like a fat man taking enforced constitutionals on medical advice.

David had even briefly managed to acquire a squirrel, which was no mean feat. Squirrels are nervous animals, and it's hard to get them to go anywhere they don't want to, but somehow David had persuaded the squirrel to enter the house, whereupon it panicked and scampered around breaking things, generally making a nuisance of itself. They were all quite relieved when the squirrel departed.

Fascinating Fact No. 199: Kerry was once ruled by the Badger King, until he was overthrown by the Otter Prince.

But bringing home a bear was another thing entirely, especially when their mother was out. She had left them with a lot of instructions about how to behave when they were alone. These included, but were not limited to: not turning on the oven; not turning off the oven if it was already on; not opening the door to strangers; not talking to strangers even through a closed door; and not climbing on any object more than six inches high. Admittedly, she had not made any rules about bringing bears into the house, but Steven was sure that this fell under the general heading of not having things to do with strangers. David was holding the bear by the paw, or the bear was holding David by the hand. Either way, he and the bear were hand in paw.

Steven put down his pencil, the letter forgotten.

"It's a bear," he said, although this was obvious, and really didn't need remarking upon.

"I know," said David.

"Where did you find it?"

"In the field behind the house."

"What was it doing?"

"Just standing there."

"Maybe it was waiting for someone."

"Who would a bear be waiting for?"

Steven considered the question. "Another bear?"

"I don't think he was waiting for another bear. I think he was waiting for one of us."

"How do you know it's a he?"

"I just do."

Steven didn't know how you went about telling a male bear from a female bear, and wasn't certain he wanted to. However you did it, he didn't think the bear would be too happy about the whole business.

Steven regarded the bear. It wasn't really like any bear he'd ever come across in photographs, on television, or even at the zoo. It was more like a big teddy bear than an actual bear. Its fur was golden brown, but thin and worn in spots. Its eyes were glassy, like buttons, and one ear was torn. It was also wearing a red-and-white-spotted tie, which was in itself unusual, Steven never having seen a bear wear a tie before.

"Hello," said Steven, in the absence of anything more profound to say to a bear.

The bear waved a paw in greeting.

"He seems friendly," said Steven. He was quite relieved. There was no telling what an unfriendly bear might do. "Do you think he's hungry?"

"I haven't asked," said David. He looked up at the bear. "Are you hungry?"

The bear shook his head.

"Apparently not," said David.

"What do bears eat anyway?" asked Steven.

"Berries, I suppose. Nuts. Fish too. And honey."

"Like Winnie-the-Pooh." Steven was very fond of Winnie-the-Pooh.

"Yes, just like him."

The bear released David's hand, sat in an armchair, and stared at the ghost of himself in the television screen.

"He doesn't say a lot," said Steven.

"I don't think bears are big on conversation."

David sat beside Steven on the floor. Together they watched the bear. He wasn't doing much but appeared fascinated by his reflection. Maybe he had never seen himself before, thought Steven, or perhaps he believed he was looking at another bear. Steven hoped the bear wouldn't attack the television. They didn't have a lot of money and couldn't easily afford to replace it.

"Should we call someone?" Steven asked.

"Who?"

"I don't know, but his owner may be worried about him. He might have wandered off from a zoo or a circus. He may have been a prisoner and managed to escape."

Steven had a vision of the bear digging a tunnel or scaling a wall, while searchlights scanned the darkness and a siren wailed.

"If he's escaped, he'll want to keep a low profile," said David.

Steven didn't think the bear could keep a low profile. He was, after all, a bear. He could possibly get rid of the necktie, which would make him harder to distinguish from other bears, but he would still be a bear.

"We should call the police," said Steven.

"If we call them, they'll come and take him away."

The bear shook his head, as if to confirm that he really didn't want them to call the police, which decided the matter. They all remained silent for a time.

"Mum will be angry that you brought a bear home," said Steven eventually. "The squirrel was bad enough."

"But she hasn't met the bear yet. She might like him."

Steven wasn't convinced that their mother would approve of the bear. She refused to even let them have a puppy. He hoped he wouldn't get into trouble for being party to letting the bear in the house. If it came down to it, he'd have to tell her that it was David who had brought the bear home.

"He might like to watch television with us," Steven suggested.

He was, to be honest, getting bored with just looking at the bear. For a bear, he was pretty uninteresting, once you got over his essential bearness.

"Okay," said David.

He turned on the television, and together they and the bear watched cartoons and a documentary about salmon—which the bear gave every impression of enjoying—and then a war film. The war film was a bit violent, so after half an hour the bear changed the channel to more cartoons.

Fascinating Fact No. 397: If you shout your name into the mouth of Kerry's famous Crag Cave, the echo always comes back as "Pardon?"

It was growing dark and beginning to rain when they heard their mother's car pull up outside, followed by her footsteps on the path and the doorknob turning. Steven's tummy gave a little lurch of apprehension.

Their mother walked into the living room. She looked at the bear. The bear looked at her. She was carrying a bag of groceries in her hand, which she set down on the coffee table. She was a little surprised to see the bear, but didn't scream or shout, as Steven feared she might, and she didn't appear angry.

"Who's this?" she asked.

"He's a bear," said David. "He doesn't have a name though, not yet."

"David brought him home," said Steven, to put himself in the clear in case their mother decided to turn nasty. "But he's not dangerous," he added. "He just sits quietly. He's no trouble."

Steven was already getting used to having the bear around. It was like he was meant to be there.

"And where did he come from?" asked their mum. She was staring quite intently at the bear.

"I found him outside, standing in the field," said David. "He looked lonely."

"Yes," said their mother, "I expect he was."

"Can he stay?" asked David.

"No, I'm afraid the bear has to go."

Steven wasn't too surprised to hear this, though he thought he would be sad to see the bear leave. But David began to cry.

"I want him to live with us," he said.

"He can't, not here."

"But where will he go?"

"That's for the bear to decide."

She spoke in her special tone of voice, the one that wouldn't brook any nonsense from bear or boy. The bear understood. He wasn't stupid. He stood to leave, and David stood too. He put his arms around the bear.

"I'm sorry," said David.

The bear patted him on the head. Steven reached out and shook the bear's paw.

"Goodbye," he said. "It was nice to meet you."

The bear nodded in agreement and padded to the front door. He paused for a moment beside their mother, and it seemed he might have tried to say something to her were it not for the fact that he was a bear, but the only sound to be heard was David sobbing.

The bear left, and their mother watched him go.

"Right," she said, once the front door had closed behind the bear. "Help me put away these groceries and I'll get started on dinner."

Fascinating Fact No. 428: Kerry pronounced backward is "Ree-Ke," which is also its Japanese name and translates as "small, lonely bird."

They ate in the kitchen. Steven tried to make conversation, but David wouldn't speak and barely touched his food. They cleared the table while their mother went to her room. The two boys sat at the living room window and stared out into the night. The bear was sitting on the garden wall, illuminated by the lights of the house and the beams of passing cars. He sat with his back to them. It was still raining, and his fur was soaking wet.

Their mother appeared from the back of the house and walked across the garden to where the bear sat. She had put on a coat, but her head was uncovered. Even from a distance, the boys could see raindrops running like tears down her cheeks. She spoke to the bear, although the boys could not hear what she said. The bear turned his head to listen to her. She put her hand to his face and stroked his torn ear. The bear reached up and removed his head, and now the rain fell on their father and mother both.

Their mother returned to them. Their father was gone. They had watched him plod off into the night, his head restored to his shoulders so that he was a bear once more. The rain had stopped and the moon was shining through the clouds. Their mother sat with her boys, one arm around each of them.

"Will the bear come back?" David asked her.

"Maybe," she said. "The bear and I will talk, and we'll see . . ."

Fascinating Fact No. 500: There are bears in Kerry.

THE FLAW

It was with some surprise that I learned of Hayden's return to London—indeed, to England, as he had been absent from these shores for more than a decade. The last anyone heard of him, Hayden had become mixed up in the business of Orabi Pasha and the uprising against the khedive. He was perceived to be on the wrong side, too, given our government's support for Tewfik, though it didn't make him many friends among the French either. But Hayden was always his own man, with a natural sympathy for the underdog. I suppose he was lucky not to have perished in the bombardment of Alexandria or the subsequent invasion, and whispers suggested that only the intervention of some distant cousin in the Ministry prevented him from being exiled to Ceylon with Orabi and his followers.

Still, there was a certain doomed romanticism to Hayden's actions, and the more progressive among us, the ones who sensed the tide turning in favor of Egyptian nationalism, believed that history might eventually adjudge him to have been on the right side after all. So it was that by the time I heard he was back in the city, any lingering doubts about his overall character were the province of a minority, albeit a powerful one: Hayden's membership in two of the better clubs had been rescinded in his absence, and his critics had ensured that no reconsideration of this decision was likely to occur in their lifetime. Consequently, he had taken up residence at the

Aetolian, founded in part on a bequest from Lord Byron following his death at Missolonghi during the Greek War of Independence, and a refuge for men of controversial repute.

I should say, before we proceed any further, that Hayden had left England quite suddenly and without explanation, apart from a general letter to his closest friends (among whom I was pleased to count myself) advising that he had decided on a whim to travel abroad and would be in touch again before long. But no additional correspondence from him was ever received, and when mutual acquaintances crossed his path—in Tripolitania, or the Sudan—Hayden was reserved to the point of rudeness. Rumors circulated of some scandal involving a woman, a gambling debt, or even a murder that had been hushed up to avoid embroiling the prime minister, the Queen, and perhaps the Almighty Himself.

But from my inquiries, it became apparent that none of these were true, and the contents of his original letter were, in large part, accurate. Hayden had determined, quite abruptly, that England was no longer for him and elected to exchange its green fields for the sands of Araby. He entrusted his legal and financial arrangements to a solicitor, Granby, whose practice had long looked after the family affairs. Hayden was unmarried, and the only surviving child of three—an older brother had been taken by pneumonia while still in his minority, while a younger sister had died of burns after her dress caught fire at a ball—and his parents were both deceased. Accordingly, there was nothing beyond habit to keep him at home. Nevertheless, the manner of his departure was so abrupt, and the silence that followed so out of character, that I did wonder if something more might have been behind that caprice of which he wrote.

Now, here was the exile returned, and a card delivered to my house advised that Hayden would be pleased if I could join him for dinner at the Aetolian the following evening—or the night after, should that prove more convenient. I showed my wife the invitation. By then, we had been married for three years and were expecting our first child within the month. As Grace could not go out as before, I was more inclined to remain home with her, even at the risk of becoming a source of amusement to those who saw more weakness than strength in my spousal devotion. But I had spoken often to Grace of Hayden, perhaps because the mystery of his departure continued to disturb me. Before our marriage, I had tried to reach him through the British Consulate in Cairo, hopeful that he might consent to serve as my best man, but a year later, the letter was returned unopened, though significantly stained and torn.

"Do you wish to meet with him?" Grace asked.

"Very much," I replied. "I bear Hayden no ill will for the absence of communication. He was always a singular man. I'm just relieved to know that he is safe, and can only imagine what stories he might have to share after all this time."

She looked at me in bemusement.

"But you were friends," she said, "and he abandoned you without explanation, unless an impulse may be regarded as sufficient."

"Because we are friends," I replied, "I can and will forgive him. As for an explanation, I'm convinced that one will be forthcoming over dinner."

"Well, then you must go," said Grace, "and I shall wait up for you, so that you can share the story of his disappearance with me upon your return."

"But what if it is unsuitable for your ears?" I asked.

She slapped me on the arm.

"I grew up with four older brothers," she said, "three of them now soldiers. I suspect my ears may have been tested more frequently and ferociously than your own. I will want to hear that story, Nicholas, unless you're of a mood to sleep with one eye open to protect your manhood from harm."

As you can tell, she was not lying about a familiarity with barrack-room talk.

"If I know you're trying to keep awake in anticipation of my return," I said, "it will cause me to worry."

"Overshadow your drinking, more like," she replied. "The story can wait until the morning then, but no later."

Thus, it was agreed that I should meet Hayden for dinner.

The Aetolian's food, like the club itself, wasn't regarded as London's best, and those members who elected to eat on the premises generally did so due to straitened circumstances, or because, for whatever reason, they didn't care to have their dining companions, or lack of them, remarked upon. The Aetolian did have this much going for it: it was undoubtedly discreet, in its eccentric fashion. In addition to a handful of central tables, the dining room boasted a series of snugs along its walls, of the type more commonly found in certain pubs, the doors of which could be closed against the idle curiosity of others. The lighting also verged on the turbid, possibly to hide the dishes from view, but the club had a decent cellar, stocked generously with wines from the Adriatic and the Balkans. If you knew your stuff, you could drink well for a fraction of what a similar French vintage might cost.

But I must admit I was surprised when the porter informed me that Mr. Hayden had requested dinner to be served in his rooms, and his instructions were to escort me there as soon as I arrived. He led me up the stairs, past portraits of Englishmen in Greek attire, Greeks in English attire, and, if only rarely, Greeks looking like Greeks. I began to fear that Hayden might have suffered some form of disfiguring wound during his time away, and I would be forced to spend the evening trying not to stare at an empty eye socket or an arm with a hook on the end.

"How has Mr. Hayden been?" I asked, hoping to pick up some clue as to what I could expect to find.

"To be honest, sir," said the porter, "we haven't seen a great deal of him. He's a quiet gentleman and keeps himself to himself. Makes a pleasant change from some, I have to say."

The Aetolian did have a reputation for boisterousness, even if it was subdued enough that evening. It was said that the young King George I of Greece had accidentally set fire to a set of curtains in the library, a consequence of a particularly spirited faux duel with some comrades during his post-coronation visit to London in 1863, and was fined five guineas for his trouble. According to club lore, the fine had never been paid, and the king had not darkened its doors since. It wouldn't have happened had they gone with Prince Alfred, the Duke of Edinburgh, for king, as the Greeks wanted. Alfred might have broken the place up occasionally—after all, this was a man who once managed to get shot at a picnic in Australia—but he'd have paid his debts.

The porter paused before a room at the end of a corridor, a plate on its door identifying it as the Constantine Suite.

"I should warn you, sir," he whispered, "that the gentleman requested some alterations to his accommodation. You may find it a trifle bare."

Upon which he knocked, and Hayden's familiar voice invited us to enter.

Hayden was standing by one of the windows, looking out over Fitzroy Square. When he turned to greet me, I saw that he was thinner than before, and his previously dark hair was now fair. At first, I took it to have been bleached by the sun, for his skin was tanned to the color of lightly creamed coffee, but when he came forward to shake my hand, it became clear that his hair was not blond but white. The right side of his face, unblemished before, was pockmarked from either disease or injury, but he showed no other signs of depredation, and his smile was as friendly as I could ever recall.

"Palmer, my old friend," he said.

"Hayden, how I've missed you."

We shook hands warmly as the porter departed. A table had been set for two, and decanters of wine and sherry were waiting to be drunk, but my attention was distracted by the walls of the room. They were entirely devoid of the paintings, daguerreotypes, and photographs that cluttered every other available space in the Aetolian, their dearth identifiable by the lighter patches of wallpaper revealed by their removal. The result was that the room appeared to be in the process of abandonment, as though the Aetolian were on the verge of closing its doors forever.

"I asked that they be taken away," said Hayden, noting the direction of my gaze.

"So the porter suggested. May I ask why? You haven't become a Mohammedan, by any chance?"

The smile faltered. "To be honest, I'm no longer sure to what faith I hold, if any," Hayden replied, "though I have grown comfortable with some ways of the Muslims."

I wasn't about to judge him for that. I was C of E, but I wouldn't have been giving the local vicar much cause to remember my face had Grace not insisted on dragging me to a service every Sunday. I didn't mind it, though. Apart from the singing, which could be distracting, it gave me a chance to think—well, "daydream" might be more accurate, but it was relaxing nonetheless, and I liked to believe that the enthusiasts in the congregation took up my slack.

"I suppose traveling in strange lands will make a man consider anew his position in the universe," I said.

"Yes," said Hayden thoughtfully. "You know, I had a feeling you might understand. Other fellows wouldn't, but you always did keep an open mind."

He went to the table, poured two glasses of sherry, and we toasted to old friends.

"You still haven't told me why the walls are bare," I said.

"Let's eat first," said Hayden. "And when we're done, I'll have a tale for you."

The Aetolian's food was worse than I recalled, the meat swimming in oil and tough enough to make my jaws ache, but Hayden was fine company. I listened in awe to his account of Orabi Pasha confronting the British and French outside Tewfik's palace, where Hayden's was the only white face among the natives, disguised from his countrymen by a headscarf and the actions of the sun. He spoke highly of Wilfrid Scawen Blunt, who was almost as anti-imperialist as himself, and all in favor of Egyptian self-government, but both men knew the game was up long before the Battle of Tel-El-Kebir, in which Hayden claimed not to have participated because he did not wish to fire on British soldiers. I wasn't sure I believed him, and despite the oddness of what was to follow, it was the only point in the evening at which I doubted his testimony.

In turn, I spoke of my marriage to Grace, described my ascent through the ranks at Coutts, and caught him up with developments in the lives of mutual acquaintances, but my existence seemed very sheltered and constrained by comparison with his. It was ever thus with Hayden, who had been captivating rooms since his youth, and for whom England was always destined to be too small. Yet I would not have exchanged my life for his, even before the cigars were produced, the brandy was poured, and he told me his reason for leaving these shores, and why the walls of this room—of every room in which he now slept—were kept bare.

• • • • • • •

Hayden's father had died in 1872, leaving his fortune to his only surviving child. It was a small bequest by some standards, but enough to keep a man like Hayden in comfort for a lifetime, if he was prudent. Hayden and his sire had never been close, and the son was surprised to find himself the sole beneficiary of a will unencumbered by onerous conditions: the obligation to maintain some unsuitable employment in the City or marry a sensible woman before midnight on the next New Year's Eve, that kind of nonsense. The estate included a number of properties, among them an apartment in Mayfair—cluttered with his father's possessions and smelling of tobacco and damp—and the family home in Kent, which had been far too large for Hayden *père* by the end of his life, hence his desertion of it in favor of the London residence. Both were immediately put up for sale, but it was Granby who informed Hayden of another dwelling, a cottage not far from St. Just, on Cornwall's Roseland Peninsula. His father had never mentioned it, and Hayden was unaware of its existence until Granby produced the deeds.

"I believe your father purchased it while your mother was alive," explained the lawyer, "in the hope that it might provide a summer retreat. Unfortunately, by the time the paperwork was signed your mother had become ill, though she had already given instructions for the furnishing and decoration of the house. Your father, I feel, was reluctant to part with it because of these associations, and unwilling to use it for much the same reason. I believe he spent a few nights there, but he was excessively lonely without her company."

Hayden was not an unduly sentimental man, but the idea of having access to a small property furnished by his mother, whom he had adored, but untroubled by the more problematic remembrance of his father, appealed greatly. Also, St. Just was said to be a delightful village, with a beautiful medieval church; Hayden enjoyed a fondness for the architecture of the period, an interest inherited from his late mother. He determined to occupy the cottage as soon as was practicable, and Granby arranged to have it cleaned and aired in anticipation of his arrival.

Hayden reached St. Just in the first week of October, when the summer crowds had departed and the village was becoming once again the sole preserve of the natives. The weather had turned cold, but there was no sign of rain, and the skies were blue with smoky wisps of cirrus cloud. The property, a modest late eighteenth-century stone building on a small hill, was within easy walking distance of the town and set on five acres, with the remains of an old stone circle visible from some of the upstairs windows. There was nothing unusual in that, Cornwall being plentifully supplied with ancient monuments: the Hurlers, the Merry Maidens, the Men Scryfa—the list goes on. The stones on the Hayden property were known locally as the Five Good Children because they stood in ascending height like obedient offspring awaiting the inspection of a parent. While Hayden was aware of darker associations with stone circles—human sacrifice, punishment for disrespecting the Sabbath, temporal gateways—the Five Good Children were to him merely one more reason to love the place, and he understood immediately why it should have called to his mother. The sight of the stones also caused him to think more kindly of his father, who must have known how much their presence would delight his wife, and would have felt great sorrow that she did not live long enough to spend a season with them.

The cottage retained most of its original features, and Hayden's mother had found furniture—some modern, some old—that complemented them without sacrificing comfort or practicality. Mrs. Paige, a local woman engaged by Granby, had made a fine job of dusting the floors and setting the fireplaces and, at the lawyer's instruction, had stocked the cupboards with enough food and drink to last its new owner a week or two, at least. Mrs. Paige herself appeared shortly after Hayden had returned from strolling the grounds. She was a small, frowning woman who quickly revealed a droll sense of humor, noting that, as a single man in possession of a good house, he was likely to find himself inundated with edibles, alcohol, and invitations to take lightly supervised tea with the unmarried daughters of the village.

This turned out to be just the case: at one point, Hayden had three warm pies—two apple, one blackberry—on his kitchen table, along with half a ham, a venison stew, and enough bottles of Cornish cider to open his own bar. As for invitations to visit, he could have stayed in St. Just until Christmas and, at the rate of one or two a week, still not have been in a position to fulfill them all. In the end, Mrs. Paige agreed to spread a rumor that the new resident had come to the village to work on a book, and would not be socializing, beyond occasional trips to the Star Inn, until his labors were complete. So as not to make a complete liar of the housekeeper, Hayden began to assemble some recollections of his schooldays and discovered that he rather enjoyed the process, especially once he had decided not to permit direct experience, or even reality, to get in the way of a good story.

Hayden took long walks on the moors, sometimes venturing as far as Land's End, a round trip of more than eleven miles. He would be sustained on his travels by a bottle of cider and selections from his stock of food, thankfully growing less daunting now the local mothers had accepted that bribery alone was unlikely to permit them to put their marriageable daughters on display. Upon his return, he would often sit in the chair by his bedroom window and watch the sun set upon the Five Good Children. On days when he elected not to wander, and the weather was good, he would sit with his back to the middle stone, and there he would read or write; and because this is not a penny dreadful, Hayden felt no sense of foreboding, nor was he troubled by the spirits of ancients trapped in the megaliths. He was most anxious to stress this as we sat in his rooms at the Aetolian.

"You have to understand that what happened wasn't connected to the stones," he told me. "It runs deeper than that, so much deeper."

At the end of his third week in St. Just, Hayden decided to ride to Penzance for a change of scenery, and rented a horse for that purpose from the local stable. He ate lunch in The Turks Head before walking along Chapel Street, peering in the windows of the antique stores and browsing inside when something caught his eye. He was in the last of them, examining a drawing of smugglers landing their goods on a beach, which the dealer claimed to be a preliminary sketch by John Robertson Reid, when his attention was caught by a larger work hanging between some over-polished horse brasses. The scene it depicted had been captured at dusk, the combination of light and shadow all the more striking for being suspended between shining metals.

"The Five Good Children," said the dealer. "They're a local landmark around St. Just way."

Hayden, perhaps wisely, elected not to share his knowledge of them, or his ownership of the land on which they stood, because it might result in the payment of a premium for his honesty. He thought the artwork might even have been painted from the window of his bedroom, so accurately did it evoke the view. Yet even that was to sell the work short, for the execution was faultless. This was more than an act of reproduction: instead, the artist had captured the quintessence of the landscape in all its uniqueness and beauty. Hayden might almost have termed it perfect.

"Who is the artist?" he asked.

"It's unsigned," said the dealer, "and I'd be lying if I said I could enlighten you as to its provenance. Judging by the frame and the canvas, I'd say it dates from the early part of the last century. The work of an amateur, given the absence of a signature, but a gifted one. I bought it as part of a job lot from a dealer in Camborne who wanted to retire, though if you ask me, he should have retired long ago, for everything he owned had a layer of dust to it that you could write your name in. I only finished cleaning that piece last week, so it hasn't been long on the wall."

Whereupon the haggling commenced, and after some good-natured back-and-forth, a price was agreed to with which both parties were more or less equally unhappy, the definition of a satisfactory compromise. The dealer agreed to arrange delivery the following day, Hayden being reluctant to risk causing damage by riding eight miles with the wrapped work tied to his saddle, a decision that became doubly sensible when the rain began to fall halfway through the return journey. Upon reaching home, he went straight to his bedroom where, while changing his clothes, he gazed out upon the Five Good Children and was convinced that the unknown artist must indeed have once stood in that very spot, and the work might have been destined to revert to the place of its creation.

As promised, the painting was delivered late the following afternoon, while Mrs. Paige was present. She was able to offer no clue as to the artist, and refused to concede that the work might be worthy of admiration or display. Hayden tried hanging it in the living room, but it looked out of place. He had been reluctant to display it in his bedroom, since it seemed odd to him to replicate in art that which he could glimpse in reality simply by turning his head. As it turned out, the painting sat well opposite the window, creating a kind of mirror effect that Hayden found pleasing. The more he looked at it, especially in conjunction with the actuality of the Five Good Children, the more accomplished it seemed to him, and for the first time, he felt a real sense of completeness about the house, and a conviction about the correctness of his place in it. He slept soundly and woke to bright morning light. The Five Good Children watched him in sunshine from his left and in shadow from his right, so that he might have been suspended outside time, with all manner of existences open to his sight.

He was dressing for the day before a mirror when his eye was caught by a mark on the reflection of the painting. At first, he thought it a trick of the light, but when he turned to examine the painting more closely, he saw that he had not been mistaken: a faint flaw was visible on the canvas, and he could not think why he had failed to notice it before now. Between the rendering of the second and third stones was a white blemish, as though the paintwork in that spot had faded slightly, or the artist, due to some distraction, had neglected to apply one final, crucial brushstroke. The flaw did not mar the work unduly—in fact, it was barely visible—and made the painting more amenable to Hayden's sensibilities, because there is nothing more human than imperfection. At the very least, it was a reminder that, when it came to shopping in dim light, one should always bear in mind two important words: caveat emptor.

Hayden spent the morning working on his memoir, into which he had now inserted a Harry Flashmanesque school bully in imitation of Thomas Hughes. For this, he had no need to exert his imagination, our alma mater having been more than adequately equipped with tormenters and oppressors, a disturbing number of whom had subsequently entered political life or the clergy. In the afternoon, he took his regular constitutional, and the evening he devoted to reading. He was now, he realized, a man of leisure. Following his father's death and the confirmation of the bequest, Hayden had handed his notice to Lloyd's. He had never been happy dealing with matters of insurance and had accepted the job only to avoid familial conflict. He had no intention of embarking on a life of indolence—that was not in his nature—but had not yet determined what might replace a deskbound occupation. For the present, he thought, he was content to remain in St. Just, where solitude and reflection might reveal the path to be taken.

Shortly after nine, he retired to bed, pausing only to glance again at the white spot on the painting. It was, if anything, more pronounced than before, despite being viewed by lamplight. Hayden put it down to his new awareness of the smudge, just as a man who detects a chip in his tooth will feel it increase in size every time he touches his tongue to it. He wondered if it might not be worth having the painting restored for fear that eventually the landscape could become secondary to the flaw, leaving the latter as the focus of his attention.

And from the window, the Five Good Children were lost to the October dark.

Hayden could not have said what woke him. The night was still, and the house quiet, yet he came awake in the manner of one suddenly aware of an intruder. He sat up and saw that the flaw in the painting had assumed a new luminosity. Hayden got out of bed and drew closer. As he did so, the blemish flickered, like a candle flame caught by a momentary gust. Hayden stared, but it did not move again, even as it continued to glow. He was inclined to attribute the whole affair to the lateness of the hour and some deficiency of his night vision when an impulse caused him to walk to the window and draw back the curtains. Between the second and third of the Five Good Children, he detected a similar radiance—less distinct than the flare on the canvas, but visible nonetheless.

Hayden looked from one to the other, bewildered. Finally, he pulled on a pair of trousers and went downstairs. He found his boots and a warm overcoat, grabbed the stoutest of walking sticks from the stand, and went outside. The Five Good Children were now hidden by the trees and shrubs in the garden, but it did not take long before they were discernible again. The glow, to Hayden's eye, had faded somewhat in that time, and now resembled the fluorescence of certain mists. He marched on, but the closer he drew to the Five Good Children, the less apparent was the light, until, by the time he reached the stones, it was gone. Again, the analogy of a mist struck him as apt—only from a distance would it register—but he remained troubled by its earlier position and its reproduction in the artwork on his bedroom wall. He even tested the spot between the second and third stones with the walking stick, half expecting to encounter resistance and most grateful when he did not.

With nothing more to be seen or done, and with the chill of the night beginning to seep through his overcoat, he headed home.

When he looked back at the Five Good Children from the brow of the hill, the only light upon them came from the moon. On the picture in his bedroom, the flaw remained: not glowing now, or flickering, but clear and present nonetheless, and larger than before.

Hayden did not sleep again that night.

The curse of morning is that it tends to cause us to doubt our memories of night. In the daylight, Hayden could no longer be confident that the flaw in the painting had, in fact, grown. As with his recollection of the mist from his nocturnal excursion, the flaw was less obvious the nearer one stood, so that it became hard to tell where the paint ended and the absence of color—if absence it truly was—began. Hayden was also used to his own company and was therefore familiar with the tricks the mind can play on one who has been spending too much time in sequestration, even one such as he, who could be alone without ever knowing loneliness. He determined to make a greater effort with his neighbors, and over the following days began to accept invitations that would previously have been rejected, as well as spending evenings among the regulars at the Star Inn, indulging in the odd game of pitch penny or dominoes, or joining in the chorus of songs that often closed the night out.

Hayden's labors bore fruit. His mood improved, and the flaw in the painting remained fixed in size, so he was able to convince himself that it had always been thus. But one evening, while walking back from the inn, the heavens opened, soaking him thoroughly. To add to his misfortune, Hayden missed his footing and twisted his ankle, which slowed his progress home. Mrs. Paige nursed him through the fever that followed, spending a night on the couch below while Hayden tossed and turned through the worst of it—and let the gossips' tongues turn to ash, Mrs. Paige thought, impugning the reputation of a respectable woman like herself, even as it gave her a pleasurable thrill to sleep under the same roof as a man who was not her husband.

In his torment, Hayden became convinced that the flaw had begun to expand once again. He insisted that Mrs. Paige cover the offending painting with a sheet, which she did, because she was not about to argue with a febrile employer. Yet even through the obstruction, the flaw seemed to Hayden to gleam, and he heard the Five Good Children calling to him in the old Cornish tongue, their voices hoarse with dirt and dead things.

On the third day, the fever broke, and the local doctor, who had been calling daily to check on the patient, confirmed that more rest would see him right, this being forced upon Hayden anyway by the damage he had done to his ankle. It was suggested that he might want to move downstairs until he could put more weight upon his foot, where he would be nearer the kitchen, the privy, and the garden, but Hayden did not care to eat, drink, work, and sleep in the same space. He assured both the doctor and Mrs. Paige that he was capable of ascending and descending with relative ease, if not dignity, by seating himself on a step and working his way up or down accordingly.

But Hayden found that once he had made his way downstairs, he was inclined to remain there until night. He read a little and tried to work on his book, but more frequently, he napped. Mrs. Paige came by every morning to make the bed, air the room, and check on her charge, and returned in the evening to set a fire in the bedroom—because, as she informed Hayden, he was still weak, no matter what the doctor might say, and a returned fever was a vengeful one. She occasionally popped by in the afternoon as well, so that Hayden began to feel slightly suffocated by her care.

After a week of this, it was with some relief that he learned from Mrs. Paige that she intended to travel to Falmouth to see her sister, and he would have to manage without her for a couple of days. That night, Hayden dined on soup and chicken, his appetite almost fully revived, and went to bed as soon as the first stars appeared in the sky. The fire still burned in the bedroom grate, but Hayden noticed that it failed to warm the room. The cottage was not drafty, its walls being solid and the frames of the doors and windows properly fitted. Shivering, and mindful of the housekeeper's warning about revenant fevers, he added more wood to the fire and prepared for bed.

Only then did he look again at the picture of the Five Good Children. It remained covered, as it had been throughout his illness. He could not remember ordering Mrs. Paige to obscure it, though she assured him he had; but neither had he asked her to reveal it again, and felt no great urge to do so himself. He decided, perhaps as a consequence of his recent trials, that he no longer cared to keep it in the house. It gave him no pleasure and had been sold to him under false pretenses. It was defective, whether in its original execution or due to the manner of its storage. If he was desirous to have the view from his window replicated in oils, he could commission an artist accordingly, even as he doubted he would ever wish to. It was one thing to come across such a painting priced modestly, but quite another to instigate its creation at significant expense.

Now, having decided to be rid of it, curiosity took hold. Hayden wanted to look at it again, to see if it was as he remembered. But the truth was also that, being restored to some measure of his old self, the draped painting made him uneasy, as though it were less a framed image than the specter of one.

Hayden reached out and pulled away the sheet.

At the Aetolian, Hayden tipped the brandy decanter toward my glass. After a pause for the sake of politeness, I allowed him to pour.

"Were this a drama, and you permitted the curtain to fall at such a point, the crowd might tear you limb from limb," I said.

"Thankfully, I have an audience of only one," said Hayden, "and unless you have changed greatly, you are not the riotous kind. I just want to emphasize something before I proceed. Yes, I had endured a nasty fever, and yes, I was troubled by a painful ankle, but the fever had cleared, I was in full possession of my wits, and had taken nothing stronger than a glass of whisky. No Battley's Sedative, no Dover's Powder, no wine with a tincture of opium. I eschew them, and always have. What I saw was real."

He spoke with such matter-of-factness that I did not discredit him, even before I had heard the rest of his story. Here was no lunatic, yet neither was he the Hayden I once knew. He was too much changed for that—not alone physically, but psychologically. It was in his eyes, which were those of a man who had looked upon queer, even brutal sights and been irrevocably altered by them.

"I believe you, Hayden," I said. "In all our years of friendship, I have never known you to utter a falsehood."

Hayden reached out and grasped my right hand, which lay on the table between us. He held it tightly for a moment, and I observed the topography of his flesh, his veins blue rivers set against the arid desert landscape of his tanned skin. Did the tributaries of the Nile look like this, I wondered, when seen from above? Hayden had sailed the river and bathed in its waters. He had visited Baghdad, Jerusalem, and Damascus. I had been no farther than Europe, and then only to France and Italy; they were different from England, but not alien. Hayden had traversed landscapes upon which I would never set foot. He had walked among ancient civilizations and experienced new worlds. And when he had concluded his narrative, I felt only pity for him.

Hayden stood before the picture and stared. The flaw was transformed. It no longer lay among the Five Good Children, but had moved down the image, drawing closer to the lower part of the frame. It was also much larger than before, and its shape was different. Hayden's recollection of it was as a kind of oval, or perhaps the white flare of a lit match, but it now had the recognizable form of something almost human: a head, arms, and legs, but all distorted and distended. The head was too large for the body and bulging with deformities; the arms were so long as to extend below the level of the knees, the fingers hooked like claws; and the legs were massive and squat, so that it could only have shuffled rather than walked, the effort required to raise them being too great.

Hayden took a step back from the picture, then another, and it seemed to him that the monstrosity in the frame advanced in turn, seeking to close the distance between them. From that misshapen head, dark eyes popped, extruded by internal pressures, the entity configuring itself, concluding its act of creation. A thin line drew itself below the eyes, a slit that opened to become a mouth, and Hayden heard a sound that was both agonized and triumphant, as of a newborn creature freed from the womb.

Hayden spun away, for the sound had come not from inside the frame but outside the house. He ran to the window and pulled open the curtains. There, moving sluggishly across the rough ground between the Five Good Children and his cottage, was the creature from the painting, bathed in a pale, liquescent light, a parturitive residue that dripped with each step, evaporating into nothingness as it fell to the ground.

Yet the nearer it approached, the smaller the beast seemed to become. Its head began to shrink, the growths subsiding, the skull growing more rounded. The arms contracted, the legs withered, and the torso became more compressed until Hayden was staring, not at some unknown horror, but at the naked figure of a man, one pale and unfinished, so that, in a certain light, Madame Tussaud herself might not have disdained to claim it. As it peered up at the window, its face was something like Hayden's own.

Hayden looked back at the picture, where a similar figure filled the canvas. He had no weapons in the cottage, no means to defend himself beyond some walking sticks, a poker, and—

Fire.

Hayden returned to the painting and yanked it from the wall. It was heavier than he remembered, and he had to use a thigh for support, putting painful pressure on his wounded ankle. Awkwardly, he maneuvered the painting toward the fireplace as, on the canvas, the mouth of the figure grew impossibly wide in a face that was now incontestably Hayden's own, and he heard that sound again, this time closer to the cottage, and he feared the rage of it. Seconds later, the front door shuddered with the impact of a body, and Hayden was grateful that the habits of city life, the locking of doors and securing of windows, should have followed him to the countryside. With a final effort, he flung the picture into the fire.

For a few moments, nothing happened. The flames licked at the frame, but the image remained intact. His face gazed back from it, the eyes black, the mouth a hole ripped in time and space, before a flare shot from between its lips, the canvas at last surrendering to the blaze. From outside, Hayden caught a roar of pain that was cut short as light bloomed from below.

Hayden went to the window. In his garden, a burning figure was beating hopelessly at the fires that consumed it, even as it stumbled onward, through the gate and along the path that led to the Five Good Children. It was halfway there when the conflagration overcame it. The figure dropped to its knees, then its side, and Hayden watched it burn.

In the Aetolian, Hayden surveyed the guttering of the candles on the table.

"It smoldered away to ash," he said. "The wind took it, leaving nothing. Perhaps it was for the best. How would I have explained the charred remains of a dead man to the police? I might have found myself accused of murder."

"And the painting?" I asked.

"Only shards of the frame remained, until I broke them up and they, too, burned. The next morning, I returned to London and left instructions that the cottage be put up for sale. I could not see myself returning there, for obvious reasons."

"No, I should imagine not."

"I had intended to remain in London, but—"

"Go on," I said. "Whatever you have left to share can be no stranger than what went before."

Hayden shook his head.

"So you may think," he said, "but here, possibly, is where it tips further into madness. I saw the flaw again, a day or two later, this time in a William Shayer landscape from my father's collection, marked for auction. It was tiny, barely visible to the naked eye, but it was there. I stayed awake that night to monitor it, for fear that it might grow."

"And did it?"

"No, but it may be that it was merely dormant, waiting."

"For what?"

"For the right moment, the right host? Having failed with me, might it not look for another? After all, I was now alert to its presence. I was watchful. There would be easier prey. The alternative, of course, was even more unnerving."

"That it might try again with you?" I suggested.

"Yes. I had hurt it, but I had not put an end to it. Whatever it is, I'm not sure it can be disposed of so easily. So I left England. I embraced the desert, a place without representations of the natural world and where art, when it is found, tends toward the nonfigurative, the decorative. There I stayed, until legal obligations forced me to return here, however briefly."

"And that's why you asked for the paintings in this room to be removed," I said.

"Now I perceive some mistrust creeping in," said Hayden. "I can hardly blame you."

"I admit only that it is straining my credulity," I said, "not shattering it. But a creature, a homunculus, that finds its way into our world through—what, pictures of landscapes or standing stones?"

"I have spent a long time considering this," said Hayden, "and have learned that I am not alone in what I have experienced. Others, too, have seen the flaw. In fact, once the eye is trained to look for it, it becomes hard to miss. It is in everything—this blemish, this imperfection—but most profoundly in art because art is so deeply human, and humans are so deeply flawed. What if there are worlds beyond this one? What if, in creating representations of what we see around us, an artist may, in moments of great vision or inspiration, capture a quintessence, and in so doing, forge a connection between the real and the unreal: a window between realms, or the expansion of a fissure, a gap wide enough for something to enter, something that seeks to be what it is not?"

To these questions, I had no answer. I rose, thanked Hayden for dinner, and wished him good night. It was time to return to my wife and leave Hayden to his sleep, however troubled it might be. Did I believe his story? He believed it, which was enough for me. I did not share it with my Grace. It did not seem appropriate to do so. Instead, I told her that Hayden had become unsettled following his father's death, and England no longer gave him peace.

Hayden and I made loose plans to meet again over the coming weeks, but he did not contact me. When I called at the Aetolian to ask after him, I was told he had left a few days earlier, permanently relinquishing his membership upon departure. I know he will never come back to England, and therefore I shall never see him again.

A few days after my final visit to the Aetolian, two packages were delivered to my home. The first contained Hayden's unfinished memoir of our schooldays, which I read more with sadness than joy because I missed those young men so. The second was a small oil on canvas by the artist George Cole, depicting a cottage on the Avon by night. It was, a note included with the painting informed us, a gift from one of Grace's aunts, who was leaving London for Somerset following the death of her second husband earlier in the year, and had decided to redistribute some of her possessions in preparation for the move. My wife was overjoyed because the little picture was lovely, even by Cole's high standards.

That night, after my wife went to bed, I stayed reading by the fire. We had positioned the painting to the right of the mantelpiece, where the light suited it best, even though it already seemed to be illuminated from within, so perfectly had the artist captured the moon's shimmer on the water by the cottage, a single candle burning behind the window. I stood before it, admiring a possession that we could not have afforded to buy.

Across the river from the cottage, a tree rose high above the bank, with thick bushes at its base. I leaned in closer to examine the details of the execution. Beside one of the bushes, between the water and the tree, was a small white mark, like a dusty smear on the canvas. I blew at it, but it remained in place. It's still there now, years later. It has not changed.

I know this because I watch it closely.

UNQUIET SLUMBERS: A TALE OF THE CAXTON PRIVATE LENDING LIBRARY & BOOK DEPOSITORY

As befits its nature and history, the Caxton Private Lending Library & Book Depository contains many tales within its walls—and not only those that have been committed to print, there to join its vast archive of manuscripts and first editions.

Like any library, the Caxton is more than just a storage facility for books: it is both a living entity, with words as its lifeblood, and a haunted house, with characters as its ghosts. But what distinguishes the Caxton from its more quotidian peers is the fact that its literary inhabitants are corporeal, each of them given physical form by the imaginations of writers and readers and rendered immortal by those same agencies. Within its walls, fiction is the only reality.

The Caxton is where the great, the good, and the not so good of literature find sanctuary when their creators die. Shortly after the passing of a noted novelist, one whose characters have become, if not household names, then at least names in the better households, the Caxton receives a brown paper parcel bound with string, containing a first edition copy—sometimes even a manuscript—of that author's best-known work. Sometimes—in the rare case of a Shakespeare, for example, or a Dickens or an Austen—the parcel will include more than one volume, but most authors would be content should even a single example of their work, or a sole character, capture the popular imagination sufficiently to earn a place in the Caxton.

Of course, if this were all that were to occur after an author's death, the Caxton would be remarkable merely for its collection and the mechanism that permitted the delivery of those final parcels. No one seemed to know how, or by whom, they were packaged and sent, and no individual had ever stepped forward to claim credit for their dispatch during the centuries of the library's existence. It had been suggested by more than one early librarian that perhaps generations of a single family, a clan embedded in the printing and publishing industries, had taken secret responsibility for the task, but this seemed unlikely. Questions of access to materials arose, particularly in the case of rare texts, while nothing in the meticulously detailed records of the institution—which contained documents dating back to Caxton himself—indicated that such a system might have been put in place. As a consequence, it was decided that some nonhuman agency—call it the Creative Spirit, the Muse, or the Divine—took care of deliveries, and any further inquiry into the matter was therefore both futile and potentially unwise. The apparatus worked, which was all that mattered.

But the Caxton is greater than the sum of its books and papers, however extraordinary they might be. Those novels and manuscripts do not appear on the Caxton's doorstep in isolation. After—or even simultaneous with—delivery, their most famous characters also manifest themselves. These dramatis personae are sometimes confused, periodically tetchy, sporadically depressed, or—once in a blue moon, and even a full one—dangerously angry, but all eventually settle down and find their place.

The Caxton, like all libraries, is capable of containing universes within its walls. New rooms materialize, furnished according to the requirements of their residents, but the physical boundaries of the library never extend, and it never runs out of space. Beyond those rooms lie entire worlds: enter the accommodation of Sherlock Holmes and Dr. Watson, and through the window of the living room you may glimpse the rooftops of nineteenth-century London; exchange a greeting with Mr. Fitzwilliam Darcy in his study, and the gardens of Pemberley stretch beyond the glass; visit Alice, and the Cheshire Cat stretches languorously on a tree outside, all smiles. The Caxton is a reader's dream made manifest.

But like any venerable establishment, it has its peculiarities, even prejudices. The collection errs on the side of Anglophone writers, particularly those born in England, and has been known to evince an especial distrust of Americans. In addition, either the library or its animating spirit—that fickle Muse again—has an odd sense of humor. For example, following the death of Samuel Beckett, a printed note was delivered to the Caxton promising that a copy of his most famous drama was on its way, but so far it has not actually arrived, although more notes have since followed, each containing a more elaborate and unlikely reason than the last for the delay. Similarly, an entry in the Caxton's ledger confirms receipt, on August 14, 1946, of a copy of *The Invisible Man* by H. G. Wells, but the volume in question cannot be found; Tristram Shandy has yet to be born, although his cradle sits waiting; and the Count of Monte Cristo is never in his room.

On occasion, too, the Caxton understands what others do not, and perceives beauty where others see only ugliness. Books that are underappreciated in their day, and characters that are disregarded, may turn up at its door, waiting for history to clasp them belatedly to its bosom.

The Caxton, one might say, knows quality.

On this subject, an odd incident occurred in the middle of the nineteenth century, during the stewardship of Mr. Hanna, a retired academic with an insatiable curiosity for the dustier corners of late eighteenth-century British history.

Mr. Hanna was, by all accounts, of a nervous disposition, and therefore possibly ill-suited to caring for the library during the resurgence of gothic literature. Upon Mary Shelley's death on February 1, 1851, Mr. Hanna took a fortnight's holiday in Weston-super-Mare and did not return until he was certain that Shelley's most famous creation had found its own way to whatever corner of the library had been arranged for its comfort. The Caxton's records show that the library sulked for some months after, and took mischievous pleasure in repeatedly relocating Mr. Hanna's pipe and slippers to the Annex of Unfinished Books, from where he had a devil of a time retrieving them.

But this temporary estrangement of library and librarian came later. For now, let us return to December 1848, when the Caxton was situated on the outskirts of the city of Ely in Cambridgeshire, within sight of the great cathedral. At that time, the Caxton's collection was much smaller than it is now, and its residents fewer. The librarian, between his daily tasks of filing and mending, could easily visit most of his charges at least once a week, a pleasure that would subsequently be denied his successors.

But even for the most garrulous of men, such social calls could prove exhausting, and Mr. Hanna, although a great lover of books, was less well equipped for conversational pleasantries than most. His preference was to communicate by letter or note, which better displayed his essential kindness and good nature while hiding his shyness, to the extent that his administration of the Caxton bore something of the complexion of the Post Office, and his morning delivery of missives became the highlight of many a character's day.

Mr. Hanna was in the habit of taking a regular evening constitutional around the city, both to give him some time alone away from the Caxton and to aid the digestion of his supper, although he made a point of avoiding the cathedral's precincts after dark owing to a preponderance of reported sightings of spectral monks. While many might have dismissed such tales as foolishness, Mr. Hanna's vocation made him very reluctant to disregard any reports of the otherworldly.

But on one particular night, having returned from his walk, Mr. Hanna discovered to his displeasure that a window was broken in the library's east wall, as though someone had attempted to gain access to the building in his absence. The effort, it seemed, had been unsuccessful, because the hole in the glass was quite small, although a series of significant cracks radiated from it, rendering the whole pane unsafe.

"Good Lord," said Mr. Hanna, to no one in particular. "I mean, really."

The Caxton was very accomplished at not being noticed. It had a way of blending into its surroundings, aided by the tendency of a great many people—some of whom should really have known better—to ignore books, or underestimate their importance and dismiss reading as a dreary pursuit, this being the natural response of the unimaginative. A very large concentration of fiction, such as that contained in the Caxton, succeeded in deflecting their attention to an unusual degree, which worked to the library's advantage. Consequently, assaults on the Caxton's physical structure were exceedingly rare.

Mr. Hanna located a brush and pan, swept up the broken glass, and fixed a board over the inside of the window until he could source a replacement pane, the Caxton's librarians being required to attain a degree of accomplishment in making minor repairs to bricks and mortar as well as leather and paper. The window was quite narrow, and only a very thin person might have been able to gain access through it, assuming they had succeeded in removing the glass in its entirety. But the damage was troubling to Mr. Hanna, for the window in question was in his bedroom, and few things are better guaranteed to come between a man and his sleep than the possibility of being roused by an intruder.

To calm himself, Mr. Hanna prepared a cup of hot milk, checked all the other windows and doors, and went to bed, where he endured a restless night. He spent most of the following day trying to make some sense of Samuel Richardson's revisions, over fourteen separate editions, to the four volumes of *Pamela in Her Exalted Condition*, the late novelist's sequel to his most famous work, *Pamela; or, Virtue Rewarded*. This was a task of such indescribable tedium that successive librarians had been bequeathing it to one another ever since Richardson had gone to the great sorting office in the sky back in 1761, but it was one that Mr. Hanna—for whom mundanity was very underrated—remained determined, even delighted, to complete. He set his work aside only to venture into town, where he purchased a new pane for the broken window and determined to embark upon its installation come morning.

That evening, as the weather turned cold, he once again took to the fields for some fresh air and exercise. Soon it would be Christmas, and the choristers were practicing in the cathedral, their songs carrying pleasantly in the still air. Mr. Hanna was still humming "Come, Thou Long Expected Jesus" when he returned to the library, only for a vague sense of unease to mute his joy. He decided to make a single circuit of the exterior and found to his displeasure that another pane had been broken in much the same manner as the first, the ground beneath the window being much disturbed by the impressions of bare feet.

Mr. Hanna had by now progressed from troubled to actively concerned. As has been established, the Caxton was practiced at concealment, but this did not mean it could remain undetected forever. It had already been required to relocate on a number of occasions, a contingency for which instructions remained available, even if the relevant envelope was marked with a wearied note written in a previous librarian's hand, reading "*Do Please Try Not To Open This.*"

As before, Mr. Hanna cleared away the broken glass and covered the hole in the window. He brewed a pot of tea and mulled over the problem. The solution, unpleasant though it was, might be to forgo his walk the following night, and instead secrete himself in some bushes from where he might be able to monitor the approach of any interloper, and discourage further attempts at damage with vague, unfulfillable threats of police intervention.

With something approaching a plan of action in place, Mr. Hanna settled into bed in the company of a comparative study of the Corn Laws of 1773, 1791, 1804, and 1815, with an emphasis on price stabilization measures. In due course, the excitement proving too much for him, he nodded off in his little closet bed, the curtain drawn over the single window to deal with the draft from the missing pane. The wind whistled beyond the walls, and the first of the winter's snow began silently to fall, but to all this Mr. Hanna remained oblivious as he dreamed of being surrounded by 490 bushels in a grain store while he struggled to remember where he'd left his hat.

In time, though, Mr. Hanna was woken by a tapping, as of a branch knocking against the glass from outside.

"Oh, bother!"

He tried to get back to sleep, but the noise persisted from behind the curtain. An old oak, overdue for pruning, stood close to the library's east side. Mr. Hanna had been waiting for the quiet of January to tackle the job, when people would be fewer and the oak would be dormant, leaving the tree to tend its wounds in spring and recover by summer. That job, he realized, might now have to be moved forward.

"For goodness' sake!" said Mr. Hanna as he pulled back the curtain to open the window. Half-asleep, he sought out the offending branch in order to break off enough to cause the knocking to cease.

But instead of touching bark, his fingers found a small, cold fist.

Mr. Hanna shrieked, and through the open window heard a girl cry out in return. He tried to retrieve his hand, but it was now held in a relentless, icy grip.

"Let me in—let me in!" said the girl, as yet unseen.

"Get out of it!" said Mr. Hanna. "Give me back my hand."

"I'm come home."

"No, you haven't," said Mr. Hanna. "This isn't your home. It's a library!"

He peered through the gap and could just make out, amid the descending snow, the features of a brown-haired young woman. She was wearing a thin white dress, and her feet were bare.

"What are you doing out there anyway?" said Mr. Hanna. "You'll catch your death. And where are your shoes?"

"It's been twenty years," said the girl.

"Don't be silly," said Mr. Hanna. "You can't be more than eighteen. You really ought to go home, you know."

"I've been a waif for twenty years!" insisted the girl.

"All right, all right," said Mr. Hanna. "Have it your way."

Mr. Hanna might have been a retiring, scholarly man, but he was far from heartless. He couldn't leave the girl out in the snow, waif or not. He'd never have been able to forgive himself if something happened to her.

"Look," he said, "let me go if you want to come in."

The girl peered at him suspiciously.

"Promise?"

"I promise."

Reluctantly, she released Mr. Hanna's hand.

"Come around to the front," he said. "I won't be long."

Mr. Hanna located his dressing gown, put on his slippers, and went to the door. When he opened it, the girl was standing on the step, shivering. Her lips were bloodless and her skin pale, but her eyes shone with a brilliance that had nothing to do with the lamp in Mr. Hanna's hand. She was, he thought, quite beautiful.

"I'm come home," she said.

"Yes, I heard all that," said Mr. Hanna. "You haven't, but never mind. I'll put the kettle on, and we'll find you somewhere to put your head down for the night. Tomorrow we'll work out what to do with you."

The lving room that doubled as Mr. Hanna's office was still warm from the fire, and some embers remained in the hearth. Mr. Hanna added paper and wood, and soon a small blaze was crackling again. He made the girl a cup of tea, and gave her a slice of ginger cake, which she nibbled while curled up in an armchair.

"What's your name?"

"Catherine."

"Look," said Mr. Hanna, "I hope you won't think me rude for asking, but you haven't been breaking my windows, have you?"

Catherine shifted her feet awkwardly.

"Might have done."

"But why?"

"Dunno. Just seemed like the right way to go about it."

"Go about what?"

"Getting in."

"Doors are the right way to go about it," said Mr. Hanna. "Very popular they are, doors, and have been for centuries. Breaking people's windows is only the right way to go about getting into prison."

"Sorry," said Catherine.

"So you should be. Forced entry is a bad habit to develop, especially for one so young."

Mr. Hanna knelt to poke the fire. He had a feeling he was missing something, like a man who has been given a jigsaw puzzle to complete without any clue as to what the final picture might be. When he looked again at the girl, she was sound asleep in the chair.

Mr. Hanna took a blanket, laid it over her, and prepared to return to bed. He did not worry about leaving a stranger alone in the library. The Caxton knew how to look after itself.

As he prepared to go, he heard a thud from outside, as though a heavy object had just landed on the doorstep.

"Ah," said Mr. Hanna. "Right."

Because it was Christmastime, and delays were to be expected.

The girl named Catherine opened her eyes and stretched. Winter sunlight shone through the window behind her. Mr. Hanna sat in a chair on the opposite side of the fire. By his feet lay a sheet of brown paper, a length of string, and the first of the two volumes of the novel that had arrived during the night. The second lay on his lap, its final pages finished by him only moments earlier.

"Feeling better?" he asked.

"Much, thank you."

Color had been restored to her cheeks and lips, so that she seemed to glow. She watched as he closed the work and prepared to set it aside.

"What is the nature of the book?"

Mr. Hanna turned the spine toward her so she could read the title.

"Seeing it in your hands," she said, "I think I recall some of its contents, but not all."

"Well, we only ever really know our own stories," said Mr. Hanna, "and oft as not, barely those."

"Did you enjoy it?"

"It was unusual. I don't believe I've ever read anything like it."

"But that's true of all the best books, isn't it?"

"Yes, I rather suppose it is."

"Did you sit up all night to finish it?"

"I did," said Mr. Hanna. "I haven't slept a wink. I was aware of the novel's existence, but hadn't been inclined to read it. I think I had judged the book by what others wrote of it, but the library knows better than any of them. It always does. Incidentally, I was wrong about something else, too. You have come home, Cathy. This is where you were always meant to be."

The girl looked concerned.

"Just the two of us?"

"No, you'll have plenty of company, and more to come, I should think."

He stood, smiled upon her, and offered his arm.

"Meanwhile, why don't I show you around? There are so many interesting characters for you to meet . . ."

OUR FRIEND CARLTON

Our friend Carlton was a friend until he wasn't—though even at the end, he was still sort of a friend. What I mean is that we liked him and were sorry we had to kill him. We didn't want him to suffer, or even know anything about it. We simply wanted to shoot him, bury him, and feel bad about it afterward. One second, he'd be there, and the next, he'd be gone. We guessed it would probably hurt a little, or even a lot, but not for very long. That was some consolation.

It wasn't our friend Carlton's fault that we had to kill him, not really. He hadn't done anything wrong, or not to us. The details aren't important, but it came down to money: money that had previously belonged to someone else and subsequently found its way to us, when maybe some people might have taken the view that it shouldn't have. A woman was also involved, because a woman often is. This woman was a prosecutor who, along with the police, began putting pressure on Carlton to talk about the money in a way that wouldn't be appreciated by its new possessors. Our friend Carlton seemed likely to buckle under this pressure, and once he cracked, who knew what might pour out? This wasn't the first time we'd been involved in the redistribution of wealth, and we doubted it would be the last. In addition, we had to answer to others, and those others didn't regard Carlton as a friend. To them, he was just a guy, and the world wasn't about to run out of guys who were just guys anytime soon.

So we told our friend Carlton that the men who weren't his friends, or ours, wanted us to retrieve something for them, and this would require a certain amount of digging in the dead of night. We'd performed similar duties before, because the unfriendly men were in the habit of burying things that occasionally had to be dug up again or, more often, had to be buried and stay that way. Our friend Carlton was about to fall into the second category.

I didn't fire the fatal shot. I offered to, but Stanhope said he'd take care of it. I think he was worried I might hesitate at the last. Carlton was a friend to both of us, but he was more Stanhope's friend than mine, or so Stanhope claimed—perversely, I suppose, seeing as how he was so willing to shoot Carlton. I disagreed but kept this to myself because I didn't suppose it mattered. We had reached the point in our relationship with Carlton where gradations of friendship were largely inconsequential.

I don't recall much about the shot. Stanhope didn't give us any warning. We were walking in the woods by Tabernacle Township, Carlton and I, with Stanhope behind, when next thing I heard the gun go off, and Carlton went down halfway through a sentence. There wasn't much blood because Stanhope used a .22 hollow point, which meant all the bullet's energy was absorbed by Carlton's brain tissue. It's the exit wound that usually creates a mess. A mess leaves evidence, which can lead to arrest and a significant loss of liberty. The hollow point made a small hole entering our friend Carlton's head, and then stayed in there, going about its business. Carlton twitched some after he fell, but it was all electrochemical. It wasn't like he was trying to get up or anything. By then, he was already deceased.

We buried him not far from where he'd died. Stanhope told me later that he'd scouted Tabernacle a few days before to pick the best spot. He'd shot our friend Carlton where he did because nearby were building materials that had been dumped by a contractor, including stone waste. The way Stanhope figured it, we could drop Carlton in a hole and put stones on top of and around the body. If we did it right, we'd avoid subsidence, as nothing says BODY BURIED HERE like subsidence.

So that was what we did: we dug a hole, dropped our friend Carlton into it, added the stones, refilled the hole, and scattered leaves and branches over the dirt so it looked like any other area of ground. We didn't bother offering a prayer, because Carlton wasn't religious, but we wished him well and told him we were sorry it had come to this. Then we checked the surrounding area to ensure none of us had dropped anything that might later prove embarrassing and retraced our steps to the car. We were quiet on the ride home. Like I said, we liked Carlton.

It's important to note where we interred Carlton, by which I mean it was a regular patch of forest. Our friend Carlton wasn't even the first guy buried out there. People in our line of work had been burying bodies in parts of Wharton State Forest and the Pinelands for so long it was a wonder there was any space left for new arrivals. During the seventies and eighties, so many holes were being made that it started to resemble a gravediggers' convention, and someone could have performed a valuable act of public service by keeping a discreet note of the resting places so nobody would be in danger of selecting a spot that was already occupied.

At least, we thought, Carlton wouldn't be lonely.

Stanhope and I picked up some Chinese food and ate it at the kitchen table. When we were done, Stanhope went to his room while I stayed up to think about Carlton. I decided that Stanhope was definately wrong, and Carlton had been more my friend than his. I was really going to miss Carlton, while Stanhope would just find a new friend to replace him. People were interchangeable to Stanhope. They were his friends until they weren't, and he liked them until he didn't. I sat there, not watching TV, and realized that someday, if the need arose, Stanhope would put a bullet in my head, and then he'd have a vacancy for a new friend. This caused me to wonder if Stanhope and I were really friends at all. Stanhope, I decided, lacked depth of feeling.

I don't recall when I went to bed, only that it was later than usual. Stanhope was sleeping silently, or I supposed he was asleep. He might have been lying awake, listening, just in case I was nursing some resentment about the manner in which he'd killed our friend Carlton. I was glad Carlton hadn't died scared or in too much pain, but I was starting to wish that I'd had a little longer with him—you know, to say goodbye. I also didn't like how Stanhope hadn't given Carlton time to complete his final sentence. It struck me as rude, like whatever our friend Carlton might have had to say wasn't important enough to allow him the couple of seconds required to finish it. Maybe Stanhope had always considered Carlton's conversation unsatisfactory at best. It was true that Carlton could be poor company, and I would sometimes find excuses to do something other than listen to him, even if that something else was a chore, like laundry. But it wasn't as though Carlton would be boring anyone for much longer, not with Stanhope walking behind him in those woods. Would it have hurt Stanhope so much to let our friend Carlton conclude what he was saying?

I wished I could recall what it was that Carlton had been talking about, but I wasn't paying attention. Had I known Stanhope would choose that moment to kill him, I'd have listened more closely. I might even have been able to finish Carlton's sentence for him. After all, his thoughts weren't so original that I couldn't have figured out the ending for myself. Maybe that was why I was annoyed with Stanhope: because it was easier than being annoyed with myself.

I woke to the sound of Stanhope calling my name. I made a point of putting on my robe before I went down because the robe had two pockets, in one of which I placed my gun. Stanhope was still playing on my mind, and I kept my hands in my pockets as I headed down, with my right clutching the little pistol. The kitchen light was on, and Stanhope was standing in the doorway. He was wearing shorts and didn't have a gun, only a glass of milk.

"What is it?" I asked.

Stanhope pointed to his right, at something I couldn't see. He tried to speak, but no words came out, so instead he shrugged and went on pointing.

Our friend Carlton was seated at the kitchen table. He had dirt on his cheek, in his ears, and clogging his nostrils. Dirt was smeared on his face and clothes, lodged under his fingernails, and stuck between his teeth. There was even dirt jammed in the bullet hole in his head. I could see it from where I stood, because Stanhope hadn't shot Carlton in the back of his balding skull but on the left side.

"Carlton?"

I didn't know what else to do other than call his name, and once I'd done that, I wasn't sure what to say next. I couldn't see any point in asking if he was okay because clearly he wasn't, and apologizing for what had happened out in the forest might have come across as insincere. But Carlton didn't react. He just stared at the kitchen table, his hands lying flat on the wood.

"How did he get here?" I asked Stanhope.

"Walked, I guess."

"It's thirty miles. That's, like, ten hours, minimum."

"Faster, if you're in good health," said Stanhope.

We both looked at Carlton.

"Okay," said Stanhope. "Ten hours, but it could be more."

I checked the clock on the wall.

"It's only been eight since we buried him."

Stanhope went to the window, giving our friend Carlton a wide berth along the way, and peered through the drapes.

"I don't see a car," he said.

"You think he drove himself?"

"Or someone else did. They could have picked him up on the side of the road and dropped him off outside."

I told him that didn't seem likely. Anyone seeing our friend Carlton on the side of the road, looking like he did, would either have put their foot down hard or called the cops. Also, Carlton didn't appear to be in any state to tell someone where he lived, and we'd removed his wallet before burying him.

"Could be they knew him," said Stanhope. "If they knew him, they also knew us, and decided the best thing was to bring him back here, where we could deal with whatever had happened."

I admitted this was more plausible than picturing Carlton behind the wheel of a car, but not by much.

"I have another question," I said. "How did he get in?"

I'd noticed that the back door was bolted from the inside. I glanced at the front door and saw the necked door bolts were in place, so Carlton hadn't come in that way either. Meanwhile, the kitchen window was closed, and I couldn't feel a breeze from anywhere else.

Stanhope went into the living room, after which I heard him go upstairs. I stayed with our friend Carlton. It was awkward, and I was glad when Stanhope returned.

"They're all closed, every window," he said.

I nodded at Carlton.

"Excuse us," I said. "We'll be right back."

Stanhope and I stepped outside, but we kept the kitchen door open so we could watch Carlton through the gap between the door and the frame.

"That bullet must have rattled around in there without killing him," I whispered to Stanhope. "It should have put his lights out completely, but instead, a couple stayed on—though it still doesn't explain how he got here."

"I don't care how he got here," said Stanhope.

"What matters is that he leaves again. We need to put him back in the ground while it's still dark."

I went to get dressed while Stanhope remained with Carlton, and then Stanhope and I swapped places. Throughout, Carlton didn't move much, or not beyond slow, irregular blinks. I didn't even notice him breathing, though he must have been getting air in somehow because I detected a soft whistling sound from either his nose or mouth.

Stanhope reappeared, carrying a black sports bag.

"Any change?" he asked.

"None. Let's get him up."

Stanhope coughed awkwardly.

"Carlton," he said, "we're going to take you to the emergency room, okay?"

I glared at him.

"What?"

"Seriously?"

It was wrong, lying to our friend Carlton like that, especially after what we'd done to him. Carlton might have been dull, but he wasn't an idiot.

"Sorry," said Stanhope.

We each took an arm, placed a hand under an armpit, and lifted Carlton. He came up easily, so we didn't have to take a lot of his weight, and he allowed us to guide him to the back door. I used my free hand to open it because Stanhope had the sports bag. I checked that the street was empty before leading Carlton to Stanhope's Chevy. Stanhope hit the remote to open the trunk.

"We can't put him in there," I said.

"Why?"

"Look at him. He's our friend. He's Carlton."

Stanhope seemed inclined to differ—maybe on both counts, since there wasn't much of Carlton left, not after what the hollow point had done. However, we didn't have time to argue. We had to get on the road. We put our friend Carlton in the back seat, and after a short discussion, I agreed to sit with Carlton because Stanhope didn't want to drive with him behind and the two of us in front, just in case Carlton panicked or began to foam at the mouth and we all ended up wrapped around a tree.

Stanhope was of the view that we should put Carlton in the same hole because it would save a lot of unnecessary digging, but I convinced him otherwise. Initially, we assumed Carlton had managed to crawl from the hole unaided. Still, the more I considered it, the more it seemed that someone must have helped him. It's one thing to dig yourself out from under dirt, and another to do it from under dirt and heavy stones. If Carlton had received help, it meant that at least one other person knew where we'd buried him the first time. When Carlton disappeared again, that would be the first place they'd look.

"If you're right," said Stanhope, "they could be watching us now. They may have been watching us from the moment they delivered Carlton to the house."

But I didn't think so. I'd been checking for signs we were being followed—which was unsettling because it meant I had to lean against Carlton—and hadn't spotted a tail, though I admit that the darkness meant I was judging solely by the absence of headlights. We were on a side road, and I hadn't seen a car behind us for some time. I'd even made Stanhope pull over so I could get out and listen for a drone hovering above, but I'd heard nothing, felt nothing. I had a sixth sense for surveillance. I don't know how I'd come by it, but it had served me well, which was why I'd never spent a day in jail. That instinct was one of the reasons Stanhope liked to work with me, and it was how we ended up sharing a house—me, Stanhope, and our friend Carlton. Sometimes, people laughed at us or passed comments, but they didn't laugh for long, and never repeated those comments.

This time, we didn't drive as far as Tabernacle, but picked a spot west of Shamong, in Pinelands National Reserve. We knew the area because the three of us used to like eating at Christine's House of Kingfish Barbecue, which wouldn't be the same anymore now that Carlton was no longer with us—or should not have been with us and was destined not to be with us again, if you see what I mean.

We parked under some trees, out of sight of Atsion Road, and walked Carlton into the woods. I guided Carlton by the arm, with Stanhope walking behind us. We'd put blue plastic covers over our shoes, held in place with rubber bands, but Carlton gave no indication that he noticed. We hadn't done it the first time because that Carlton, the old Carlton, would have begun to wonder why we might have wanted to avoid getting dirt caught in the soles of our shoes while he didn't have to worry about it. But this Carlton, the new Carlton, wasn't worried about anything, or not that I could see, and the covers would save us having to scrub our shoes when we got home, like last time.

I'd asked Stanhope to cough when he was ready, as I didn't want to be deafened or injured. When I heard him cough, I let go of Carlton's arm and stepped smartly to the left so Stanhope would have a clear aim. Stanhope had loaded the sawed-off with 00 buckshot, so one second, our friend Carlton had a whole head, and the next, he had part of one, since the top half had vanished from the bridge of his nose up. Carlton pitched forward and lay on the ground but didn't twitch this time. Stanhope took two carbon steel folding shovels from his sports bag, and together we dug a fresh grave for Carlton before rolling him in. The sawed-off had made a mess, so we cleaned that up as best we could. We didn't have any discarded construction materials to hand this time, so we made do with thick branches, forming a mound of wood and dirt over Carlton. When we were finished, Stanhope produced a bottle of bleach from his bag and emptied it over the shovels. We got back to the car, where we took the covers from our feet, folded the shovels, and put the covers and shovels in a black garbage bag that we threw into Atsion Lake as we neared the 206.

Afterward, we went home directly and retired to our respective bedrooms. Within minutes, I heard Stanhope snoring, but I couldn't sleep. I'd thought about sharing with Stanhope what I'd noticed about our friend Carlton while sitting next to him in the car, but in the end, I'd opted against it. I told myself I might have been mistaken. Even if I wasn't in error, I doubted Stanhope would have believed me.

The pumping of blood by the carotid arteries produces pulses in a person's neck. You can feel the carotid throbbing if you put your finger in the groove alongside your windpipe. If you look closely, you can see it too. But the action of our friend Carlton's left carotid pulse wasn't visible, even with the light on in the car. When I helped him out, I made a point of taking him by the wrist, where I couldn't feel a pulse. I could only conclude that Carlton was dead, but the message hadn't made it to his brain. I didn't know how or why. I wasn't a doctor. It might have been an intriguing avenue for medical science if I'd been able to tell anyone about it without going to jail. But the only person I could have told was Stanhope, a negativist, so I kept it to myself.

Our friend Carlton returned the following night. I don't know what time, only that when I went downstairs to make a cup of coffee at around 8 AM, there he was, sitting at the kitchen table, just as he had been the previous night. His head was more or less intact, apart from the original hole made by the .22. Even the dirt on his face and in his nose and ears looked the same.

I called Stanhope, and once he'd gotten over the shock, which took a while, the two of us ended up sitting with Carlton, trying to figure out what we should do.

"I ought to tell you," I said to Stanhope, "that I think our friend Carlton is dead."

I watched Carlton as I spoke, to see if he might react to the news, but he didn't.

"He ought to be, but he isn't," replied Stanhope. "He ought not even to have much of a head, but he does."

"What I mean," I continued, "is that he was dead the first time as well. I checked when I was getting him out of the car, and I couldn't find a pulse."

"And you didn't think to inform me of this?"

"I was worried about being mistaken, or called crazy."

Tentatively, Stanhope touched two fingers to Carlton's left wrist.

"Nothing," he said.

He brushed his fingers against his shirtfront before figuring that might be an insufficient precaution to take. He went to the sink to scrub his hands clean with soap.

"We can't keep him here," said Stanhope.

"I never suggested we should."

But Stanhope just kept talking, as though I had, in fact, done just that, and only by steamrolling me would he get his way.

"The whole point was to make him disappear before he could be arrested or subpoenaed. The police could show up anytime, not to mention some of our associates."

By "associates," Stanhope meant the men to whom we answered. They wouldn't understand about our friend Carlton, no matter how hard we tried to explain. They'd think we were screwups who couldn't even put a guy in the ground right. Most probably, they'd do what we had done, which is try to kill Carlton again, except this time they might kill us too. That was the kind of men they were. If they'd been reasonable, they'd have found a different line of work. And it wasn't as if we could call anyone else—like, I don't know, the American Medical Association, or Ripley's—because then we'd have been forced to explain how our friend Carlton had come by the hole in his head.

"So what do you want to do?" I asked.

"We go again."

Stanhope went down to the basement, leaving me with Carlton. I spent a while looking into Carlton's eyes, but I couldn't figure out whether there was life in them, not then. If anything was going on in his head, it wasn't showing.

Stanhope kept a roll of plastic sheeting in the basement, for emergencies. By the time he told me to bring Carlton down, he'd spread the sheeting on the floor, and we positioned Carlton in the middle, facing away from the stairs. Stanhope, who had stripped to his underwear, then hit Carlton on the head with a sledgehammer, hard enough to break his skull. Carlton dropped, but Stanhope kept hitting him until his arms got tired and Carlton didn't have any head at all. Stanhope took a few minutes to catch his breath before going to work with his power tools. I left him to it. I'd only have been in the way.

By the time Stanhope was done, our friend Carlton had been cut up into fourteen or fifteen pieces, each of which Stanhope placed in its own garbage bag. He wrapped the pile of garbage bags in the plastic sheeting, added some old dumbbells for weight, sealed the package with T-Rex Brute Force tape, and took a shower. That night, we drove to Oswego Lake, where a buddy of Stanhope's kept a boat. We put the package in the boat, rowed out to the middle of the lake, dumped our friend Carlton, and were home by midnight. Stanhope admitted to being cautiously optimistic that this might mean the end of it, but I wasn't so sure. We both tried to sleep, but I wasn't too surprised to wake up just before 4 AM to hear Stanhope's bedroom door opening, followed by footsteps on the landing. I went to join him.

"I just thought," he said, "you know . . ."

We went downstairs. The kitchen door stood open. Stanhope sagged with relief. He turned to me.

"Let's never speak of this again," he said.

We shook hands on it, and when we looked again at the table, our friend Carlton was back.

You might have expected our sanity to have taken a hit, or for one or both of us to have fled, but we didn't. First of all, our associates would have found us in the end, which wouldn't have gone well. Had they not found us, the police would have, and that wouldn't have gone well either.

But for Stanhope, our friend Carlton also represented a problem to be solved. Carlton was an affront to Stanhope's professionalism and sense of order. If he'd left Carlton for someone else to deal with, he'd never have slept well again. It would have bothered him forever. Stanhope didn't even like leaving dishes unwashed after a meal.

That afternoon, Stanhope went on a buying expedition. It took him a while, because he couldn't purchase everything he needed in one store for fear of attracting attention. He spent the evening getting the mix right before instructing me, once again, to bring Carlton down to the basement. He handed me a mask as soon as I arrived—he was already wearing his—and again hit Carlton on the head with the sledgehammer, but not so hard this time, just enough to knock him out. Then Stanhope and I carried our friend Carlton to the big, new metal tub and carefully lowered him into the acid. Stanhope asked me to stay and help him stir. I could hardly refuse, as he'd done all the heavy lifting up to then.

Dissolving a body in acid is a time-consuming process. If the acid solution is too strong, it'll burn through the container; too weak, and you'd better clear your schedule for the week. Thankfully, Stanhope was an expert, and within twenty-four hours, our friend Carlton had been reduced to soup. We drained the acid and poured what used to be Carlton into a barrel, which we then buried near the Costco Wholesale up by Manahawkin. By then, it was after midnight, and only as we were nearly home did I realize we'd buried the barrel about three or four miles from Lazarus Preserve, as the crow flies. This I took to be a bad omen, but again, I elected not to share it with Stanhope, on account of how he'd tried so hard to solve our problem.

Our friend Carlton didn't appear that night, but he did appear the following night. What I took from this was that it had something to do with when he was put in the ground, disposed of, or however you want to phrase it. If it happened before midnight, he'd be back by the morning of the next day; after midnight, and it would be sometime the following day. To be fair, hindsight may be at work here, as we were given ample opportunity to test the theory.

Over the next week, Stanhope and I tried dismembering Carlton a second time and burying the body parts in different spots; burning him in a crematorium oven; tying weights to him and dropping him in the water from the Hudson River Palisades; putting him, limb by limb, through an industrial meat grinder; sticking him in a car crusher; and interring him deep in wet concrete before watching from an Airbnb as the construction workers arrived and started work above him. On that last occasion, Stanhope remained at the Airbnb while I returned to the house to check the kitchen and call Stanhope after.

"He's here," I told Stanhope, who was so annoyed that he left a bad rating for the Airbnb owners, even though the place was perfectly nice.

Someone once told me that you can apply Kübler-Ross's five stages of grief to any difficult situation. If so, Stanhope never got beyond depression, which is stage four, though he also remained angry, which is stage two. He couldn't understand why our friend Carlton wouldn't, or couldn't, accept that he was dead and do what dead people did, which was stay that way. Stanhope became obsessed, and it got so that even his personal hygiene, about which he'd previously been very mindful, grew to be neglected. I started leaving the Carlton problem to him because I had other things to do, like trying to keep a roof over our heads while explaining to our associates why Stanhope couldn't make it to work that day.

I should add that we stopped disposing of Carlton on a regular basis, as nobody has that kind of time on their hands. Sometimes, we'd leave him in the basement for days and days, though we kept him chained to a galvanized steel ring as a precaution. We also left the TV on, for company. We were lucky that, on the two occasions the police came by, Carlton was absent by reason of attempted destruction, and we claimed to have no knowledge of where he might be. The police had their suspicions, though, and we were both questioned. A few of the neighbors told the police that they often heard us coming and going late at night, but it happened so often that it wasn't as though the police could look at one instance and say, "Ha! That must have been the night you killed your friend Carlton"—not unless we were doing it every night, which for a while we pretty much were. Even if they had somehow tracked us to one of those disposal spots, they wouldn't have found anything. Out of curiosity, Stanhope and I dug up that first grave in Tabernacle Township, only to find it empty. We weren't completely shocked. In fact, had we discovered our friend Carlton's rotting corpse down there, it would have raised more questions than it answered.

After a while, the police gave up calling, but not before they obtained a final warrant to search the house. They brought in a forensics team, and Stanhope and I had to stay at a motel for a couple of nights under police guard. The forensics team came up with nothing. There was no trace of Carlton, even though I'd lost count of the number of times Stanhope and I had butchered him in the basement, or periodically the bathroom for a change of scenery. I think it might have been for the same reason that his grave was empty. Each time we eliminated our friend Carlton, he dispersed, every atom of him, only to be reconstituted as recently deceased Carlton, complete with bullet hole.

The funny thing was that I had started to come to terms with Carlton's continued presence in our lives. I suppose I'd reached Kübler-Ross's fifth stage, or some version of it, the one Stanhope couldn't quite get to. In fact, so frustrated and unhappy was Stanhope becoming that, unbeknownst to me, he stopped drugging, shooting, or stunning Carlton before attempting to get rid of him. Only when he admitted to feeding our friend Carlton to hogs while he was still conscious, or what passed for it, did I begin to experience serious reservations about Stanhope. His disclosure also explained something I'd noticed lately about Carlton: his eyes had changed. I might have been wrong, but I thought I saw pain in them. Somewhere in there, our friend Carlton was remembering, and with remembrance came suffering.

Meanwhile, Stanhope was proposing ever more inventive ways to liquidate Carlton, many of them completely impractical. I remember something about jet engines, or maybe it was rockets, and another to do with a volcano in Iceland. Finally, Stanhope produced a design for a contraption based on a work of conceptual art that he'd read about in the *New York Times*. It involved putting our friend Carlton in a tank filled with maggots, which would consume his flesh. Those maggots would then grow into flies, which, upon taking their first flight, would zoom straight into a bug zapper, whereupon they would fall back into the tank, providing sustenance for more maggots, which would become more flies, which—

You get the picture. It was undoubtedly ingenious, our friend Carlton undergoing perpetual destruction in a closed-loop system, but I couldn't countenance it and told Stanhope so. I'd had enough. I told him he ought to leave Carlton be, but Stanhope couldn't. It simply wasn't in his nature.

I buried Stanhope down at Swan Bay, not far from Lower Bank Cemetery, where his parents were interred. He didn't suffer. He didn't even know anything about it. That night, I sat in the kitchen until long after sunrise, but Stanhope didn't return, not that day or any other, which was a relief.

Now it's just Carlton and me. He stays in the basement during the day, with the TV. At night, I take him outside to the back porch, where we sit in companionable silence. Some might regard it as a mundane existence, but I don't mind. I don't think Carlton does either. He always was more my friend than Stanhope's anyway.

HORROR EXPRESS: EXTENDED EDITION

AUTHOR'S NOTE

While this monograph deals in part with the making of the film of the same name, it was really an opportunity for me to explore the importance of nostalgia in our lives (very underrated, nostalgia) and reflect on aspects of my childhood, notably my relationship with my father. In that sense, it's as much memoir as film criticism, though I was also fascinated by the process through which a disparate group of individuals can come to together to produce, if not necessarily a work of art, then at least a perfectly entertaining demonstration of craft. While *Horror Express* might not even make the list of my hundred favorite pictures, it was, curiously, the first that came to mind when I was invited to write at length on a genre film of my choice. The reasons for this are examined in the piece itself.

I don't think the reader needs to have seen *Horror Express* to find something interesting in what follows—at least, I hope not—but should you choose to engage with the film, I'd suggest first reading Parts I and II of the essay, then watching the film, before continuing to Parts III and IV. For complicated historical reasons, *Horror Express* is easily available to watch for free on the Internet, including via YouTube, but Arrow Video also released a restored version on Blu-ray in 2019. The numbering system in Part III refers to minutes and seconds, just in case you feel like fast-forwarding, rewinding, or pausing the film. Because versions of the film vary in length depending on the starting point, the numbering is approximate, but I did my best to begin from the moment the train whistle is first heard against a dark screen.

Horror Express—or my *Horror Express*—was originally published by PS Publishing in 2018, but it has been revised, corrected, and expanded for *Night & Day*, not least because the film's director, Eugenio Martín, passed away in 2023, at the age of ninety-seven.

Railroads are a great prop. You can do some awful wild things with railroads.

BUSTER KEATON

5

I
THE EXCAVATION

— 1 —

In 2017, I published a novel entitled *he*, a (barely) fictionalized account of the life of the comedian Stan Laurel. I think I'd lived with the book for most of my writing life, as I'd first considered Laurel as a possible subject for a project back in 1999, although it was then little more than a passing thought.

It's sometimes erroneously assumed that ideas are the currency for writers. Some variation on "Where do you get your ideas from?" is the question most frequently asked of authors by readers, but it is a subject in which many of those practitioners remain studiedly uninterested. (I suspect this is partly superstition, a fear that, if overanalyzed, the delicate operation of making stuff up might collapse entirely.) Ideas manifest themselves with maddening frequency, rather like the six impossible things believed before breakfast by the Queen of Hearts in *Through the Looking-Glass*. The real currency for writers, as for readers, is time. Just as there will always be more books to read than hours in which to read them, so too writers will always have more ideas to set down than hours in which to write them.

Thus it was that a decade elapsed before I finally committed myself to writing the Laurel book (at some point), and a few more years had to pass until I resigned myself to the fact that the ongoing business of clipping magazine articles and buying expensive treatises on the history of British comedy and the development of Hollywood, along with biographies of long-dead comedians, meant this work had already commenced.

But during that time I became fascinated by the processes

through which films come into being. I don't mean the mechanics of filmmaking, although obviously these constitute an important element, but the human entanglements that produce movies: the manner in which various individuals may be brought together, sometimes only for one project, before dispersing, often never to be reassembled as a unit, leaving behind a piece of work that, in an ideal world, may represent a lasting cultural artifact or, at the very least, engage an audience for the duration of its running time.

—2—

Horror Express brought together five such individuals: a war hero who fell into acting for want of anything better to do; a widower who wished only to die so he could be reunited with his wife in the next world; a philanderer and gambler who yearned to be the handsome lead, yet appeared destined to play only the villain; an alleged communist sympathizer who, in a Kafkaesque twist, was never formally accused, and therefore never given an opportunity to confront his accusers, but found himself blacklisted nonetheless; and the Catholic product of a fascist regime who moved to the left in his teens but remained intent throughout his career on resisting all efforts to force him into making political statements in his films, seeking only to entertain.

These five men would work together only on this single occasion. In fact, one of them would never make another picture, despite living for many more years. The film that resulted from their sole collaboration is not great, but it is good, and certainly much better than it has any need to be. It is a product of craftsmanship and a love of the medium. It wants to be all it can possibly be and, perhaps, just a little more.

—3—

I once interviewed the American mystery author George Pelecanos, who remarked that none of us is writing for the ages; we just have to write as though we are. Every creative endeavor should aspire to the condition of art.

—4—

Before we proceed, a brief word on the subject of this monograph. *Horror Express*—or *Pánico en el Transiberiano*, as the Spanish-British coproduction was titled in Spain—is a 1972 horror/science-fiction piece, set on the Trans-Siberian Express as it travels from China to Moscow. The film deals with the discovery of the frozen remains of a primitive, apelike creature and the consequences of this discovery for the passengers on the train transporting it to its ultimate destination. It stars Christopher Lee, Peter Cushing, and Telly Savalas, was directed by Eugenio Martín, and produced by Bernard Gordon.

Its British stars do not appear to have regarded the picture with any great fondness. Peter Cushing lists it in the filmography at the back of each of his two memoirs, but tells us nothing about the film itself. Christopher Lee, in his 2003 autobiography, *Lord of Misrule*, gives it a single mention, but only to complain about the quality of the catering. Its Spanish director, Eugenio Martín, was either a jobbing filmmaker who accepted whatever work was offered to him or, according to the only significant study of his output, "an auteur in every genre," which is certainly a nicer way of putting it, though it rather stretches many accepted definitions of "auteurism." *Horror Express* is Martín's best-known and best-loved film, if only because most of the others aren't very well known or loved at all.

—5—

Some years ago, when I was touring Australia as a newly published author, I decided to take what is often described as one of the great railway journeys of the world: the Ghan, the passenger train that runs coast-to-coast from Adelaide in the south to Darwin in the north via Alice Springs, at the nation's heart. It's a three-thousand-mile trip named, according to some sources, after the cameleers—mostly Pakistanis mistaken for Afghans, hence "Ghan"—who made inroads into the Red Centre of Australia at the end of the nineteenth century.

I didn't have enough time to take the entire four-day jaunt, so instead settled for the first leg from Adelaide to Alice Springs. Since this was to be a once-in-a-lifetime experience, it seemed appropriate to travel in some luxury, so I booked the best compartment available. It was eye-wateringly expensive, but I had seen *Murder on the Orient Express* and figured that one got what one paid for.

I arrived at the platform in Adelaide and was directed to what I was informed was the first-class section, or whatever fancy equivalent the company had applied in lieu, Australians being funny about class. Upon reaching my assigned compartment, I discovered a not-excessively upholstered chair, a stainless steel sink of the kind familiar from prison films, and little else in the way of furnishings, not to mention luxury. It had more than a hint of the monastic to it but without the ultimate promise of salvation. It was, not to put too fine a point on it, a cell with pretensions. Clearly, some mistake had been made, and I said as much to the guard on the platform as I hauled my luggage back to terra firma.

"You see," I explained, "I booked first class."

"That is first class," he replied.

I looked at him. He looked at me. I looked at the piece of paper in my hand, which stated in black and white just how much I'd paid for one day and one night on this train.

"You're joking," I said.

"I'm not."

And he wasn't.

Reader, you may have sensed by now that the Ghan was not a happy experience for me. I did get to view the promised landscape, but there wasn't a whole lot to see in it, desert tending toward the monotonous after a while. I found myself passing the time by calculating how much each mile was costing me, and thus slowly made my way to Alice Springs. When I eventually arrived—sadder, wiser, and much poorer—my taxi driver asked how long I planned to spend in "Alice." I pointed out that, since I had just stepped from the train, and he was taking me to the airport, I patently wasn't planning to spend much time there at all. I was, I told him, going to visit Uluru—or Ayers Rock, as the sacred Aboriginal site was formerly known—which is the main reason anyone makes the journey to Alice Springs.

"But there's loads to do in Alice," protested the driver. "That's just a rock."

Leaving aside the merits of the taxi drivers of Alice Springs as ambassadors for Australia's natural and cultural heritage, what was missing from the Ghan—in addition to a four-figure sum from my wallet—was any hint of romance. I'm not talking about a woman, even if one might have helped, but about the sense of mystery and excitement associated with great journeys, and with the great railway journeys in particular; the feeling of leaving behind the quotidian and immersing oneself, however briefly, in a man-made environment of great charm, even exoticism. Admittedly there was a certain alien quality to what was passing before my window as I ventured into the outback, but it was rather undone by any equivalent sense of the remarkable in my immediate surroundings.

The Ghan was not the Orient Express, but it may be that the imagined experience of the Orient Express differs from the actual Express. I've never traveled on the Orient Express, so I can't say for sure, but perhaps it's the case that even the most comfortable of trains remains, well, a train. Unlike the Ghan, the Venice-Simplon Orient-Express is apparently devoid of showers, and guests share a single toilet at the end of each carriage, unless they choose to spend their children's inheritance on a Grand Suite. In other words, you can have all the velvet and champagne your heart desires, but you still can't use a toilet that hasn't been warmed by someone else's behind.

— 6 —

Is it the case that the romance of long railway journeys is largely manufactured, a product of other media? My conception of long-distance rail travel remains colored by the films I've seen and the books I've read, which was why the reality of it in its (admittedly Australian) luxury form came as such a crushing disappointment. Then again, here is Baz Luhrmann, director of *Strictly Ballroom* and *Romeo + Juliet*, describing his experience of traveling by train through Russia:

> In 2001, I'd just finished *Moulin Rouge!* and I decided that this time I would take the Trans-Siberian express across Russia, from Beijing through Manchuria and Irkutsk and on to Moscow. Alone. I suppose I thought this would be romantic. A first-class cabin was reserved and off I went. And, well, my cabin was a sardine tin, with a rackety air-conditioner and an old babushka handing me a hose and yelling "This! You go! Now! Shower!" I quickly realised that this was not going to be the great poetic experience I'd had in mind—it was going to be more like *Crime and Punishment*. (*The Sunday Times Magazine*, November 28, 2017)

And that's if you're *not* traveling on the Horror Express.

The notion of the luxury train may, therefore, be substantially historical both in origin and contemporary replication, but perhaps it must also be accepted that this representation of railway travel could itself be a romanticized version of the reality of the past, since journeys by rail back in the nineteenth and early twentieth centuries were considerably longer, more uncomfortable, more difficult, and more dangerous than they are now.

For example, early nineteenth-century steam engines had the unfortunate habit of exploding. On July 31, 1815, the boiler of Brunton's Mechanical Traveller, an experimental locomotive, blew up on the Newbottle Waggonway in County Durham in England, killing up to sixteen people and injuring a further forty. On February 28, 1818, the driver of the *Salamanca*, the first commercially successful steam locomotive, made the error of fiddling with the engine's safety valve. He was, according to a report in the *Leeds Mercury*, "carried, with great violence, into an adjoining field the distance of one hundred yards," with, unsurprisingly, fatal consequences.

Such incidents set the pattern for what was to come, and a cursory examination of the history of the first century of commuter rail travel reveals a disturbing litany of fatal detonations, crashes, collisions, derailments, fires, and collapsing bridges. Even 1906, the year in which *Horror Express* is set, saw three major accidents on Britain's railways, resulting in more than 160 fatalities, and two in the United States, which killed 106 people. More recently, the Trans-Siberian Express itself was struck by a gas explosion in 1989, which resulted in the deaths of more than five hundred people on two trains; and in 2016, a woman was decapitated by a passing locomotive, apparently while having sex by the Trans-Siberian track, as one does.

—7—

The idea for the Great Siberian Way (the name "Trans-Siberian" is a Western invention), a railway line that would link Vladivostok in the east to Moscow in the west, a distance of 5,772 miles, was first mooted in the 1850s. Construction was delayed for decades by technical difficulties and financial considerations, including the reluctance of the Russians to involve foreign investors in such an important infrastructure resource. Planning eventually began in the 1880s, during the reign of Tsar Alexander III, but the main instigator and driving force behind the project was the Russian finance minister, Sergei Witte.

Despite Witte's involvement, or perhaps because of it, unwise economies were made from the start, including the use of lighter rails and fewer sleepers per mile, and the building of some bridges using wood instead of iron or steel. At one point, almost ninety thousand men were laboring on the line, many of them under hostile conditions, and not all of them of their own volition. Soldiers and conscripts, including convicts and local peasants, were called upon to bolster the workforce as construction progressed over rivers and tundra and through mountains, at a rate of more than four hundred miles of track per year, resulting in the line's completion in just twenty-five years. The line's Lux Blue Express would later be used by Communist Party apparatchiks to travel across the country in splendor, their dining experience enhanced by Russian caviar and imported cigarettes, while considerably less glamorous carriages transported Stalin's enemies to the gulags. The Trans-Siberian remains the world's longest single-railway journey: add in the Mongolian stretch, and it extends to 6,850 miles.

I've struggled a bit in finding out just how many people might have died while constructing the Trans-Siberian. I suspect it was rather a lot. Mind you, at least the Trans-Siberian was completed, unlike a similar enterprise undertaken during Stalin's rule: the Trans-Polar Mainline, later known as the Dead Road, a proposed thousand-mile track linking the eastern and western parts of Siberia, to be constructed entirely by "enemies of the people," some 100,000 of them (though I've seen estimates as high as 300,000), most of whom had been jailed for stealing food during the famine of 1946–47.

By the time Stalin died in 1953, just over 370 miles of the Trans-Polar had been laid, and the project was shelved by his successor, Nikita Khrushchev, though not before tens of thousands of slave laborers had given up their lives for it. Many of them had come from the 501st Construction Camp, or gulag, which still exists today. It has been renamed FKU IK-3, but is better known as Polar Wolf, and it's where Russian president Vladimir Putin imprisons his political opponents. It was home to the Russian opposition leader Alexei Navalny until his unexplained death in February 2024.

— 8 —

Until I began writing this monograph, I had not seen *Horror Express* in more than three decades. Yet when I was initially approached about writing a film monograph, *Horror Express* was the first picture that came to mind, and the only one I wished to examine at length. In part, the monograph itself is an attempt to understand why.

— 9 —

The Swiss physician Johannes Hofer first coined the term *nostalgia* in 1688 to describe the mental and physical symptoms experienced by mercenary soldiers who desired to return to their homes. The roots of the word are Greek: *nostos*, or "return home," and *algos*, meaning "pain." Nostalgia was regarded as a psychological and emotional malady, and for centuries it was associated with depression. In 1938, the psychodynamic scholar Isaac Frost described it in the *British Journal of Psychiatry* as an "immigrant psychosis," while for the psychoanalyst Nandor Fodor, writing in 1950 for the *Psychoanalytic Review*, it was a "compulsive disorder," a "yearning for the prenatal home," the womb. Nostalgia and melancholia, it was believed, went hand in hand, and suggested remedies that varied from harsh military discipline and bracing mountain hikes to public shaming and the ingestion of opium.

Nevertheless, most parties agreed that nostalgia was potentially dangerous, even fatal. In "So Lonesome I Could Die," an article written for the *Journal of Social History* in 2007, Frances Clarke recounts instances of Union soldiers in the American Civil War weeping and begging to be allowed to return home. One man, William Scott, wrote to his family to say that "if I did not keep up good spirits I should die," and J. Theodore Calhoun, a surgeon-in-chief in the Army of the Potomac, recorded that "men have sickened, and I doubt not died, from home sickness . . ." In 1863, Meeta Melgrove, a hospital worker and columnist for the *Tioga County Agitator*, described how one young Union private, desperately homesick, took his own life by jumping from the Provost Marshal's window. During the First World War, the depth of soldiers' attachment to home was evinced by the sheer quantity of letters they sent to their families. In 1917, British troops on the Western Front were posting 8,150,000 letters home each week—mostly to their mothers, since it is estimated that three-quarters of those who died in the war were unmarried.

But these young men, like their mercenary predecessors, were craving a place that no longer existed, or not as it once had. As Michael Roper writes in "Nostalgia as an Emotional Experience in the Great War" (*The Historical Journal*, 2011), the scenes they constructed in their minds were "actually composed from past experiences. While people on the home front were adjusting to the war in all sorts of ways, coping with food shortages and rationing, and taking up voluntary or paid war work, in the soldier's mind, life remained unchanged." The return to a fundamentally altered society was not always easy for soldiers and is the subject of one of the first great serial killer novels, *In a Lonely Place* (1947) by Dorothy B. Hughes, in which the sociopathic ex-airman Dix Steele, lost without the meritocracy of the armed services, stalks post–Second World War Los Angeles, directing his rage at the women who, in his absence, have been empowered to explore new roles beyond the domestic.

More recently, the *OED* has defined *nostalgia* as a "sentimental longing for the past," although this definition is imperfect and allows considerable latitude for the negative. After all, a sentimental longing for the past has variously given us Brexit, resurgent right-wing nationalism in Europe and the US, and a Russian presidency that has more than a whiff of tsardom about it. For some, the past may be not only a nice place to visit but also to live. It is, perhaps, the difference between personal nostalgia, which draws on significant memories of family, friends, spouses, even pets, and a more generalized, dangerous nostalgia that peddles idealized fantasies of yesteryear, of a better past that didn't even exist at the time. Culture as much as politics has a part to play in this, an example being the 1939 film adaptation of Margaret Mitchell's novel, *Gone with the Wind*, whose opening title crawl celebrated "a land of Cavaliers and Cotton Fields," a "pretty world" where "gallantry took its last bow," which required one to ignore the 3,500,000 slaves held in the South by 1860, a situation that meant nine out of ten Black Americans were in a state of involuntary servitude. The title crawl did at least manage to acknowledge the existence of slavery, but only in a somewhat wistful manner: "Here," it told us, "was the last ever to be seen of Knights and their Ladies Fair, of Master and Slave . . . A Civilization gone with the wind . . ."

In 2020, when the South Korean film *Parasite* won the Academy Award for Best Picture, much to the annoyance of US president Donald Trump, it was to *Gone with the Wind* that Trump turned. "Can we get, like, *Gone with the Wind* back, please?" he implored a rally in Colorado Springs, Colorado, on February 20, 2020. One could argue that what he was seeking was the revived celebration of epic filmmaking of a particularly American stripe, but while correlation does not imply causation, by 2023–24 slavery denial had become a theme of the Republican Party presidential primaries. At a town hall meeting in Berlin, New Hampshire, on December 27, 2023, presidential hopeful Nikki Haley, former governor of South Carolina, replied to a question about the cause of the Civil War by mentioning only "how government was run, the freedoms, and what people could and couldn't do"—including, presumably, own slaves, though she didn't specify this. "Make America Great Again" is a perfectly legitimate campaign slogan, but it raises the questions of when America was supposedly greater, and for whom?

— 10 —

In 1999, a pioneering psychologist named Constantine Sedikides—who is, appropriately enough, Greek—suggested looking at nostalgia in a new way. His personal experience of thinking about the past was generally positive: it gave him a sense of belonging and continuity. For Sedikides, nostalgia had beneficial connotations. As he put it in an interview with the *New York Times* in 2013: "It provided a texture to my life and gave me strength to move forward."

This, it seems to me, is crucial: the past as an engine of forward motion rather than an avenue of retreat, and nostalgia as an instrument of contextualization and progression rather than negative comparison and ultimate regression. It is the difference between individual nostalgia—or even nostalgia shared among small, intimately connected social groups—and collective nostalgia, which may have a thornier basis in a yearning for a past that never was, and can give rise to separatism and chauvinism.

Sedikides, now Professor of Social and Personality Psychology at the University of Southampton in England, and the director of its Centre for Research on Self and Identity, even helped create what is known as the Southampton Nostalgia Scale, a seven-item questionnaire, with each answer measured on a sliding scale of one to seven.

THE SOUTHAMPTON NOSTALGIA SCALE

---

1. **How valuable is nostalgia for you?**

1	2	3	4	5	6	7
Not at all						*Very much*

2. **How important is it for you to bring to mind nostalgic experiences?**

1	2	3	4	5	6	7
Not at all						*Very much*

3. How significant is it for you to feel nostalgic?

1	2	3	4	5	6	7
Not at all						*Very much*

4. How prone are you to feeling nostalgic?

1	2	3	4	5	6	7
Not at all						*Very much*

5. How often do you experience nostalgia?

1	2	3	4	5	6	7
Very rarely						*Very Frequently*

6. Generally speaking, how often do you bring to mind nostalgic experiences?

1	2	3	4	5	6	7
Very rarely						*Very Frequently*

7. Specifically, how often do you bring to mind nostalgic experiences? (Please check one.)

_____ At least once a day
_____ Three to four times a week
_____ Approximately twice a week
_____ Approximately once a week
_____ Once or twice a month
_____ Once every couple of months
_____ Once or twice a year

In 2006, seven studies of nostalgia provided the core of an essay for the *Journal of Personality and Social Psychology* titled "Nostalgia: Content, Triggers, Functions," by Sedikides and others. The collated results revealed that most of us are nostalgic at least once a week, although almost half of respondents experienced nostalgia up to four times a week. Curiously, feelings of nostalgia may be instigated by negative stimuli—loneliness, or social and political disruption—but the effect of them is to make the subject feel *less* depressed. It appears that nostalgia, far from being the adverse, disruptive force of conventional wisdom, may instead offer a powerful source of consolation and respite.

The day after writing the previous paragraph, back in November 2017, I opened the *Irish Times* to find an article on homelessness in Dublin. It included an interview with two brothers, Andrew and John McDonnell, both in their early thirties, who had been sleeping rough for eight years. They had previously lived with their mother, but struggled to cope when she died, especially with two younger siblings to look after. They sought solace in alcohol and narcotics and ended up on the streets. They now lived in a tent. (Those few simple sentences sketch the lineaments of a small, desperate tragedy.)

"Sometimes," Andrew told the *Irish Times*, "to keep ourselves going, we tell each other about our favourite episode of *Only Fools and Horses* or *Friends*. It's not much, but it's a memory of time we spent together as a family."

Andrew McDonnell's comments encapsulate so much of Sedikides's theories about the beneficial effects of nostalgia, including its capacity to provide solace, trigger empathy, and combat feelings of loneliness and alienation. As Sedikides's colleague Dr. Tim Wildschut told the *Guardian* in November 2014: "Nostalgia compensates for uncomfortable states, for example, people with feelings of meaninglessness or a discontinuity between past and present. What we find in these cases is that nostalgia spontaneously rushes in and counteracts those things. It elevates meaningfulness, connectedness, and continuity in the past. It is like a vitamin and an antidote to those states. It serves to promote emotional equilibrium, homeostasis."

Nostalgia can also have physical benefits. Chinese scientists at Sun Yat-sen University have discovered that feelings of nostalgia are more common on cold days than hot, and those who waxed nostalgic reported feeling warmer as a consequence. These discoveries always sound more convincing when rendered in academic terms, so, for fear of being doubted:

An explanation for the nostalgia-warmth association is that (a) nostalgia fosters feelings of interpersonal affiliation (Zhou, Sedikides, et al., 2008), and (b) a strong mental association exists between feelings of interpersonal affiliation and warmth that might develop early in life due to repeated juxtaposition of affiliation and physical warmth in interactions with nurturing caregivers (IJzerman & Semin, 2009; Williams & Bargh, 2008). We have a further reason for focusing on the feeling of temperature.

Considering the close integration of temperature and pain sensations in the central nervous system (CNS), which reflects their shared evolutionary significance for maintaining body integrity (Craig, 2003), it is surprising how little is known about the role of positive emotions in regulating the feeling of temperature relative to their role in pain regulation (Roy, Peretz, & Rainville, 2003; Zhou, Feng, He, & Gao, 2008; Zhou & Gao, 2008; Zhou, Vohs, & Baumeister, 2009). We aimed to redress this imbalance.

To summarize, we propose that nostalgia is integral to a hierarchically organized system of homeostatic correctives that serves to restore and maintain thermoregulatory comfort. Thus, the thermoregulatory discomfort one feels on a chilly day or in a cold room reflects homeostatic drive and mobilizes homeostatic correctives to restore comfort (Craig, 2003).

From "Heartwarming Memories: Nostalgia Maintains Physiological Comfort,"[1] American Psychological Association, 2012

Nostalgia, then, is a psychological condition that can instigate physiological change, or at least cause sufficient alteration in one's perception of a difficult situation to enable one to persevere. The

---

[1] American Psychological Association, https://psycnet.apa.org/record/2012-05385-001

reason for this may lie deep in our evolutionary past. As winter approached, memories of the comfort of caves, fires, and the company of our tribe, and the feelings of safety and security associated with such memories, might well have spurred our primitive ancestors to begin preparing for the hard times to come by stocking up on food and fuel for fires, and ensuring that shelters were dry and secure.

As an addendum to the temperature debate, I suspect I feel more inclined to read supernatural fiction in autumn and winter than in spring and summer, and the effectiveness of such stories is greater as a consequence. I wonder if this, too, has similar atavistic roots: an activated fear of the dark, based on very real threats from wild animals and enemies, that led our forebears to seek warmth and sanctuary.

Mind you, consorting with seasonal specters does have its limits. Some years ago, during my annual January writing binge, I took with me to Maine Michelle Paver's *Dark Matter* (2010), an extraordinarily creepy tale of polar explorers succumbing to supernatural forces during a lightless northern winter. I was sitting in bed reading it one night, and thought, You know, I think I might leave this until morning.

Not because I was scared, you understand, but because I was feeling a bit tired.

— 11 —

Nostalgia also colors the past. To return to "Heartwarming Memories":

> In nostalgic reverie, one remembers an event from one's past, typically a fond, personally meaningful memory such as one's childhood or a close relationship. One often views the memory through rose-tinted glasses, misses that time or person, and may even long to return to the past.

And this is where we come to the meat of it, I think: my reason for writing this monograph.

My memories of first viewing *Horror Express* are tied up with childhood, and more specifically my early teenage years. I was raised in Dublin by parents who didn't socialize together very much. My father liked to join his exclusively male associates for a pint or two in the Rialto House pub each evening, while my mother had a circle of female friends accrued largely through shared interests in singing, drama, and community work. Only a handful of times each year would my parents go out as a couple, usually at Christmas or on their wedding anniversary, leaving me in control of the television with no concerns about their returning before midnight.

It was on one of those parent-free evenings that I watched *Horror Express* for the first time. I'm sure it was shown by the BBC as the late-night film, and I am certain my parents wouldn't have allowed me to settle down in front of it had they been present—not because it was terribly frightening, but its running time took it well past my bedtime. (A helpful note from the monograph's first editor suggested that the screening could have been either on Wednesday, January 2, 1980, or Thursday, July 15, 1982. I'm leaning toward the former, as it would make sense for my parents to have ventured out together over the festive season.) I have a recollection of following its final moments from the doorway of our living room, listening for the sound of my father's car pulling up in our driveway so I could have the TV turned off and be in my bed before his key was in the lock of our front door.

I loved my father, but I was always a bit frightened of him and his moods. I was twenty-three when we buried him, and probably still angry, as young men often are when it comes to their fathers. We were also very dissimilar, my father and I. He regarded me as an impractical dreamer, and was frustrated beyond measure when, in 1988, I quit my permanent, pensionable council job to study

English at Trinity College Dublin, with vague ambitions of becoming a journalist. He thought I'd end up living on the streets.

In 1991, the year he died, I traveled to the United States for the first time to work in Delaware and, later, Maine. The night before I departed, he came home from the pub and said that, had he known I'd be around, he'd have asked me to come for a farewell drink with him. I shrugged it off. I was busy anyway, and there would be other times.

In late August, as I was visiting New York, I received a call from home informing me that, shortly after leaving his doctor, my father had collapsed, his body riddled with undiagnosed cancers. I suspect he knew how ill he was but was afraid to admit it, either to his physician or himself. He was already hospitalized by the time I returned home, would never leave that bed, and only briefly regained consciousness in the weeks that followed. It's the strange gift that cancer gives before it finishes its work: a few days, or even just a couple of hours, during which the patient is offered clarity and a chance to say goodbye. My father spent some of this time drawing a map of the hospital and its surroundings on the back of a cigarette packet, the irony of plotting his escape with the aid of the instruments of his self-destruction entirely lost on him.

I have not thought of him so fondly in so long.

All these memories.

— 12 —

In October 2017, Dr. Catherine Loveday, a lecturer at the University of Westminster, in England, contributed a fascinating piece to *BBC Music Magazine* titled "Notes to Remember," on the ways in which we attach significance to music. She noted the manner in which musical memories could survive traumatic brain injury and the onset of dementia. "Even those who have become entirely divorced from their former life—desperately lost and confused—can be dramatically reawakened when they hear the right music," Loveday wrote. "Familiar melodies seem to provide a conduit to their past and a means to reconnect with friends and family."

Musical memory, it emerges, is stored in a "safe" area of the brain, and we gravitate strongly toward music first heard in childhood or young adulthood. This is known as the "reminiscence bump" and applies not only to music but also to books, films, and even television personalities. "A popular theory," Loveday went on to say, "suggests that memories from this time are important in defining our identity—who we are, what we like and where we come from. . . . These memories tend to be particularly emotive."

So we're back to the territory of the milestones identified by Sedikides, the pitons in the rock face of our progress from birth to death. But Loveday's analysis provides a reason for the potency of these recollections from our youth: they are associated with a crucial period in the formation of the self, and therefore have a value to us that may be out of proportion to their objective cultural or artistic worth.

Loveday found that "a large percentage of musical memories are bound up with our relationships. People often refer to songs that their mother, father, or grandparent used to sing around the house when they were very young, or a cassette that was played on every family holiday. . . . Melody, pitch, rhythm, and timbre are fundamental to our communication of emotions—they signal joy, sadness, grief, surprise, excitement; they add crucial meaning to our words, and are the substance of universal pre-linguistic expressions such as laughter and crying. In one form or another, it is music that enables us to connect, empathise, build friendships and regulate our own feelings."

Can a movie or TV show do all this? Possibly, but almost certainly not to a similar degree. A book might—but then I would say that, wouldn't I? Still, there is a point of connection here with my memories of viewing *Horror Express*, and I realize that it's family. My recollection of watching the film is tied up with circumstance, with all the love and frustration that is so much a part of family life and the grief that accompanies inevitable loss.

So I return to my father, who was already forty when I was born in 1968—and an old forty at that, with little or no interest in cinema, fiction, or music; who disliked—or tolerated at best—his job as a rate collector for the city council; who dreamed of taking a boat trip around the South China Sea upon retirement, even though he didn't enjoy driving very far from home; who smoked too much, drank a couple of pints of beer a night, and refused to consume any meal that didn't include some form of potato; and who was so frightened of illness and death that he refused to make a will, as though to acknowledge the reality of his own mortality would be to encourage the Reaper to quicken his step, and consequently wouldn't consult a doctor about the pain he was experiencing until it was too late, so that he died barely a month after his initial cancer diagnosis.

I return to my mother, who, aged fifty-eight, went back to work after my father died, not just because she had two sons in full-time education and money was tight, but also because she had been forced to give up her job upon marriage (until 1973, married female civil and public servants in Ireland, along with bank officials, were required to resign their positions so as not to occupy a job that could otherwise be filled by a man); who learned to drive at fifty-nine; who, having never ventured farther from Ireland than the island of Jersey (and then only on her honeymoon), was determined to see more of the world as a widow, and did so, traveling to Europe, the United States, and Africa; who had escorted her elder son, when he was of reading age, to the local library and signed him up for a library card; who bought him a desktop computer because he aspired to become a novelist; and who remains alive and well at the age of ninety-one as I write.

I can see them both now, can almost smell my father's cigarette and my mother's perfume, can hear their voices as they enter the house. I can visualize our living room and the huge, tomblike television. I could project *Horror Express* onto its screen from memory, but the film would not be the same because I am no longer the same. In the years since I first saw it I have buried my father and become estranged from my brother. I have watched my mother grow old. I turned fifty-six this year and am resolutely middle-aged. The *Horror Express* I knew is part of a cache of memories from childhood, each imperfectly preserved and inordinately fragile. To expose them to the light is to risk their destruction, and with it something precious from my past.

There was, therefore, a part of me that did not want to watch *Horror Express* as an adult, as so much of its significance for me is tied up with the circumstances of that first viewing. I was also still just a child when I first saw it, and children experience emotion with a purity and intensity that can only be eroded by maturity. But in taking this position, was I not open to charges of indulging in a kind of anti-nostalgia, a belief that a cultural encounter from the past cannot be as potent if disinterred in the present? The solution lay in admitting that my original exposure to *Horror Express* could not be replicated but that the film itself might be examined anew. It was not about judgments of superiority or inferiority, but the acceptance of difference.

Cultural artifacts are not fixed objects. We bring our constantly altering selves to everything we consume, and so a book read in adolescence will be experienced in a new way if taken up in adulthood. I wrote a novel about this, *The Book of Lost Things*, almost two decades ago, and it is the work of mine that has resonated most profoundly with readers over the years. We may pick up the right book at the wrong time and set it aside unread—or, more commonly, finished reluctantly, because readers are disinclined to abandon books without very good cause. Years later, for whatever reason, the book may find its way into our hands once more, to be read with new eyes.

I think of the number of times I struggled to come to grips with *Bleak House*, *Ulysses*, or *War and Peace*. The last of them took three attempts: the first in adolescence, the second in my early twenties, and the final, successful assault in my late twenties. *War and Peace* waited for me to embrace it, but the book was never the same each time. It seemed to shimmer, as though viewed through a wall of heat. I could offer similar examples in other media: the music of Arvo Pärt or Van Morrison, the poetry of E. E. Cummings, the films of Preston Sturges. Even now, they continue to morph, to assume new forms. I would worry if they did not, because it would mean that I had begun to atrophy, to stagnate.

So *Horror Express* need not be better than I remembered, or even as good; it just has to *be*.

— 13 —

The train has figured frequently in mystery fiction, though the popularity of its carriages as settings for murder and intrigue began to dwindle with the demise of steam. Wood and leather vanished, replaced by plastics and artificial fibers. Compartments were removed in favor of more open seating arrangements with the result—possibly counterintuitively—that the opportunity for interaction between individual passengers, whether voluntary or forced upon them by proximity and circumstance, was reduced.

Whereas in the past the soundtrack to a rail journey came from the rhythm of the wheels upon the track, the rattle of the cars, the rustle of book pages and newspapers, the subdued hum of speech, it is now largely electronic in nature—the bleeping of cell phones and laptops, the seepage of noise from cheap headphones—abetted by the consequent surge in imperfect dialogues as the brain tries to deal with the distraction of being privy to only one side of the conversations taking place in its immediate vicinity. It is easier to ignore two interlocutors speaking in person than it is to block out the noise from one individual apparently conversing with an unheard, unseen other. In the latter instance, the ear keeps listening for an expected response that never comes, with the result that this ingrained anticipation itself becomes a form of intrusion.

In an age in which most people did not have access to a motorcar, the railway represented a partial democratization of mechanized travel, albeit one that continued to emphasize the connection between income, class, and comfort. In effect, the train not only symbolized a more mobile society but also represented society itself in mobile form. It would be decades before a similar process of democratization would occur in the air, since airplane travel would remain beyond the reach of many until the latter part of the twentieth century. (In 1975, eighty percent of Americans had never flown, but that decade would see rapid advances in engine technology, followed by a process of deregulation in the 1980s, leading to the flying buses of today.)

But why should the train be more suited to horror and mystery than, say, an airplane or boat? As the lamentable *Snakes on a Plane* (2006) demonstrated, the problem with using an aircraft as the setting for horror is precisely the aspect that would appear to make it most fitting: the sense of containment, of entrapment. Unfortunately, it is constraint with very limited room for maneuver and no prospect of survival beyond reaching the ground safely, which requires specialist knowledge unavailable to the majority of passengers. In addition, escape while the plane is in flight remains difficult. (I have flown a lot over the years and have yet to be told where the parachutes might be concealed in the event of a catastrophic accident.) Finding a hatch and clinging to the fuselage is the preserve of James Bond or Tom Cruise in Ethan Hunt mode. In the end, the plane either lands or crashes, but that fate is out of the hands of the kind of characters who make life-and-death dilemmas engaging for the general viewer, that is, those most like ourselves.

Meanwhile, the manifestation of a threat on a plane, and its effect, is difficult to conceal. As with a train, a plane is divided according to class and ability to pay, but those divisions take the form of curtains, or a flight of stairs. It remains a single aluminum tube, with only the flimsiest of barriers preventing a complete perspective. In the end, the airplane is best suited to thrillers, not mystery or horror.

A boat offers a more amenable environment for horror—and as a rule of thumb, the bigger the boat, the better. (The greatest horror ship of all time moved not through water but space: the *Nostromo* in Ridley Scott's seminal 1979 shocker *Alien*.) A ship at sea is a contained habitat, but those on board have vertical and lateral freedom of movement. Like Dante's hell, a large ship offers the prospect of descent into increasingly deeper and darker echelons. With each level explored, the terrain becomes less and less familiar until, at last, the passengers—who are, once again, our representatives in this Hadean murk—find themselves in the bowels of the ship, lost in storage spaces and engine rooms. (*The Poseidon Adventure*—from 1972, ignoring the later, unfortunate remake—offers a literal inversion of this, but with the same result.)

Unlike an airplane, a ship in motion presents opportunities for escape: lifeboats, rescue by the occupants of another craft, and, in the most extreme circumstances, lifejackets followed by immersion in a cold sea. Even then, new threats may emerge: exposure to the elements or hostile organisms. We may drown or be eaten alive. Our putative rescuers may betray us. Still, our chances of survival are better than they would be on a plummeting plane.

What a large vessel lacks is real velocity. It moves, but at a pace that is often quite sedate. (*Speed 2: Cruise Control* [1997] was a challenging production and a huge flop, but a passing child could have pointed out in advance the disjunction between the stately progress of a vast ocean liner at sea and the relative concept of "speed.") Also, the very unfamiliarity of its below-deck areas, and the expertise required both to navigate them and to influence their operation, can be as much a disadvantage as an advantage in engaging the viewer.

Finally, an ocean liner is just *too* big, and we might also argue that the effectiveness of a piece of horror is inversely proportional to the number of those in peril. It's hard to care about the destiny of more than a handful of individuals in a movie, so horror films must, of necessity, narrow their focus. The first step is to get rid of as many nonessential human distractions as possible—or, as in *Alien*, dispense with them entirely by giving us a massive craft, but a small crew and no passengers. Another option is to create a ghost ship and lure a group of explorers on board to uncover the reasons behind its apparent abandonment and, better still, share the fate of the missing.

The third choice is just to use a smaller boat. Phillip Noyce's *Dead Calm* (1989) takes a yacht and a cast of three, and manufactures from those elements an effectively nasty little thriller. It's not difficult to imagine the same film altered only marginally by the addition of a supernatural component to Billy Zane's homicidal Hughie. But the selection of a modest vessel presents another complication for us to consider: by restricting the space through which the characters move, we must also reduce the number of those characters.

For narrative purposes, give me the train, but only an old-fashioned model. Give me relative freedom of movement. Give me social interaction. Give me the prospect of escape but also the possibility of intrusion, because speed permitting, one can get on a train almost as easily as one can get off. Yet it may also be the case that the train, with its forward motion on set tracks, offers an analogy for a particular form of storytelling. It is the perfect setting for propulsive narrative.

— 14 —

Eighteen Interesting Train Films

The General (1926)
Night Mail (1936)
The Lady Vanishes (1938)
Strangers on a Train (1951)
The Narrow Margin/*Narrow Margin* (1952/1990)
The Train (1964)
The Incident (1967)
Horror Express (1972)
Emperor of the North (1973)
The Taking of Pelham One Two Three/*The Taking of Pelham 123* (1974/2009)
Murder on the Orient Express (1974/2017)
Breakheart Pass (1975)
The First Great Train Robbery (1978)
Runaway Train (1985)
Europa (1991)
The Darjeeling Limited (2007)
Snowpiercer (2013)
Train to Busan (2016)

— 15 —

I haven't had much direct experience with filmmaking, horror or otherwise. I made assorted appearances—including inadvertently driving on the wrong side of a Maine highway during a snowstorm—in *Of Blood and Lost Things*, a documentary about my work shown by RTÉ in 2009. More recently, my novel *The Book of Lost Things* was acknowledged as an influence on the Academy Award–winning animated film *The Boy and the Heron* (2023). But my principal involvement in filmmaking has been as the author of a supernatural short story titled "The New Daughter" that became a movie of the same name in 2009.

To have a short story adapted to film is a gentle way of dipping a toe in those waters. A short story involves, to borrow William Trevor's phrase, "the art of the glimpse," so it leaves plenty of space for a screenwriter to expand the central idea or develop new ideas of their own to complement it. A novel, on the other hand, will require more cuts and compression, which can be painful for the author of the book being adapted, whether they choose to write the screenplay themselves or leave it to another. I spent a year trying to adapt my novel *The Book of Lost Things* for the screen, so I speak from experience. I found dealing with producers' notes and rewrite after rewrite very frustrating, and in the end the film never got made. Ultimately, I fear that I am not psychologically conditioned to filmmaking. I became a novelist because, by and large, I don't play well with other children. I'm not collaborative by nature and filmmaking is, of necessity, a collaborative process. But I also know that, when I begin a novel, the finished work is likely to be published—so far, I have no rejected manuscripts in a drawer—whereas there are no such guarantees when it comes to film. I would prefer, therefore, to spend a couple of years writing a novel than writing a script, even if the latter might pay better—but if anyone in Hollywood is weeping at this news, I'm struggling to hear them.

— 16 —

The New Daughter came together relatively quickly, or that was my impression. A writer named John Travis—whom I had not met at that point, but who is now a friend—wrote the script, essentially on spec, and sold it. Bruce Willis apparently read it at an early stage but didn't want to star in another supernatural thriller after *The Sixth Sense* and *Unbreakable*, so Kevin Costner signed on instead. Luiso Berdejo, the Spanish screenwriter of the films *Rec* and *Quarantine*, agreed to make *The New Daughter* his directorial debut, and Ivana

Baquero, the young star of Guillermo del Toro's brilliant *Pan's Labyrinth*, was cast as the titular child, Louisa, with Samantha Mathis and Noah Taylor taking supporting roles.

John and I visited the set of the film in Charleston, South Carolina. Everyone was perfectly lovely, though Kevin Costner seemed to think I'd criticized his acting, having misheard something I said. That caused a bit of a chill to settle, or such was my impression. Otherwise, I recall one of the producers showing me "the monsters," one of the departures from the source material, which didn't have any monsters. In the short story, the narrator remains uncertain whether the change in his daughter's behavior is being caused by something in the fairy fort on their property or by the advent of adolescence. That question remains unanswered at the end, but a feature-length film—like a novel—requires a resolution. In addition, while the short story played on myths of fairies, the film relocated the action to the United States, which doesn't share that mythology. Hence, the monsters.

On set, I also served as a walking buffet for the local insect population. Apparently, the house chosen as the main location was situated on land used to test mosquito repellent, and the two things you need to test mosquito repellent are repellent and mosquitoes. Of the latter, there was no shortage. On set, the crew wiped themselves regularly with sheets of fabric softener, boxes of which they kept nearby at all times; the mosquitoes, it seemed, hated the scent of fabric softener. Unfortunately, I didn't have any fabric softener, and word of this spread fast and far among the local mosquito population. They descended on me while I was filming an interview for the film's electronic press kit. Under duress, I tried to stay still for the questioning, until I felt something crawling up my leg and decided I'd given enough blood for one day. Somewhere, there is footage of me leaping from a chair and fleeing.

The New Daughter didn't have much luck from that point on. Due to problems that had nothing to do with cast or crew, it received a very limited contractual release before going to home viewing. Costner was reportedly unhappy with the film's treatment, and some of the reviews were harsh. But what I took from the experience, and what I'll always remember, was how committed everyone involved was to the project. This was a horror film, modestly budgeted, but the cast and crew set out to make the best modestly budgeted horror film they could.

In that, I find echoes of *Horror Express,* and much else besides.

— 17 —

The Plaza Cinema in Dublin no longer exists. For a time, after its demise as a picture house, it became a wax museum, containing desperately poor simulacra of the pope, some Irish prime ministers, and U2. It's now a hotel, the original cinema having long since been demolished.

The Plaza was a peculiar entity, one that simply could not exist in the present day now that most old movies, however poor, are easily available on DVD and streaming services. It showed mainly second-run films, or even third-run, as well as new releases that represented something less than the finest work of those involved. It was in the Plaza that I watched *Buddy Buddy* (1981), Billy Wilder's final misguided gasp as a director; *Zulu Dawn* (1979), the prequel to *Zulu* ("It's like Zulu, except the Zulus win!" "Oh. What else is on?"); and *At the Earth's Core* (1976), in which Doug McClure and Peter Cushing battled men in rubber suits à la the Japanese Godzilla movies.

What links these films, apart from their generally flawed nature and the role that the Plaza played in ensuring that someone, somewhere, made money from them, is the presence of my father. Every Christmas, he would take my younger brother and me to dinner and a movie in the city center. We nearly always seemed to end up at the Plaza—not only because it was cheap but because my brother and I quite often wanted to watch the films that it showed, poor though many of them might seem in retrospect.

I saw Ray Harryhausen's *The 7th Voyage of Sinbad* in the Plaza. I don't remember the year in question, although the film itself was made in 1958, which meant that, even by the Plaza's fairly lax scheduling standards, it was a bit on the old side when I sat down to it. I can only assume it was the bottom part of a double bill, but the title of the main attraction has been forgotten. It doesn't matter, because whatever it was, it didn't match up to *Sinbad*, in which Kerwin Mathews tries to foil the machinations of the magician Sokurah and find the necessary ingredients for the potion that will restore his love, a miniaturized Kathryn Grant (Mrs. Bing Crosby), to her full height.

This is the best of Harryhausen's three Sinbad movies, for a host of reasons. Harryhausen didn't direct it, but that's beside the point. It belongs to him as much as *The Thing from Another World* (1951) belongs to Howard Hawks, regardless of Christian Nyby's director's credit on the latter. *Sinbad* has a decent script, a Bernard Herrmann score, and special effects that were, for their time, quite groundbreaking. I can still recall my horror at the sight of a sailor being spit-roasted—in the nonsexual sense; one can't be too careful about these things—by the Cyclops, a scene that distressed me so much, I think I may have cried. It may be my earliest cinemagoing memory, and despite all the difficulties in our relationship, I owe it to my father.

I was fortunate enough to meet Ray Harryhausen some years ago. He was signing copies of *Ray Harryhausen: An Animated Life* with Ray Bradbury at the Los Angeles Times Festival of Books. I shook his hand. That's important. I shook Ray Harryhausen's hand. Because here's the thing: creaky though those special effects in *The 7th Voyage of Sinbad*, *Jason and the Argonauts*, or even the much later *Clash of the Titans* may seem to the modern eye, and by that I mean those unfortunate children and teenagers brought up only on CGI, they have a substance, a density, that modern computer imagery lacks. Harryhausen's creatures—the Cyclops, the Roc, the Gorgon—exist on the same level of reality as the actors on the screen. They have weight, breadth, height. They are created from plaster, plastic, fur, and metal. They can be touched and moved by hand. And they were so moved, because every action of the creatures, however minuscule, resulted from a moment when the craftsman and his creation came into intimate contact, which is as it should be.

The first trip overseas I made after the easing of COVID lockdown restrictions in 2022 was to Edinburgh for the *Ray Harryhausen: Titan of Cinema* exhibition at the National Galleries of Scotland. There, for the first time, I saw Harryhausen's original models and found myself growing quite emotional at the sight: how he must have labored over them, how he must have loved them, and how I had loved them in turn. I had a similar experience at London's Museum of Childhood in 2016, where I attended a retrospective of Smallfilms, a company formed by Oliver Postgate and Peter Firmin to make short children's television programs for the BBC. Basically, Smallfilms operated out of a shed, but their creations—Bagpuss, The Clangers, Ivor the Engine, all lovingly crafted and animated by hand—were integral to my childhood. What I remember most vividly about that presentation is standing beside a man my age who was weeping silently. When his wife asked what was wrong, he pointed at one of the exhibits and said, "Look, it's the Mouse Organ." And it was the Mouse Organ, a little pipe organ that played rolls of music and was serviced in *Bagpuss* by tiny stop-motion singing mice. What was happening to that man was hugely complex and wonderfully life-affirming. Sedikides, had he been present, would have understood and approved.

This is not to denigrate the art involved in creating computer-generated figures and worlds, the hours and hours spent manipulating code in an effort to create a simulacrum of reality. Rather, it is to point out that a virtual representation remains just that: virtual. It has the same relation to the real that a symphony listened to over headphones on an MP3 player, one that has been cleaned up and then compressed into a file, has to a live performance of the same piece by an orchestra—or, indeed, that the Plaza's waxworks had to their human models.

Lest I be tarred a Luddite, let me reiterate my love of spaceships exploding, rampant armies of Orcs, and the creation of new worlds through which I can wander for a time, but I may temper it with the qualification that I would preserve for posterity the wonderful model effects in John Carpenter's *The Thing* before any scenes in George Lucas's cold, mechanized *Star Wars* prequel trilogy; that I will take Wes Anderson's compromised *Fantastic Mr. Fox* (Roald Dahl by way of *The New Yorker*) over *Up*, even as I acknowledge the genius of Pixar's best work; that Nick Park deserves a statue to himself for Wallace and Gromit alone, and every time I see a fingerprint on Aardman's creations my eyes grow hot, but *Flushed Away* is problematic for pretending to be similarly crafted throughout when it is not; and that, in all things, I will seek the sticky, imperfect human touch over the inhuman perfection of images generated by computers or, horror of horrors, any effort by a computer to artificially replicate flaws in an effort to suggest humanity.

So it is that my affection for *The 7th Voyage of Sinbad* is, in the end, tied up with the quaintness of its animation to modern eyes—its defects, for these are what make it the product of people, not machines. I cherish its trust in its audience, its faith in that audience's willingness, its desire, to suspend disbelief. It represents an affection for ingenuity, for a time when not everything that could be imagined was capable of being presented on the screen. The viewer was required to reach out to the filmmaker, just as the filmmaker reached out to the viewer, each acknowledging the gap between dream and reality while at the same time respecting the efforts being made to bridge it, forging a bond between the cinemagoer and the creator of the image.

But I accept, too, that my love for *The 7th Voyage of Sinbad* is entwined with my feelings for my father, now many years dead, and for those hours spent sharing the fantastic with him.

So many of my early experiences of cinema are associated with him. He took me to see *Star Wars* in 1978, and rescued me when I went to the toilet halfway through and got a bit lost. In 1982, he decided we should see *Gandhi*, since it had swept the Academy Awards that year, winning in eight categories. Unfortunately for my dad, he failed to book in advance and the screening was sold out, so instead, we went to see Paul Newman in *The Verdict*, which was much better and remains among my favorite Newman performances. Secretly, I think my dad might have preferred it to *Gandhi* as well, though neither was as memorable as that sailor being roasted alive by the Cyclops in *The 7th Voyage of Sinbad.*

If I sound as though I want to turn back the clock, it is as much out of a desire to be reunited for a time with my father as it is out of my affection for the efforts of Harryhausen and those who have followed in his footsteps.

I shook the hand that made the Cyclops.

I shook the hand that made the Gorgon.

I touched genius.

— 18 —

The term "*ontology*" may be familiar to readers versed in critical theory. Before anyone offers me a berth in Pseuds Corner, let me state for the record that, while I studied critical theory as part of my English degree at Trinity College Dublin, I was absolutely hopeless at it, and you should feel free to take all that follows with a pinch of salt. On the other hand, based on my experience of a year of the subject, I came to the conclusion that it was largely the preserve of scoundrels and flimflam merchants, although I accept that a 2:2 in the final exam—a GPA of about 3.0, in American terms—may be contributing to some residual bitterness.

Ontology is the philosophical study of being. At its most basic level, it asks: What is the thing? But in his book *Specters of Marx* (1993), the philosopher Jacques Derrida came up with the concept of "hauntology," a blend of "haunting" and "ontology." It refers, if I understand it correctly (see above), to the idea of the ghost that is neither present nor absent, and is therefore, one supposes, also simultaneously both absent *and* present. We think of ghosts as entities from the past, yet they exist in the present and therefore cannot be regarded as definitively part of one temporal reality or another.

In "What Is Hauntology?", a 2012 essay for *Film Quarterly*, the critical theorist Mark Fisher noted that *Specters of Marx* repeatedly referred to Hamlet's response to the visitation by his father's ghost and the revelation that Claudius was responsible for his death: "The time is out of joint . . ." (*Hamlet*, 1.5, 210). Fisher went on to observe of hauntings that they happen "when a place is stained by time or when a particular place becomes the site for an encounter with broken time." For Fisher, even the future was experienced as a haunting because it "impinges upon the present, conditioning expectations."

In terms of critical thinking, hauntology has become an element of the discourse surrounding retrofuturism: the use of older sources to create new forms, particularly in music but also in visual art. It connects to nostalgia at the point where the yearning is neither for the past nor the future, but for past *visions* of the future.

In a sense, all art is haunted: by the Platonic ideal to which it aspires but of which it must, by necessity, fall short; by those aspects of it that defy a definitive interpretation or explanation; and by the ghost voices and shadows of the art and artists that have preceded it, so it is both current and also the echo of a preexisting fragment. The internet has amplified this artistic echo, since nothing ever truly dies now: old television series, half-remembered songs, and films major and minor find themselves eternalized on the internet, and because they are open to constant rediscovery by new generations, their place in the temporal landscape becomes disrupted. Everything old becomes new when processed for the first time, and what is new can now more easily be identified as the sum of its influences because those influences are so much more accessible than they once were. It is no longer only a question of one's engagement with one's own past, but an engagement with a past that was never one's own to begin with, but for which one nevertheless experiences a hunger. The creation of new art emerges from that hunger. Eventually, I suppose, this process may lead to art that is haunted by itself.

— 19 —

"Folk horror," a term usually attributed to the filmmaker Piers Haggard, is a fine example of a hauntological art form. In *Folk Horror: Hours Dreadful and Things Strange* (2017), Adam Scovell provides a useful formulation. For Scovell, folk horror is:

- A work that uses folklore, either aesthetically or thematically, to imbue itself with a sense of the arcane for eerie, uncanny, or horrific purposes.
- A work that presents a clash between such arcania and its presence within close proximity to some form of modernity, often within social parameters.
- A work that creates its own folklore through various forms of popular conscious memory, even when it is young in comparison to more typical folkloric and antiquarian artefacts of the same character.

Its power arises from a suggestion of the persistence of primitive, pre-Christian beliefs in modern times and the idea that these terrors are somehow ingrained in the rural landscape, as though the very soil itself were steeped in blood—that the ground has gone "sour," as Stephen King puts it in his 1983 novel *Pet Sematary*.

Folk horror is a peculiarly modern phenomenon, its potency linked to our increasing distance, both physically and psychologically, from the countryside. In 1801, fewer than twenty percent of people in England and Wales resided in cities or towns, with the remainder living close to the land. Just over two centuries later, those proportions have become almost exactly reversed: more than eighty percent of the population of England and Wales now lives an urban existence. The rural environment is alien territory to many of us, and a tendency to patronize or denigrate its inhabitants masks a deeper lack of understanding, even fear, of its landscape, rhythms, and history. As the writer Joe Kennedy has wittily remarked, it is "the terror in the *terroir*," the "psycho" lurking in psychogeography.

Folk horror, in its modern British cinematic form, probably begins in 1971 with Haggard's *Blood on Satan's Claw* and quickly reaches its apogee with Robin Hardy's *The Wicker Man* (1973), in which the unfortunate Sergeant Neil Howie, a Christian, is dispatched from the Scottish mainland to investigate the disappearance of a young girl from the remote Hebridean island of Summerisle and discovers a community in thrall both to pagan gods and to nature itself. As Lord Summerisle (Christopher Lee) explains to Howie, the people of the island not only "love nature," they "rely on it." This is not Howie's world, and he will pay dearly for his trespass.

Michael Reeves's *Witchfinder General* (1968) is another useful reference point in folk horror, but television proved even more fertile ground for the subgenre: consider "Robin Redbreast" (1970), "Penda's Fen" (1974), and *Children of the Stones* (1977); Nigel Kneale's final TV iteration of *Quatermass* (1979); and even *Doctor Who*, which, with "The Daemons" (1971), produced a startling piece of folk horror that preceded by a couple of months the release of *Blood on Satan's Claw*.

— 20 —

Horror Express, by contrast, is closer to retrofuturism than pure folk horror. What initially appears to be an ancient evil permeating the present is slowly revealed to be something odder still: an extraterrestrial life-form that has concealed itself in a specimen of early man, hibernating until it can be rediscovered by a new generation of suitable hosts. It is science fiction in the garb of period horror, but also, thanks to the presence of Lee and Cushing, a version of a Hammer horror future that never came to pass.

Whatever its flaws may be, *Horror Express* is more interesting and entertaining than any film released by Britain's Hammer Film Productions during the same period—or indeed, until the demise of the studio's first incarnation in 1979. Initially a pioneer of gothic horror, by the early seventies, Hammer, under pressure from its US partner, American International, had discovered nudity. The gateway drug was Sheridan Le Fanu's vampire novella *Carmilla* (1872), with its lesbian undertones:

> Sometimes after an hour of apathy, my strange and beautiful companion would take my hand and hold it with a fond pressure, renewed again and again; blushing softly, gazing in my face with languid and burning eyes, and breathing so fast that her dress rose and fell with the tumultuous respiration. It was like the ardour of a lover; it embarrassed me; it was hateful and yet overpowering; and with gloating eyes she drew me to her, and her hot lips travelled along my cheek in kisses; and she would whisper, almost in sobs, "You are mine, you shall be mine, and you and I are one for ever." (*Carmilla*, Ch. 4)

Carmilla provided the inspiration for Hammer's so-called Karnstein Trilogy—*The Vampire Lovers* (1970), *Lust for a Vampire* (1971), and *Twins of Evil* (1971)—in which the studio increasingly tested the British censor's tolerance for explicit sexual content, but these films also marked the beginning of a race to the bottom that would see Hammer produce a series of low-budget quickies derived from British television comedies, with more risqué content than would have been permitted in their small-screen incarnations. The nadir was the *On the Buses* trilogy, which somehow contrived to take an already unfunny TV show and make it less funny still. *Holiday on the Buses*, the last of the films, and mediocre even by their desperate standards, was released in 1973, leaving Hammer to linger ineffectually for another six years, the cinematic equivalent of some dreadful radioactive half-life.

So *Horror Express* appears, in retrospect, to be the sort of film that Hammer didn't make anymore, even while Hammer continued to exist. The casting of Lee and Cushing now seems to mark it as a form of homage to the British studio, though at the time the actors' recruitment was occasioned more by an attempt to replicate Hammer's earlier successes and earn a quick profit by drawing in English-speaking cinemagoers than any effort to suggest the error of Hammer's ways.

But *Horror Express* also exemplifies the ease with which folk horror and science fiction can coexist. Like Nigel Kneale's *Quatermass and the Pit* (1967), the high-water mark of later Hammer (it had previously been serialized by the BBC from 1958–59), *Horror Express* explores the tension between reason and superstition, between the rational and the antirational. As in *Quatermass and the Pit*—or, to offer a near-contemporaneous literary equivalent, John Wyndham's *The Midwich Cuckoos* (1957)—what initially appears to be some form of curse or supernatural activity is eventually revealed as extraterrestrial in origin, but the potency of this intrusion is directly related to the persistence of old beliefs unrelated to the alien presence.

— 21 —

It is appropriate that *Horror Express* should have been an Anglo-Spanish coproduction—a hybrid, as it were—since not only is the film a fusion of two genres (horror and science, or speculative, fiction) but Spanish horror cinema is itself a peculiar synthesis of influences, an anomaly in continental cinema of the uncanny.

Unlike Germany or France, Spain does not appear to have wholeheartedly embraced the gothic, and the gothic is the cornerstone of horror. It's worth considering what lies behind this relative absence. In cinematic terms, we may look to the influence of Generalissimo Francisco Franco and his fascists, who ruled Spain from 1939 until Franco's death in 1975. Centralized control by the fascist regime extended to cinema, and the National Commission of Film Censorship policed Spanish film production for content unacceptable to the state, including anything that might undermine morality and public order. Since horror is frequently concerned with questioning assumptions about the former and delights in pushing the kind of boundaries delineated by society's guardians, whether state- or self-appointed, it found little favor with the Francoists. If the stick of censorship were not enough to discourage such experimentation, the carrot of state subsidies available to approved cinematic forms—largely musicals and religious epics—helped tip the balance.

But where Franco went, so too did the Catholic Church. As in neighboring Italy, the influence of the Church, as much as that of the fascists, helped to stifle all but the most resilient manifestations of the gothic. This was not due solely to a Catholic distrust of creative forms that delight in the occult. A strong streak of anti-Catholicism runs through the early literary gothic, so much so that it is tempting to regard it as a primarily Protestant art form.

— 22 —

In her 2012 essay "Anti-Catholicism and the Gothic Imaginary: The Historical and Literary Contexts," Diane Long Hoeveler traces the historical origins of the gothic novel to the rise in anti-Catholic sentiment in England following the Jacobite rebellions of 1715 and 1745, and the later backlash that resulted from the attempted Spanish invasion of 1779, leading to the Gordon riots of 1780. Allied to these are the rise of scientific rationalism in Enlightenment Europe and a concomitant distrust of superstition and priestcraft, leaving the stage set for the emergence of Catholic clergy as the principal villains in Protestant literature. The results include Denis Diderot's *The Nun* (1796), Matthew Lewis's *The Monk* (1796), and Mrs. F. C. Patrick's *The Jesuit* (1799)—I think you can see a pattern emerging here—along with any number of novels featuring the worst excesses of the Inquisition offered up for popular consumption in exquisite, and explicit, detail.

One should always be suspicious, though, of those who protest too much, and the enthusiastic Protestant embrace of the gothic is indicative of a certain appalled fascination with occultism and ritual, and particularly any Catholic associations with the same. It also suggests no small amount of fear. In *Anti-Catholicism and Nineteenth-Century Fiction* (2004), Susan M. Griffin notes that, by the eighteenth century, Protestants had already begun to regard Catholicism as a "retrograde religion," a relic of the past in the form of the uncanny, "manifested in monsters both literal and metaphoric . . . the living dead, bloody bodies, vampires." The fiend, in other words, is Catholicism itself, feasting on the flesh and blood of a god incarnated in human form. In Europe, this extreme anti-Catholicism was most prevalent in England, France, and northern Germany. These, then, are our gothic crucibles.

Or take the example of my homeland of Ireland, a small Catholic island forcibly settled by English Protestants. The Irish gothic tradition should more correctly be termed Anglo-Irish, since it is not native in origin and has bequeathed to us a quartet of the great gothic novels of the nineteenth century: *Melmoth the Wanderer* (1820) by Charles Maturin; *Uncle Silas* (1864) by Sheridan Le Fanu; *Dracula* (1897) by Bram Stoker; and *The Picture of Dorian Gray* (1890) by Oscar Wilde. All four novelists were Protestants, and of them Maturin—eccentric "almost to insanity," as one contemporary profile noted—was by far the most anti-Catholic. He was, like Le Fanu, of Huguenot descent. The Huguenots were a Protestant sect that emerged in France in the middle of the sixteenth century, which wasn't a good time or place to be Protestant. In 1598, the Edict of Nantes gave the Huguenots a brief respite from torture and execution, bringing an end to the Wars of Religion, but their persecution resumed in the seventeenth century, culminating in the revocation of the edict in 1685. Forced conversion of the Huguenots to Catholicism followed, although many of them fled France for more sympathetic surroundings, including Ireland. Perhaps understandably, they brought with them a virulent hostility toward the Catholic religion. In *Melmoth the Wanderer*, the titular rover at one point explains to his lover that Catholicism is typified by a dedication to sadism and masochism, but he lumps in Judaism and Hinduism as well, thus demonstrating a prejudice both deep *and* wide.

The critic Roy Foster has argued that the Protestant Irish were defined by fears of their eradication by the Catholics surrounding them, and it may be no coincidence that each of the Anglo-Irish gothic novels mentioned above features a man either cut off from his Big House—the term applied to the mansions of the landed gentry in Ireland—or trapped in it and surrounded by a hostile population, which was very much the situation of the Protestant Ascendancy in nineteenth-century Ireland. But it may also be the case that Anglo-Irish Protestants became infected by the very culture and society they found so threatening to begin with: a realm of violence and uncertainty, one that was comfortable with ambiguity and antirationalism, myths and folklore, and superstitions that long predated the arrival of Catholicism. These are strange texts, rendered stranger still by the land in which they came to fruition.

— 23 —

If Catholic Ireland was gifted its gothic tradition by Protestant colonizers, Spain, as a colonial power itself, could enjoy no similar infusion of fresh blood. Instead, the Catholic Church maintained its stranglehold on the home of the Inquisition and in the twentieth century allied itself willingly with Franco as a means of reversing the earlier process of secularization begun under the Republicans. The clergy controlled the school system, dictated the filling of university positions, and became an extra-judicial arm of the state, authorized to investigate the past and current behavior of its citizens. Spain itself had even been consecrated to the Sacred Heart by King Alfonso XIII in 1919.

All of which—the absence of homegrown gothic literature, the strong grip of the Catholic Church, and a censorious right-wing dictatorship—goes some way toward explaining why Spain was largely ill-disposed to the horror tradition in cinema, or at least to the kind of consistent development found in contemporary Germany and France. Jonathan Rigby, in his excellent *Euro Gothic* (2016), identifies various early Spanish incursions into the genre—1919's *El otro* (The Other); 1935's *Las cinco advertencias de Satanás* (Satan's Five Warnings); 1944's *La torre de los siete jorobados* (The Tower of the Seven Hunchbacks)—but pickings remain slim until the 1960s and the emergence of Jesús "Jess" Franco (1930–2013). Franco's 1962 *Gritos en la noche* (Screams in the Night) was the first true Spanish horror film in almost two decades, inspired by a screening of Terence Fisher's *The Brides of Dracula* (1960), thus marking a point of contact between Hammer and the embryonic Spanish tradition.

Jess Franco was the great journeyman of Spanish cinema, directing 173 feature films between his debut, 1959's *Tenemos 18 años*, and his death. He was legendary for the speed at which he worked, and has a justified reputation as an exploitation merchant, with a fondness for "women in prison" pictures. The most famous, or infamous, of these is certainly 1977's *Ilsa, the Wicked Warden*, also variously known as—deep breath—*Greta, the Torturer*; *Greta, the Mad Butcher*; *Greta, the Sadist*; and *Wanda, the Wicked Warden*. "Her Prison," the tagline informs us, "Was HOTTER THAN HELL! Young Girls . . . CHAINED . . . CONDEMNED to a Life of TORMENT at the Hands of their Beautiful, BRUTAL Captor!" (Ladies and gentlemen, the prosecution rests.) But Franco also worked with Orson Welles, shooting second-unit footage on *Chimes at Midnight* (1965), and was even announced as the substitute director for an ultimately doomed version of *Treasure Island* after Welles fell ill. Franco is interesting not only for his role in rejuvenating Spanish horror cinema, but also for taking us one step closer to *Horror Express* through his association with Christopher Lee.

In the 1960s, Spain, in common with much of Western Europe, was experiencing the effects of a growth in prosperity and consumerism. Censorship was relaxed, resulting in a more commercial Spanish cinematic output. As Eugenio Martín remarked in an interview reflecting on this period:

> This "boom" in horror is something that's really happened. It's corresponded to a set of circumstances directly related to the Censorship, and to the general circumstances of Spanish cinema. The difficulties of dealing with the Censor made it impossible to portray Spanish subjects in the movies in any critical or realistic way. This leads to an attitude of mimicry, of copying elements of foreign themes; so at one point adventure films were copied, at another the western, and finally, horror. But the adventure film is very expensive to make, the "western" had saturated the market (and it was just too much, besides), so we fell back into horror, since it was easily exportable. The genre was doubly favored, then, once economically and once by the Censor. The "boom" lasted a couple of years, give or take, and in my opinion it's almost completely passed. I think that we're starting to create a critical cinema from the real Spain, as a result of this openness we're coming into.
>
> In a certain way, Spanish horror cinema could be compared a little to the Universal films of the 1930s (in the sociological sense of escaping from an uncomfortable reality), but with the great difference that the Anglo-Saxon countries have always had a literary tradition that explored this in other ways. Also, this "boom" has followed the economic demands of producers and exhibitors, of movie buyers . . . at the market level, in short, because the horror movie could be sold abroad—even if at low prices—which allowed an easy amortization. It seems to me much more about the economic demands of the cinema than about the needs of the filmgoing public. ("Testimonios—Eugenio Martín" in *Cine español, cine de subgeneros*, edited by Fernando Torres, 1974.)

If anyone was attuned to the "economic demands" of cinema—the understanding that to continue making movies, the movies one made had to turn a profit—it was Jess Franco. By 1968, he had started working with Harry Towers, a prolific British producer who had progressed from making radio series in the forties to television in the fifties, and finally to cinema in the sixties. Towers had what might charitably be referred to as a checkered past. He was close to Stephen Ward, the English osteopath who, in 1961, introduced John Profumo, the then-British secretary of state for war, and also a married man, to nineteen-year-old showgirl Christine Keeler. Keeler may also have been having an affair with a Russian military attaché named Yevgeny Ivanov, and the subsequent scandal ended Profumo's political career, brought down the Conservative government of the day, and led Ward to commit suicide. It was through Ward that Towers met Mandy Rice-Davies, a friend of Keeler's and a peripheral figure in the Profumo affair. Towers would later cast Rice-Davies in one of his films, *Black Venus* (1983).

Ward was also friendly with Horace "Hod" Hidden, a London nightclub-owner who brought his wife, a topless dancer named Mariella Novotny, to Towers's attention. Towers and Novotny commenced an affair, and the pair traveled together to the United States in 1961, ostensibly to cast Novotny in commercials and modeling. Instead, Novotny was arrested by the FBI and charged with soliciting, while Towers was accused of transporting her from the UK for the purposes of prostitution. It seemed that, as a sideline to producing, Towers might also have been running an escort agency, resulting in his being charged under the White-Slave Traffic Act. To make an already bad situation worse, Novotny told the FBI that Towers was a Soviet agent, tasked with compromising important individuals through the use of honey traps. Released on bail, Towers did a runner back to England, and the charges were eventually dropped. Towers decided to concentrate his future efforts on film production far from American shores, while Novotny hosted sex parties in London, which were apparently so popular with British politicians that Novotny took to referring to herself as the "government's chief whip."

Towers may have been the catalyst for Franco's prison fetish, as among their earliest collaborations was *99 Women*, "The Demented Mother of All Women-In-Prison Movies!" *99 Women* featured quite a cast, including Herbert Lom, Maria Schell, and Oscar-winner Mercedes McCambridge (she won for 1949's *All The King's Men*, I hasten to add, and not for *99 Women*), still a few years away from voicing the demon in *The Exorcist*. I've only seen the trailer for *99 Women*, as I'm not much for women's-prison pictures, but it looks suitably sleazy and has been available in a more explicit version since 2005, should you be seeking a Christmas present for your grandma.

Between 1965 and 1970, Towers also produced five Fu Manchu movies, all starring Christopher Lee, two of which were directed by Franco. Lee must have enjoyed the experience because he would also work with Franco on *The Bloody Judge* (1970), *Count Dracula* (1970), and *Eugenie* (1970), each produced by Towers. *Count Dracula* is the most interesting of the bunch, mostly because it spawned *Cuadecuc, vampir* (1971), a black-and-white documentary on its making by Pere Portabella, which is more unsettling than the film itself, thanks to an experimental soundscape by Carles Santos and the near absence of speech throughout. *Cuadecuc, vampir* was shown at the Cannes Film Festival in 1971, but was quickly banned by the authorities in Spain, who detected in it a subtle critique of the fascist regime.

Lee would later claim, in an undated audio interview, that Franco's *Count Dracula* was "in some ways better than the Hammer films," based on Lee's approval of the vampire's depiction. "I do appear entirely dressed in black as an old man with white hair and a white mustache, and I do gradually get younger in the film—indeed, as he does in the book . . . It's the nearest I ever got to portraying the character as Stoker wrote him."

So it is Towers and Franco who can be credited with introducing

Lee to the joys of Spanish filmmaking, making him amenable to the approaches that would result in *Horror Express*.

— 24 —

Lee, as we have already learned, was hardly unique among British and American actors in his willingness to earn a little foreign currency in mainland Europe. He was not even the most famous horror icon to do so. That honor can properly be claimed by Boris Karloff, who, in 1967, found himself in the unlikely surroundings of Torremolinos, Spain—the epicenter of British package tourism—filming *El coleccionista de cadáveres* (The Corpse Collector) for Santos Alcocer. The picture, also variously known as *Blind Man's Bluff* and *Cauldron of Blood*, would not receive a release until 1971, and is, by all accounts, not particularly good.

But Karloff still had one last great performance in him, as the retired horror actor Byron Orlok in Peter Bogdanovich's *Targets* (1968). By then Karloff was very unwell and would soon be relying on a wheelchair and an oxygen tank to complete work on a series of four Mexican horror films, his scenes being shot in Los Angeles due to his deteriorating health. When Karloff eventually retired to Britain in 1968, he immediately contracted bronchitis and died in a Sussex hospital from a combination of emphysema and pneumonia in February 1969.

But the real boom in Spanish horror begins not with elderly British actors who had seen better days, but with two men boasting roots closer to Spanish culture. The first is the Uruguayan-born Narciso Ibáñez Serrador, whose *Obras maestras del terror* (Masterworks of Terror) and *Historias para no dormir* (Tales to Keep You Awake) provided Spanish-speaking television audiences with adaptations of Poe, W.W. Jacobs, and Fredric Brown, alongside original material by Serrador himself. The second is Jacinto Molina Álvarez, better known as Paul Naschy, a former weightlifter turned actor and writer. Naschy actually met Karloff while the horror legend was filming in Spain in 1967 and this, combined with a lingering affection for the old Universal monster movies, may have spurred Naschy to write what would become 1968's *La marca del hombre lobo* (The Mark of the Wolf Man). There is a touch of the William Shatners about Naschy in his fondness for appearing shirtless on-screen, but *La marca del hombre lobo* proved a huge success, and Naschy reprised the role of Waldemar Daninsky, the Wolf Man, a further eleven times. Naschy's career in horror films continued until the start of this century, if with diminishing returns. He was, apparently, a very nice chap who managed to stay married to the same woman—the sepulchrally named Elvira—for forty years.

The Spanish horror genie was now well and truly out of the bottle, to the extent that it was already being regarded as the nation's most exportable cinematic form. Profilmes was founded in Barcelona in 1965 with the intention of creating a Spanish iteration of Hammer, while the Basque filmmaker Eloy de la Iglesia would produce a loose quartet of successful, politically aware horror pictures between 1970 and 1972. To this list can be added the work of Miguel Madrid (or Michael Skaife, as he styled himself), Alfonso Balcázar, José Ramón Larraz . . .

And, finally, Eugenio Martín.

II
THE PROTAGONISTS

— 25 —

On February 24, 1988, Peter Cushing made his fourth—and final—appearance on BBC TV's *Wogan*. He was publicizing *"Past Forgetting": Memoirs of the Hammer Years*, his second autobiographical volume. Like his first, *An Autobiography*, published two years earlier, it was a slim book, and revealed little about the actual process of making films, Hammer or otherwise. *"Past Forgetting"* did at least find space for one of my favorite theatrical anecdotes. Cushing worked with Oliver Messel, the flamboyant and openly gay stage designer, who was part of the British Expeditionary Force evacuated from Dunkirk in 1940. When asked about the experience, Messel reputedly replied, "My dear! The *noise*—and the *people*!" (This anecdote is spoiled only slightly by the fact that Messel wasn't actually at Dunkirk, but was instead based at Aldershot in England. Still, it's the kind of thing Messel might have said, though it has also been attributed to the actor Ernest Thesiger, who may have used the phrase in reference to his experience of trench warfare during WW I.)

Cushing was a thespian of the old school, with hardly any interest at all in the technical aspects of cinema and an abhorrence of idle gossip and tittle-tattle. As a result, the reader seeking tales of Hollywood debauchery or BBC bitchiness will close both Cushing volumes feeling decidedly unsated. His reminiscences read like products of the nineteenth century, not the latter part of the twentieth. They are creations of restrained elegance and elegant restraint.

Why, then, did the BBC's flagship early-evening chat show see fit to invite him onto its couch four times? The answer, thanks to the glories of the internet, can be ascertained for oneself: Peter Cushing was simply the most delightful of men. To watch him being interviewed is to feel slightly better about the world, although with an accompanying sense of regret that Cushing is no longer in it, accentuated by a suspicion that we're probably not making individuals like him anymore.

I watched the final *Wogan* interview on the night it was broadcast—I would then have been nineteen—and it was the first time that I contemplated writing a fan letter. I didn't, in the end, because I wasn't even sure how one went about contacting authors or celebrities. I supposed that one could have written to them c/o their publishers, but Ireland in 1988 was still a somewhat isolated place, with a provincial mindset. People like us, or certainly people like me, did not go around writing to London publishers asking them to forward letters to film stars we'd never met. My god, they might have sent the police around.

And what would I have said to Peter Cushing anyway? Well, I would have mentioned the films and television series in which I had seen him perform, and the Hammer productions in particular. I might have brought up *Dracula: Prince of Darkness* (1966) as a Hammer favorite, since that was the first horror film I ever watched, although I'm not sure how Cushing would have taken that, since he wasn't in it.

In fact, that's not entirely true. Cushing wanted to reprise his role of Van Helsing, with Christopher Lee returning as the Count, but prior commitments prevented the former's involvement. Anthony Hinds, who oversaw much of Hammer's output during its glory years, contacted Cushing to ask if he'd mind terribly if they used the final sequence from the original *Dracula* (1958) as the prologue to *Dracula: Prince of Darkness*. Hammer's problem was that it hadn't expected *Dracula* to be such a success—or, indeed, to have such an afterlife. (See what I did there? Comedy gold.) As a consequence, Hammer had rashly reduced the Count to ashes at the end of the film, leaving only his ring intact. (That sounds wrong, but you know what I mean.) The ring (we're moving on) would provide the opening (still moving on) needed to explain the Count's resurrection for the next installment.

Cushing, ever obliging, gave his consent. After all, he'd been paid once for the role and saw no reason to be greedy, even though he and his wife, Helen, had recently acquired a London residence and were making expensive repairs to the roof. When the work was completed, a receipt from the builders arrived for Cushing in the mail, which came as a surprise as he hadn't yet paid for the work. He was informed that Hammer had settled the bill as a gesture of appreciation for his earlier kindness, which says a lot about the Hammer folk.

But we've become sidetracked slightly: I was speculating about what I might have said to Peter Cushing in my great, unwritten fan letter. Ultimately, the contents could probably have been summarized as "I think you're a gentleman, and life would be better if more people behaved like you." That, I imagine, would have been enough.

It's possible that some readers may feel I'm sentimentalizing a man with whom I was acquainted only through film and television, but this is what Christopher Lee, who appeared with Cushing in twenty-two films, had to say about him: "He really was the gentlest and most generous of men," Lee recalled in *Lord of Misrule*. "It could be said of him that he died because he was too good for this world."

And, as we shall soon discover, only a fool would take issue with Christopher Lee.

— 26 —

Peter Wilton Cushing was born in 1913, so some of his earliest memories were of German zeppelins bombing London. To his mother Nellie's regret, Cushing came into this world a male, but she did her best to undo nature's work by dressing him as a girl in infancy and buying him a fully equipped dolls' house. These measures failed to alter his gender in any marked way, so she eventually settled for leaving him as he was, although she did retain a lock of his long blond hair as a memento of what might have been. (Cushing's mother certainly appears to have been an unusual woman. Whenever he disappointed her, she would sing the refrain from "Love Will Find a Way," with the lyrics altered for maximum tragic impact, before pretending to die.)

Meanwhile, his father, George, was a shy man, but could claim some credit for putting an end to his wife's predilection for sending their younger son out to play in female clothing. In early childhood, Cushing wandered off and was found by the police, who brought him to the nearest station. His worried father rang to report a missing boy and was informed that, while they hadn't picked up a boy, they did have a little girl. A mortified George, suspecting the truth, asked the duty sergeant to make sure, presumably by means of observation. Thus was Peter Cushing restored to his parents, and the frilly dresses were mothballed. Less happily, George Cushing was also responsible for giving his son a morbid fear of the dark, having once locked him in a lightless cellar as punishment for some breach of discipline. The boy's nyctophobia would persist until his late teens, when he managed to conquer it by forcing himself to walk down poorly lit alleys at night. "It got me in the mood for horror films," he later reflected.

Cushing had theatrical roots. His grandfather, Henry Cushing, was a member of Henry Irving's company—and therefore peripherally connected to Dracula through the Count's creator, Bram Stoker, who was Irving's business manager at the Lyceum Theatre. Similarly, his Aunt Maude had acted in touring companies; his step-uncle, Wilton Herriot, was a stage actor; and an Uncle Bertie had been banished to Australia in 1901 due to what was darkly described by his family as an "artistic temperament." Eventually, after a false start in the Drawing Office of the Surveyor's Department at Coulsdon and Purley Urban District Council—I include this detail to give you, dear reader, some sense of the dullness from which our subject sought to escape—Cushing followed the path of Grandfather Henry (if not Uncle Bertie) and took to the stage.

Having briefly contemplated suicide in Exmouth to escape Coulsdon and Purley UDC, Cushing instead settled for a Devonshire cream tea in town and was taking the train home when he spotted a newspaper notice concerning scholarships to the Guildhall School of Music and Drama. Despite being afflicted with chronic shyness, he applied—at first unsuccessfully—and was ultimately accepted. This marked the start of a vocation that would commence in the theater, proceed briefly to Hollywood, return to England to be forged in the fires of early live television broadcasting, and finally bloom into a long (and, at that time, unusual) career balanced between high-profile TV and film work.

— 27 —

A strain of wistful yet determined English eccentricity runs through Cushing's life. He was no shrinking violet: at school he won medals for rugby, athletics, and swimming, and grew to an impressive six feet in height. He appears smaller on-screen, partly because of the thin build of his middle and later years—a consequence of illness, diet, and grief—but also because he starred so often with Christopher Lee, who topped out at six-five. Cushing had wide, size-twelve feet, which presented difficulties when it came to costumes, requiring his footwear to be ordered specially for him. While playing Grand Moff Tarkin for George Lucas in *Star Wars* (1977), time constraints meant there was no opportunity to have jackboots made to fit, so he suffered in agony through the early setups. Unable to endure the pain any longer, he asked Lucas if he could be filmed from the waist up for the remainder of his scenes. Lucas agreed, and Cushing spent the rest of the picture stalking the Death Star in carpet slippers.

When the Second World War broke out, Cushing was in Hollywood. (Feeling homesick, Cushing, who was an accomplished artist, painted a scene of the Devonshire countryside on his bedroom wall, and assuaged his loneliness by gazing upon it until he fell asleep.) Although unsuited to military service due to sporting injuries to his knee and a perforated eardrum, he felt obliged to make a contribution to the war effort, and worked his way back to England via Canada, finally reaching Liverpool as a mate on a ship despite having no experience as a sailor. He ended up with ENSA, the Entertainments National Service Organization, established to provide amusement for the troops.

After the war, Cushing would be recruited personally by Laurence Olivier to join the company at London's Old Vic theatre, but such opportunities were fleeting and he enjoyed no lasting success. When money was tight, he took employment as a designer and painter of ladies' silk scarves, one of which ended up in the wardrobe of Queen Elizabeth II. By his late thirties, he was still struggling to earn a living, to such a degree that his father offered to lend him some evening clothes so he could work as a front-of-house theater manager. "You are nearly forty," Cushing's father informed him solemnly, "and a failure."

Television saved Cushing, followed by Jimmy Carreras and Hammer Studios. Hammer did not share the general film industry snobbery toward actors who had appeared on TV, reasoning that a face familiar to viewers from the small screen might entice those same viewers to the big one. So keen was Hammer to recruit Cushing for the role of the Baron in *The Curse of Frankenstein* (1957) that they arranged a private screening of their earlier production *X the Unknown* (1956) to convince him of their bona fides.

Cushing's subsequent relationship with Hammer spanned decades. He would pass the time on set by painting, drawing, and making elaborate models out of balsa wood and card. He was a teetotaler (though a pub in Whitstable, where Cushing lived for thirty-five years, is named after him) and a strict vegetarian. Christopher Lee recalled him subsisting entirely on apples and cheese, day after day, week after week, year after year. When Lee complained to him about the quality of the food on the set of *Horror Express*, Cushing continued peeling an apple and quietly admonished him with the words, "Well, there's no good belly-aching about it, you know." These were, according to Lee, the most severe words Cushing had ever uttered to him, leaving the former quite unsettled. Cushing's only vice was cigarettes, which he smoked while wearing white gloves in case telltale nicotine stains should be picked up by the cameras.

— 28 —

Cushing's relative shortness with Lee on the set of *Horror Express* can be attributed to the great tragedy of his life. In 1942, Cushing met Violet Helene Beck—or Helen, as she was universally known—when she starred with him in a production of Noël Coward's *Private Lives*. Helen was a divorcée and eight years his senior. It was love at first sight, and she and Cushing were soon inseparable. They married the following year, though Helen's health would always be fragile. Following a hysterectomy, she was found to be carrying a dead fetus in her womb.

While Cushing made his name on television (he appeared so often on the BBC that the definition of television was once said to be "Peter Cushing with knobs on"), he suffered horribly from nerves, daunted by the thought of the sheer number of viewers who would be watching his performances, which, in the early days of the BBC, were broadcast live. Helen suggested that he visualize a single viewer for whom to perform, but Cushing pointed out that he only ever thought of her when he worked. The solution, with the consent of the BBC, was that Helen should be on set while he acted, and this situation prevailed until her health deteriorated to such a degree that she could no longer be there for him. "I missed her presence in the control box," he later wrote, "which gave me the confidence I lacked."

— 29 —

There remains the strange tale of his 1986 involvement with the British television and radio celebrity Jimmy Savile, who was revealed after his death to have been a voracious sexual predator and a committed abuser of children.

Cushing, like many British celebrities, had previously encountered the culturally omnipresent Savile, but with no obvious awareness of the presenter's dark side. In the mid-eighties, Cushing wrote to *Jim'll Fix It*, Savile's primetime Saturday evening BBC TV show, wondering if it might be possible to have a rose named after his deceased wife. A rose grower named Christopher Wheatcroft added the pollen from a Silver Jubilee to the stigma of another varietal named Deep Secret. A year later, Cushing was invited to choose one rose from the resulting bushes, which he named the Helen Cushing. He selected a solitary whitish flower, which was then propagated by budding.

In March 1986, Cushing's *Jim'll Fix It* segment was broadcast, and it can easily be found on the internet. Cushing, as always, is delightful, and had even gone so far as to handcraft some cardboard medals as tokens of appreciation for Savile, Wheatcroft, and Roger Ordish, the show's producer. It's possible that any experience of watching Savile in action is now colored by our knowledge of his behavior, but it's interesting to view the clip and see Savile's attention wandering, even in the course of the two minutes he spends speaking with Cushing and Wheatcroft. His eyes are devoid of interest and warmth throughout, and I'm certain that Cushing's carefully hand-lettered cardboard medal went in the trash immediately after the show.

— 30 —

Cushing had a happier experience with the British comedy duo Morecambe and Wise, making repeated appearances on their television show during the 1970s to protest that he hadn't yet been paid for his role as King Arthur in one of Ernie Wise's terrible plays. "Until I get my money," Cushing warned, "wherever you go, I shall go. . . ." He never did get paid.

— 31 —

If Christopher Lee's attitude occasionally suggested a degree of ambivalence about his work with Hammer, and particularly its handling of the figure of Dracula (rarely will more diplomatic words be used in this book), Cushing was less troubled by his intimate association with the horror genre. Helen warned him of the dangers of becoming typecast, and Cushing took her point, but he had endured too many lean years and feared being unable to provide for his wife and himself in old age. He was also, I believe, relieved just to be working. An actor was all he ever really wanted to be, and he was a man largely devoid of pretension.

— 32 —

On January 14, 1971, Helen Cushing died of emphysema. "My life as I knew and loved it," Cushing wrote, "ended with the death of my beloved wife . . ." Grief rendered him smaller. He lost weight, aging visibly and rapidly. He no longer believed himself to be capable of working. But contracts had been signed, and *Horror Express* had to be made.

— 33 —

For the purposes of this book, as for so much of their own careers, where goes Peter Cushing, so goes Christopher Lee.

I owe something of my fascination with horror to Lee, but my primary engagement with the genre came first through books, not film. This is hardly surprising. I was born in 1968, and until the

1980s, most of my exposure to horror cinema was limited to whatever might be shown as the early half of the BBC's occasional Saturday night Hammer double bills, assuming my mum and dad didn't want to watch something else instead; or, as in the case of *Horror Express*, was subject to the vagaries of television programming on weekday nights in a house only rarely untroubled by adults.

But my parents did not police my reading, so any restrictions on genre exploration were determined by our local library (which tended toward the classics, the council's buyers being a conservative bunch back then) and the stock of the city's various secondhand bookstores, which were staples of Dublin's cultural life until quite recently.

If I can be permitted another slight digression, I may well belong to the final generation for whom hardback books were once unaffordable objects. For many years, new hardbacks were the preserve of libraries or, at a push, mail-order book clubs, which discounted heavily but tied the subscriber to the kind of long-term commitment more usually associated with mortgages and pacts with Satan. Even a paperback was expensive as a proportion of income, to the extent that I can recall the first time I bought more than one in a single purchase: it was in the old Penguin bookstore on Dublin's Nassau Street at the end of 1985, and I had just received my inaugural paycheck from my council employers, which probably amounted to less than £200 for two weeks' work. I must have spent a third of it on a long-planned buying spree that included *Mishima on Hagakure: The Samurai Ethic and Modern Japan* by Yukio Mishima, Boris Pasternak's *Doctor Zhivago*, *The Great Shark Hunt* by Hunter S. Thompson, and a boxed set of paperback reference books, including a dictionary and thesaurus. (Even at seventeen, I knew how to have a good time.) The fact that I can still recollect the titles, and remain slightly in awe of my immoderation, indicates the seriousness of the outlay involved.

For the most part, though, I relied on used books to fill my shelves and reading time. From an early age, I retained a fondness for supernatural short stories, perhaps understanding, even then, that they possessed a potency often lacking in a longer narrative. A supernatural novel requires some explanation or conclusion to be offered to the reader, but this is often far less interesting than the mystery posited at the start of the book, and the worst thing one can do as an artist is explain away the monster. Thomas Harris made this error with *Hannibal Rising* (2006), which attributes Hannibal Lecter's cannibalistic urges to the consumption of his sister by ravenous Russians during the Second World War. I admit that I'm no expert on pathologies, but this strikes me as psychologically dubious. More recently, Ridley Scott set about methodically sabotaging the *Alien* sequence by divesting its xenomorphic predators of any background mystery at all, and shifting his attention to the nature of artificial intelligence and the threat it might pose to humanity. The latter is all well and good but is not perhaps the main reason that people pay good money to see a movie with "Alien" in the title.

A supernatural short story, by contrast, is under no obligation to elaborate or elucidate. Its power lies in offering the reader a peek behind the curtain, a fleeting revelation of the true queerness of the universe. Most of the oeuvre of M. R. James, probably the greatest British writer of eerie short stories, centers on incidents of brief, traumatic exposure to the otherworldly. Memorably, this is what befalls the unfortunate Professor Parkins in what remains James's best-known story, "Oh, Whistle, and I'll Come to You, My Lad," the academic's view of the universe being irrevocably altered by his unwise decision to pick up an ancient whistle and, worse, blow into it, thereby summoning "a horrible, an intensely horrible" presence to his bedroom. James never explains the intruder. We get no history, no rumors of old curses, and barely any description of the entity itself. It is enough that it exists, and Parkins has been made aware of it. The world is far weirder and more threatening than he once believed, and he will never be comfortable in it again.

This may be why the horror genre is so appealing to adolescents, who are gradually beginning to understand that the adulthood into which they are growing is set to be confusing and frightening, and may involve no small amount of physical, emotional, and psychological pain. The horror genre enables teenagers to put names and configurations—ghost, vampire, werewolf, zombie—to existential terrors and thereby interrogate the concept of fear itself. Most will dispense with the genre in time, but the more interesting among them—like you, dear reader—will continue to engage with horror, accepting that terror never leaves us; it just assumes new forms.

So it was that the little library in my attic bedroom contained enough anthologies of supernatural fiction to threaten the structural integrity of the house. Not all of them were good. I retain a soft spot for the original *Pan Book of Horror Stories*, first published in 1959, because it exhibited a level of quality control, including, as it did, tales from Bram Stoker, L. P. Hartley, Muriel Spark, and Nigel Kneale. Not all of the volumes that followed could hold a head up in quite the same way, and one could argue that as the covers of the *Pan* collections became more garish—and they were hardly understated to begin with—their contents grew trashier. The original editor of the series was Herbert van Thal, who went the way of all flesh in 1983, and could most charitably have been described as "unusual looking," which might explain the paucity of available photographs. (Johnny Mains, who published a biography of van Thal, *Lest You Should Suffer Nightmares*, in 2011, claimed that it took more than a year just to track down a picture of him.) He served on the jury that, in 1953, convicted the serial killer John Christie, who murdered eight people in his flat at 10 Rillington Place, London. Van Thal didn't want Christie to hang, believing that he should instead be imprisoned and studied, but Christie was sent to the gallows anyway, dying at the end of a noose in Pentonville prison in July 1953. This suggests a progressive streak to van Thal that I find rather appealing.

These various anthologies fought for space alongside novelizations of films, most of which I had not seen, either because I was too young or because nobody had yet got around to showing them on television. In the pre-video/DVD/download age, novelizations were the only way one could revisit previously viewed films or television series, or even get some sense of their contents if one had no direct experience of them at all. John Burke adapted eight Hammer horrors as novellas for two volumes of the *Hammer Horror Film Omnibus*, including *The Gorgon* (1964), *The Reptile* (1966), *The Plague of the Zombies* (1966), and—the clincher for me—*Dracula: Prince of Darkness*, because it was the first adult horror film I had seen. (Lee refused to speak in the film because he regarded the script as appalling. As he remarked in the documentary *The Many Faces of Christopher Lee* [1996], "I'd read the script, and the lines were literally unsayable. . . . It's a silent film, as far as I'm concerned.")

I watched *Dracula: Prince of Darkness* on a small black-and-white portable television at the vacation home owned by the parents of my then best friend, Dan. Neither of us could have been more than six or seven at the time, because I lost touch with Dan shortly after I began attending Synge Street CBS in 1975. The film was sufficiently disturbing to give him nightmares, and I have a vague recollection of an unfortunate bed-wetting incident—Dan, not me, honest—but this may be incorrect. In any case, *Dracula: Prince of Darkness* put me on the path that has brought me to this juncture: nearly forty books to my name, the majority of a supernatural bent, and a pressing desire to spend tens of thousands of words examining *Horror Express*.

Thank you, *Dracula: Prince of Darkness*.

Thank you, Christopher Lee.

— 34 —

Christopher Lee always stood out from the crowd. As he reminds us in his autobiography, *Lord of Misrule*, the average height of the

British soldier during the Second World War was only five feet, four inches, which meant that when Lee reached his majority, in 1943, he was at least a foot taller than many of those around him. "To me, anybody under six foot is a midget," he wrote in *Lord of Misrule*. "The reader is more than likely a midget. I am surrounded by midgets."

Lee's mother was a famous society beauty, Contessa Estelle Marie Carandini di Sarzano, who could trace her lineage back to imperial Rome, although the origins of the name seemingly lay in *Carandus*, a maker of carts. Lee's Italian blood would encourage the xenophobic instincts of his fellow pupils at assorted schools, resulting in taunts of "dago" and "wop." His father was Lieutenant Colonel Geoffrey Trollope Lee, who fought in the Boer War and the Great War before leaving the family home when his son was four, under circumstances that were never completely clear but concluded, two years later, in divorce. Lee the elder would die of pneumonia in 1941.

At Summer Fields School, Lee acted alongside Patrick Macnee, later to find fame as John Steed in the TV series *The Avengers*, and was interviewed for Eton by M. R. James—"a little old man in glasses with a skin like parchment," as Lee remembered—though Lee failed to obtain a scholarship and so was consigned to the less prestigious Wellington College for his further education. Later, he would play James in a series of BBC readings of his stories, so at least he had some first-hand knowledge on which to base his performance.

In a similar vein, his stepfather's sister, Evelyn, was the mother of Ian Fleming, and Fleming would refer to Lee as his "cousin," giving the actor a familial connection to the James Bond franchise when he played the villain Francisco Scaramanga in *The Man with the Golden Gun* (1974). He was also the only actor on the set of Peter Jackson's *Lord of the Rings* films to have met J. R. R. Tolkien. In addition, he was introduced as a child to the men who had killed Rasputin, whom he later portrayed on-screen, and was subsequently invited to meet Rasputin's daughter, Maria. He also spent time with

Mussolini's executioner and was present at the last public execution by guillotine in France. Christopher Lee was that kind of guy.

— 35 —

In 1941, perhaps spurred by the death of his father, Lee volunteered for the Royal Air Force, where he accumulated a variety of nicknames including Lofty, Tiny, Toff, Duke, and, curiously, Lee of Babbacombe, after the Victorian murderer John Lee, who survived a death sentence after the gallows failed to work on three separate occasions, leading to a commutation of the sentence to life imprisonment, followed by his eventual release. (It is said that the phrase "third time lucky" was inspired by Babbacombe Lee's good fortune.)

The other Lee—Christopher—served in Rhodesia and Egypt before being transferred to the No. 260 Squadron of the RAF as an intelligence officer. He saw combat in North Africa and Europe, contracting malaria as well as being injured—embarrassingly but painfully—in the buttocks.

"The worst hour of the war for me," he wrote, "came with the assault on Monte Cassino. . . . When at last that heap of rubble was taken, and we'd gone through it past the immense litter of corpses lying in scummy water, I had the sense of having reached the nadir." Lee was decorated for his service in the war by the governments of Great Britain, Yugoslavia, Czechoslovakia, and Poland but rarely mentioned these accolades.

In a letter to the author Mark A. Miller, Lee's former schoolmate—and later, costar—Patrick Macnee had this to say about Lee's wartime service:

> Of course, the secret about Chris Lee is the heroism that nobody can tell. I heard about it, and just by accident, from Buckmaster, the famous spy chief in the Second World War. Chris worked behind the German lines in Russia and all over the

> place. It couldn't be told in his autobiography, unfortunately, because of the Official Secrets Act. He was one of the most distinguished men of Intelligence. He served loftily and with great distinction. This comes straight from Buckmaster, certainly not from Lee. . . .

After the war, Lee was involved with CROWCASS, the Central Registry of War Criminals and Security Suspects. He was, essentially, a Nazi hunter. His hands-on experience of warfare would prove useful when it came to film the death of Saruman for Peter Jackson's *The Lord of the Rings: The Return of the King* (2003). Saruman is stabbed in the back by his acolyte Wormtongue, and Jackson spent a long time explaining to Lee how he wanted him to react, and the sounds of agony he should make. As Lee noted, "I seem to recall that I did say to Peter 'Have you any idea what kind of noise happens when someone is stabbed in the back? Because I do.' " The director didn't argue the point further. "He seemed to have expert knowledge of exactly the sort of noise that they make," said Jackson.

Lee returned to England following his service but was unable to settle. It was his cousin Nicolò, the first Italian ambassador to the Court of St. James's following the fall of Mussolini, who suggested he might consider acting. Lee knew nothing at all of the profession beyond his experience in school plays, but he had little better to do now that the war was over. The only obstacle was his mother, who suggested that acting was for men of low moral character, but she eventually acquiesced when it was pointed out to her that the Carandinis themselves had a theatrical background.

— 36 —

In 1947, thanks to Nicolò's contacts, Lee ended up on a seven-year contract, at ten pounds a week, with the Rank Charm School, even though the producer Josef Somlo told him he was "too tall" to be an actor. Somlo wasn't totally mistaken: Lee's height worked against him, denying him the matinee idol roles that his good looks might otherwise have attracted. He landed his first film part in the 1948 drama *Corridor of Mirrors*; the picture's novice director got around the problem of Lee's height by filming him sitting down. The director in question was Terence Young, who would go on to direct three of the first four James Bond films.

The Rank Charm School was theoretically an effort to develop talent and manufacture a star system similar to that of the Hollywood studios. In reality, it was regarded as something of a joke within the industry and even inside the Rank Organization itself. Olive Dodds, who was responsible for the Charm School during Lee's time there, would regularly be asked, "What have you got to amuse us with this week?" at the end of board meetings. Young actresses were often recruited based on a passing resemblance to more famous stars, becoming easy pickings for predatory directors and producers, who viewed the company's weekly cocktail parties as an opportunity to select future sexual conquests. Lee remembered his time at Rank as being mostly without benefit, although he acknowledged the Charm School as "a brave idea, even a good idea."

Lee continued to work as a supporting actor, picking up roles alongside John Mills in *Scott of the Antarctic* (1948), during the filming of which he claimed to have lost his virginity to an obliging director's assistant named Jacqueline; Gregory Peck in *Captain Horatio Hornblower* (1951); and, in *The Crimson Pirate* (1952), Burt Lancaster, from whom he learned the skills of screen fighting. (Lee's mangled little finger resulted from a sword fight with Errol Flynn in 1955's *The Dark Avenger*, which almost severed the digit from his hand. It was, Lee later declared, "one of those unfortunate little accidents.")

Thanks to the Carandini family's exotic connections, Lee also managed to enjoy the kind of social and cultural life that would have been beyond the reach of most jobbing actors, including cultivating the friendship of the oil billionaire J. Paul Getty. Lee had a fine singing voice, auditioning at various points for Noël Coward and the Swedish Royal Opera, and could reputedly whistle all nine of Beethoven's symphonies from memory, which must have worn thin after the first two. While he remained committed to a career in acting, music would continue to fascinate him. Most famously, he would go on to sing "The Tinker of Rye" for *The Wicker Man* and record a number of heavy metal records in his eighties and nineties.

In 1956, Lee crossed paths with Boris Karloff, who had returned to England to play John Dickson Carr's detective Colonel March in the BBC series *Colonel March of Scotland Yard*. Lee appeared in the fourth episode, entitled "At Night All Cats Are Gray," which was broadcast in March of that year. That same month would see the broadcast of the sixth episode, "The Invisible Knife," directed by a man who would soon have the greatest single impact on Lee's image and career, Terence Fisher, for whom Lee had acted eight years earlier in Fisher's directorial debut, *A Song for Tomorrow*.

"It did not bother [Karloff] that he had become typecast," Lee wrote. "Types, he said, are continually in work. If they weren't types, they wouldn't be popular. I wasn't desirous of being a type, though I could see the force of his argument. Nor was I in any way eager to emulate him and become a type in the field of horror. . . ."

Eager or not, it's ironic that Lee would go on to do precisely that, even commencing his employment in horror films with the same role made famous by Karloff back in 1931: the Creature in *Frankenstein*. Reflecting later on his agent's recommendation that he accept the role, Lee remarked that he considered it "one more indignity on a grander scale," but acknowledged that after a decade in his chosen profession, he remained "as tall and as foreign and almost as unknown as when I started."

— 37 —

By 1956, Hammer Film Productions was not yet the horror powerhouse of lore. The original company was founded in 1934 by William Hinds, a jeweler turned music-hall comedian, who adopted the stage name of Will Hammer. Hinds expanded from performance into theater production and, finally, into film with Hammer Productions Limited, as well as a distribution arm called Exclusive Films, created with the aid of a former cinema owner named Enrique Carreras. Hammer's initial incarnation was short-lived, forced into bankruptcy in 1937, but Exclusive survived. Carreras's son James took over the running of the company following his demobilization from the army in 1946, and resurrected Hammer to make so-called quota-quickies.

Under the Cinematograph Films Act of 1927, amended in 1938, British cinemas were required to show a certain number of domestic films to counter the huge influence of Hollywood pictures. It was an attempt to stimulate growth in the industry, based on the hope that an artificially created market might blossom into one capable of being self-sustaining. The result was a torrent of £1-a-foot films, which meant that the total budget for any production would rarely exceed £5,000–£6,000, and filming had to be completed within ten days. (In defense of those pared-back budgets, it's worth noting that then, as now, stars' salaries represented a significant proportion of the production cost of a film, so dispensing with big names made financial sense.) About sixty percent of these quickies have been lost forever, and in most cases that's probably no great tragedy, but the films did provide a training ground for artists who would go on to achieve far greater renown: David Lean, Terence Rattigan, and Vivien Leigh all began their careers in the quota industry.

In 1951, Hammer began using Down Place in Berkshire as its principal base, renaming it Bray Studios, and two years later the company diverged from its staple of detective stories, melodramas, and war films to make a pair of science-fiction features, *Four Sided Triangle* and *Spaceways*, both directed by Terence Fisher. (The former, with its laboratory scenes and a plot concerning the creation of an artificial being, could be seen as the director's dry run for

The Curse of Frankenstein.) These genre experiments were successful enough for Carreras to green-light *The Quatermass Xperiment* (1955), based on the BBC series, to be directed by Val Guest.

With *The Quatermass Xperiment*, Hammer was attempting to push the boundaries of what was permissible in the science-fiction genre, consciously moving it in the direction of horror, to the extent that the film received an X rating from the British censor, which meant access was denied to anyone under the age of sixteen. "This is the best and nastiest horror film I've seen since the War," enthused Paul Dehn, film critic of the *News Chronicle*, and *The Quatermass Xperiment* has since received plaudits from Stephen King and John Carpenter. Although it can't lay claim to being the first great science-fiction/horror hybrid, it's certainly the first great *British* science-fiction/horror hybrid, and therefore provides an interesting marker on the path to *Horror Express*.

— 38 —

Phil Leakey designed the special effects makeup for *The Quatermass Xperiment* and would hone them on the following year's *X The Unknown*, before tackling the Creature for *The Curse of Frankenstein*, which had to differ radically from the Karloff incarnation due to copyright issues. Lee wasn't very happy with the result—the critic Leslie Halliwell described the Creature's appearance as "excessively nasty, as though he had been pickled for a year or two in formaldehyde"—but was distracted by having plenty of other things about which to be unhappy, not least the fact that the Creature was mute, which meant Lee didn't have any lines. When he moaned about this to his costar, Cushing replied, "You're lucky. I've read the script."

It could have been worse. The original draft for *The Curse of Frankenstein* was written by Milton Subotsky, who would found Amicus Productions in the 1960s. Amicus is remembered mostly for its portmanteau horror films—*Dr. Terror's House of Horrors*

(1965) and *Tales from the Crypt* (1972) among them—but rarely for the quality of its scripts, particularly when Subotsky was involved. Hammer engaged Jimmy Sangster, the former production manager who had scripted *X the Unknown*, to refine Subotsky's effort, assisted by producer and Hammer lynchpin Anthony Hinds, the son of studio founder Will Hammer. Their contributions represented enough of an improvement to enable production to commence but, as Cushing's comment indicated, the final draft still wasn't going to win any prizes. (Sangster's 1997 autobiography was titled *Do You Want It Good or Tuesday?*, which tells you all you need to know about the strictures under which he worked.)

For the most part, Lee seemed to enjoy working on *The Curse of Frankenstein*. He liked Cushing, whose birthday turned out to be one day before his; the catering was good, although Lee's makeup meant that he subsisted on soft foods and had to drink through a straw; and the limitations imposed on him by the costume meant that he had to reconsider the use of his physicality, which advanced his acting. "It was absorbing work," he said. "I never felt so content."

That contentment lasted only until the film's release. The critical response was hostile, even venomous: "not so much frightened as nauseated"; "a preoccupation with the disgusting"; "depressing and degrading." As late as the 1950s, the idea of British-made horror films was still anathema to some, despite the genre's prevalence in English literature. A small proportion of British silent films had flirted with horror, and a handful of sound pictures could be added to their number, most famously *Dead of Night* (1945), but horror was definitely regarded as infra dig in the better circles.

Yet even those critics with some appreciation of horror cinema were uneasy about *The Curse of Frankenstein*. In *The Dead That Walk*, his 1986 study of horror icons, Leslie Halliwell observes:

> *Curse* was a film without Hollywood expertise. It set out its horrors plainly: there was no sheen of lighting, no dazzling editing,

> no playing with shadows, no subtlety of narrative. It simply went hammer and tongs for the most gruesome effects, hoping to collar an audience by its sheer bravura. After all, who would have expected that so outlandishly violent a film could ever come from a British studio?

But Halliwell also took Lee to task, complaining that he "was not enough of an actor to create anything but revulsion for this particular monster." By contrast, Halliwell argued that Peter Cushing "presented a chilling but amusing figure, partly from his own personality. . . ."

Terence Fisher, on the other hand, opined: "Lee, more than Cushing, uses his body as a means of expression. Lee is a superb silent actor, very good at expressing himself with gestures and facial expressions. . . . He can convey emotions very well without dialogue and is good at adding a 'human touch' to a monstrous character."

This raises an interesting point, namely just how accomplished an actor was Christopher Lee? He was certainly good at being Christopher Lee, but it wouldn't be unfair to suggest that his imposing physical presence and dark charisma impressed more than his range, even if he was capable of greater subtlety than Halliwell was willing to admit. Cushing was perhaps the more versatile of the two, though his apparent ease was a product of huge amounts of preparation. Knowing every detail of his performance in advance gave him the security to adapt. Halliwell also hints at Cushing's greater likability and accessibility on-screen, whereas Lee always seemed to maintain a certain distance, both from his fellow actors and the audience. This was partly a consequence of the roles he played and his physical stature, but there was an aloofness to Lee that infused his performances. It could be useful, particularly in parts such as Dracula or Saruman, but it tended to inspire admiration more than affection.

Richard Pasco, who would come to be remembered as one of the finest classical actors of his generation, acted alongside Lee and

Cushing in *The Gorgon*. Interviewed by Mark A. Miller, he remembered Lee as "very much like his screen image. Christopher is—we have an expression in this country—a bit 'grand.' He appears to be rather withdrawn, rather unapproachable, and a highly intelligent man who doesn't suffer fools gladly. Don't get me wrong. He's a very nice man, but he's not an easy man to know." Of Cushing, Pasco said: "He's one of the world's saints, you know, Peter. He would help anybody in trouble and is so patient. Peter is one of the kindest, gentlest men I've ever known in my life, the antithesis to what he often appears to be on screen. He's a darling man."

Yet the undeniable edge to Lee's personality goes some way toward explaining why he also possessed a sensuality that Cushing lacked. At a press conference to announce the production of *Dracula*, James Carreras announced his intention to make a film suffused with sex. "Not you, Peter," he assured a mildly taken aback Cushing. "We'll leave that to Chris Lee."

As soon as shooting on *The Curse of Frankenstein* had concluded, Lee went off to make *A Tale of Two Cities* (1958), as though to compensate for playing to the cheap seats. Still, any concern he might have felt at the potential damage to his critical reputation would have been assuaged by the box-office success of *Curse*. The film was a worldwide hit on a modest budget of £65,000, and Lee's performance as the Creature resulted in a call from Hammer requesting that he play Dracula.

"It was the one that made the difference," Lee confessed. "It brought me a name, a fan club and a second-hand car, for all of which I was grateful. It also, if I may be forgiven for saying so, brought me the blessing of Lucifer . . . Count Dracula might escape, but not the actors who play him."

Lee's chilliness would combine with his lowering looks to imbue the character of Dracula with a carnality and a level of sexual threat lacking in earlier incarnations of the Count. He also earned his money—what little of it there was: in *Lord of Misrule*, Lee claimed to have been paid £750 for the first picture—particularly when it came to suffering for his art. The red contact lenses used in some of his Dracula outings irritated his eyes, and when one of them fell out on the set of *Dracula: Prince of Darkness*, a makeup man handed it back to Lee without wiping off the salt doubling as snow, with predictably painful results.

Dracula finally gave Lee security as an actor, but at the cost of playing various iterations of the Count and other aristocratic vampires for Hammer, Italian directors, Spanish directors—for anyone who came knocking, really, alongside the Mummy, Henry Baskerville in *The Hound of the Baskervilles* (1959), a magician in *The Hands of Orlac* (1960). . . . The list of genre roles goes on. "I always looked for some redeeming feature in any script that I was offered," Lee claimed.

Even if it was only the check.

— 39 —

Along the way, Lee finally got round to getting married. The bride was Birgit "Gitte" Kroencke, daughter of the director of the Tuborg Brewery in Copenhagen. They wed in 1961—they would have one child, Christina—and were still together when Lee died in 2015.

The couple honeymooned in Portugal, but decided to settle in Switzerland for tax reasons, which restricted the amount of time Lee could spend in England. His Swiss base meant that he began working increasingly often for Italian directors: Antonio Margheriti (*La vergine di Norimberga*/The Virgin of Nuremberg, 1963); Camillo Mastrocinque (*La cripta e l'incubo*/Terror in the Crypt, 1964, based on Le Fanu's *Carmilla*); Giuseppe Vegezzi (*Sfida al diavolo*/Katarsis, 1965); and the great Mario Bava (*Ercole al centro della terra*/Hercules in the Haunted World, 1961, and *La frusta e il corpo*/The Whip and the Body, 1963).

Lee grew increasingly ambivalent about some of his films, particularly the canonical reiterations of characters such as Dracula and Fu Manchu. "I never had any sense of embarrassment over the first *Dracula* nor *The Face of Fu Manchu . . .* ," he wrote. "Alas, in the follow-ups to both there was much to make me look shifty and suck my paws. Knowing this, I nevertheless repeated each character many times over. I did so because they were my livelihood."

The Face of Fu Manchu (1965) was filmed in Ireland under what Lee would describe as "execrable" conditions, while Lee dismissed *The Brides of Fu Manchu* (1966) as "tosh." He remarked of the allegations of racism directed at the films: "I heard there were objections in San Francisco and other cities with large Chinese populations, Hong Kong too. Apparently, some people objected to this presentation of the Chinese, as an insult to the Chinese people. I can only say that I never played Fu Manchu in a way that the Chinese could find offensive. I always played him as a man of immense power and dignity together with remarkable intelligence." (As a side note, when Sax Rohmer's Fu Manchu novels were banned in Germany in 1936, possibly in the mistaken belief that the author was Jewish, Rohmer—born Arthur Henry Ward in Birmingham, England, to Irish parents—argued that he was "a good Irishman" and his books "were not inimical to Nazi ideals.")

Rasputin: The Mad Monk (1966) was made back-to-back with *Dracula: Prince of Darkness*, and a close watching of the two films reveals the replication of sets, but Lee didn't care for the latter because—again—he didn't have any lines, and the gore quotient was increased. Our friend Leslie Halliwell didn't warm to *Dracula: Prince of Darkness* either, describing it as "unpleasant and cheap-looking. It had no style. Its sets were cardboard, its back-projected skylines quite unnecessarily inept."

Halliwell may be correct in his criticisms—he's certainly right to argue that the film suffers from the absence of Cushing's Van Helsing—but I don't really care. We're back to the curious workings of nostalgia and the ways in which a flawed cultural relic may lack universal significance while serving a transformative function on an individual level. I think I have watched *Dracula: Prince of Darkness* only once in its entirety since that first childhood viewing. It was duller and slower than I remembered; when I gave it another try a few years back, I stopped the film halfway through. So, what is important to me is not the picture itself, but the *memory* of the first viewing of the picture—a combination of age, circumstance, and the shock of the new—along with the importance of the horror genre to my subsequent creative life. The error lies in attempting to re-create an experience in the expectation of an emotional or psychological effect of similar impact. It is to anticipate heat but receive instead only gentle warmth. It is to expect the arrival of a person but see only a ghost.

— 40 —

To consider Lee's filmography in the periods both before and after *Horror Express* is to encounter the résumé of a jobbing actor. In 1970 alone, Lee appeared four times as Count Dracula: for Jess Franco in *Count Dracula*; for Peter Sasdy in *Taste the Blood of Dracula*; for Roy Ward Baker in *Scars of Dracula*; and in a cameo as 'The Vampire' for Jerry Lewis in the aptly titled *One More Time*, which featured Peter Cushing as Baron Frankenstein.

But in 1970 Lee also got to play Mycroft Holmes for Billy Wilder in *The Private Life of Sherlock Holmes* and Artemidorus in a widely panned film of Shakespeare's *Julius Caesar* from which, perhaps surprisingly, only Charlton Heston as Mark Antony emerged with any credit. (The critic Roger Ebert accused Jason Robards, playing Brutus, of bringing the production to its knees, reciting his lines as though "reading from idiot cards.")

The following year saw Lee essay the role of Bailey in Burt Kennedy's *Hannie Caulder*, a film that remains an uneasy viewing experience to this day, being a peculiar mix of rape, violence, parody, and nascent feminist revenge porn; but as with *Cuadecuc, vampir*, it represents one of the better Lee performances witnessed that year. By 1972, the year in which *Horror Express* was released in Spain, it was back to Dracula in the barrel-scraping *Dracula A.D. 1972*, but the two years that followed may well represent Lee's midcareer peak: the villainous Rochefort in Richard Lester's *The Three Musketeers* (1973), and its sequel, *The Four Musketeers* (1974); Lord Summerisle in *The Wicker Man* (1973), which Lee regarded as his greatest performance; and Scaramanga, complete with third nipple, in the ninth James Bond outing, *The Man with the Golden Gun* (1974).

But of the sixty films Lee made between *The Man with the Golden Gun* and Tim Burton's *Sleepy Hollow* (1999), the picture that might be considered to mark the beginning of his late-career resurgence, only four or five are of any real interest, and this includes Steven Spielberg's divisive *1941*. One starts to feel that Lee really should have been more effusive about *Horror Express*.

— 41 —

I should confess that, at this stage of writing, I have still not rewatched *Horror Express*. I'll get to it, but the longer I continue mining my memories of the film, the more reluctant I am to be confronted by its possible, even probable, weaknesses. I tell myself they won't really matter, and there is a truth to this: they won't matter because I am finding the journey to the point of the film's creation interesting in itself, and I have that memory of my first childhood viewing to which to cling. Nevertheless, I have noticed the expressions of puzzlement on the faces of those with whom I've discussed this project. The majority don't know the film, and most of those who do can't understand why someone might devote many months to researching and recounting the manner in which it came into being. I try to explain that it is about what *Horror Express* signifies as much as it is about the film itself, but they just shrug.

— 42 —

Peter Cushing and Christopher Lee made twenty-two films together over a period of thirty-five years, but only twenty of them count as formal collaborations; they did not share the screen in Laurence Olivier's *Hamlet* (1948) or in *Moulin Rouge* (1952), John Huston's biographical film about the artist Henri de Toulouse-Lautrec. It's an indication of their respective statuses at the time that Cushing gets a named role in *Hamlet* (Osric)—and a speaking one, to boot—whereas Lee is a spear carrier without credit, heard at one point shouting "Lights!" but otherwise unseen. In *Moulin Rouge*, as the painter Georges Seurat, Lee does at least get a line, singular. Despite this, Lee makes an impact, thanks to an impressive beard and an even more impressive hat. He also got to see Paris, which was more than Cushing did, who filmed his single scene as a racehorse owner at Kempton Park in Surrey.

The two men narrowly missed becoming costars for the first time in 1955. Cushing was asked to appear in a film version of the Edana Romney play *That Lady*, to be directed by Terence Young, but was committed to Sam Wanamaker's new production, *The Soldier and the Lady*, at the Wimbledon Theatre. Cushing had been offered the part of King Philip II of Spain. In his absence, Paul Scofield got the role, and Christopher Lee played his Captain of the Guard.

Their career as costars, therefore, really begins with *The Curse of Frankenstein* in 1957 and ends, rather less happily, with *House of the Long Shadows* in 1983. It is an astonishingly lengthy professional and personal relationship, one that appears to have passed without rancor or regret, which says much about the men in question: Cushing, the elder, driven to become an actor from an early age and willing to endure poverty rather than give up on the profession; and Lee, the younger by nine years, with a degree of privilege behind him, an actor less by compulsion than inclination, and then only in the absence of anything more interesting to engage his attention.

— 43 —

The first meeting between the two men, legend tells us, occurred on the set of *The Curse of Frankenstein* and involved the exchange, mentioned earlier, about the quality of the script. Lee and Cushing shared a sense of humor and a similar cultural refinement: while Cushing painted to fill the hours between setups, Lee would sing.

They reunited in 1958 for *Dracula* (or *Horror of Dracula*, as it was titled in the US), still regarded by many critics as the best entry in the series. (It was Cushing who persuaded Lee to stay in the theater during the American premiere, after the ambience of the film's opening sequence caused the audience to jeer, only to be silenced by the appearance of Lee's Count.) *Dracula* was followed by *The Hound of the Baskervilles* (1959), in which Cushing played Sherlock Holmes while Lee took the role of Sir Henry Baskerville. Three years later, Lee himself would play Holmes in an unfortunate German-Italian-French coproduction entitled *Sherlock Holmes und das Halsband des Todes* (Sherlock Holmes and the Deadly Necklace), though his voice was later dubbed into English by another actor, for reasons lost to time.

Despite the quality of the finished product—"disastrous," "a very unpalatable dish," and "a mess" were some of the views Lee expressed about it—the actor was pleased with his own performance, which may not come as a shock:

> My portrayal of Holmes is, I think, one of the best things I've ever done because I tried to play him really as he is written—as a very intolerant, argumentative, difficult man—and I looked extraordinarily like him with the make-up on. . . . Everyone who's seen it said I was as like Holmes as any actor they've ever seen—both in appearance and interpretation.

And, perhaps, also in certain aspects of his own character. The actor Francis Matthews, discussing Lee with Mark A. Miller, described Lee thus:

> I soon found he is an extraordinary man of myriad parts, few of which explain why he became an actor. He is a fluent linguist, expert in martial arts and ballistics, and a mine of knowledge in literature, science, and technical matters. . . . They inform his performances with an authority and contained strength which are the genuine articles.

If ever a man were born to play Sherlock Holmes, Lee was he, and the actor would reprise the role later in life, making him, I believe, the only actor to have played on film both Sherlock Holmes and his brother, Mycroft.

— 44 —

The collaborations between Lee and Cushing continued, with both Hammer and Amicus, throughout the 1960s and into the next decade. Some are better—and better-known—than others: *She* (1965); *The Skull* (1965); *Night of the Big Heat* (1967), released in the US as *Island of the Burning Damned*, of which I'd never even heard until I began researching this book; and *Scream and Scream Again* (1970). Occasionally, one or the other would be permitted to play against type—Cushing as the obsessive Dr. Namaroff in *The Gorgon*, Lee as the troubled and fearful Sir Matthew Phillips in *The Skull*—but for the most part they settled comfortably into the kind of established roles that offered them steady work.

Nearly twenty years after its release, *The Skull* would bequeath to cinema a great sight gag, in two senses of the word. The film's most famous image features Cushing staring through a looking glass, his left eye hugely magnified. In the 1984 comedy *Top Secret!*, Cushing would cameo as the "Swedish bookstore proprietor," introduced while peering through a looking glass, once again with his left eye greatly magnified. When he removes the magnifying glass—

Well, you're probably ahead of me here.

Curiously, and very unpleasantly, Cushing was diagnosed with prostate cancer two years before the release of *Top Secret!* The cancer was found to have metastasized in his left eye, resulting in the very bulging parodied in the film. The prognosis was poor, and Cushing was given only eighteen months to live. The cancer, he said, "didn't worry me at all" since it meant he "would be with Helen at last." He would defy the doctors and live for more than a decade.

For *Scream and Scream Again*, Lee and Cushing were teamed with horror icon Vincent Price, with whom Lee had previously starred in *The Oblong Box* (1969). Price was fond of Lee, and they remained in touch until Price's death in 1993. "If you get him on a subject that he likes, he's very warm and vibrant," Price said of Lee. "I think he's got a wonderful sense of humor, but I don't think everybody knows how to get at it." Price remembered Cushing, with whom he would later star in *Madhouse* (1974), as being "nothing like Christopher Lee" and "a very gentle sweet man," but also as "one of the strongest men I ever knew in my life. . . . He doesn't fake it at all."

— 45 —

With the dawning of the 1970s, Lee and Cushing could reflect on their ongoing good fortune and congratulate themselves on their contribution to Hammer's financial success. Between them, they had starred in more than thirty Hammer features since *The Curse of Frankenstein*; Lee had played Dracula four times for the studio, and Cushing had portrayed Baron Frankenstein on five occasions. The Frankenstein and Dracula franchises were consistent earners.

In 1969, James Carreras claimed that the films brought in a gross of £1.5–£2 million each, although the British Film Institute's Screen online entry for *Dracula: Prince of Darkness* suggests that by 1968 the picture had made £463,000 worldwide, before television receipts, on a budget of £220,000.

But the best of Hammer was already in the past, and Lee and Cushing would appear together only twice more for the studio, in *Dracula A.D. 1972* (1972) and *The Satanic Rites of Dracula* (1973). In the interim, they would keep each other company on more Amicus features, including the regrettable *I, Monster* (1971). Helen Cushing was so ill during the filming of *I, Monster* that her husband insisted on traveling home each night to be with her, arriving after 10:00 PM and rising early to be back on set. She would die shortly after the film's completion, leaving Cushing, as we have established, bereft but not inconsolable. He tells in *An Autobiography* of picking up a piece of newspaper on a beach in the immediate aftermath of Helen's death and looking at it only upon his return home. Printed on the page was a Bible verse: "Ye now therefore have sorrow: but I will see you again, and your heart shall rejoice, and your joy no man taketh from you" (John 16:22). He also found solace in a letter left for him by his wife. "Do not be hasty to leave this world," she advised him, before promising that "we will meet again. . . ."

So Cushing commenced what would be a twenty-three-year wait for death, and the reunion with his wife that he was convinced would follow. (One actress claimed that, upon being invited to dine with Cushing years later, she arrived to find the table set for three. The third place, Cushing informed her, was for his dead wife, which probably cast a pall over the evening.) It was in this frame of mind that he joined his friend Christopher Lee in Spain for the filming of *Horror Express*.

Which brings us to the final significant international name on the *Horror Express* call sheet. . . .

— 46 —

The narrator's tones were undeniably familiar. It was definitely Telly Savalas, star of the popular television series *Kojak*. He was even eulogizing an urban landscape not dissimilar to the one he policed as the eponymous New York detective. Admittedly, it looked a bit less glamorous, even by comparison with seventies Manhattan, and appeared to be hosting an over-forties disco competition, but if it was good enough for Telly, it was good enough for us. Birmingham, England was, it seemed, Telly's "kinda town."

I have a clear memory of seeing *Telly Savalas Looks at Birmingham* at a cinema in Dublin in the 1980s, but I can't imagine I was terribly happy about it. Quota filler or not, it was poor stuff, and the disjunction between the commentary and visuals was abundantly clear. Frankly, Birmingham looked like a bit of a hole.

"Birmingham's road system is revolutionary," said Telly, clutching at straws. "The Inner Ring Road; Queensway; a four-mile circuit of dual carriageways, tunnels, and overpasses linking up with the main arteries of the city and the Aston Expressway." Telly was either on drugs or lying through his teeth. Or both.

I was even less happy to visit Birmingham in person some years later, when I was promoting my first novel, *Every Dead Thing*. That was in 1999, and the city center had yet to commence its phoenix-like emergence from the ashes of neglect. I remember parking my car near a strip club by the Bull Ring shopping district, adjacent to a particularly insalubrious curry house, and reflecting that being an author was a less glamorous experience than I'd hoped. "You know, it's an adventure to shop in this city," Telly had advised in the course of his tribute to Birmingham, and in 1999 I had to agree, given that I wasn't entirely sure my car would still be in one piece when I returned to it. Mind you, the city is much nicer now, though that wouldn't be hard.

The reason for the existence of *Telly Savalas Looks at Birmingham* (and its similarly liberal-with-the-truth companion pieces *Telly Savalas Looks at Portsmouth* and *Telly Savalas Looks at Aberdeen*) was our old friend the Cinematograph Films Act of 1927, which forced cinemas to show one British film for each American one, even if the British offering was required only to be one-third the length of the main feature. (As if centuries of English oppression weren't bad enough, Irish cinemas somehow also got inveigled into showing these shorts, which wasn't fair at all.)

Telly Savalas Looks at Birmingham was the work of one Harold Baim, the quickie king, who was friends with Savalas's agent. The three films in the series were already almost complete by the time Savalas was hustled into a studio at De Wolfe Music in London, where he recorded the scripts over two days, all without ever setting foot in the cities in question. But the Birmingham contribution has a kind of surreal quality that elevates it above the rest, and even demonstrates an occasional rare prescience: "Guns and Birmingham go together," Telly enthuses, as a posh chap points an expensive shotgun at the sky, a whole thirty-five years before Birmingham would overtake London as the gun crime capital of the United Kingdom. It is quite an odd film, but then Telly Savalas was quite an odd man.

— 47 —

Telly Savalas was born Aristotelis Savalas in Garden City, New York, in 1922, but he would regularly fudge the year of his birth. The son of Greek immigrants—Nick, a restaurant owner, and Christina, an artist—Savalas would use his mother's paintings to decorate the walls of his dressing room when he became a star, and she would continue to exert a strong influence over him for the duration of his career. He was one of five children, and unusually tall and strong. He claimed to have talked his way into the National Guard at age twelve, aided by his older brother, Gus, in order to learn how to drive heavy vehicles, and to have briefly taken up boxing at sixteen until his mother's dislike of violence caused him to quit. As with much of what Savalas shared about his early life, these tales should be approached with a measure of skepticism.

What is true is that he joined the US Army in 1941, reaching the rank of corporal as a member of the 4th Medical Training Regiment, but little is known about his military service. He did receive a Purple Heart, and a damaged finger on his left hand was the most obvious manifestation of injuries he professed to have received in combat, but we only have his word for it. He studied psychology at Columbia University under the GI Bill, but grew disenchanted with his studies, describing them as "seven wasted years." He maintained a particular animosity toward Sigmund Freud, whom he considered "one of the great criminals of the world. . . . The guy blew five or six generations of young people with his ludicrous interpretation of the human personality through sexual terms and motifs."

By then Savalas had met his first wife, Katherine Nicolaides, whom he married in 1948. They named their first child Christina, after Savalas's mother, and Savalas found work as a host on Voice of America, the US State Department's main propaganda network, a broadcasting bulwark against Communism and anti-Americanism. It was the beginning of a media career that would eventually lead Savalas into acting, although he was already on the kind of nodding terms with veracity that would ultimately lead him to Harold Baim's door: he claimed to have won a Peabody Award for the *Your Voice of America* show and is also often credited with another Peabody for his ABC Radio talk show *The Coffeehouse in New York City*, although his name does not appear in the lists of winners for those years.

— 48 —

The end of Savalas's time with ABC in the late 1950s coincided with the disintegration of his marriage, and he left the network to manage a theater in Connecticut. His efforts were unsuccessful, but by then he had met his second wife, Marilyn Gardner, with whom he started a second family. He worked as a teacher to make ends meet before a chance phone call landed him a role in a 1959 New York teleplay entitled "And Bring Home a Baby" on NBC's *Armstrong Circle Theatre*, followed by his film debut in 1961's *Mad Dog Coll*. He would come to be mentored by Burt Lancaster, who cast him as Feto Gomez in *Birdman of Alcatraz* (1962), in which Lancaster starred as Robert Stroud, the imprisoned avian expert of the film's title. Unfortunately, Savalas suffered from an acute fear of flying—he preferred to drive everywhere—so Lancaster had to get him drunk in order to put him on the plane to the film's Alcatraz set.

At this point, Savalas was still in possession of a head of hair, until George Stevens appeared on the scene. Stevens was casting his biblical epic *The Greatest Story Ever Told* (1965) and wanted Savalas to play the part of Pontius Pilate. Stevens's vision for the character involved a shaved head, and he was unwilling to compromise: a bald skullcap wouldn't suffice. Savalas was concerned that his hair wouldn't grow back, but he was also worried about the effect his enforced baldness might have on his young children, so they came to the set to watch him being shaved, and it didn't bother them one bit.

As a Christian, Savalas invested a great deal of himself in Pilate and always maintained it was the role of which he was proudest. Unfortunately, the picture tanked and, like Christ, was crucified by critics, though Savalas escaped the worst of the carnage, which was one of the benefits of being a character actor. No film would stand or fall on his performance, and the chances of escaping with his dignity intact would therefore be greater.

— 49 —

Savalas could have regrown his hair after Stevens was done with him, but he didn't have time. He was now in demand as an actor and smart enough to keep working while the opportunities were available. He also came to realize that his baldness marked him out in a crowded field, giving an extra edge to the psychopath roles that were quickly becoming his bread and butter. He still entertained hopes of being a handsome male lead in the Paul Newman/Rock Hudson mold—like his future costar Christopher Lee, it could be said of Savalas, as we put it in Ireland, that he always had a great welcome for himself—but this was not to be his destiny.

In 1966 he headed to England to star in Robert Aldrich's $5 million adaptation of *The Dirty Dozen*, after Jack Palance, the first choice for the role of Maggott, declined it over discomfort with the more distasteful aspects of the character, who is depicted as both a rapist and a racist. While *The Dirty Dozen* could easily have been filmed in the US, British subsidies meant it was cheaper to make in the UK. The production was occasionally fraught, mostly due to testosterone-fueled clashes of ego, as recounted in Dwayne Epstein's book *Killin' Generals* (2023). "Telly felt he was the star of the movie," remembered Jim Brown, who played Robert Jefferson in the film. "When his character Maggott got killed, Telly told me, 'Well, Maggott got killed. This movie is over.' " The film's lead actor, Lee Marvin, was often drunk, and a fire destroyed one of the sets, but by the end of filming, Savalas had become a committed Europhile. He liked London, and developed a fondness for its casinos, but he also had an eye for its women, and they for him: his *Dirty Dozen* costar Dora Reisser described him as "the most charming, intelligent man."

Although he publicly portrayed himself as a devoted husband and father, committed to Marilyn and his daughters back home, Savalas began an affair with a British actress, Sally Adams, during the filming of *The Dirty Dozen*, and lived with her when he was in London. Eventually, they would have a son, Nicholas, together, but Savalas would not openly acknowledge the relationship for seven years, and then only when it was revealed by the tabloid press. He maintained that he and Marilyn had been separated for many years, and "because I was working in Europe, I couldn't clear up the legal status." It is more probable that he was very much enjoying this clandestine extramarital affair, one easily concealed from his wife with the excuse of filming abroad.

And film work was readily available to him in Europe. The Italian and Spanish film industries were in resurgence, and American actors were regarded as eminently bankable. Savalas dabbled in comedy, and started dividing his time between Rome and London, where he could be close to Adams and enhance his reputation as a committed gambler. On one occasion, according to Marsha Daly's 1975 biography of Savalas, he won $125,000 in a single sitting at a Mayfair casino, only to lose $117,000 of it because he was unable to walk away from the table. On the set of *The Dirty Dozen*, a poker game ran almost continuously from April to September 1966, with Savalas, Charles Bronson, and Clint Walker among the more committed participants. The stakes were high. One of the British actors, Colin Maitland, lost $1,000 in ten minutes, the equivalent of almost $10,000 today, and never played again.

This kind of profligacy needed to be fed, so Savalas decamped to Spain to make quickie westerns such as *Land Raiders* (1969) and *A Town Called Bastard* (1971), in addition to a high-profile turn as Ernst Stavro Blofeld in the sixth James Bond outing, 1969's *On Her Majesty's Secret Service*, taking over the role from Donald Pleasence. But TV executives back in the US were also paying attention, noting Savalas's popularity and versatility. In time, this interest would lead to the part that would make him most famous: NYPD lieutenant Theo Kojak.

"One day they will realize I can do a romantic story," Savalas would later complain, even amid the wealth and fame that *Kojak* would bring him. "Forget the gorilla exterior. Inside is a sixteen-year-old Romeo."

But in 1971, American producer Bernard Gordon wasn't interested in the sixteen-year-old Romeo inside Telly Savalas. Instead, he had something much older and deadlier in mind.

— 50 —

In the fall of 1947, seventy-nine Hollywood writers, directors, and producers were subpoenaed to appear before the House Un-American Activities Committee (HUAC) in Washington, DC, forty-three of whom were put on the witness list. Formed in 1938, HUAC was a committee of the House of Representatives tasked with investigating subversive activities by suspected communist and fascist sympathizers. After the war, HUAC's focus narrowed to concentrate almost wholly on communism, and in 1947 it commenced a series of hearings into possible communist influences in Hollywood.

In truth, left-wing sympathies were prevalent in Hollywood, then as now, but not everyone went so far as to join the Communist Party of the United States of America (CPUSA). The comedian Charlie Chaplin, thanks in no small part to the deficiencies of his childhood, said that he was "ever haunted by a spirit, the spirit of poverty, the spirit of privation," and thought communism might create a fairer society. He was also a committed anti-fascist, with the result that he spoke at events backed by communists or shared a stage with them. "I am not a Communist," he announced in 1942, "but I am proud to say that I feel pretty pro-Communist." This wasn't enough to stop the FBI from assembling a nearly two-thousand-page dossier on Chaplin because of his political beliefs, ultimately forcing him into a twenty-year European exile, although his sexual behavior, including a predilection for underage girls, also did him few favors.

Those first forty-three individuals, Chaplin among them, were alleged to have introduced communist propaganda into their films, claims that were largely unsubstantiated and therefore difficult to defend oneself against. Nineteen of those subpoenaed refused to cooperate with HUAC; of the nineteen, ten appeared before the committee and used the protections offered by the First Amendment to refuse to answer questions about their political beliefs or the political convictions of colleagues. They were charged with contempt and convicted, fined, and jailed. Eric Johnston, the president of the Motion Picture Association of America, announced that the "Hollywood Ten," as they became known, were to be fired or suspended, and would not work in Hollywood again until they had purged themselves of their contempt.

It was the beginning of the Hollywood blacklist, which would ultimately blight the careers of some three hundred individuals until the mid-1960s, with repercussions that continue to divide the film community to this day. In 1999, the Academy of Motion Picture Arts and Sciences chose to award an honorary Oscar for lifetime achievement to the director Elia Kazan, a former member of the Communist Party who, in 1952, had testified before the committee. Under pressure to cooperate—Kazan was one of the most important witnesses summoned before HUAC, and the committee was determined to secure his testimony—he named eight actors who had been fellow communist activists when he was part of New York's Group Theatre in the 1930s and '40s.

It was a pivotal moment in the hearings. Kazan was the most acclaimed theater director of his day, responsible for the first stage productions of Tennessee Williams's *A Streetcar Named Desire* (1947) and Arthur Miller's *Death of a Salesman* (1949), and an Oscar winner for the 1947 film *Gentleman's Agreement*. Because of his commercial success and critical reputation, it was felt by many that Kazan could safely have defied the committee and refused to name names, presenting an example to others in the process. Instead, Kazan caved, and two years later would win a second Best Director Oscar for *On the Waterfront* (1954), perhaps the most famous defense of snitching in cinema history. Kazan justified his testimony on the basis that it reflected his "true self," arguing "secrecy serves the Communists." (Arthur Miller, Kazan's former friend and collaborator, acidly responded that "the public exposure of a bunch of actors who had not been politically connected for years would never push one Red Chinaman out of the Forbidden City, or a single Russian out of Warsaw or Budapest.")

The move to honor Kazan at the 1999 Oscars exposed the lingering bitterness over events surrounding the blacklist. A full-page ad in *Variety* condemned the Academy's decision, and when a frail Kazan arrived onstage to receive his award from Martin Scorsese and Robert De Niro, many of those present, including the actors Nick Nolte and Ed Harris, refused to applaud.

But in an interview with the *New York Times* (February 6, 2018), the actor Christopher Plummer offered a more compassionate view of Kazan's conduct. Plummer had worked with Kazan—or "Gadge," as he was known—on the 1958 play *J.B.*, which earned the actor his first Tony nomination. Plummer regarded the experience as one of the "great moments" of his life, and had this to say about Kazan's naming names to HUAC: "You see, he was an immigrant, and really I think maybe he was scared. So as hard as it is, it might seem pitiable in a way that someone with such authority and courage in the theater could be timid and scared about his position in the United States."

Perhaps the greatest irony of the HUAC hearings is that, in relying on denunciation as an integral part of its investigative process, the committee was replicating the very systems used in the Soviet Union during the Red Terror. As Hannah Arendt puts it in *The Origins of Totalitarianism* (1951):

> The consequence of the simple and ingenious device of "guilt by association" is that as soon as a man is accused, his former friends are transformed immediately into his bitterest enemies; in order to save their own skins, they volunteer information and rush in with denunciations to corroborate the nonexistent evi-

dence against him; this obviously is the only way to prove their own trustworthiness.

— 51 —

Among those at the forefront of the campaign to deny Kazan his honorary Academy Award was Bernard Gordon, whose experience of the blacklist demonstrates its insidious, pernicious nature.

In 1952, Gordon, a union activist and former member of the Communist Party, was beginning to make a name for himself as a screenwriter. (Though few in Hollywood rated writers, let alone screenwriters. Jack Warner, for whom Gordon worked at one point, referred to all writers as "shmucks with typewriters.") Gordon was conscious of the threat posed to his career by his political leanings, which were familiar to many in Hollywood. The film of his first produced screenplay, *Flesh and Fury* (1952), starring a then largely unknown Tony Curtis, had only recently been released when Gordon was subpoenaed to appear before the committee. It would duly emerge that the writer and producer William Alland, who provided the original story for *Flesh and Fury*, had named Gordon in the course of testimony before HUAC in 1953. (Alland was completely without principle when it came to the hearings: he gave up his ex-wife, the mother of his daughter, to the committee, and would later try to convince Gordon to turn informer.) Charles Katz, one of the attorneys representing the "unfriendly witnesses"—those who refused to cooperate with HUAC—had objected to Alland's testimony, protesting that Gordon was not present and should be permitted the opportunity to defend himself. Gordon was subpoenaed, but his appearance before HUAC was then postponed, leaving him in limbo. Alland's allegations were enough to destroy Gordon's career, and he became one of those banned from employment by the major studios.

With a wife and young daughter to support, Gordon took a job as, in his own words, "the world's worst plastics salesman," until the producer Charles Schneer approached him to write a western. Gordon assumed that Schneer knew about his blacklisting; if he did, Schneer elected not to mention it. *The Law vs. Billy the Kid* (1954) became the first of a series of pictures that Gordon would write under the pseudonym "Raymond T. Marcus," after his boss at the plastics company. It says much for the lack of communication between the institutions of American government that he did so while retaining his original Social Security number. When the blacklist ended, that number provided the evidence Gordon needed to claim proper credit for the pseudonymously written films, credit that other blacklisted writers struggled for years to be awarded.

Between film assignments, Gordon was employed as a private investigator, and also wrote for television, where it was easier to work under the radar. He even scripted *Hellcats of the Navy* (1957), which starred the rabidly anti-communist Ronald Reagan, who had been a friendly witness before HUAC. At that time, most of Hollywood was unaware of the extent of Reagan's cooperation with the FBI during his presidency of the Screen Actors Guild, when he would regularly share with the feds the names of SAG members suspected of communist sympathies.

Hellcats of the Navy was apparently Reagan's favorite among his films and was screened regularly at the White House during his presidency, which gave Gordon considerable satisfaction. "Imagine: him making love to Nancy, speaking my words," Gordon told the journalist Hank Rosenfeld of the *Los Angeles Times* in 2000. "I never had the heart to tell him that his favorite movie was written by a blacklisted writer."

— 52 —

Gordon's connection with Spain and its film production facilities began in 1960, when he was offered $5,000 by the producer Philip

Yordan to work on the script for a proposed screen adaptation of John Wyndham's 1951 sci-fi novel *The Day of the Triffids*. Yordan was, by any measure, a fishy character. A former Chicago lawyer, he had reputedly helped a pair of feuding Chicago fraudsters escape conviction in 1936 by accepting a subpoena on their behalf before taking flight to California. As a token of their gratitude, the fraudsters gave Yordan $35,000 and promised him a further $50 a week while he tried to establish a career in writing. In this, Yordan was mostly unsuccessful, and following the Japanese attack on Pearl Harbor in 1941, he was told to report for duty at an airfield in Bakersfield to train air force recruits in navigation and meteorology, Yordan having rapidly secured a qualification in this area to avoid more dangerous service.

The owner of the airfield proved to be quite the anti-Semite, which worked to Yordan's advantage. They agreed between them that Yordan should remove his Jewish self from the airfield to find employment elsewhere, and the airfield's owner would keep Yordan's pay in return for saying nothing to the authorities about his absence. Yordan began writing for the King brothers, slot machine suppliers turned bargain-basement film producers, and never looked back. His first big hit was *Dillinger* (1945), and he won an Oscar for Best Story for *Broken Lance* (1954), but by then Yordan had developed a nice racket in taking salaries from multiple studios for the same script, problems with this arrangement arising only when it came time to deliver the screenplays in question. Yordan was also happy to employ surrogates to write for him while he claimed the credit, which made him a useful front for blacklisted writers.

Yordan finally became unemployable in Hollywood and left for Europe to work for the producer Samuel Bronston, who had elected to make Spain the base for his film epics to keep costs down, while Yordan was also developing his own projects, including *The Day of the Triffids*. Under Bronston, Yordan would work on scripts for *King of Kings* (1961), *El Cid* (1961), and *55 Days at Peking* (1963), among others, but the extent of his actual authorial input may have been limited to keeping an eye on his factory of proxy writers ensconced on the top floor of the Madrid Hilton. In return, Bronston paid Yordan $300,000 per script and a cut of the profits. "Philip Yordan has never written more than a sentence in his life," Ben Maddow, one of the factory writers, claimed in an interview with the author Patrick McGilligan. "He's incapable of writing."

Bronston would ultimately go bust, but Yordan continued to produce films in Europe and the United States. He remained admirably committed to a life on the peripheries of legality: in 1984, while a defense witness at a murder conspiracy trial in Florida, he was caught trying to dispose of crucial documents in a toilet in the court building.

— 53 —

So Bernard Gordon settled in Europe—first in Paris, then Madrid—bringing over his wife and daughter to join him, and traveled between France and Spain to work on the films being made by Yordan and Bronston, either individually or together. But Gordon did not always receive a writing credit, and when he did, it was shared with Yordan.

The Day of the Triffids was released in 1963, but its tortured path to the screen alerted Gordon to the flaws in Yordan's approach to filmmaking. Yordan would cut so many corners during production, and pinch so many pennies, that it would cost more to fix the flaws in postproduction than sensibly budgeting to begin with might have done. Nevertheless, their relationship enabled Gordon to work with directors such as Nicholas Ray (*King of Kings*), Anthony Mann (*El Cid*), and Henry Hathaway (*Circus World*, 1964), if not on their best films. Gordon was earning $2,000 a week, owned two cars, and vacationed in St. Moritz. For him, the cloud of the blacklist had developed an appealing silver lining.

Samuel Bronston's operation collapsed following the box-office failure of *The Fall of the Roman Empire* (1964), but Yordan and Gordon continued to hustle. Gordon had also been working for some time with his childhood friend Julian Zimet, who was another victim of the blacklist. Zimet had attended City College of New York with Gordon in the 1930s, before heading to Hollywood to become a script reader at Republic Pictures, a Poverty Row studio that specialized in churning out cheap genre pictures. He served in the Second World War, but on his return found Republic no longer had a job for him and turned to screenwriting to make ends meet, producing western scripts for Roy Rogers, Alan Ladd, and Gene Autry, until his blacklisting made him unemployable. By 1955, he was living an impoverished existence in Mexico, where he had begun work on a novel titled *The Young Lovers*, which would be published later that year under the pen name Julian Halevy, the pseudonym he would continue to use into the 1970s. *The Young Lovers* was reasonably successful, and spawned a film version starring Peter Fonda, released in 1964.

Zimet reunited with Gordon for the screenplay of *The Case Against Brooklyn* (1958), which led him to the door of Philip Yordan. Together, Zimet and Gordon also wrote the generally derided *Custer of the West* (1967), with Costa del Sol serving as Little Big Horn, and Zimet wrestled uncredited with the script for the volcano drama *Krakatoa*, which would be released in 1969, to Gordon's eternal embarrassment, as *Krakatoa: East of Java*, despite Krakatoa actually being west of Java.

— 54 —

Bernard Gordon returned to the United States in 1967. The blacklist was effectively over by then, although since it had never officially existed, the concept of an ending was difficult to contextualize. The damage it had caused to the careers of hundreds of professionals could not easily be undone, and in many cases never was. As Gordon put it in his memoir, *Hollywood Exile, or How I Learned to Love the Blacklist* (1999):

> After almost twenty years of not working in the industry (or working under pseudonyms or fronts), after almost a working lifetime as salespeople, bartenders, or whatever, after such a long time of being in the closet and out of the circuit, most of the affected people never did get back to work.

The aftereffects were evident not only in the wreckage of lives but also in the enduring animosity that would lead, three decades later, to the Kazan protests. As Gordon and his wife settled into their new home above Sunset Strip, they were visited by FBI agents, who quizzed them about some of their acquaintances in Europe, indicating that the agency's interest in Gordon had persisted while he was abroad. The agents suggested that Gordon might be investigated for treason, at which point he sensibly showed them the door, although his lawyer later pointed out that he shouldn't have admitted them in the first place. Gordon heard nothing more about it, but it was hardly the kind of welcome he had hoped for after his years in the wilderness.

— 55 —

Philip Yordan, meanwhile, had found new financing in England, and he and his partners acquired land at Daganzo, outside Madrid, where they began building a studio complex, to be named Madrid 70 Studios. Yordan approached Bernard Gordon, who was finding it hard to sell his scripts in the US, to help with developing projects for the Spanish base. Gordon would not receive a salary; instead, he would be a producer alongside Yordan, and earn a piece of every picture. If the films were a success, Gordon would make far more than he would as a salaried employee. Gordon took the deal, and by 1970 was back in Madrid, attempting to salvage the studio's first film, *A Town Called Bastard*, starring Robert Shaw and Telly Savalas, and preparing for work on the second, *Captain Apache*, with Lee Van Cleef.

Van Cleef had made his name as a villain on television and in films, mostly westerns, including a memorable, wordless debut as the killer Jack Colby in Fred Zinnemann's *High Noon* (1952), but in 1958 he was involved in a car accident that nearly crippled him for life. His first marriage collapsed afterward, and he developed a drinking problem. As the popularity of westerns faded, Van Cleef was reduced to working as a house painter to make ends meet. His salvation came in the form of Sergio Leone, who cast him as the bounty hunter Colonel Douglas Mortimer opposite Clint Eastwood in *For a Few Dollars More* (1965), the sequel to the previous year's hugely successful *A Fistful of Dollars*. The film gave Van Cleef a new career in so-called spaghetti westerns, and he would make more than twenty of them before their era came to an end in the late 1970s.

Gordon didn't care much for Van Cleef, particularly as the actor was being paid $300,000 for two pictures to be filmed back-to-back—which was hardly chump change—yet appeared intent on being, in Gordon's words, "sullen," and "a clod." For one scene in *Captain Apache*, Van Cleef was required to simulate sex with the female lead, Carroll Baker, with both of them naked under the covers.

"What if I get an erection?" Van Cleef inquired worriedly of one of the producers, Milton Sperling.

"Fuck her," advised Sperling.

While all this was going on, Yordan busied himself with purchasing the rights to foreign films, usually westerns, that could be dubbed quickly into English for the American market, and arranging coproduction deals with the French and Italians, a complex business that involved ensuring each film hired sufficient workers from the coproducing country, or used enough of its facilities, to gain "nationality," which meant the picture would be considered a local product. It could therefore avail of tax breaks and favorable distribution deals while not being subject to any restrictions on non-domestic product.

With *Captain Apache* (1971) in the bag, the producers still had to find another project to justify their investment in Van Cleef. Yordan dug up *Bad Man's River*, a western he had conspicuously failed to sell to anyone in Hollywood, and engaged in a hasty rewrite that did nothing to improve it. Gordon identified *Bad Man's River* as the stinker it was, but Van Cleef was on his way from America and production needed to commence so Yordan could gain access to the budget and pay his bills. Gordon knew no director in his right mind would take on *Bad Man's River* in its existing form, but the task of finding someone who might was made marginally easier by the necessity of hiring a Spanish director to ensure Spanish nationality for the film.

A name was suggested: Eugenio Martín.

— 56 —

Eugenio Martín Márquez was born in the Spanish-controlled North African port city of Ceuta in May 1925. His earliest memories were of police sympathetic to the Spanish Nationalists stopping and frisking anyone who looked like a worker, and therefore a leftist, as the country teetered on the verge of civil war in 1936. The uprising, when it came, began in Spanish Morocco, so Ceuta was immediately on the front line. A few days after the conflict commenced, the Republican battleship *Jaime I* bombed the Francoist Ceuta. When interviewed almost seventy years later, Martín could still recall the sight of blood on the pavement near the door of his home where a child had been killed in the shelling.

The post–civil war period was difficult for Martín's family, as it was for many in Spain. Although he loved the cinema, he could rarely afford to go and learned to cherish the memory of those films he was fortunate enough to see, recounting their details to entertain his friends. "I would tell the movie in multiple ways," he told the writers Carlos Aguilar and Anita Haas for their book *Eugenio Martín, autor para todos los géneros* (2008), "making changes in the story every time so they'd believe it was another, and another, and another, usually within the same genre. I saw that they were listening to me with great interest, and over time I started to think I had some innate storytelling skill, the ability to create a story as I told it."

Later, the adolescent Martín would apply his zeal for stories to religious broadcasting, writing tales for radio in association with Catholic Action, an international lay organization formed in the nineteenth century to promote Catholic teaching and counteract anticlericalism. Only when his family moved to Granada, a more left-wing and cultured environment than Ceuta, did Martín begin to shake off the influence of Franco and the Church. He attended university in the city, supporting himself by teaching, and began reading proscribed writers such as Federico García Lorca and León Felipe. He was, he said, "becoming more skeptical, agnostic, or whatever you want to call it." In 1949, Martín even published a book of his own, a volume of poetry entitled *On Any Street*, and always regretted not attempting a work of fiction, regarding his lack of narrative experience as one of his "worst shortcomings" as a filmmaker.

Martín's love of film flourished in Granada, but he would ultimately fail to complete his studies. He established a cinema club in one of the university's lecture halls, only to close it in a rage when the Jesuit authorities attempted to censor the club's offerings, though the rector of the college, Luis Sánchez Agesta, was more tolerant of the young student's efforts. Still, Martín was growing increasingly anti-fascist in his convictions and decided to leave Spain for Mexico to join other exiles from Franco, once he had completed his compulsory military service. At this point, Sánchez Agesta intervened, and suggested that Martín might be better off studying cinema. To assist him, the rector offered Martín a scholarship to Madrid's exotically named Institute of Cinematic Investigation and Experiences, which he accepted, and in the years that followed Martín would accrue qualifications in art history and information sciences, specializing in images. Information sciences, he would declare ruefully, did him no good at all.

— 57 —

Following a series of short films, Martín made his full-length Spanish debut in 1957 with *Despedido de soltero* (Bachelor Party), which he also cowrote. Unfortunately, according to *A History of Spanish Film*, Martín didn't manage "to create a film capable of satisfying the least demanding." Aided by his facility with the English language, he also worked as an assistant to the soon-to-be Hammer stalwart Terence Young on *Zarak* (1957), which was making use of Spain as an inexpensive location, and Martín would follow this with stints on various other Anglo-Spanish coproductions helmed by the likes of Roy Ward Baker, Nathan Juran, and, most notably, Nicholas Ray, including *King of Kings*, which brought Martín into the orbit of Philip Yordan.

Meanwhile, Martín continued to work on his own films as a director. He made the pirate picture *Los corsarios del Caribe* (Conqueror of Maracaibo) in 1961, with funding from the extreme right-wing Catholic institution Opus Dei, which left him to his own devices on the condition that he made sure the finished product was devoid of sex. His best film of this period is generally regarded as *Hipnosis* (or *Dummy of Death*, as it was titled in the UK), a 1962 black-and-white thriller about a malevolent ventriloquist's dummy that Martín again also cowrote. Perhaps to make up for the kicking it gave *Despedido de soltero*, *A History of Spanish Film* describes *Hip-*

nosis as "a crime movie in which all the ingredients have been handled with care" and "a work that honours our cinema."

But it would be the western that brought Martín his first real taste of significant critical acclaim. In 1966, at the instigation of his former screenwriting lecturer, José G. Maesso—an associate of Sergio Corbucci, director of the best non–Sergio Leone spaghetti western, 1968's *The Great Silence*—Martín signed on to direct *El precio de un hombre*, better known by its US title, *The Bounty Killer*, but also sometimes referred to as *The Ugly Ones*. Adapted from a novel by Marvin H. Albert, the film is a compelling siege western in which Luke Chilson (played by British actor Richard Wyler) attempts to claim the bounty on the outlaw José Gómez (Cuban actor Tómas Milian, in a career-making performance), a folk hero whose actions gradually cause the people to turn against him in favor of the hunter.

Martín might have hoped that *The Bounty Killer* would lead to further westerns, but a falling-out among the producers meant that his next three films were instead musicals, one of which starred the singer Julio Iglesias, who hardly stretched himself by playing a character also named Julio Iglesias.

But Philip Yordan hadn't forgotten Martín, and by the early 1970s he had a western ready to go. Yordan had seen *Hipnosis*, liked it, and signed the director to a three-picture deal. Martín duly started work on Yordan's western, *Bad Man's River*.

And quickly wished he hadn't.

—58—

Bad Man's River was Bernard Gordon's producing debut. He and Eugenío Martín got on well once the latter came to accept that Philip Yordan was about as trustworthy as a scorpion, and Gordon was the one he needed on his side when it came to rewrites and decision-making. For both Gordon and Martín, the film would prove to be a difficult experience. Yordan had no script ready, only an early treatment based on an aborted Nicolas Ray project entitled *Badman*, but Martín refused to begin filming without one, so three weeks were spent cobbling together something that vaguely resembled a screenplay, as long as one didn't examine it too closely.

Two days before he was due to start work, the British actor James Mason, who was cast as the villain, Montero, had still not been in touch with the producers, and no one knew if he would even show up. Gordon contacted the actor in Switzerland, but Mason claimed never to have heard of him. After some cajoling, Mason agreed to catch a flight from Geneva to Spain, and arrived in time to have a wardrobe fitting before his first scenes.

Mason's career was firmly in the doldrums, but he had also entered a kind of second adolescence. He grew his hair long and commenced a relationship with the much younger Clarissa Kaye, an Australian actress with whom he had performed a sex scene in Michael Powell's 1969 film *Age of Consent* and whom he would soon marry. Mason's former sister-in-law from his first marriage described him as "transformed, reborn, his joy in living restored, his confidence buoyant," thanks to Kaye.

Which was all well and good, but Mason's newfound romantic bliss appeared to have clouded his critical faculties, or perhaps he just needed money very badly after his divorce from his first wife, Pamela Kellino. In 1970, he played a half-Chinese, half-Mexican criminal mastermind in *The Yin and the Yang of Mr. Go*, directed by the actor Burgess Meredith and filmed partly in Hong Kong. Mason and Meredith couldn't stand each other and eventually ceased communicating both on and off the set. The budget ran out, the investors vanished, and many of the cast and crew were left waiting for payments that would never be made. The film was finally released on video years later, with narration and animated scenes added in an effort to make some sense of what remained. Also in 1970, another project, this time the Italian film *Crepa padro, crepa tranquillo*, similarly failed to reach completion before Mason, now on a roll, added to his filmography a Charles Bronson europudding, *De la part des copains* (Cold Sweat), a picture so poor, even allowing for Bronson's pragmatic/erratic career choices, that it wouldn't receive a US release until four years later.

In time, a resurgance would come for Mason—he still had *Cross of Iron* (1977), *Heaven Can Wait* (1978), *The Boys from Brazil* (1978), and *The Verdict* (1982) ahead of him, as well as the TV adaptation of Stephen King's *Salem's Lot* (1979)—but for the present he was in Spain, Kaye in tow, for another shambles, in which he would put on a Mexican accent while consoling himself with the check, and the likelihood that the film would never be seen anywhere outside mainland Europe. Later, Mason would mournfully reflect, "When shooting a film in Spain, one should never say to oneself, 'Never mind, no one is going to see it,' because that will be just the film the Rank Organisation choose to release in England."

To add to the production's challenges, the female lead, Gina Lollobrigida, felt she was slumming by accepting $50,000 to star in a western, especially when the money failed to appear in her account with one day of filming still to go; and Lee Van Cleef, the final member of the film's major acting trinity, initially refused to ride a horse, which was tricky for a western. Van Cleef was not a fan of horses at the best of times, and not a fan of Bernard Gordon at any time. He spent the production complaining about the cold and envying what he regarded as the preferential treatment being offered to Mason, but was professional enough not to cause serious trouble. Apart from some dialogue looping for *Captain Apache* in April of that year, Van Cleef and Gordon would never work together again.

The script for *Bad Man's River*, credited to Philip Yordan and "Gene Martin" (Eugenio Martín's name is also anglicized for his director's credit), is a peculiar mix of comedy and action, since Yordan's solution to structural problems was to drop in some comic business, leaving the original difficulties unresolved. The finished effort has an intrusive soundtrack, and none of the principal cast is better than adequate, but Martín's direction isn't entirely terrible. The film is still rubbish, though.

— 59 —

After *Bad Man's River*, everyone involved might have been forgiven for never wanting to meet again. As Martín would observe of his three-picture deal, "The first script didn't exist, the second one was terrible, and the third one was a work in progress." But script deficiencies, or even the nonexistence of any script, were no obstacle to progress, and Gordon, Yordan, and Martín moved straight to their next project, a film about a raid by the Mexican revolutionary Pancho Villa on the town of Columbus, New Mexico, on March 9, 1916. Had he been around, Villa might have appreciated the intention, if not the final product. Villa was an early convert to the power of moving pictures, and in 1914 signed a contract with the Mutual Film Company permitting his battles to be filmed, a deal referenced early in *Pancho Villa* when he and his men watch scenes of their attack on Durango.

Yordan agreed to release the pathetic sum of $1,000 a month to develop a script. Gordon's friend Julian Zimet continued to flounder and consented to write the screenplay while living in Gordon's spare bedroom, but the result was even worse than the script for *Bad Man's River*. Still, Yordan had now settled in Britain, which at least meant that *Pancho Villa* would be the first film on which Gordon had free rein as a producer without the threat of Yordan's direct interference.

The picture was cast before the script was completed, with Telly Savalas, who had starred in *A Town Called Bastard* for Yordan, signing on as Villa. He was joined by one of his costars from *The Dirty Dozen*, Clint Walker, who, two months earlier, in May 1971, had narrowly avoided death when a ski pole pierced his heart at the Mammoth Mountain resort in California, causing him to immediately embrace religion; and the former star of TV's *The Rifleman*, Chuck

Connors, a staunch Republican and supporter of the Vietnam War, who was also a huge star in the Soviet Union, where *The Rifleman* was one of the few American shows permitted to be shown. (The Soviet premier, Leonid Brezhnev, was such a fan of the actor that Connors wanted to attend his funeral in Moscow in 1982 but was refused permission to travel with the US delegation.)

The climax of the film would involve a train chase, with Savalas's Villa in one locomotive being pursued by Connors, as Colonel Wilcox, in another. Two radio-controlled miniature trains, each about six feet long, were built in London specially for the production before being shipped to Spain, where suitable tracks had been constructed at the studio. This expense would become crucial when a decision had to be made about Yordan and Co.'s next film.

For now, though, *Pancho Villa* was the project—and problem—in hand. Savalas was a pragmatist, and happy to be earning decent money, since he was by now juggling one ex-wife and a child from that marriage; a wife and two more daughters by this marriage; a mistress in London; and a heavy gambling habit. But Savalas was also bald, which represented an obstacle to progress, as Pancho Villa was most certainly *not* bald. A hairpiece was suggested, but it seemed pointless to cast Telly Savalas only to conceal his distinguishing feature. Finally, it was decided to incorporate into the script an opening scene in which Villa's head is forcibly shaved. "You know, I look more interesting this way, more intelligent," Villa announces upon viewing his freshly shorn head. "Like a professor."

Savalas made the most of his leisure hours. According to Bernard Gordon, he spent his downtime drinking and enjoying the company of women, assisted by a one-legged factotum who would scout local bars for suitable female company to introduce to his boss. Savalas settled into a comfortable threesome with a pair of English girls, perhaps because they reminded him of Sally Adams back in London—or perhaps not. When he wasn't boozing, having sex with his English conquests, or gambling, Savalas amused himself by riding on top of the period train being used for some of the action and baiting Clint Walker, who most certainly wasn't boozing, having sex with English girls, or gambling now that he was right with Jesus.

Having finished his scenes, Savalas headed to Rome to film Alberto De Martino's *I familiari delle vittime non saranno avvertiti* (or *Crime Boss*, to give it its more manageable 1972 US title). Unfortunately, Gordon required Savalas to return to Spain for some close-ups and didn't have enough money to pay the actor for the extra days. Savalas asked for three first-class roundtrip tickets from Rome to Madrid in lieu, suggesting that a) he might not have been alone in the Eternal City and b) his stamina remained impressive. Savalas and Gordon settled on two first-class tickets, presumably leaving one unhappy concubine back in Rome.

I've tried to watch *Pancho Villa*, but it's quite awful. Savalas doesn't even attempt to moderate his New York accent, making him the only Garden City revolutionary on the team. Standing six-six, with a torso like a refrigerator, Clint Walker is impressively built but acts as though speaking and walking are two actions that have never previously been demanded of him simultaneously. Martín's direction makes his work on *Bad Man's River* look practically Kubrickian in its attention to detail. The model trains are the best things in it, and having spent so much money on their construction, Yordan was determined they should not go to waste.

— 60 —

Which brings us, at last, to a viewing of *Horror Express*. I'm in my office, in the house in which I have lived and worked since 2007. Perhaps I should have returned to my childhood home for this, but so much has changed there since I first watched the film. My father is dead, that massive television set is no more, and—more to the point—I am different. Like those Swiss mercenaries of old, whatever I yearn for is as much within as without, and this process of research and writing has already evoked feelings and recollections without the necessity of replicating scenes from my youth. This may be the beauty of memory, of nostalgia: whatever we seek is already there. We carry it with us. We carry it in our heart.

III
THE AUTOPSY

— 61 —

0:00

Horror Express doesn't mess about with the viewer's expectations. The first sound one hears over a dark screen, just before the titles begin to roll, is the mournful whistle of a steam train, followed by the rumble of its wheels against the tracks. The screen is lit by what is intended to represent, at least in part, the main headlight of a locomotive engine, but it's distorted and slightly refracted, and changes position throughout the entire title sequence, which is more futuristic than might have been anticipated. Combined with the visual effects, it subtly signals the science-fiction aspect of the film, although these effects prove rather unfortunate for the director of photography, Alejandro Ulloa, whose name is obscured as a result, which must have left him feeling legitimately aggrieved. The credits were created by Iván Zulueta, who later became known as the writer and director of the 1980 Spanish arthouse film *Arrebato* (Rapture), and for designing the posters and promotional materials for Pedro Almodóvar's early films. The locomotive headlight is actually the bulb of the slide projector through which Zulueta fed the film, with a camera placed in front.

The Ennio Morricone–influenced title music is by John Cacavas, who had worked as an assistant to Morton Gould, the Pulitzer Prize–winning American composer and conductor. Gould was that rare creature: a classical composer who was comfortable experimenting with popular idioms, including jazz, folk, and marching band music, and was as happy—if not happier—writing for movies and television as for the symphonic repertoire.

Cacavas, a former music arranger with the US Army Band, and later a second conductor at CBS, came to the film through Telly Savalas. Like Savalas, Cacavas was the son of a Greek emigrant father, and the two men became friends after meeting accidentally in London in the early 1970s. Savalas invited Cacavas to his hotel room to hear some of the actor's musical recordings, which the composer was forced to admit were "terrible." Cacavas agreed to help improve them if Savalas secured him some film work in return. Savalas recommended the composer to Gordon and Martín, and encouraged them to listen to his compositions, resulting in Cacavas being given his first big break on *Pancho Villa*, for which he composed the song used over the closing credits, "We All End Up the Same," sung by Savalas. It helped that Cacavas was willing to work cheaply to gain a screen credit, which made Yordan amenable to employing him. "All he asked was, 'How much will it cost?' " Martín recalled of his conversation with Yordan about Cacavas. "Since he didn't ask for much, they hired him."

On *Horror Express*, Cacavas was assisted in his efforts by the film's associate producer, Irving Lerner, himself a musician. It was Lerner who suggested that Cacavas compose a fugue to go with the closing sequence of the film, the section of the soundtrack with which the composer professed himself most content. "I spent most of the money on the orchestra," Cacavas remembered of *Horror Express*, "and little left for myself, but in the end, it was the way to go. I had a strange orchestra: I had no violins. There wasn't enough money for a big violin section, but I had four violas and four cellos, which really took their place, and did it very well."

Cacavas would compose the score for the next Lee–Cushing collaboration, *The Satanic Rites of Dracula* (1973), before returning to the United States to commence a long and successful career in Hollywood, principally in the area of television series and made-for-TV movies. In a nice piece of circularity, Cacavas would provide much of the music for *Kojak*, including the series theme for its final season.

2:20

Screenplay by ARNAUD D'USSEAU and JULIAN HALEVY, from an original story by GENE MARTIN

Even before the release of *Pancho Villa*, Philip Yordan had decided that westerns were no longer a saleable proposition, or at least not in the United States, which was a market on which he relied for the profitable distribution of his product. Yordan and his London-based business partner, Ben Fisz, determined that cheap horror pictures might prove more attractive to a variety of distributors worldwide, so these were what their company, Scotia International, would now make.

Scotia's financial affairs were complex, involving not only backers in the UK and the US but also a line of credit with Banco de Bilbao in Spain, and the company was always hustling. It couldn't afford to let its studio space in Madrid lie dormant for any length of time, and believed it was better to be making poor films than no films at all. With this in mind, Yordan summoned Julian Zimet and Arnaud d'Usseau to London to ensure they cranked out the horror script he required.

Bernard Gordon claimed it was his idea to find another use for the miniatures used in *Pancho Villa* and suggested to Yordan the possibility of setting a horror movie on a train: *Murder on the Orient Express*, but with a supernatural tinge. Gordon, by his own account, also came up with the English-language title for the film, but lived to regret it, believing it "sounded cheap and lessened the value of what was otherwise a good effort." Gordon preferred *Pánico en el Transiberiano*, the title given to the film by the Spanish distributors, which is hardly much classier. (In *Euro Gothic*, Jonathan Rigby suggests that *The Plague* was also briefly considered as an alternative title.)

Whatever its genesis, Yordan gave the idea the go-ahead, and a reorganization of the Spanish operation enabled the company to reduce its overheads before filming commenced. While Scotia's westerns had cost about $1 million each to make, Gordon budgeted *Horror Express* at just $300,000, rising to $350,000 once salaries for the British and American stars were taken into account. Gordon was now in sole charge in Madrid, a situation that caused difficulties with the Spanish authorities. Spanish law did not permit foreign ownership of any media, film studios included, but the Daganzo facility was only nominally owned by Spaniards so as to circumvent the regulations and avail of Spanish nationality for tax and export purposes. The reorganization, which included the firing of producer and studio fixer Gregorio Sacristán, temporarily attracted the attention of the Spanish fiscal inspectors. Gordon made himself difficult to find and waited for the storm to blow over.

D'Usseau was recalled to Madrid from London and set to work on a first draft of the script, which involved circus performers on a train at the beginning of the twentieth century. Unfortunately, d'Usseau's script lacked the action and horror that Yordan and Gordon required, and rewrites only compounded the problem. D'Usseau was replaced by Zimet, who brought in the frozen creature, the Trans-Siberian Express, and a hint of science fiction: the idea of the creature as a hiding place for an alien being that had been trapped on Earth.

All this was going on while Martín was shooting *Pancho Villa*, and although he was present for some early production meetings and offered input, his attention was focused on the film already underway. Martín was an intelligent, not untalented director, and must have recognized that, with *Pancho Villa*, he was presiding over an unfolding catastrophe. Like most such cinematic failures, the difficulties could be traced back to the script, which had never been good enough to begin with and wasn't enhanced by Yordan's salvage efforts.

Yordan might have been an Oscar winner, but he had long since ceased to care about the quality of the screenplays for his films—or if he did care, he had learned to live with his shame. What mattered to Yordan was coming up with a product, however poor, that could be manufactured cheaply before being handed over to the distributors who had already paid for the rights to show it. The script was largely incidental; the film would be sold on the basis of a story and the guaranteed presence of a couple of international stars. But if a script is poor to begin with, any director will struggle. Discussing *Bad Man's River* and *Pancho Villa* many years later, Martín concluded: "I blame myself, to some extent, and it's my fault that I couldn't get good movies from bad scripts. That's something only geniuses can do, and that's not me."

Whether even a genius can make a good film from an inferior script is debatable, but what is undeniable is that Martín, although a journeyman, retained a degree of professional pride. This goes some way toward explaining why, with *Pancho Villa* completed and *Horror Express* next on his slate, he began digging in his heels. In September 1971, at a meeting in London attended by all the principals, Martín refused to direct the film unless more work was done on the script.

Yordan was insistent that *Horror Express* should go into production immediately, arguing that even with a better script "it won't make a dime more at the box office." In the end, he was forced to relent or lose his director, but the commitments he had made to the moneymen and distributors meant that filming of *Horror Express*, on a thirty-day schedule, had to be completed by the end of the year. It would have to go before the cameras in November, with whatever script was to hand.

Julian Zimet returned to Madrid with Bernard Gordon, and the rewrites began. Zimet worked on *Horror Express* for another month, but by now he was tired of the project and missing his family in Rome. Zimet went home, but Martín remained unhappy with the script and refused to film its current draft. The long-suffering Zimet was brought back from Rome, arriving in Madrid only after Gordon threatened to hand the script over to another writer, which would have affected Zimet's screen credit. Another ten days were spent hammering the screenplay into a form with which both Zimet and Gordon were content, further delaying filming. There was no way that *Horror Express* would wrap before the end of the year, but it finally had a script.

Martín, by the way, probably had little input into the original story and was credited only to satisfy the quota of Spanish input required by Scotia to reap the financial benefits of coproduction. He would later recall discussing the project on weekends with Gordon while mired in *Pancho Villa* on weekdays, but it seems likely that Zimet, aided by Gordon, did the lion's share of the work.

2:28
Directed by Gene Martin

Despite all the efforts of Zimet and Gordon to produce a satisfactory script, Martín still refused to commit to *Horror Express*. With only three days to go before filming was to due commence, he advised Gordon to hire another director. Martín, it emerged, had scheduled surgery to coincide with the start of production. It appeared that he really, *really* didn't want to make *Horror Express*. Gordon harried him on the nature of his upcoming procedure. Under pressure, Martín admitted that he was going to have his hemorrhoids seen to. Production was postponed for a week so that Martín could sit in comfort. In the second week of December 1971, with his room for maneuver gone, Martín began directing *Horror Express*. The fact that his name is anglicized as "Gene Martin" in the credits to *Horror Express* but remains "Eugenio Martín" for the version titled *Pánico en el transiberiano* indicates a degree of marketing compromise.

2:45
Provincia de Szechuan, CHINA, 1906

Christopher Lee's narration commences, informing us that this is a "true and faithful account" to the Royal Geological Society by Professor Alexander Saxton of events that befell the society's expedition in Manchuria.

The province of Manchuria had a complicated history. It was originally the homeland of the Manchus, who displaced the Ming dynasty to rule China as the Qing dynasty for almost three hundred years, until the early part of the twentieth century. The Manchus attempted to keep their homeland free from the influence of the Han Chinese, the majority ethnic group in China, who made up more than ninety percent of the population. It was a fight the Manchus were always destined to lose, and by the beginning of the twentieth century they were no longer the dominant force in Manchuria.

The Hans were not the only threat to the security of Manchuria. To the north lay the massive Russian territory of Siberia, and from the middle of the nineteenth century the vulnerable Manchus found themselves ceding more and more of their province to Russia. By the 1860s, Manchuria had become divided into two regions: Outer Manchuria, ruled by the Russians, and Inner Manchuria, which remained Chinese, but only under the shadow of increasing Russian influence.

And to the east lay the Japanese, who were growing alarmed by Russia's colonial expansion, particularly when Russian control of Outer Manchuria gave the tsar access to the Sea of Japan. This would ultimately lead to the Russo-Japanese War of 1904–05, during which Chinese guerrillas sided with the Japanese against the Russians, their animosity fueled by memories of Russian military actions against the Chinese during the Boxer Rebellion of 1899–1900. The Russians sued for peace after the defeat of their army at the Battle of Mukden in February–March 1905 and the annihilation of their fleet at the Battle of Tsushima in May, leaving Japan as Inner Manchuria's controlling influence. The defeat further weakened Tsar Nicholas II, who was already dealing with social and political unrest at home, forcing him to share power with a newly formed parliament and sowing the seeds for the Russian Revolution of 1917.

Horror Express, therefore, is set in the immediate aftermath of war.

4:13

Our first glimpse of the creature, which is almost totally concealed by ice, apart from the front section of its skull. Martín's slow reveal is skillful, as Saxton explores a cave system, any stone of which might represent some frozen horror. Cacavas's musical accompaniment is less successful. Once again he nods to Morricone with an eerie whistle, before undoing this good work with the kind of incidental guitar twangs that would become a staple of his scores for *Hawaii Five-O* and *The Bionic Woman*.

"That was a brilliant idea," Martín later noted of the whistling, which becomes a recurring motif in the film, "but I don't remember whose it was. Gordon's or mine, logically. Anyway, in movies it's often very difficult to determine who's responsible for each success. Everybody takes credit, but they usually come out of collaboration, at a point where no one knows to whom each contribution belongs."

This is also our proper introduction to Christopher Lee as Saxton, Lee being the first actor to commence work on the film. Martín maintained that he had originally intended to cast Lee and Cushing in two different films but decided to put them together in *Horror Express*. (Martín, as you may already have gathered, was rarely shy when it comes to the ownership of good ideas.)

According to Bernard Gordon, Lee was pleased with both his role and the script, and arrived on time each day with his lines learned. When not on set, he would sing operatic selections while roaming the hallways of the dressing-room building. He would also prove invaluable in averting disaster following the arrival of Peter Cushing.

5:04

We see the train for the first time. The decision to show a full-sized locomotive early in the film was made in the hope that it would add veracity to the later sequences featuring the miniatures, and it works. Much of the credit for the look of the film goes to Ramiro Gómez, production designer on both the ill-fated *Bad Man's River* and *Pancho Villa*, and the cinematographer Alejandro Ulloa, with whom Martín had worked on *Hipnosis*. Martín described Ulloa as "a very American cinematographer . . . that is, he's very good and very fast, and lights things in a way that makes colors pop and creates beautiful shades between light and shadow. Without the superb work of Gómez and Ulloa, *Pánico en el Transiberiano* would be a much poorer film."

The production was also fortunate to be able to film at the Delicias railway station in the heart of Madrid, which stands in for what the intertitle informs us is "Peking: Russian Concession." I'm not sure that there was a Russian concession in Peking, a concession being a colony of the nation leasing the land, from which Chinese nationals, as well as citizens of other countries, could legally be excluded from entry, residence, or the ownership of property. As far as I can determine, in 1906 the Russians only had concessions in Tianjin, Harbin, and Hankou, but never mind.

Delicias was no longer a transport hub by the time *Horror Express* came to use it and had instead become a storage facility for older locomotives and carriages. This meant that Martín could position his actors on, and around, actual trains, in scenes that might otherwise have necessitated the construction of large sets. The icing on this particular cake was Delicias itself, an impressive nineteenth-century edifice of iron and glass in which Martín was able to film an establishing crane shot of the station that would not have been out of place in an epic. Even just five minutes into the picture, it's difficult to believe *Horror Express* is the work of the same director who gave us *Bad Man's River* and *Pancho Villa*.

The design of Delicias is often erroneously attributed to Gustave Eiffel (Bernard Gordon makes this mistake in *Hollywood Exile*), but Eiffel was involved in the rebuilding of the older Atocha station after the original was almost completely destroyed by fire. Delicias was the work of another Frenchman, Émile Cachelièvre, aided by a Spanish engineer named José Antonio Calleja. It is now home to Madrid's Museo del Ferrocarril (Railway Museum), and should the mood strike, one can have a drink in one of the old dining cars while fantasizing about fighting zombie Cossacks, of which more later.

5:55

Dr. Wells (Peter Cushing) enters.

Shooting had already been ongoing for a week when Cushing arrived in Spain. Bernard Gordon went to the airport to pick him up. Gordon knew of Cushing only by reputation, as the producer was not a fan of horror films and claimed never to have seen any of Cushing's performances.

The desire to distance the production from Hammer, whether contemporaneously or in retrospect, was not unique to Gordon. Martín also informed interviewers that he had never watched a Hammer film before making *Horror Express* and was more influenced by older black-and-white pictures, particularly the classic Universal monster movies; the work of Danish director Carl Theodor Dreyer, responsible for *The Passion of Joan of Arc* (1928) and *Vampyr* (1932); and Jacques Tourneur, director of *Cat People* (1942) and *Night of the Demon* (1957). Both Gordon and Martín may well be telling the truth, but even if they are, the atmosphere conjured by Hammer for its films had already seeped into the visual language of contemporary horror cinema. Whether Gordon and Martín liked it or not, *Horror Express* was a child of Hammer.

But let us return to Bernard Gordon, waiting at the airport for his first sight of Peter Cushing. "He was slender, not tall, very fair, with delicate features—not what I had expected from one of the world's leading actors of horror films," Gordon wrote. "No Frankenstein monster he."

The reader may be forgiven a sigh here. Cushing was, in fact, quite tall, but more to the point, he had never played Frankenstein's creature, only its creator. Gordon published his memoir in 1999, but it seems that after almost thirty years he still hadn't bothered to find out much about one of the two leading men in the best film he would ever produce. Then again, Gordon can be forgiven some residual ambivalence toward Cushing. As they were driving to the studio, the actor told the producer that he had no intention of making the film and had only traveled to Spain because Ben Fisz, Yordan's partner in Scotia International, insisted that Cushing inform Gordon in person of his refusal to work.

Cushing was scheduled to begin filming the following day, which left Gordon no time to find a replacement. When he asked the actor to explain his reasons for bowing out, Cushing claimed to have signed on the basis of the first draft of the script, which had since been substantially rewritten, "but when I read the final one, the one you're shooting, I told Mr. Fisz that I didn't care to work on the film." (Given how poor the first draft had been, one can only conclude that Cushing had latched on to this as an excuse to return home and continue mourning his wife.)

Gordon managed to get Cushing to the studio before calling Ben Fisz in London. Fisz pointed out that Gordon was the producer, and Fisz had fulfilled his duty by getting Cushing to Spain. It was up to Gordon to convince him of the necessity of adhering to his contract. Gordon, sensible man that he was, tracked down Christopher Lee, who agreed to act as an intermediary. Lee advised Gordon that Cushing was always nervous before embarking on a new role, and his reluctance to commit was part of an established routine. The three men gathered at Cushing's hotel later that evening, but the only one to speak at length was Lee, who engaged in a virtual monologue for more than half an hour with the sole aim of putting Cushing at ease, as well as preventing him from making any further complaints about the script. When he was finished, Lee stood, made his farewells, and told Cushing he would see him on set in the morning. Cushing appeared the following day and commenced work. (Eugenio Martín gives a slightly different account of the Lee–Cushing encounter, which excludes Gordon's participation, but the substance remains the same: Lee's intervention was crucial to ensuring that Cushing remained in Spain.)

According to Gordon, Cushing approached him about a week later to apologize for his conduct on the day of his arrival, and to compliment the script and the working environment. By then, Gordon says, he had been made aware of the death of Helen Cushing the previous year and learned that this was the first time the actor had left England since her passing.

If true, this was a considerable oversight on the part of Gordon and his colleagues. Being a producer is undoubtedly a difficult job, but to be unaware of the personal circumstances of one of your lead actors, especially when they involve such a painful bereavement, seems careless to an unusual degree. Ben Fisz was responsible for casting the leading roles in London, and should have alerted Gordon to the extent of the actor's grief, which was common knowledge in the British film community. To Cushing we should allow some latitude: he had signed on for *Horror Express* after Helen's death, perhaps believing himself ready to work abroad again, but when it came time to leave, he must have realized his mistake.

So here, finally, we have Lee and Cushing in their first scene together in *Horror Express*. Lee's Saxton doesn't look overjoyed to learn that he may be sharing a train with Cushing's Dr. Wells. There is history between these two men—in fiction, as in life.

7:35

The first corpse, as a Chinese thief takes an unhealthy interest in Saxton's crate and suffers for it. When the thief's face is uncovered, his eyes have turned white. The effect was achieved by fitting plastic covers under the actor's eyelids. In a nice touch, the final note of Cacavas's accompanying music resembles the steam whistle of a train.

8:10

Saxton—who is being denied a place on the train—and Wells disagree on the ethics of bribery, or "squeeze," as Wells terms it. This may be a bastardization of the Chinese *shòuhuì*, although I wouldn't swear to it. One of the pleasures of *Horror Express* is the interplay between Lee and Cushing, who—once Cushing had settled into his role—spark off each other in a manner that is atypical of most of their other collaborations, where they are frequently presented as being in dramatic opposition.

8:31

As Saxton sweeps the stationmaster's possessions from his desk in an effort to secure passage, an officer appears and announces himself, in clipped British tones, as Captain O'Hagan. He is wearing a Chinese uniform, is accompanied by Chinese soldiers, and says he is in the service of a General Wang. I'm not sure what the historical precedent might be for having a British officer with an Irish name in the service of the Chinese, but I have decided not to worry about it. The actor playing O'Hagan is Allen Russell, sometimes credited as Allen E. Russell. I can find only seven film credits for him, all but one of them in westerns, and none before 1971 or after 1975, which is curious.

8:57

We see a monk kneeling by the body of the dead thief, praying for his soul. This is Pujardov, a Rasputinesque monk who will be revealed as the spiritual advisor to Count and Countess Petrovski. For now, his role is to draw attention to the white eyes of the thief, initially mistaken for a blind man because of the absence of pupils. Pujardov suspects "the work of the devil" and attempts to open the crate containing the missing link but is prevented from doing so by the judicious application of Saxton's umbrella. A Russian policeman, Inspector Mirov (veteran Spanish actor Julio Peña, making his one of his final cinematic appearances), becomes involved, and asks about the contents of the crate. "Fossils," Saxton replies, but Mirov suggests it may contain gold. Pujardov, by contrast, perceives only evil, and is hardened in this conviction when he tries—and fails—to mark with a cross the tarpaulin covering the crate.

Alberto de Mendoza, the tall, charismatic Argentine-born actor who plays Pujardov, starred in more than a hundred films (some sources put it closer to 200) before his death in 2011 at eighty-eight. De Mendoza was orphaned at age five and sent to Spain to be raised by his grandmother, Isidra. She died in 1939, and the teenage de Mendoza returned as a refugee to Argentina, where he became a cabaret dancer, working for ten pesos a dance and a mortadella sandwich. "Many women have abused me," he told an interviewer from *Clarín* shortly before he died—although given that he was six feet tall and quite the looker, this may have been laying it on a bit thick. "I bring to mind the phrase of Gassman, a teacher and friend: When one has come to know life and all its mystery, then comes death. And he was right: when you get to know women and no longer screw up, then you're old."

12:20

The crate is loaded on to the train, supervised by Saxton and Wells, and an audible growl is heard from within. Saxton checks its contents, but is satisfied with what he finds, which is odd given that it has started making noises.

The train pulls out of the station, giving Martín one of his best shots as the beautiful vintage locomotive departs amid clouds of steam, the farewell waves of passengers and bystanders, and the sound of the whistle blowing. This is the last we will see of the real train. From now on, only miniatures will be used, but these early scenes at Delicias have done the heavy lifting for Martín in selling the illusion.

13:54

"And what are you going to astound the scientific world with this time?" Wells asks Saxton, as he secures the crate once again.

"A remarkable fossil," replies Saxton, causing Wells to point out that this can hardly be the case since it's showing definite signs of being alive. Saxton, though, insists otherwise.

"You won't need to feed it, then," says Wells.

"The occupant hasn't eaten in two million years."

"Well, that's one way to economize on food bills," Wells concludes.

Saxton's scientific arrogance is interesting. Lee never played Baron Frankenstein, only his creature, but Saxton's refusal to acknowledge the peculiar events associated with his find comes close to Frankenstein in spirit.

14:39

Saxton meets the beautiful Countess Irina Petrovska, a Pole whose dog is being made anxious by the fossil in the crate. They exchange some banter about England's betrayal of Poland to the Russians in the fifteenth century, which is the kind of thing that passes for foreplay among the better classes. Countess Irina is played by Silvia Eulalia Tortosa López, better known as Silvia Tortosa, who first became known on Spain's TVE as an actor and presenter, went on to have a career as a director, and started her own YouTube channel before dying in March 2024. One of her most famous roles, aside from Petrovska in *Horror Express*, is probably that of Elke Ackerman, a professor at a girls' boarding school, in Amando de Ossorio's *Las Garras de Lorelei* from 1973, which also starred another *Horror Express* alumna, Helga Liné. *Las Garras de Lorelei* was released in the US as *The Swinging Monster*, and later as *When the Screaming Stops*. (It's also available as *The Loreley's Grasp*, although the voice-over on the trailer insists on calling it *The Claws of Loreley*, which means it might be possible to inadvertently see it four times.) Ticket holders for *When the Screaming Stops* were given vomit bags in case of "stomach distress," and the film was re-edited so that the screen flashed blood-red before any scenes deemed especially disturbing. Tortosa retains her dignity by remaining fully clothed throughout.

15:46

The miniature train in all its glory. Various accounts of the film declare it to have been salvaged from the set of *Doctor Zhivago* (1965), or *Nicholas and Alexandra* (1971), but it's definitely one of the *Pancho Villa* models running over some of the thousand meters of track laid in the Madrid studio.

15:52

We're now seeing more of the train's cars and furnishings. The production could not afford to build full-size reproductions of the carriages, and instead relied on a series of lightweight timber frames, or "flats," to represent the dining car, the corridors, etc. These were mounted on springs to simulate the movement of the locomotive. Only two interiors were available, one of which was permanently maintained as the freight car in which the fossil crate is stored, while the other was re-dressed according to the filming requirements of the day.

16:09

In the corridor, Saxton finds a key belonging to a young engineer, Yevtushenko (Ángel del Pozo), who asks Saxton why the monk's chalk failed to work on the crate. "Hypnosis," says Saxton. "Yoga. These mystics can be very convincing. . . ."

While this exchange is taking place, Wells bribes the baggage man, played by one Victor Israel (born José María Soler Vilanova), to drill a hole in the crate and take a peek at whatever is inside. Israel was among the most famous of Spanish character actors. He acted opposite Orson Welles, Yul Brynner, and Kirk Douglas, among others. In 2010, a year after his death, his career was celebrated in a documentary entitled *The Perverse Faces of Victor Israel.*

17:37

Helga Liné arrives on the scene as the femme fatale Natasha, seeking to share Wells's accommodation as she tries, she says, to get away from Shanghai. The distance from Shanghai to Peking is 819 miles, so it's not clear why she has chosen this particular means of escape from what is a port city.

Unfortunately for all involved, the privacy of Wells's compartment is also set to be invaded by Saxton, who has been given the upper berth. "I'm sure we can all get along very well together," declares Natasha, somewhat optimistically. We're witnessing some nice comic interplay between Cushing and Lee, who give the impression of enjoying themselves enormously. One can trace something of the characters' heritage back to Charters and Caldicott, the two English cricket enthusiasts (played by Basil Radford and Naunton Wayne) who assist Iris (Margaret Lockwood) and Gilbert (Michael Redgrave) in Alfred Hitchcock's locomotive mystery *The Lady Vanishes.*

19:00

The baggage man sets about earning his bribe from Wells by investigating the contents of the crate while whistling the refrain of Cacavas's theme tune. Having partially opened the container, he turns his back on it and steps away, permitting a monstrous hand to reach out and begin picking the lock. When the baggage man returns he is exposed to the creature's red-eyed gaze. His own eyes begin to bleed and go white. He falls to the floor, seemingly dead, although the whistling eerily persists . . .

While the white-eye effect was easy to achieve, the red glow was more complicated. The first attempt involved strips of reflective material being placed over the actor's eyelids, but this didn't impress the crew. Bernard Gordon complains in his memoir that they didn't try hard enough to get the lighting right, but it's possible that this particular piece of penny-pinching offended their professional sensibilities. Their solution was to place a tiny flashlight bulb behind a red lens and wire it to a battery pack and switch concealed in the actor's hand. The lens was placed over one of the actor's closed eyes (the creature only has one functioning eye) and switched on as required. The actor, Juan Olaguivel, couldn't see properly once the lens was in place, and so couldn't perform long scenes involving complicated movement. As the film progresses, more and more characters become possessed by the creature, requiring the actors affected to wear white lenses over both eyes. Martín rehearsed with the cast beforehand to make them familiar with the steps necessary, but was happy to allow them to grope for support when necessary, since he felt it added to the mystery and horror.

23:37

The whistling is heard again as we join Count and Countess Petrovski, along with the monk Pujardov, in the Petrovskis' sumptuous private car.

Let's pause here for a quick word on the subject of dubbing. It's sometimes erroneously assumed that Spanish actors in these films spoke their lines in their native tongue, which were then overdubbed by native English speakers, or non-English actors with a better command of the language. This was typically the case with foreign films dubbed for the British or US market, but the Spanish actors in *Horror Express*, as in most such films with an eye on distribution in English-speaking markets, were asked to deliver their lines in phonetic English, whether they were familiar with the language or not, and their lines were later re-voiced by other actors. Then again, even the leads had to rerecord their dialogue later in a studio to make their speech audible, or even understandable, to an audience, a process known as ADR (Automated Dialogue Replacement) or "looping." Dialogue work on *Horror Express* was completed at a sound studio outside Madrid before the principal cast returned home.

The creation of the final sound mix for *Horror Express* was, as Bernard Gordon notes, the textbook definition of a compromise: a situation in which everyone is left more or less equally unhappy. In any production, the actors, the composer, and the Foley artist—the sound-effects creator—all want their work to feature as prominently as possible in the finished film, but for the actors to be heard, the music must be muted and vice versa. Gordon makes an interesting point in his memoir: each craftsperson on a film set, he says, is often more worried about his or her contribution in isolation than about the overall effect when these elements are combined for the finished picture. Even the director is not immune to such concerns. As the producer, Gordon felt it was his role to make the final decisions, and this he did after input from the various interested parties. The use of the word "auteur" about Eugenio Martín is therefore incorrect in this instance. Instead, the production model was much closer to that of the old Hollywood studio system than the director-driven pictures that would become increasingly prevalent as the decade went on.

25:46

Under pressure from Mirov to open the crate following the disappearance of the baggage man, Saxton throws the key out of the window of the moving train. We have already observed the miniature moving across a frozen landscape, and here we see a rudimentary icy-blue backdrop beyond the window. As the train travels deeper into Siberia, the backdrops become more detailed, but each represents the work of the art department which, in a production that counted every dollar, painted the scenery on a large roll of paper that was unfurled to give the impression of the locomotive's progress.

Eventually, Mirov instructs two soldiers to break open the crate with an ax, revealing the body of the baggage man and the absence of Saxton's fossil.

"Are you telling me," Wells says to Saxton, "that an ape that lived two million years ago got out of that crate, killed the baggage man and put him in there, then locked everything up neat and tidy, and got away?"

"Yes, I am," Saxton replies.

Julian Zimet, tongue lodged gently in cheek, was getting paid less than he deserved for the script.

28:07

We are given a glimpse of the creature's face, as it lurks in a compartment in which two children are sleeping. We're about a third of the way into the film, so Martín is maintaining his careful pacing, aided by judicious editing. Although short, this scene ramps up the tension, cutting between the children, the creature, and a soldier searching the carriage. Frustratingly, Cacavas's score threatens to undo much of the good work, having once again veered off into TV detective territory.

30:24

The most sumptuous of the train's interiors: the dining car. Wells is sharing a table with Natasha, who may be a spy and is recognized by Yevtushenko. He believes they have met at the "governor's palace," which she denies, causing him to reconsider. Wells, meanwhile, is distracted by the pale eye of the fish being served for dinner. The engineer points out to him that this is to be expected, since the fish has been boiled. This sparks a certain set of associations for Wells, although he does not yet disclose them to his companions. Wells, we are about to learn, has a medical background, because Mirov arrives seeking his expertise with the baggage man's corpse.

"What are the symptoms?" Wells asks.

"He's dead," Mirov replies.

Which is a fairly conclusive diagnosis, obviating the need for a doctor, but Mirov is actually seeking a cause of death, and Wells agrees to give up his dinner to help. He approaches Miss Jones (Alice Reinheart), an American nurse, and announces that he needs her assistance.

"Yes, well, at your age I'm not surprised," she says, indicating that Zimet may well have missed his calling as a purveyor of double entendres.

"With an autopsy!" declares an appalled Wells.

"Oh, well," replies Miss Jones, "that's different."

Alice Reinheart was best known as a television and radio actress, with few films to her résumé, but according to Donna L. Halper's *Invisible Stars: A Social History of Women in American Broadcasting* (2014), Reinheart—or sometimes "Reinhart"—also had a nice sideline as a "yowler," a supplier of screams that could be recorded and later used as needed, since she could produce the kind of spectacular shrieks that were much prized by the producers of mystery shows.

32:41

The autopsy, in which Wells takes a scalpel to the baggage man's skull. When asked by Mirov what he's doing, Miss Jones replies "Trepan," which is not technically correct, trepanning being the drilling or scraping of a hole in the skull. Wells is, I believe, performing a craniotomy, which implies that he might have been better off leaving Miss Jones in the dining car. The hands performing the autopsy during these scenes are not always those of Peter Cushing, who left before principal photography was completed. When another close-up of his hands was later required, a suitable pair of non-Cushing limbs had to be sourced. Cushing begged to be allowed to return to do his own handwork, but the budget didn't extend to bringing him back for a scene in which his face wouldn't be seen.

Wells removes the top of the skull, revealing a brain that is devoid of marks or wrinkles.

"Smooth as a baby's bottom," says Miss Jones. (Wells *really* shouldn't have bothered with her.)

"Learning and memory are engraved on the normal brain," Wells tells Mirov, who wants to know what all the fuss is about, "leaving a wrinkled surface. This brain has been drained."

Wells is mistaken: a fetal brain is wrinkled by forty weeks, and we retain throughout life the wrinkles we have at birth. Even for the time, Wells is significantly behind the curve in terms of neuroscience. In 1906, the year in which *Horror Express* is set, Camillo Golgi and Santiago Ramón y Cajal won the Nobel Prize in Physiology or Medicine for their work on formulating the "neuron doctrine"—that the functional unit of the brain is the neuron. The surface of the brain, the cortex, contains our neurons, so the greater the surface area of the cortex, the greater the number of neurons, and the higher our processing power. Our brains have ridges (gyri) and folds (sulci) because this increases the surface area, a feature common to larger mammals. (Rats and mice, for example, have smooth brains.)

A human brain without gyri or sulci is known as a lissencephalic brain. The condition can be the result of a rare genetic condition or a viral infection of the uterus or fetus early in pregnancy. This leads to severe developmental problems and a shortened life expectancy.

36:05

The creature, which has been clinging to the outside of the train all along, returns to the freight car containing the remains of the recently autopsied baggage man. Martín, understanding that less is more, allows the creature's shadow to play on the white shroud instead of focusing the lens directly on the intruder itself. It's also interesting to see how long Martín allows between cuts and how stationary he is willing to keep his camera. An exercise often practiced in film schools is to ask students to watch a scene and clap each time there's an edit. With older pictures, this tends to produce a sporadic sound, but with newer films the result is near-constant applause.

In this case, almost twenty seconds pass uninterrupted from the moment the creature's shadow first touches the shroud until its features are finally revealed.

38:10

Natasha, now confirmed as a spy, opens the Petrovskis' safe and removes a box, but is attacked by the creature before she can leave. Martín gives us more of the monster, but since everything from the neck down is an ape suit, he keeps as much of it as he can in shadow and works the single red eye for all it's worth.

40:20

Wells goes to the freight car and is attacked by the creature, but Mirov intervenes, shooting it in the arm. The creature attempts to hypnotize Mirov, but he manages to fire again, and it falls, its arm trailing beside the dead spy.

41:45

A very fine shot of the miniature speeding over the frozen wastes of Siberia. Once again, it's difficult to equate the stylishness of *Horror Express*, these small, elegant touches, with the mess that is *Pancho Villa*.

41:50

Mirov wakes in a sleeping compartment and stares at his right hand as though seeing it for the first time. Saxton arrives to speak with Mirov, and informs him that Natasha's brain, like that of the baggage man, has been completely erased. Here, Saxton makes the kind of logical (or illogical) leap of which only the most brilliant men, or the most straight-faced of actors, are capable.

"Supposing that creature," he tells Mirov, "the one you killed, was capable of taking ideas directly from other people's brains and transferring them to its own."

"You mean it sucked other people's brains?"

"Absorbed," Saxton corrects him. "Through the eyes."

But Mirov is distracted when a train attendant brings him a package that, Mirov says, "belonged to Count Petrovski."

Petrovski, we learn in the next scene, has in his possession a sample of steel "harder than a diamond," and it was this that Natasha was seeking when she searched the safe.

"What really matters," Petrovksi informs Mirov, "is the formula, and that is safe"—he taps his head—"up here." The monk, Pujardov, who has been listening to their conversation, is convinced the creature is not dead.

"The unholy one is among us," he warns, as a candle goes out, and an icon falls mysteriously to the floor—possibly, it is implied, at Mirov's instigation.

46:00

Saxton, Wells, and Jones remove the creature's eye so Saxton can examine its ocular fluid, a procedure that allows Martín to indulge in a bit of gory business involving needles and an animal eyeball. When placed under a microscope, the fluid sample contains within it a fleeting glimpse of Inspector Mirov.

"Why," Wells exclaims, "it's the last thing the creature saw!"

Saxton concludes that the creature's visual memory is contained not in the brain but in the eye itself. The belief that the final image seen is imprinted upon the eye at the moment of death was a popular one in the late nineteenth and early twentieth centuries, and became something of a staple of mystery fiction. James Joyce even alludes to it in *Ulysses* (1922): "The murderer's image in the eye of the murdered. They love reading about it."

This area of ocular history is the subject of a fascinating essay by

Arthur B. Evans in *Science Fiction Studies* (November 1993), upon which I shall now shamelessly draw. In 1876, a researcher named Franz Christian Boll at the University of Rome identified a red pigment in the retina of a frog, which he named visual red, later known as visual purple, or rhodopsin. Boll concluded that rhodopsin permitted the initial absorption of light that ultimately culminated in vision. His work was subsequently advanced by Professor Wilhelm Kühne of the University of Heidelberg. (Kühne coined the word "enzyme," and at first refused to permit women—whom he referred to as "skirts"—to attend his classes before Ida Henrietta Hyde, a female student, successfully passed the physiology examination without access to Kühne's classroom or laboratory, graduating in 1896.) Kühne was a pioneer of optography, the procedure whereby an image is generated from the retina after death by fixing the rhodopsin in alum. Kühne's experiments involved any number of unfortunate rabbits, which were permitted a brief sight of sky through a barred window before being decapitated to remove the rear part of their eyeballs. It will probably constitute small consolation for rabbit lovers (and, indeed, the rabbits themselves) that Kühne was proved correct in his theory that "the retina behaves like an entire photographic workshop," for the likeness of the barred window was revealed upon the retinas of the dead animals.

Kühne's discovery was widely reported, and immediately captured the public imagination. While Kühne's work involved the careful application of laboratory techniques to produce an image, the dumbed-down version of his research supposed that if a person died with his or her eyes open—and the more dilated the pupils, the better—an optogram of the final vision would be recorded on the retina. In 1888, the eyes of Annie Chapman, believed to be the second victim of Jack the Ripper, were pried open and photographed in the hope of discovering an image of her killer; and in 1927, the murderer of Essex policeman George Gutteridge fired a shot through each of his eyes, probably inspired by a similar belief in telltale eyeballs. Meanwhile, Jules Verne, Rudyard Kipling and, more recently, the American mystery novelist John Sandford (in 1991's *Eyes of Prey*) have all utilized the device in their fiction.

47:30

As with Chekhov's gun ("If in the first act you have hung a pistol on the wall," the playwright once advised, "then in the following one it should be fired."), if you place an eyeball in a dish in Act One, then in the following act it should be pierced with a large needle, preferably accompanied by a sound like an egg cracking. This time, the ocular fluid reveals images of dinosaurs.

48:27

This is the point at which *Horror Express* begins to take its most interesting leap, as the ocular fluid is found to contain a likeness of Earth as viewed from space. We'll come back to this shortly, but the film's fusion of horror and science fiction probably wouldn't have occurred had it been a solely Spanish production. Spanish cinema was still smarting from the failure of 1964's *La hora incógnita* (The Unknown Hour), written and directed by the prolific Mariano Ozores, which made Spanish investors skittish about science fiction. Mashups like *Horror Express* were the stuff of coproductions.

49:17

The Countess, who has been invited to examine the fluid through the microscope, calls on the monk Pujardov to join them and see it for himself. Unsurprisingly, it hardens Pujardov in his conviction that the creature is Satan, who, the monk says, once looked down upon Earth from heaven.

Pujardov steals the eyeball.

52:18

While searching for Pujardov, Miss Jones is confronted in the freight car by Inspector Mirov, to whom she offers a thousand rubles for the safe return of the missing eye. When he expresses disbelief at a mere eye being worth so much, she explains to him that it contains "pictures of the Earth in prehistoric times, pictures of the Earth seen from space," and goes on to reveal that Wells, Saxton, and "that pretty Countess" have all looked at them, too. Miss Jones is quite the Chatty Cathy, and so brings a nasty death upon herself when Mirov removes his right hand from his pocket to reveal that it is, in fact, an appendage of the creature. The red bulbs are working perfectly, and both of Mirov's eyes glow impressively as Miss Jones meets her end, watched from the shadows by Pujardov.

Miss Jones's loss is medicine's gain.

54:02

Pujardov reveals himself to Mirov and offers him the eyeball. "Have pity," Pujardov begs, whereupon Mirov throws the eyeball in the furnace and announces he has no intention of killing Pujardov, since "there's nothing in your head of any use." Saxton and Wells arrive with a search party, to be informed by Mirov that there has been another killing. Mirov now assumes control and forbids anyone to leave the train. To ensure that his command is complied with, Mirov kills the conductor, whom Saxton has instructed to contact the next station.

59:09

Saxton discovers the conductor's absence.

1:00:09

A communication is now received by the station, informing it of the train's arrival in fourteen minutes.

"Fourteen minutes," a familiar voice repeats, and we are instantly transported to Birmingham, the city that will later hold a special place in his heart. With two-thirds of the film elapsed, Telly Savalas finally makes his appearance as the Cossack, Captain Kazan.

"Christopher Lee and Peter Cushing were two very good actors in their own way," Martín told Aguilar and Haas, "and Telly Savalas was a very good actor in his. Lee and Cushing were both very orthodox and disciplined, incredibly professional, who could do seven identical takes of a single shot, because they know what they have to do, and they know they're doing it well. They never made mistakes in their lines or their blocking, they were always ready, they never slowed anyone else's work down. They hit their marks, knowing exactly what fans of the Gothic expected of them. Savalas was the opposite: an impulsive, emotional actor, a lover of improvisation, someone who enjoyed finding new things in each take, in order to react spontaneously. I enjoyed working with Savalas more; as a director of actors, I found him more inspiring."

Savalas had arrived in Madrid accompanied by Sally Adams and seems to have set out to steal the film from the start. In this, his first scene, a woman can be glimpsed in bed with him as he instructs his Cossacks to prepare for the train's arrival. Gordon claims that this wasn't part of the script, and Savalas just fancied some company while he lay in a cold, uncomfortable bunk on a drafty film set.

Historically, the Cossacks were supportive of the tsarist regime and helped to suppress dissident elements during the Revolution of 1905. In return, the Cossacks were granted a degree of autonomy and were not taxed, although they were required to perform up to twenty years of military service, most of which could be served in the reserves.

1:01:48

Mirov approaches Yevtushenko and asks if he knows how to measure, or even overcome, Earth's gravity. The engineer admits to a degree of knowledge of the subject, thanks to one of his mentors, thereby dooming himself. The science-fiction element of the picture is about to become more pronounced, and this is confirmed when, in the next scene, Mirov visits Saxton and requests an explanation for what is taking place on the train.

"Millions of years ago," Saxton tells him, "something, some form of intelligence, came to the Earth from another planet. The atmosphere of the Earth was new to it, different, but it learned how to survive . . . by entering into the body and brain of an Earth creature . . . The animal that you shot was only the host, and when that animal died, the alien intelligence transferred, somehow, to another host. It's alive, in someone on this train."

This brings us to one of the loveliest exchanges in the film, as Wells interrupts Saxton's disquisition by arriving with a shotgun.

"But what," Mirov wonders, attempting to sow mischief, "if one of you is the monster?"

"Monster?" Wells replies, affronted. "We're British, you know."

This is the stuff that made Britain great, and while the film plays it for gentle laughs, all that snow and ice and those stiff upper lips remind me of an interview I did some years ago with the writer Fergus Fleming, who was then publicizing *Killing Dragons: The Conquest of the Alps*, his 2001 book on early Alpine exploration. *Killing Dragons* contains fascinating material on the nature of the British character in adversity, and I was particularly taken by the tale of Charles Fellows and his companion, William Hawes, who, in 1827, decided to ascend Mont Blanc. Dispensing with the usual niceties, such as proper provisions, equipment, and weather reports, they loaded themselves with eight joints of meat, a dozen fowls, various breads and cheeses, and "forty-two bottles of red wine, brandy, capillaire and syrup of raspberries." Fellows and Hawes, accompanied by a hastily assembled team of guides, slept in temperatures of minus five degrees Fahrenheit on two shelves of rock, measuring four feet square and eight feet by four feet, respectively, on the very edge of a three-hundred-foot drop. It was so cold that the silk tassel on Fellows's nightcap kept freezing; it says a lot about Fellows that he was wearing a nightcap with a silk tassel in the first place.

When the climbers reached the summit of Mont Blanc on July 25, they were bleeding from every orifice due to the thin atmosphere. On the way back down, a thunderstorm hit them (Fellows described it as "extremely irksome"), and a two-hundred-foot block of ice fell on a spot where they had been standing only minutes before. They returned to Chamonix, in France, on the morning of July 26, having spent forty-eight hours on the mountain. The two Englishmen immediately went on a two-hour walk through the valley to stretch their legs, caroused until midnight, and were up at six the next morning to catch the train back to Geneva. They really don't make men like that anymore, which may be just as well.

But returning to *Horror Express*, Saxton's reflections on the nature of the creature signal the film's debt to *Who Goes There?*, a novella by John Wood Campbell first published in the August 1938 edition of *Astounding Science Fiction*. In *Who Goes There?*, a group of male Antarctic researchers discover an alien spaceship that has been buried in ice for millions of years. From it they salvage the remains of a creature, but as soon as it thaws, it begins to attack. What makes the entity especially lethal is its ability to replicate the physical form of its victims and absorb not only their bodies but also their character and memories. Suddenly, anyone and everyone could potentially be a hostile alien life-form, and the men are faced with the challenge of determining who is infected before the alien finds a way to escape Antarctica.

Who Goes There? can claim the distinction of having inspired two classic—and radically different—film versions: 1951's *The Thing from Another World*, directed by Christian Nyby, but with considerable input and assistance from Howard Hawks; and 1982's *The Thing*, directed by John Carpenter. A third version, a prequel to Carpenter's picture, also entitled *The Thing*, released in 2011, isn't bad, but does little more than hang on the coattails of Carpenter's masterpiece.

Rereading *Who Goes There?*, it's striking how much of what is great about the Carpenter version is already present in the novella.

The Nyby-Hawks adaptation is far looser, leavening the testosterone-heavy source material with the introduction of a female character, and almost sabotages itself by giving us an alien that is, in essence, a giant walking carrot. Carpenter, though, sticks closely to Campbell's novella, which includes such memorable elements as the initial confrontation with the alien as it attempts to replicate a dog; the infamous "blood-test" scene, in which McReady, the assistant commander, tries to discover who may be infected by testing samples of the survivors' blood with a hot wire; and most interestingly, in terms of *Horror Express*, the creature's plan to build a ship to effect its escape.

Who Goes There? may well have been influenced by H. P. Lovecraft's earlier novella *At the Mountains of Madness*, written in 1931 but not published until 1936. *At the Mountains of Madness* also features an Antarctic expedition, the discovery of hostile alien life-forms, and a messy end for some dogs, but Campbell's story is more rationalist and science-based than Lovecraft's (Campbell had a degree in physics), which, in typical Lovecraft fashion, veers off into all sorts of odd business about "shoggoths," "the elder pharos," and "the windowless solids with five dimensions." Campbell also offers a resolution to his tale, with the destruction of the alien by the "grace of God" and a blowtorch, while Lovecraft ends with the narrator, Dyer, and a graduate student named Danforth fleeing the site of an ancient (yet not uninhabited) civilization and warning others to stay away from it.

Lovecraft became more liberal as he grew older, which doesn't excuse the toxic racist and anti-Semitic opinions he had previously espoused. Campbell, by contrast, was always regarded as extremely right-wing, with a low opinion of Black people that revealed itself in approving remarks about slavery and support for the presidential campaigns of the Alabama segregationist George Wallace. But to give the devil his due, Campbell can be credited with further popularizing the term *science fiction* as a genre descriptor, as it was he, as editor, who retitled the influential periodical *Astounding Stories of Super-Science* as *Astounding Science Fiction* in 1938.

Bernard Gordon, in his account of the genesis of *Horror Express*, makes no mention of *Who Goes There?*, but it's not difficult to perceive its influence on the finished film. Then again, there is little that is new in any genre. What matters is how one builds on what has gone before. With *Horror Express*, d'Usseau and Zimet, aided by Martín, fashioned from their antecedents a light, witty, and entertaining vehicle. Campbell, whatever his qualities as a writer (the prose style of *Who Goes There?* is leaden), doesn't raise many smiles. *Horror Express*, by contrast, does.

Finally, although Gordon never ascribed political connotations to the film, we bring ourselves and our experiences to everything we encounter, and elements of *Horror Express* bear some similarity to Don Siegel's 1956 *Invasion of the Body Snatchers*, in which alien seedpods assimilate the memories of sleeping human beings to create precise duplicates. I mention Siegel's picture because it was created in the shadow of the HUAC hearings, of which Gordon and Zimet were victims, and has been read both as an allegory of the dangers of McCarthyism and an anti-communist warning. In an interview for the book *Don Siegel: American Cinema* (1975), Siegel remarked of the film: "The political reference to Senator McCarthy and totalitarianism was inescapable, but I tried not to emphasize it because I feel that motion pictures are primarily to entertain and I did not want to preach."

1:06:20

Just as Mirov is questioning the Count about the capacity of his revolutionary new steel to deal with high temperatures, Kazan and his Cossacks board the train. The Countess threatens Kazan with the tsar's wrath, promising to have him sent to Siberia. Most viewers will have immediately spotted the inefficacy of this punishment under the geographical circumstances, but Kazan still takes the time to point it out:

"I *am* in Siberia."

Kazan promises to smoke out the killers, the troublemakers, and the "foreign influences."

"What's he raving about?" Saxton asks, not unreasonably.

Savalas, it must be said, would be chewing the scenery if the budget permitted its consumption, and Martín has acknowledged that the actor appeared to be involved in a completely different film from everyone else.

1:10:35

Having already given Saxton a firm elbow in the belly for accusing him of babbling, Kazan whips Pujardov to the floor after the monk calls him a fool. Kazan spots that Pujardov seems to be trying to protect Mirov by distracting the Cossack's attention from him—revealing Kazan to be more perceptive than anyone else on the train, and the snow has barely melted from his boots. Kazan's comment provides Saxton with the final clue he needs. Saxton kills the lights in the carriage, revealing Mirov's red eyes glowing in the dark. Kazan responds by lobbing a sword into Mirov's back before shooting him. The wounded Mirov flees, Pujardov at his heels.

1:13

With no better option presenting itself, the alien entity jumps from the dying Mirov to Pujardov, who plunges the train into darkness before advancing on the Cossacks. What follows is a tense thirty seconds or so—aided by the chiaroscuro effect created by Savalas's bald head, glimpsed half in shadow—as Kazan and his men direct their fire toward what turns out, unhappily for them, to be the wrong end of the railway car. Martín handles the ensuing slaughter well, the implacable Pujardov mowing down the Cossacks in semi-darkness, their bleeding white eyes contrasting with the red glow of his own.

1:15:52

As the passengers descend into panic, Saxton and Wells arm themselves, adding a lamp to their reserve on the grounds that the creature "always kills in the dark. He can't play his little tricks in the strong light." I'm not convinced this is true, since the Chinese thief at the start of the film died in a brightly lit station, but we'll bow to the Englishmen's superior knowledge, now that they have some kind of handle on affairs at last.

1:16:10

Kazan, the last survivor of the Cossacks, tries to get away from Pujardov, but is prevented from doing so by the creature's power. He falls, sword in hand, his eyes white. The final frames of this scene are quite beautiful, reminiscent of a piece of Baroque art, with Pujardov, his pale breast exposed, hovering almost Christlike above the carnage.

1:17:10

Saxton and Wells break into the carriage of dead Cossacks. Again, it's worth remarking on the use of contrast by Martín and his crew, even in this incidental moment. After all, the director could just as easily have presented us with a scene showing the two scientists already in the car, taking in the sight of the bodies, but Martín, like Savalas, is enjoying himself. I like to think of him as metaphorically shaking the viewer by the lapels and shouting, "See! *This* is what I can do!"

1:18:22

The creature, still in the guise of Pujardov, at last reaches the opulent quarters of Count Petrovski, where the lights remain on. After chiding the Count for his treatment of the monk, the creature plunges the car into darkness and sucks the Count's knowledge from him. No screams here, and no sound but the rattling of the train's wheels on the track, intercut with scenes of the speeding locomotive. Martín, like the train, is rolling now.

Before the creature can attack the Countess, whom he claims Pujardov loved "more than the promise of Heaven," Saxton intervenes, arriving with shotgun in hand for his big confrontation with the entity, which cleverly begins to play on the explorer's scientific curiosity to aid its survival.

"Who are you?" Saxton asks.

"I am a form of energy," the creature replies, "occupying this shell."

"Where do you come from?"

"Another galaxy. I came with others like myself. I was left behind—an accident. I survived in protozoans, fish, vertebrates. The history of your planet is part of me. Pull the trigger, and you will end it."

When Saxton asks the creature what he should do, it proposes that he should let it go.

"I will teach you to end disease, pain, hunger," it promises, but Saxton declines the offer, and the creature enters a trance.

1:20:50

The dead begin to reanimate: first the Count, followed by the Cossacks, Kazan among them, all accompanied by some of Cacavas's loveliest music yet. Saxton and the Countess run, battling their way through the train, Saxton using gun and blade, the Countess mostly relying on a lot of screaming to keep the threat at bay.

1:23:47

Pursued by the undead, Saxton and the Countess reach the last car, where the remaining passengers, led by Wells, are about to uncouple it from the rest of the train. We flash to a signal office, where instructions have come through from Moscow to "stop the Express at the switching point. . . . That means killing everybody on board."

1:25:08

Pujardov, at the controls of the engine, realizes that the tracks have been altered and tries to stop the train, but it's too late. Wells and Saxton manage to detach their car before the locomotive, having been shunted on to a spur line, plummets over a ravine and explodes.

Bernard Gordon claims that Martín and his cameraman insisted on trying to find a suitable three-hundred-foot cliff near Madrid to film the final sequence, but this is questionable. Martín was an experienced director and used to shooting with miniatures after *Pancho Villa*. He and his assistants would surely have known that the scale of the miniature, which was one-sixth to one-seventh that of a real train, meant a forty- to fifty-foot height would suffice. Whatever the truth, the train finally plunged from a forty-foot tower on the Madrid set, against a matte backdrop of a mountain. Four cameras were used to achieve the desired effect, including one capable of filming at ninety-six frames per second, or four times normal speed. By intercutting between the four cameras, Martín was able to overcome the impression of slow motion that would have been too obvious had they used only normal cameras running at high speed. This is known as "overcranking": frames of film captured at a high rate and played back at a slower one will reveal the action in slow motion. The term comes from silent-film days when cameras had to be hand-cranked. The opposite effect—fast motion—is achieved when a camera is "undercranked," and the film is played back at a faster rate. I always think of the first two *Mad Max* films when it comes to undercranking, as George Miller was forced to resort to it to give the impression of speed in some of his action sequences, though the sometimes-spasmodic motions of the actors in early silent comedies is another example of its effect. Also, thanks to the ingenuity of the Spanish craftsmen, it wasn't even necessary to destroy the beautiful original model of the train: instead, a wooden miniature was constructed and wrecked in its place.

And with that, *Horror Express* comes to an end.

IV
THE AFTERLIFE

Bernard Gordon had reason to be happy with his solo production efforts on *Horror Express*, despite the coproducer credit at the start of the picture, another sop to the Spanish quota. "The end result was gratifying," he writes in *Hollywood Exile*, adding that he felt he had "controlled the process enough to take pride in my accomplishment."

The critics generally concurred, with a consensus emerging that what set the film apart was its lightness of touch, the dry wit of its script enhancing the pleasure of watching Lee and Cushing in roles that permitted them to work together as reluctant allies rather than mortal enemies. They had always enjoyed a chemistry, but part of the appeal of *Horror Express* lies in the suspicion that, in Saxton and Wells, they found parts and a relationship between the characters, that reflected something of their respective personalities in real life: Lee, slightly distant, with a demeanor communicating a firm belief in his superiority; and Cushing, more eccentric, with an inherent gentleness and considerateness. As with all such generalizations, this takes complexity and whittles it down to simplicity, but there is a truth here nonetheless.

One of the more welcome positive responses to the film was that of Dilys Powell, the film critic of the *Sunday Times*. Powell had never been a great fan of Hammer's horror output, which meant that Lee and Cushing had experienced the lash of her tongue in the past. Powell accused *The Curse of Frankenstein* of debasing cinema, and by the time *Dracula: Prince of Darkness* made its appearance, she had resorted to ridicule ("I admit to a guffaw, not stifled, now and then"). But she found *Horror Express* "enjoyably absurd" and declared it was "always a pleasure to see Peter Cushing and Christopher Lee together," somewhat belying the available evidence of her earlier reviews. Alexander Walker, in the *Evening Standard*, decided that the film had "far more style and much, much more speed than home-grown horrors but catches the national characteristics nicely," while Margaret Hinxman of the *Sunday Telegraph* felt "Lee and Cushing have developed a dapper way of saying an idiotic line straight, while still communicating the joke of it to the audience," which is unfair to a script that is quite aware of its farcicalities. But Hinxman was at least less guilty of damning with faint praise than Tom Milne in *Monthly Film Bulletin*: "As bad horror films go . . . it isn't all that bad."

In Spain, *La Vanguardia* was more enthusiastic (maybe excessively so), describing *Horror Express* as a "very distinguished horror film which is on a higher technical level than many of the pictures we see these days." To the Spanish movie magazine *Cineinforme* it was a "quality film, without the shrill effects so common in the genre."

At the 1972 Sitges Film Festival, devoted to fantasy and horror, *Horror Express* lost out to the Czech production *The Cremator* for best film. (In *Hollywood Exile*, Bernard Gordon erroneously claims that the main prize was awarded to Robert Mulligan's *The Other*, but Mulligan won for best director.) *Horror Express* did not depart Sitges entirely empty-handed. In a decision that probably haunted Julian Zimet to his grave, Eugenio Martín won the award for best script, despite having written little or none of it.

Unfortunately, Martín appeared to have missed all these encomia. "It went down really well abroad, but nobody thought much of it here," he reflected gloomily in an interview with *Fangoria* in 1999. "The Spanish critics reviewed it following their usual negative criteria." Then again, Sitges wasn't Martín's ideal jury, given his tendency over the years to describe *Horror Express* as "adventure" rather than horror.

But Martín's relationship with the Spanish critics was always spiky. He believed they were "openly contemptuous of what we genre directors were doing, because we didn't deal with the immediate reality around us. They wanted a cinema committed to attacking the Franco regime and trying to save Spain, or they wanted us to shut up. That was how extreme the situation was. What I say is that it's good to have that kind of committed art, but also to be free to do other things. Things that are exciting for human beings and don't pretend to be saving human destiny."

I have a degree of sympathy with Martín here. In Ireland, genre fiction was regarded as barely beneath contempt for much of the twentieth century, perhaps because it was not deemed serious enough for a young nation struggling to define itself after years of colonial oppression. But to be an Irish writer also brought with it a requirement to engage with the nature of Irishness, and I could think of few things with which I wanted to engage less as a young writer than the nature of Irishness. My decision to set my novels in the United States, and work in genre literature, was a deliberate attempt to distance myself from such expectations.

Toward the end of his life, Martín reached a happier accommodation with *Horror Express*'s legacy, and accepted its status as a cult work. "Now, when I look back," he remarked in an interview accompanying the 2011 Severin Blu-ray release of the film, "when you have Christopher Lee, Peter Cushing, Telly, the train, the sense of humor of the story, and the sense of adventure that pervades the picture, maybe it works. . . ."

— 63 —

If Martín at least received a prize for *Horror Express*, albeit one he probably shouldn't have been awarded, there were fewer comforts for Bernard Gordon. Even before the film was released, Scotia's convoluted financial affairs threatened to undo all his hard work. At the end of the 1960s, when Philip Yordan was making his film version of Peter Shaffer's play *The Royal Hunt of the Sun* (1969), he and Ben Fisz had found a financial backer in the form of one Bobby Marbor, a London real estate developer. By 1972, Marbor was enduring a reversal of fortune, and was unable to repay a loan of $150,000 advanced to the production by Banco de Bilbao, secured against the negative of *Horror Express*. Because of the nature of Spanish coproductions, the signatories on the loan were Gordon's nominal coproducer, Gregorio Sacristán, and the film's accountant, named Ramon. Since these two gentlemen had no desire to be stuck with the bill from Banco de Bilbao, they seized the film's negative from the laboratory in Madrid.

Back in London, Fisz was screaming for the negative to enable release prints to be made, and in a fit of panic sold the US distribution rights for just $100,000. This money was then used to manufacture the release prints using the work print. According to David Gregory, cofounder of Severin Films, subsequent VHS and DVD releases of the film were taken from an old analog tape master, probably created for broadcast in the 1980s or '90s. "They looked terrible," he says, "non-anamorphic or cropped, and with muted color. In addition, the title was widely bootlegged in the US, so a lot of those releases were several generations removed." In 2011, Severin issued a HD Blu-ray transfer of *Horror Express*, sourced from the original negative stored in Madrid. In 2019, Arrow Video released a new version, further restored.

Horror Express would cover its $350,000 budget in Spanish ticket sales alone but was never the hit it might have been. Nevertheless, its reputation has only grown in the decades since its release, and it has built a sizable cult following. *Fangoria* anointed it "one of the greatest fright films ever unleashed," and Jonathan Rigby, in his book *Euro Gothic* (2016), compliments its "unbridled lunacy" and "consistently witty and inventive script," but saves his highest praise for the two leads: "Pride of place, however, goes to Cushing and Lee, both of whom are at their considerable best."

— 64 —

As for the principal players, both in front of and behind the camera, they enjoyed diverse fortunes in the years that followed.

Bernard Gordon returned to Hollywood in 1973 but was unsuccessful in his efforts to maintain a career in movie production. He received only one further screen credit, for his adaptation of the Margaret Atwood novel *Surfacing*, released cinematically in 1981. In 1997, he and ten other surviving blacklistees were honored at a ceremony in Los Angeles organized by four Hollywood unions. Gordon died in 2007, aged eighty-eight.

Eugenio Martín worked as a writer and director until the end of the last century, mostly in Spanish film and television. His final film was *La sal de la vida* (The Salt of Life, 1996). He died in 2023, aged ninety-seven.

Telly Savalas continued to make films in Europe and America, and eventually got around to divorcing his second wife, Marilyn, in 1974, although by then he had moved in with Sally Adams, who had assumed the name Sally Savalas, even though the couple remained unmarried. By 1978, Adams and Savalas were no longer an item, and she was forced to sue him for palimony as well as support for herself and her daughter from a previous relationship, who would grow up to become the actress Nicollette Sheridan.

By then Savalas was more famous than he could have ever imagined, thanks to Lieutenant Theo Kojak. Savalas first played a version of the detective in a 1973 TV movie before reprising the role for five seasons from 1973 to 1978, and a further seven TV movies between 1985 and 1990. Along the way, he reached number one in the UK pop chart with a version of Bread's "If" and eulogized the joys of Birmingham. He was married for a third time, in 1984, to a travel agent named Julie Hovland with whom he remained until his death on January 22, 1994, aged seventy-two.

Christopher Lee and **Peter Cushing** collaborated on five more films: *The Creeping Flesh* (1973), *Nothing but the Night* (1973), *The Satanic Rites of Dracula* (1973), *Arabian Adventure* (1979), and *House of the Long Shadows* (1983). The two men remained in touch over the years, mostly in the form of telephone conversations, during which Lee enjoyed entertaining Cushing with impressions of cartoon characters.

After *Horror Express*, Cushing threw himself into a period of continuous work that lasted thirteen years, accepting any role offered to him in order, he said, to forget himself and numb his grief. "I think that saved my reason," he concluded. He wore Helen's wedding ring on a watch chain, which he kept in his pocket, but seemed to reach an accommodation with his bereavement. In a letter she left for him, Helen wrote: "Remember we will meet again, when the time is right"; this, and his Christian faith, sustained Cushing. "I didn't lose her," he said. "She's just elsewhere."

Older than Lee and in increasingly poor health, Cushing did not appear on-screen as often as his friend and proved difficult to insure for productions. "All I am is a bit tired now," he said, "and unfortunately I can't work as much as I would like to." He turned down the role of Samuel Loomis, Michael Myers's psychiatrist, in John Carpenter's *Halloween* (1978), with Donald Pleasence cast in his place. By then, Cushing had already played the part for which he would become best known by a new generation: the villainous Grand Moff Tarkin in George Lucas's *Star Wars* (1977). Cushing confirmed that he had been considered for, and preferred, the role of Obi-Wan Kenobi. It went instead to Alec Guinness, but Lucas has always maintained that Cushing was his first choice for Tarkin. Cushing agreed to a daily rate of £2,000, almost as much as the combined weekly salaries of his younger costars Mark Hamill, Carrie Fisher (who remembered Cushing as smelling of "linen and lavender"), and Harrison Ford. It must have seemed like a shrewd bargain to Cushing, though not as astute as the one struck by Guinness, who agreed to play Obi-Wan for $300,000 and 2.25 percent of the gross profits, which had netted him an estimated $95 million by the time of his death in 2000.

Cushing made what seemed to be his final appearance on the big screen in 1986's *Biggles: Adventures in Time*—he would controversially be digitally "resurrected" as Tarkin for 2016's *Rogue One: A Star Wars Story*—and received an OBE from Queen Elizabeth II in March 1989, the same year he gave up his sixty-a-day cigarette habit. He was finally reunited with his beloved Helen on August 11, 1994, aged eighty-one.

Christopher Lee moved back to England in 1985. In the spring of that year, he underwent open-heart surgery for a leaking valve, but was back working two months later. Like Cushing, he would make an appearance in the *Star Wars* franchise, taking on the role of Count Dooku in *Attack of the Clones* (2002) and *Revenge of the Sith* (2005). He renewed his acquaintance with J. R. R. Tolkien, whom he had once encountered by chance at the Eagle and Child pub in Oxford, by playing Saruman in Peter Jackson's adaptations of *The Lord of the Rings* trilogy (2001–03) and two installments of the *Hobbit* trilogy (2012–14). Yet one of the films of which he was proudest was also among those destined to be seen least in his homeland: *Jinnah* (1998), a biography of Muhammad Ali Jinnah, the founder of Pakistan, which struggled to find distribution outside that country.

Like Telly Savalas, Lee also found time to indulge his love of music, if rather more successfully than Savalas. He released two solo albums of standards and cover versions—*Christopher Lee Sings Devils, Rogues & Other Villains: From Broadway to Bayreuth and Beyond* (1998) and *Revelation* (2006)—before commencing a late-period dalliance with heavy metal. Lee had become a fan of the genre in the 1970s after hearing Black Sabbath. (Sabbath guitarist Tommy Iommi would credit Lee's horror performances as part of the band's inspiration.) In 2010, Lee released *Charlemagne: By the Sword and the Cross* (2010), a symphonic metal concept album recorded with the Italian composer Marco Sabiu, and in 2013 followed it with a sequel, *Charlemagne: The Omens of Death*, a more traditional metal album arranged by Richie Faulkner of Judas Priest. Lee also worked with the New York metal band Manowar, and released two heavy metal Christmas EPs, one of which includes a version of "The Little Drummer Boy" that I'm still trying to unhear.

Christopher Lee died on June 7, 2015, aged ninety-three, after appearances in almost three hundred films and television dramas.

— 65 —

As I was making the final corrections for the original version of this monograph, I took time out to interview the writer Neil Gaiman for an event at the Irish Film Institute in Dublin. Gaiman had been asked to introduce a film of his choice and had nominated Jan Švankmajer's *Alice* (1988), an adaptation of Lewis Carroll's *Alice in Wonderland*. (Frankly, I was slightly relieved when *Alice* ended, but never mind.)

In the course of the interview, I asked Gaiman what films might have resonated with him as a child. He selected Robert Siodmak's *Son of Dracula* (1943).

"Terrible film," Gaiman recalled. "I tried watching it as an adult and it's pretty awful, but as a seven-year-old, the discovery that you couldn't keep evil things out by shutting the door, because they could come underneath in mist form—it ruined me for years."

The audience laughed, but I understood how *Son of Dracula* might have stayed with Gaiman, just as the memory of watching *Dracula: Prince of Darkness* as a child has remained with me—even if I still feel a faint sense of regret that it did not stand up terribly well to a second viewing, despite all that I have written here about the actions of nostalgia. I sometimes want to be that boy again, so open to enthusiasm, so hungry for new experiences.

On the other hand, I viewed *Horror Express* twice in full for the purposes of writing this monograph, in addition to dipping into it as research required, and I have returned to it again for this extended edition. In the years since this study was first published, I have also watched the film with a cinema audience, after providing a brief introduction to the screening. I have no regrets about the hours spent in the company of *Horror Express*. In fact, I probably like it more now than I did before. I better understand the effort that went into making it and the personal struggles that informed its creation.

Most of all, it has made me think again about my childhood, and the cultural influences that have combined to create the writer, and the man, I have become. I have gazed into the pool of the past and glimpsed, reflected back at me, the face of my younger self. He appears puzzled and slightly fretful. Perhaps I have not changed so much after all.

It has, in addition, made me less angry at my father. I don't think he ever had much faith in me, and felt that the best thing would be for me to find a job from which I couldn't be fired and keep my head down until retirement. But then, he was of an Irish generation from which a great deal of the optimism had been excised, if that optimism had ever existed to begin with. His son was not destined to be a writer because people like us did not become writers, and so it was better not to pursue a dream that would remain beyond reach. It may be that he feared I would be left disappointed and hurt, or become a burden to society—or, more worryingly, to him and my mother.

For a long time, my memories of my father involved mostly conflict. In writing about *Horror Express*, I discovered happier echoes of our time together, mostly of afternoons and evenings spent in the dark, watching films flicker. What is grief, after all, but a kind of nostalgia, an intense longing both temporal and spatial, a desire not only to return but to have someone returned. It may even be that grief is the ultimate form of nostalgia, because what is being sought can never be restored, only recalled.

But I wish I could have seen *Horror Express* with my father. I think he would have enjoyed it.

BIBLIOGRAPHY

The following books proved invaluable in putting together *Horror Express: Extended Edition*.

Aguilar, Carlos, and Anita Haas, *Eugenio Martín, autor para todos los géneros*. Bilbao: Quatermass, 2005

Company, Juan M., and Vicente Vergara, Juan de Mata and José Vanaclocha, "*Testimonios—Eugenio Martín.*" In *Cine español, cine de subgéneros*, edited by Fernando Torres, 31–33. Valencia, 1974

Cushing, Peter, *An Autobiography*. London: Weidenfeld and Nicolson, 1986

Cushing, Peter, "*Past Forgetting*"*: Memoirs of the Hammer Years.* London: Weidenfeld and Nicolson, 1988

Daly, Marsha, *Telly Savalas: TV's Golden Greek*. London: Sphere, 1975

Epstein, Dwayne, *Killin' Generals: The Making of* The Dirty Dozen. New York: Citadel Press, 2023

Gordon, Bernard, *Hollywood Exile, or How I Learned to Love the Blacklist*. Austin: University of Texas Press, 1999

Grant, Kevin, *Any Gun Can Play: The Essential Guide to Euro-Westerns*. Godalming: FAB Press, 2011

Halliwell, Leslie, *The Dead That Walk*. London: Grafton Books, 1986

Halper, Donna L., *Invisible Stars: A Social History of Women in American Broadcasting*. Armonk: M. E. Sharpe, 2001

Lee, Christopher, *Lord of Misrule: The Autobiography of Christopher Lee*. London: Orion, 1997

Lisanit, Tom, *Fantasy Femmes of Sixties Cinema: Interviews with 20 Actresses from Biker, Beach and Elvis Movies*. Jefferson, NC: McFarland & Company, 2001

MacNab, Geoffrey, *Searching for Stars: Stardom and Screen Acting in British Cinema*. London: Continuum, 2000

McGilligan, Patrick, *Backstory 2: Interviews with Screenwriters of the 1940s and 1950s*. Berkeley: University of California Press, 1991

Mendez Leite, Fernando, *Historia del cine español, Vol. II*. Madrid: Ediciones Rialp, 1965

Miller, Mark A., *Christopher Lee and Peter Cushing and Horror Cinema: A Filmography of Their 22 Collaborations*. Jefferson, NC: McFarland & Company, 1995

Rigby, Jonathan, *English Gothic: Classic Horror Cinema 1897–2015*. Cambridge, UK: Signum Books, 2000

Rigby, Jonathan, *Euro Gothic: Classics of Continental Horror Cinema*. Cambridge, UK: Signum Books, 2016

Sweeney, Kevin, *James Mason: A Bio-bibliography*. Westport, CT: Greenwood, 1999.

AFTERWORD AND ACKNOWLEDGMENTS

I don't write a lot of short fiction, relatively speaking. It's been nine years since *Night Music* appeared, and *Night & Day* contains nine tales, so I don't think you really need help with the math. For me, part of the difficulty is that writing short stories requires recalibrating the creative machinery: a short story is such a different beast from a novel, so I need to find the time to allow for that recalibration, which isn't always easy.

I sometimes get the impression that, in certain creative writing circles, short stories are regarded as a kind of dry run for novels, the equivalent of training wheels on a bicycle, though I've never felt that way about them. In fact, before beginning work on my first novel, *Every Dead Thing*, I'd written only one short story in the decade or so since leaving school. It was rejected by *Icarus*, Trinity College Dublin's literary magazine, on the perfectly reasonable grounds that it was terrible. Only after I'd published *Every Dead Thing* and submitted the manuscript of my second novel, *Dark Hollow*, did I feel properly equipped to contemplate tackling short fiction in earnest.

A short story requires greater economy and discipline than a novel. It offers fewer places for the writer to hide, but it can also provide the reader with more imaginative space to explore. While a novel generally requires a beginning, a middle, and an end, a short story frequently involves an incident—a single crucial moment or a small series of such moments—that the reader is permitted to observe before moving on, like an encounter witnessed from the carriage of a train while it's stopped at the platform. The best short stories leave hooks trailing in the imagination, allowing the reader to speculate on what came before and what might come after. A novel, by contrast, is required to do more heavy lifting, particularly at the close, because an open-ended novel can feel perilously close to an unfinished one. Short fiction is also an outlet for ideas that might otherwise be discarded or forgotten—as I remind budding writers, ideas aren't the currency, time is the currency, so I don't tend to stress about those ideas that fall by the wayside—or simply aren't suited to novel length.

Basically, I struggle to switch tracks easily between short fiction and novels. They're two different modes of storytelling, and I find I have to commit to one or the other. This may help explain why I'm not terribly prolific when it comes to short stories but also why the six previously unpublished tales in *Night & Day* were written in the space of about a year. Four of those tales—"The Pilgrims' Progress," "And All the Graves of All the Ghosts," "The Flaw," and "Abelman's Line"—arose out of my doctoral studies, as well as my earlier efforts in researching and compiling the *Shadow Voices* history-cum-anthology of Irish genre fiction. "And All the Graves of All the Ghosts" and "The Flaw" represent the fruits of one of those challenges writers will occasionally set themselves: in this case, to take similar starting points—and, indeed, similar endings—and use them to craft quite different narratives, the first hauntological and the other more traditional. With "Abelman's Line," I wanted to produce a piece of short science fiction, having discovered, in the course of working on *Shadow Voices*, a thin thread of science fiction running through Irish writing. Then, having spent three years immersed in the history of books and writers, a new Caxton Private Lending Library & Book Depository tale began to nudge its way to the fore, and so "The Pilgrims' Progress" was written. I'm grateful to Dr. Eibhear Walshe and Danny Denton, my PhD supervisors at University College Cork, for their input into these four stories, and for enriching my life.

Of the two remaining new stories, "The Mire at Fox Tor" emerged from another challenge. I was lying in bed, wondering what story I might write if someone put a gun to my head and told me to produce something there and then, or else. (I admit that I may occasionally have too much time on my hands.) I had the structure in place when I got up to shower, and the first draft was completed two days later. Finally, the basic premise of "Our Friend Carlton" had been rattling around in my mind for a while, and *Night & Day* offered an outlet for it. Worryingly, once I'd set the short-fiction mechanism in motion, I was tempted to keep going. There's something satisfying about producing short stories, which may be to do with the novelty factor of working rapidly in different idioms and genres, and with disparate characters rather than spending years living with a single narrative that spans hundreds of pages. But this can easily tip into procrastination, and there were novels to be written.

Of the remaining stories, "The Evenings with Evans" was written for *Trouble Is Our Business* (2016), an anthology of new fiction by Irish crime writers edited by Declan Burke, with whom I'd worked on *Books to Die For*. I think Declan might have been hoping for a crime story, but I've never been comfortable working with short stories in the mystery genre. I prefer writing mystery novels and supernatural short fiction, so "The Evenings with Evans" was what Declan received, and he was kind enough not to object. "The Bear" was included in *Once Upon a Place* (2017), a collection edited by Eoin Colfer as part of his work as Ireland's children's laureate, and illustrated by the gifted P. J. Lynch. While the anthology was aimed at younger readers, I think "The Bear" has an adult undertow of sadness that suited it to *Night & Day*. Finally, "Unquiet Slumbers: A Tale of the Caxton Private Lending Library & Book Depository" was my contribution to *First Edition*, a limited-edition anthology published in 2020 to mark the twenty-first anniversary of London's Goldsboro Books, whose proprietors and staff have long supported my work.

My thanks, as always, go to Emily Bestler, my editor at Atria/Emily Bestler Books, and to Sue Fletcher and Jo Dickinson, my editors at Hodder & Stoughton, for continuing to make my work better and giving it a home. I'm also grateful to the larger teams at Atria/Simon & Schuster and Hachette, particularly, at Atria, Lara Jones, Sarah Wright, Gena Lanzi, Hydia Scott-Riley, Dayna Johnson, and David Brown; and, at Hachette, Katie Espiner, Swati Gamble, Alice Morley, Catherine Worsley, Rebecca Mundy, Eleni Lawrence, Oliver Martin, Alastair Oliver, Dominic Smith, and his team, Jim Binchy, Breda Purdue, Ruth Shern, Siobhan Tierney, and Elaine Egan, as well as Laura Sherlock and Becky Hunter for all their hard work on promotion and publicity. Dominick Montalto once again did a fine job of fact-checking and copy-editing, saving me many blushes. Any errors that persist are mine alone.

My agent, Darley Anderson, and his lovely team remain bulwarks of support, as do my film agent at APA, Steve Fisher, and his assistant, Chip Draper. Ellen Clair Lamb, my long-suffering assistant, continues to suffer and assist with good grace and much kindness and, with Jennie Ridyard and Cliona O'Neill, cast a cold eye over the page proofs of *Night & Day*. My older son, Cameron Ridyard, is responsible for my nifty website.

Finally, love, as always, to Jennie, Cameron, Alistair, Megan, and Alannah—and to Maxwell and Otis, the Nicest Dogs in the World™, who are keeping me company in my office as I write these words.

John Connolly, Fall 2024